The Furies

JANET HOBHOUSE

DOUBLEDAY

New York London Toronto Sydney Auckland

PUBLISHED BY DOUBLEDAY
a division of Bantam Doubleday Dell Publishing Group, Inc.
666 Fifth Avenue, New York, New York 10103

DOUBLEDAY and the portrayal of an anchor with
a dolphin are trademarks of Doubleday,
a division of Bantam Doubleday Dell
Publishing Group, Inc.

Library of Congress Cataloging-in-Publication Data
Hobhouse, Janet, 1948–91
The furies / Janet Hobhouse.—1st ed.
p.   cm.
I. Title.
PS3558.03369F8   1993
813'.54—dc20   92-30326
CIP

ISBN 0-385-24547-5

1   3   5   7   9   10   8   6   4   2

FIRST EDITION

CONTENTS

PUBLISHER'S NOTE

Janet Hobhouse was still writing *The Furies* when she died, although for the most part she was at the stage of editing and refining a finished text.

In preparing the novel for publication the editors have made every effort to fulfill her intentions. A few passages were still in first draft, and here it has seemed preferable to allow a break in the narrative rather than include material concerning which the author was ambivalent. These are marked by a three-dot ellipsis: [. . .] In the case of the final chapter, the fragments and synopsis have been presented as they stood.

PROLOGUE

PHOTOGRAPHS ARE NOT MEMORIES . . .

For a long time my mother and I lived such a solitary life, city-trapped and economically precarious, so isolated from anything resembling family or stability, so utterly dependent on one another to provide a lovable human universe, that the existence of fore-bears, documented in hundreds of photographs—brown as leaves and dog-eared, but vivid, stylized, ornate, above all theatrical—seems to me even now a kind of fairy tale, not only in relation to what then seemed plausible but even in the terms in which it was cast. For if there were no princes among the assembled generations that posed for the photographer, smiling beneath top hats and parasols on the croquet lawns of summer residences, or sitting stiffly in the vast, treasure-cluttered reception rooms of New York town houses, there was princely wealth, exotic origins and, more fantastical than any of this, the very image of a large and loving single family, self-contained and desirable as any magic kingdom.

That my mother, who viewed herself as related to very few other beings in the universe, should have descended in a mere three generations from this world of wealth and kindness, this reliable multiplicity of connected others, this cohabitation of cousins, aunts, servants, etc., says something about the speed of American life in this century, which can not only provide a solitary immigrant with the means to create, in a matter of decades, a secure and well-populated dynasty, but can also, and at the same rate, take all these steps in reverse, reducing, as in our case, a huge, prosperous, civically active and internationally connected clan to a mere hand-ful of desperate solitaries, operating like loose ball bearings in outer space.

3

It is not just the size and magnificence of this photographed family that seems so curious to me: stranger still is the silence that surrounded its existence. Never during all my childhood was there any talk of family history, no accounts of origins or journeys, no sense of heritage or, more relevant, or a paradise lost, no characters cherished, handed down, nothing ever outside the explosive range of sister, mother, grandmother. Instead, it was as though each of us had been sprung by a kind of parthenogenesis, found ourselves fatally assigned the two or three women that were to shape or hinder us, and thereafter struggled years after childhood to free ourselves from the grip of our, inevitably female, adversaries.

And in this respect my story is the same as my mother's, my aunt's, my grandmother's. Each of us led our lives in terms of a good mother and a bad, a face of fortune entirely female that began by smiling and grew carnivorous. "Mother," "Grandmother" were only the shifting terms by which each of us identified our particular angel or gorgon, and against whom each carried on a war for survival. And maybe that was the beginning of disasters, the fact that my mother forgot the rules, forgot that you wrest your destiny from the generation above you—or when, having failed in the first stage of the conflict, she decided to play out the whole drama, the whole ancient, intergenerational ritual, entirely between herself and me.

Yet clearly there had once been another version of family life, seemingly stable, horizontal rather than vertical, and there were pictures to prove it. At the very time when my mother and I were living, between evictions, in a series of small, dreary apartments, a time when my great-aunt signified for us only as a last resort for phone and Con Ed bills, when my grandmother loomed in my mother's mind as a monster of indifference, there existed some-where—probably in the old Chinese chest of my great-aunt Shrimp—this large cache of photographs of unmentioned and not-so-long-gone family from which, theoretically, we had all descended with such speed.

These pictures would have been no less accountable to me then than when I found them later, but faded as they were, flat and cracked, unlooked at and unmentioned, with no power of provoking memories in me or my mother, they would nevertheless have offered a link to another universe, one that in its contrast to the life we led then—a life far grayer, bled out and dead, it now seems—might have promised survival. Potent, erotic, sensuous, they refer to a world of light and greenery, rich odors and fabrics, above all a world of untroubled femininity, and, more miraculously, of untroubling masculinity in the shape of evidently benign and providential patriarchs, jocular uncles and beloved brothers, images which in the context of my entirely female family (fatherless, uncleless, brotherless) and particularly in the context of my mother's life—in which all men were ominous lurkers or heartbreakers, but nevertheless walk-ons merely, utterly without permanence— can only have arrived with the force of revelation.

And these unproblematic women—satin-draped, tiny-waisted, high-bosomed, elaborately coiffed and hung with pendants, rose-scented, fresh from buying sprees in Paris and Tokyo—they too might have seemed figures of redemption. In the world that my mother and I inhabited, this drawerful of images lay like an unexploded bomb of beauty, love and safety, the secret buried kingdom to which none of us could find the key, of which, seemingly, the existence had long been forgotten.

They came to America sometime in the middle of the last century, arriving from Frankfurt with their wealth and standing intact. In New York and Baltimore they started businesses, intermarried and socialized among the same sets they knew at home, other "advanced" Jews of the professional classes, for whom being Jewish was only another way of being European, a cultural endowment and civic obligation, a source of self-respect, but not a religion and not even something anyone thought it important to mention. (Certainly not, later, to my mother or me. My mother once told me that as a child she had envied her school friends because they were Jewish.) Rabbis officiated at weddings and funerals, but there were no bar mitzvahs, no seders, no temple, no shul. Instead, the heritage meant piano lessons, foreign languages and frequent trips abroad. America was only an outpost of an empire, a place to continue, as best one could, the pleasant times in Germany.

And they don't look very American, these mysterious relations. Formal, in full self-possession, they betray no anxiety of recent arrival, no eagerness to appease or conform. They wear their extravagant fashions without apology or bravado, as though they know they can make the New World dance to their tune. They did well because they expected to; the men married beauties and the beauties bore them children, and the family looked after its own. They didn't need America to survive.

Perhaps it was not until 1907, the year my great-great-grand-father Samuel sold the small Rhinish castle on Riverside Drive, the house where his children and granddaughters were born, that the family became its recognizable American self. The list of items up for auction at that sale makes a small book, a catalogue of treasures: carved ivories, oriental screens and statuary, English and German antiques, Persian rugs, Italian madonnas and jeweled crucifixes, the contents of stables and billiard rooms. His wife Elizabeth took her Paris gowns and Irish servants to a more modest dwelling, a newly built apartment block a mile further down on West End Avenue. It was only then, in that year after the great earthquake and fire of San Francisco, the year of Picasso's *Demoiselles d'Avignon*, that my own family of sirens set foot in the twentieth century, letting go of the Old World and embracing the new, and acting out for the first time a version of the generational imperative to cut ties and create a life in the present.

Let us start with them, Samuel and Elizabeth Woolf, he of the walrus mustaches, she of the sloping eyes and dark hair, not just for this first act of faith in America, but because they were father and mother of Mirabel, the Angel of my mother's life.

In 1877 Samuel had founded the Japanese Fan Company. At first it was a simple enough enterprise, providing an everyday summer necessity for both men and women in that era before air conditioning. Later it expanded as an importer of oriental scrolls, prints and screens, tea and camphorwood chests, jades, ivories, kimonos. It has premises on lower Broadway, an office in Tokyo and agents in Shanghai, Peking, Hong Kong, Canton, Foochow and Kobe. Every year Samuel crossed the American continent to take the steamer to China, Indochina and Japan, often in the company of his wife and in-laws, his sons or his daughter, Mirabel. Often they would return via Europe, stopping to visit cousins in Germany, to distribute the presents ("bullybuffskis" was the term) for which Samuel was famous. Being a family business, the Fan Company as it prospered took into employment the lame ducks of the clan, nephews that were a little simple, husbands of sisters who had married for love. At times there were so many of these that the company ran less profitably than it might. Nevertheless, for a long time it provided splendidly, an oriental milch cow.

Thanks to the company, Mirabel and her brothers had an exotic childhood. Playing in kimonos and Kabuki masks, they swung ornamental swords, performed conjuring tricks and set off intricate fireworks. Furthermore, they were given to understand the world as a vast place, covered with water and full of foreigners.

Mirabel, this small child of the photographs, moving regally in elaborate costumes or playing with her Chinese dolls, led at home a perfect life, except for one small matter, evident in the first instant portraits and increasingly clear as she grows. Always prettily dressed, surrounded by exquisite objects, placed in beautiful settings, she is set apart from these by the sad fact that she is not and never can be, like her mother and cousins, beautiful. She is a homely child, with a square jaw and large nose, thick brows and a short body—looks made all the more pathetic as she gets older by the fashionable and meticulously cut clothes, the elaborate hats that as her mother's daughter she is required to wear.

"Mirabel was no beauty." This curious fact was full of significance to the famously beautiful daughters and granddaughters who loved her. My mother's word for her was "homely," an admission which would make her wince a little, protectively. On the other hand, my great-aunt Shrimp would say, "Of course, Mother was no beauty," with a certain pride, in the same conspiratorial tone the family would use when speaking of Eleanor Roosevelt's plainness, as though such missing endowment implied virtuous renunciation, as though both Eleanor and Mirabel had had better things to do with their time than be beautiful.

But the truth was that Mirabel was not just "homely," a word which might pleasantly describe the comfortableness of her shape, the reliable unflightiness of her looks, nor just "plain" as we say in America with theological assurance of pleasing, but downright— and I, the only member of her family outside her orbit of powers, I, who did not know her long enough to fall in with the adulation, I am the one to tell you: she was downright ugly. True, by the time I met her she was hardly more than a heap of thick clothing and expensive smells, a little pile of old-lady colors, lace-fringed, with thick ankles in sensible shoes, and the wafts of dusty drapery and silver polish in the air around her. My mother brought me to see her, or rather be seen by her, a few times before her death, each occasion like a ritual visit to royalty, her court a vast and gloomily furnished apartment on Central Park South. Seated, crumpled in her armchair, not much smaller there than when she stood, she hardly emanated the magnificence with which her family invested her person. But for my mother and her sister Constance, she was no less than a deity. This small shawl-covered parcel, whose fleshy ankles folded over her shoes in dewlaps that matched the overhang of her brooched and collared throat, whose blue eyes held like buttons the softest, loosest flesh, complicatedly lined and faintly powder-scented, whose smile threw into chaos the creases and contours of those creamy, down-covered cheeks, this little bundle of female mortality was for them the very image of human good- ness, the still center of a harrowing universe, and ultimately the weapon with which they chose to keep their own bad mother and some of the very bad men at bay.

Mirabel's life was created by wounds and pleasures at which I can only guess. There was travel and wealth in her childhood, the shelter of Samuel's castle and a large, loving family. There was a buoyant, mustachioed and tobacco-scented father, a somewhat stiff, conventionally dull and conventionally beautiful mother. There were two elder brothers and seven young uncles who danced with her at parties and never forgot her birthday; dark-haired cousins who drank lemonade in white cotton gloves in summer and arrived out of blizzards in winter, leaving their horses to steam on the sidewalk, their drivers to shiver and wait, while they discarded sealskin capes and muffs in the hallway and brought in presents to place under a grand, candlelit pine. There was all this regulated, scented, musical happiness, and then there was, too, there had to be, in the cracks and margins of this existence, the dull, constant thump of Mirabel's understanding that she was somehow incorrectly placed in this perfect and privileged family living. Her failure was not in her spirit or will, but in her person, and there must have been a moment—indeed, apparently, there was—when life changed with the knowledge that her failing was fixed, never to be overcome.

Beauty seemed to be all they talked about in her mother's circle, about features that were "favored," flattered by clothes, overprized by suitors. Love, the women said, was a dizziness that could blur distinctions between the beautiful and the merely handsome. But no one claimed for it heroic blindness. Among the chattering belles, Mirabel dwelt like an oversight, happiest when alone or invisible, in her thoughts or in movement, in a world without mirrors. And she was so perfectly costumed as her mother's daughter, so evidently accepted wherever she went, that sometimes she forgot, and imagined herself as of one piece with her life.

One day she stands in front of her dressing table observing her reflection in the early morning light. The sun behind her gives her disordered waves a pink, pre-Raphaelite glow. She is sleepy still, and the light feels like a soft hand on her head, pressing her forward into her life. Her shoulders, waxen under the straps of her chemise, curve like the arms of a beautiful chair. She sees the strength in their line and the promise of pleasures, still unnamed, still distant. She is careful not to look too closely or to fix her eyes as they move across her image. She has a sense of herself only, and its vagueness makes her happy. She studies the flow of her hair as it frames her face and falls behind her back. She thinks of her mother's tresses (she thinks of them with that word) which it is her custom to arrange each morning. Elaborate, official, ceremonial hair, as in an archdukedom (such a word? such a place?). She has seen the silver-framed portraits of her great-aunts and older cousins, dozens of them, set out like calling cards on her mother's dresser, in rows among the ivory brushes and buttonhook, the cloisonné boxes and pincushion, standing upright, gleaming over the yellowing, rose-patterned lace. Her mother's hair is of this kind, thick, entwined, triumphant as a victor's wreath, proud as a warrior's shield, carrying her into her day, the meetings with her civic peers, the councils of ladies who fund public works and organize charitable teas.

But Mirabel still has unmatronly hair, maiden's hair, unadorned as nature. She looks again, turning her head slowly against the light. She doesn't know, she says, perhaps it will be all right. She is demure, she says, elfin this morning, a rose-haired fairie queen. She likes this morning mirror that gives her to herself so gently. She feels affection for its mahogany frame, the patches of darkening silver. Today she welcomes herself. On other days, other hours of the day, she sees herself as she is sometimes afraid she really is: brutal, squat, even dwarfish, a changeling in this aesthete's castle. But at this moment she is simply herself, with a strong not "unfortunate" nose, a firm not "mannish" jaw, with intelligent blue eyes and creamy not "pallid" skin. She is sixteen. It is all right for her to wonder what the future will bring.

And then the door of her bedroom opens and her governess stands behind her, towering, shattering the aureole light, darkening the mirror, casting Mirabel's reflection to the corners of the room. Her voice destroys the perfect silence, and Mirabel's invisibility.

"Whatever are you doing?"

Mirabel sees her governess look past her, into the treacherous mirror, appraising her image, weighing her words.

"At least you're quite clever," she says in a tone to end speculation. "And that is fortunate for you, Mirabel, because you'll certainly never be beautiful."

Mirabel accepts this with a display of good humor. She knows that one day the governess will be gone and that she, Mirabel, will remain. She knows that Papa loves her and Mama respects and depends upon her. Here in this house no one tries to make her feel less than perfect. But the peace in her own image is gone forever. Twenty years later Mirabel will tell the story of the governess to her elder daughter. It will be the only part about

looking in the mirror she can remember. And that is how it will be
fixed.

And if it was not on that day, it was certainly one day that
Mirabel ended the discussion with herself and ceased to imagine
she might ever be pretty. (You say it doesn't happen that way, but
actually it does. A little valve is closed off and the whole course of
a life can change.) She never thought about her looks, or at least
not in that way, again. Instead, she agreed to be clever. She played
cards with her mother and discussed politics with her father. She
informed her parents she wished to become a doctor. Perhaps
because no one, least of all she, thought she would marry, she was
allowed to pursue her studies.

And then, into this predeterminedly self-effacing life, modest,
upright and plausible, came an implausible element, an unlikely
older man, a beautifully mannered, exceptionally dignified traveling salesman from Tennessee, who one day sat in the cherub-
ceilinged salon with Mirabel's parents, hanging his manicured
hands in his lap, addressing his remarks to his summer-weight
shoes.

A physically unfavored rich man's daughter might have been,
here as elsewhere, the heroine of matrimonial tragedy, but my
heiress of Riverside Drive had a different story. Late, but not too
late (she was twenty-six), her suitor presented himself, no fortune
hunter despite his humbler connections, but a gentle, rather
handsome man, something of a dandy, yet modest, a Southern
Jewish beau some fourteen years her senior, whom life had dealt a
blow in the deaths of his wife and only offspring in childbirth.

Nor did Mirabel act with becoming gratitude toward the Tennessee widower. On the contrary, far from welcoming this unexpected
reprieve from spinsterhood, she regarded marriage as certain catas-
trophe, as sure and unbearable humiliation. Six weeks before the
wedding, she collapsed and had what she later described as a
nervous breakdown. She cried and protested, or lay lifeless, refusing to speak, staring at the ceiling. But her mother also cried (the
invitations had all gone out), and in the end Mirabel agreed to be
married.

From my mother I know certain things about my great-grandfather in later years: that he kept a canary and listened to the radio, that on Sundays he read the comics and presided over formal family breakfasts of kippers, squabs and scrambled eggs, served on silver dishes, the height of glamour, to his small granddaughters. In Shrimp's memory her father was a "magnificent specimen," but undemonstrative and somewhat stuffy. He told jokes which his daughters thought were corny, never made an eccentric remark, objected to any off-color story (he must have made an odd traveling salesman), and was throughout his life a good, even Rotarian, Republican.

He is white-haired, very tall and elegant in the photograph I have of him, standing on a crowded beach with my mother in his arms, overdressed among the half-naked bathers, in a three-piece linen suit and straw boater. "Gentle" was always the word used to describe him, which I suspect politely implied some mental dimness. Certainly upon marriage he was taken into the Fan Company, a usual indication of deficiency. And I suspect that though his wife and daughters were fond of him, proud of his fine figure and Southern manners, they more or less ignored him. Mirabel's husband was simply absorbed into the family home and the family business, assimilated into the previous life as though this husband were just another gift from Papa, another souvenir from a buying trip abroad.

I have no picture of him as a young man. But then, he never was a young man. He arrived in Mirabel's life when he was forty, a widower, wounded perhaps, shunted sideways by the deaths of his wife and infant, though shunted is too romantic a notion for such a fastidious Rotarian. He was exactly what he seemed: dress, manners and predictability (style is substance to children). He was his gold watch chain, and those comics and kippers, jokebook-level jokes and the barely tolerated running gags by which he expressed his affection to his family. He was, I imagine, at sea in that feminine household, annexed at first by Mirabel's family, then done in by his own. Far from ruining Mirabel's life, he never stood a chance in her matriarchy—a lone male fish, there for the procreations. He hovered about them, addressing his peculiarly accented remarks, or retreated into his gentleman's world of office life and clubs, a realm of politics and tailoring, the one as important as the other. With his Southern elegance and dandified beauty he ornamented the household the way Mirabel could not. He therefore played the traditional female role, providing physical charm and social convention, and left Mirabel unexpectedly free to be her own person.

And Mirabel? She had pleased her mother and married against her will. She'd given up medicine under protest, but in the end had accepted her "magnificent specimen" with the same good humor with which she'd taken her governess's verdict on her future. She loved him, no doubt, to the best of her ability, and the more so as she discovered how little further sacrifice of the old life was involved. For she remained first and always her mother's daughter, continuing to dress the part in gowns from Worth, with pearls in her ears and one of her mother's pekes in her lap when they went out in the brougham to shops or weddings or meetings of the Ladies' Auxiliary. Even after her daughters were born, when Samuel sold his castle and the families moved into separate apartments, Mirabel traveled to her parents' home each morning and, just as always, helped to arrange her mother's hair. Four years after that sale, in 1911 when Samuel died, his widow came to live with Mirabel. And it must have been then, while the overrun man of the family went off each morning to work in his wife's family's business, that Mirabel's matriarchy was established. And it was then, as daughter to Elizabeth Woolf, mother to Shrimp and Emma, but not, I suspect, as wife to her husband, that Mirabel was born again as Angel.

They had two daughters in quick succession in the first three years of their marriage, and if Mirabel was ever bride or lover, it was a stage that yielded soon enough to the pleasures of motherhood. Her husband was allowed to hold and be photographed with the babies, but his interference with their upbringing was restricted. His realm, as he was soon made to understand, remained the company and the clubs. He had few friends of his own, though he may have been encouraged to make them. His Tennessee relations visited occasionally, but their visits were not returned. He received his social life, like his living, from his wife's family. Yet he was barely aware of his lack of power in the household, because the shifts were made in the gentlest, most subversive manner, through the unrestrained blossoming of Mirabel's family devotion.

In the summers they went, *en famille* of course, to Shokan, their place in the Catskills, where they let the carriage horses frolic and rest (Geisha, the favorite, was often harnessed and ridden by the nephews and nieces with which the family abounded), and spent long summer weeks fishing, reading, picnicking and painting in the open air. The property was rented from a retired Hudson River boat pilot whose son, a shy, effeminate youth (and therefore a trusted companion for the children), was an amateur photographer. In tweed cap and knickerbockers, he stalked the New York visitors over several summers with camera and tripod, capturing the white-muslin-dressed girls and sailor-suited boys, the flowering orchard trees and high grasses that swarmed with crickets and flies. He followed them along the muddy river walks where they took fishing poles and summer reading, and posed them formally at country feasts: vast meals of cold meats and baked pies, beer and lemonade, to which they were summoned by a large iron bell, and after which they reclined on lawns and in high wicker chairs, cooling themselves with the hand-painted fans from which the family first derived its fortune.

In the long, late-lighted evenings, the adults drew baths and dressed for supper, played whist and gathered in rooms that smelled of cologne and tobacco and the exotic must of rained-upon, sunned-upon wooden country houses. In the upstairs rooms, the children ran wild, formed alliances and suffered infatuations during days that ran in waves with the hot spells and rainy stretches throughout June, July and August.

The men who earned their livings in the city came up by train on Friday afternoons, filling the special cars added on in the summer season to accommodate weekend visitors. Then a certain formality was restored to the summer place. The women turned their attention from nursery matters (during the week it was simplest to exist on the same level as the children, responding with wonder to birds' nests and fish slaughter, commiserating over insect bites and summer chills, fretting over near-drownings and riding accidents). They refastened their corsets and put on less comfortable clothes, made an effort with their conversation and, in the presence of the men, began noticeably to twitter. The exception was Mirabel, who was happiest among the children and altered as little as was politely possible when the men invaded. As for Tennessee, he took his lemonade on the wide, pillared porch with the rest of the family, but kept his city collar on, his vest buttons buttoned from late Friday evening until his departure sometime on Monday morning.

At Shokan, among the children and elders, Mirabel was happiest. That was where she loved life best and where she taught her daughters to love it best. The invisibility she had once practiced in childhood there became translucence as she made herself indispensable to the family around her. She offered her life as a link, clear as a glass bead, between her own charmed infancy and that of her nephews, nieces and daughters. To everyone she was Angel, go-between, protector, caretaker, a beacon of accommodation to the lives around her.

It seems likely that Mirabel went from cherished daughter to cherished mother without taking much interest in the interval as cherished wife. I have as evidence not only the drastic ambivalence she felt toward the idea of marriage, but the way she insisted on filial continuity once she was wed, the way she accepted the role as duenna to her mother, and later to her daughters and granddaughters. She ruled by cheerful service throughout her life, as handmaiden to the beauty and brilliance around her. Consistently, her self-appointed role was as provider, settler of arguments, arranger of solutions. Three generations of women and at least two of men depended on her radiant generosity.

There was nothing self-denying in her devotion. On the contrary, giving fulfilled her; it was the way she tried to hand on the solid happiness of her childhood. But perhaps that kind of love and safety isn't transferable, perhaps at best you can only live it out, demonstrate it's there, as pure possibility. Certainly no one afterward ever had that placid clarity of hers, that ability just to *be*, to create an excess by simple existence. The rest of us always argued with the given, began by shaking our fortunes like apples from a tree, ended by suing for peace.

"Mother did everything," Shrimp says simply, and if there is any criticism in her remark it is only because in doing everything Mirabel may have made those around her helpless. Shrimp thinks this is true of herself; everyone believed it of my mother. And Emma, my grandmother, must have feared it because she escaped from home as soon as she was old enough to run away. On the other hand, no one ever called my aunt Constance helpless. Yet even she used Mirabel as the measure by which the rest of the world was judged and found disappointing. As for me, as I say, I never came within the orbit of Mirabel's corrupting love, but only got the effects secondhand via the broken pieces of my mother.

The two daughters born so soon after Mirabel and Tennessee were married were strikingly similar in appearance, having both inherited Elizabeth Woolf's dark hair and eyes, her pale skin and delicate coloring, and their father's tall, slender figure. In formal photographs, conventional children's portaits, the unlived lives are captured and held back from where they are heading. If I clothe these two as Mirabel clothed them, if I see them as the photographer saw them, my great-aunt and grandmother are a pair of dark-ringleted, coal-eyed girls in pale high-button boots and satin-sashed white dresses, entirely innocent and nearly indistinguishable. But if I feel them as they became and as they existed for my mother, as the two sides of a ferocious female destiny, then even their baby pictures can make me anxious. For these adorable sisters were the first generation of pairs: the good child and the bad, the survivor and the victim, which twice divided the family and set up such torrents of destruction and remorse in my life with my mother.

My great-aunt Elizabeth (Shrimp) was born in 1905, a year and a half before Emma. Until Samuel sold his castle on Riverside Drive, they lived rather formally with their parents and grandparents in a house full of servants. It was a life regulated by rigid schedules and fixed prohibitions. There were expensive, temperamental animals in the stable and exotic plants in the greenhouse,

16

and in almost every room objects one must not touch. Once the families separated, they lived more simply, in a large, airy apartment on West End Avenue, with only one servant, apart from the nursemaid, to clean and cook for them. But the two worlds remained closely linked. Shrimp remembered visits from the beautiful wives of her mother's young uncles and how they would come in together on a winter afternoon, their cheeks pink from the cold, with hats like festive birds' nests perched on top of their pompadours and anchored by veils drawn tight over their pretty, unpowdered noses. There would be violets or gardenias pinned to their furs and high-button shoes peeping from voluminous dust ruffles. She must have been allowed once or twice to attend her grandparents' evening parties, because she remembers the small, formal orchestras, and the jewels and gowns of the women, wasp-waisted and décolletée, with puffed sleeves in dark colors of satin, velvet, and bead-encrusted taffeta. She remembers light on white shoulders and wafts of perfume mingling with the men's cigars and the scent of their carnations, worn in lapels next to the gold watch chains that flashed from the black of their evening dress.

At the new home there were other, simpler, sensuous pleasures: the luxuries of illness, the fevers, dizziness and languors of a long early quarantine with diphtheria, when my great-aunt lay in bed with the shades drawn, hearing the ragmen and flower sellers call up from the street, or the strolling musicians that serenaded in the evenings from the courtyard at the back of their building and to whom she was allowed to throw coins, wrapped in paper so they would not scatter. She remembers the cats in the courtyard and the mournful horses that pulled the street vendors' wagons, the organ grinder's monkey in his gold-braided red uniform and the beautiful dalmatian who sat up front on the fire engine as it came down the block with its crank-up siren going, breaking through the sound of streetcar bells on Broadway and the rattle of the cars as they rocked along the rails.

When Shrimp was six, and after Samuel's funeral, which she was not allowed to attend, their grandmother came to live with them, taking up a small suite of rooms off the foyer. She had by then a heart condition, and the girls were instructed to be silent whenever

17

they passed her door. Mirabel brought her breakfast on a tray, and late in the mornings the children would glimpse Elizabeth Woolf taking her tea in an embroidered Chinese bed jacket, her hair under a sleeping net, flowers next to her on a small table, among the silver-framed photographs and medicines in opaque blue and brown bottles.

In the evenings their father returned from work, bearing a newspaper which he would read word by word in an armchair under the light of a fringed standing lamp. Again, they were asked to make no noise, but they must have interrupted him often. There was a player piano in the sitting room, and he would sit with them on the stool, placing his long, elegant fingers over their small hands as they followed the dips and trills of the ivories, pretending it was they who created the sounds ("Moments Musicaux," "The Dance of the Hours") which came from the rolling brass teeth in the heart of the black, mahogany instrument.

On Saturday afternoons, when Mirabel sent them out for air, Tennessee would often take the girls to the pictures instead, preferably a Wallace Reid or Lillian Gish drama, after which he would sheepishly confess that they had "slipped and fallen into a movie." Other times it was a vaudeville show to watch the pratfall comics he loved, part of the family fare at the Palace, nothing, to be sure, at Minsky's.

For Shrimp, however considerate, however engagingly childlike his amusements, her father remained removed from them by virtue of his office hours, his dignified bearing and greater age. Even his exotic trace of accent and his great height set him apart from Mirabel and the children. Their grandmother, of course, was also a remote presence, protected from the daily activities of the household by both her precarious health and her station. The Irish cook had little to attract them, and they mostly resented their nurse. As for their beloved mother, she was simply a kind of order in the universe, present everywhere, protective, loving, but indistinguishable from the rest of their physical environment, being herself a form of safety, continuity and light. The obsessive passion of Shrimp's infancy was not for any of her elders but for her baby sister. From the first, and for a long time, Emma was her love object. Home and childhood were simply the background of this overwhelming passion.

Mirabel had a tendency, perhaps born of practicality, to treat the sisters as though they were one, an extension of herself, and therefore a version of one another. She dressed them identically, bought them identical dolls, and sent them, when they were of age, to the same schools, Madame Tisney's at first, and later PSJ. For a time they seemed to conspire with her idea of them, pleased to behave as well as look alike. They were always exclusive and inseparable, both at home and at school, where, though they were in different classes, they arranged to be together at every opportunity, just as though no one else in the world existed, and in spite of the fact that they were often teased for it, at times set upon by other children, and even punished by their teachers.

But if Mirabel didn't and they wouldn't differentiate between themselves, nature had other intentions. Like a single cell, they soon began to divide and, still as though there were no one else in the world, to form themselves in relation to one another. It was the reverse of what should have been, however, because it was the younger sister who seemed the more emerged form of the older. Physically, and from the start, Emma's features were more defined, her eyes darker, her cheekbones higher, her coloring more subtle, just as though the artist in question, having roughed out the general idea in the first child, had had the time and knowledge to perfect it in the second.

In matters of character, too, Emma always had the qualities you'd expect of an older sister in relation to a younger. It was she who invented their games and initiated expeditions, she who was adventurous, far braver, from the start more independent, as though in any situation she had nothing to fear because she'd done it all already. At Shokan, while Shrimp hung back on walks, worried about mud on her clothes or the depth of water in a pond, wouldn't learn to dive, wouldn't dance with boys, Emma never hesitated. With unfailing and yet bafflingly unconscious superiority, she inevitably swam further, climbed higher, ran faster, kept a secret longer or performed a dare sooner, and nevertheless accepted without impatience or judgment her elder sister's limitations.

But Shrimp did judge herself. Her failings and timidity were a torment to her. Self-reproach became a constant burden, and soon an inseparable part of her sense of who she was. Furthermore, she began to anticipate the inevitable rejection of her sister. She became certain that their closeness was founded on the younger sister's temporary ignorance of her own virtues. Perhaps for a while Shrimp had got away with it, been just enough older for Emma to treat her as an equal, just enough taller, stronger, around in the world enough longer to disguise from Emma what Shrimp already knew: that she was simply duller, more easily frightened, less imaginative, less pretty, in short, far less gifted for life than her sister. Not just now, but in the unchangeable absolute was it so. And what made it even more hopeless was that she knew the implications of their differences and Emma did not. At school and at Shokan, Emma never even saw how the other children admired her daring, how Shrimp was respected simply for being Emma's sister. Later, but not much later, she had no idea of her effect on boys. At fourteen, fifteen, Shrimp would watch her visitors—the same young males who squirmed and looked at their watches in her company—come to life, grow pink and begin to swagger whenever her younger sister entered the room. A photo of them around this age: Shrimp is fifteen, Emma thirteen, but Emma seems the more matured beauty. Shrimp is a pale, blurrier, more puppy-fleshed version of her poised and elegant sister. But while Shrimp fussed over her hair and clothes and makeup, Emma never took the slightest interest in or trouble with her appearance. She could wear anything, leave her hair anyhow and still be dazzling. For Shrimp there was no possible response but capitulation to the inequality. Jealousy was halfhearted at best, given her own adoration and Emma's indifference. Beauty, bravery, independence, were her sister's natural condition. She was as unaware of her virtues as of breathing.

Shrimp therefore accepted her own ordinariness and hence inferiority to Emma, and began to create for herself a secondary way through the world. If she couldn't be a magic creature like her sister, she would settle for commendation and conventional excellence. She became a good student, ladylike, well mannered and well dressed. She converted timidity into decorum, adjusted her desires, and watched the adventures of her sister with increasingly fainter regret. Always closer to Mirabel, she became the reliable one, a believer in her grandmother's world of family sentiment, romantic love and the pursuit of fashion. It was Emma who became rebellious, grew to disdain the bourgeois pleasures of her family, the oppressive life among the cousins, but above all the all-providing of Mirabel. Instead of love, beauty, success in the world, things she disregarded because they were already given, she began to pursue the one thing she felt she'd have to work for, freedom. Early on, she was determined to arrange things for herself, be beholden to no one, and live like an artist.

Under her grace and originality, there was always something a little hard about Emma, an intransigence in her notions of freedom and moral rectitude that was to affect everyone in her family. But the qualities that could wound her mother and sister, and which nearly devastated her daughters, also probably saved me, when I was a child and later. Yet still, even as a child, and totally enamored of the woman warrior I knew, even then I might have confused her with the heroine of a book of fairy tales she used to read to me. However much I loved her, she was always the Snow Queen, cold, beautiful and a little ruthless.

For Mirabel, Emma was simply her enchantingly favored, wonderfully talented if headstrong daughter, and if she missed in her the closeness which she'd had with her own mother, she contented herself with the company of Shrimp, with the planning of parties and trips to Europe, the talk about boys and relatives, the constant shopping and conferring on colors and hem lengths. And once Emma began to go her own way, Shrimp flourished in her mother's care, blossomed in a world for which she now had no rival. If she sometimes suspected that Emma had chosen the better if harder way through life, she nevertheless enjoyed her own. She became a chic young woman and, despite her constant self-deprecations, accomplished. She was one of the first women at the Columbia School of Journalism, which she attended after high school, a dashing figure by this time, flashing dark eyes under angled felt hats, by now able to disguise her fearfulness, and giving every indication of optimism.

It was all still happy enough, I think, in those early days before the marriages, or at least before Emma's declaration of war on Mirabel. It was her manner of leaving that must have ended the idyll, all that picture-perfect family living, ended it then, no matter how much Mirabel later tried to restore the former Eden. Emma had already quit school to study painting at the Art Students' League when she one day disappeared from home, without warning, without a note. For an entire week her frantic parents tried to find her. "I can remember Dad when he got the telegram," Shrimp said, "his body stooped over the high radiator, weeping with relief." It had taken the Pinkerton men six days to track her down, to a hotel room in Minneapolis, the hometown of the twenty-six-year-old sculptor with whom she'd run away. She was still only seventeen.

Now this was the situation with my grandmother just before she was found by the Pinkerton men in a motel room in Minneapolis. I should describe her to you as she sits waiting for Vergil to come back from looking for work, cross-legged on the utility bed in that drab room and in a storm of conflicting emotions. None of these was betrayed by her features, which were cool as always. Her dark, glossy hair was thick and boyishly cut in the fashion of the day, naked at the nape and swept from her face in the "classic" way Vergil liked because he could see her bone structure, her "armature" he called it. She had high cheekbones and a long, delicate nose, large, often fierce dark brown eyes, penetrating, sometimes unnervingly direct for a girl so young. Her skin was fair, very pale without makeup. She was tall and slender, which you could see even under the thick navy sweater and shapeless wool skirt, with long, graceful arms and legs. She looked like the athlete she was—she swam every day at the public baths near the school, and she walked everywhere and in every weather: you could see her striding with a long gait, carrying her notebooks and brushes in a satchel on her back, traveling the thirty blocks between home and school twice a day even when it made her late for dinner. Her profile was very fine and rather regal. Vergil drew her face many times when he first knew her, and later she agreed to pose for him without clothes in his room on lower Broadway. He drew her lying, sitting, standing, lovingly, respectfully, slowly, making long charcoal lines of her limbs, emphasizing, darkening over and over, the jutting bones of her hips and shoulders, the waves of her fine, dark hair. He thought she was the most beautiful girl he had ever seen, still half a child, but already with a commanding presence, self-possessed and unaffected, with something noble and sometimes a little frightening about her beauty and bearing. He had been mad about her—everyone could see that, and it had been getting difficult for them to stay on at the League.

Sitting on the bed, moving her hand back and forth over the cheap coverlet, she tried to think about what it was she was feeling. There was, first of all, a wild, heartless, animal joy in having escaped from the little world in New York, all that upholstered, regularly dusted life on West End Avenue, all the prying and insinuating of her chalk-stained colleagues at school. She had a feeling of triumph, too, in having walked off with one of the handsome art teachers only four months after she'd started there, the brooding, dark-browed, blond sculpture instructor whom all the other girls in her class—or, rather, young women, they were mostly a good deal older than she—used to court with a shameless Victorian simpering. From the back of the room they would sigh with faked distress over their work, which Vergil would patiently correct without the least indication that he'd seen through their efforts to seduce him. With my grandmother it had been a different story from the start. To be sure, she'd stood out in his class on the very first day because she was so young, and for a while she'd mistaken Vergil's attentions: the slightly quizzical glances cast in her direction, his solicitude when helping her construct her armature or damp-wrap her work—all that might have been, and was, confused in her mind at first with the kindness of an older teacher with a much younger student. But then some of the girls had begun to tease her about it, calling her teacher's pet and the "It" girl and such things, and she'd begun to see it all herself.

But now there were coming, black and regularly since she'd run away, spasms of panic about what they'd done. She gave not the slightest thought to the terrors of her parents. It wasn't that she was indifferent; she simply couldn't imagine it, couldn't conceive of any reaction in them other than surprise, even a little awe at her daring. They certainly knew by now she intended to make her life without them. How many times had they fallen out in the past year and a half until Mirabel told Dad that Emma's will was too strong and perhaps she did know what she wanted? And so she'd left school before graduation and started that fall at the Art Students' League. And now they would simply say to one another again that Emma knew what she wanted, and they would bow to it. Hadn't her mother been forced by *her* parents to go against her desires when she married Dad, and wasn't this an opportunity for her to behave unselfishly with her own daughter? And if they didn't understand, they would just have to accept it. She, Emma, was not her sister and never would be satisfied by what satisfied *her*, taking instructions about life from women's magazines when life was the great adventure, *the great adventure*, calling her so fiercely from her room on West End Avenue that she'd simply had to go. And that was all, she'd gone.

She was going to be an artist and she meant to continue somewhere else after this thing they'd done to be together. They certainly couldn't have been together in New York. Even the idea of introducing him to her mother and father, bringing him to the house with all those good, dull things in it and Dad with his jokes and laborious gentility and then Mother with her patient dignity and solicitude. She would have *sympathized* Vergil to death. So she'd gone off with Vergil, and they were together, and now this black, blind panic thing that something had gone wrong or why wasn't she feeling free anymore about the adventure that was her life—had it suddenly and incredibly *at this age* just stopped?

Vergil had parents, too, which she hadn't counted on, drab, fat Lutherans, more conventional than her own, to hear him tell it. He even seemed, once on home ground, a little frightened of them. He was getting to be sheepish whenever she mentioned them, when he'd never been anything but sure of himself in New York, which was why she believed in him and part of why she liked him, because his free, determined nature was a match for her own. But here in this windswept place, with only a few days' money left between them and some decision to make, it was all going thin. He'd been short with her a few times, even a little nasty. And sometimes she felt lonely when she was with him. He could go into his black mood for hours, cut her off and make her not exist even to herself. He was blackest when he came from seeing his folks or his sister, who was pleased as anything, you could tell, that the big art job in New York had burned out. How Vergil wasn't so damned special after all, and would have to work and scrimp and be bored with life like the rest of them.

Emma was almost relieved when the Pinkerton agents showed up, except that she was furious at the way they'd been tracked down. She did not speak to her parents for days after they brought them back to New York. There were long conferences between her father and Vergil behind the closed door of the living room, after which Vergil went home without being allowed to talk to her, and Mirabel came tapping gently at her door offering her supper on a tray. She was restless and gloomy at home, and of course not allowed back at school. They would have to be married, her father said—and Emma was trapped. The only way to escape home, clearly, was to go off with Vergil and the only way to do that was to marry him. The problem was, Emma didn't know any longer what she wanted. Mirabel's kindness was overpowering, and Vergil succumbed, and then she had to. They offered him a job at the Fan Company, and paid six months on a little apartment, and it was all over. And then it really was all over when Emma discovered she was pregnant. She had a daughter in the first year of her marriage, and eighteen months after that—just as though Emma were living Mirabel's life all over again—a second girl. There they were, two babies before Emma was twenty. No more art, no more freedom and not much more love. Just babies and no sleep, fights with Vergil and the constant fretting and interference, the victorious and thwarted grandmothering of Mirabel, whom Emma had only wanted to get away from and now never could because her mother owned Vergil, body and spirit (she would never own *her*, however).

And as for what was left of Vergil, that was soon somewhere else, somewhere bizarre and horrible, and beyond my trapped and exhausted grandmother even to think about.

"There was always a terrible tension in the house. I remember nothing but fear in that house. I don't remember one minute of happiness as a baby. Or of no fear."

This is my mother when I asked her about her childhood, fifteen years ago.

"I heard the fighting in the other room, I didn't understand. I heard what sounded like pillows being beaten. I was afraid of my father's hitting me . . . It was always on the surface ready to happen. I knew the violence was on my mother, too, but I wasn't really worried for my mother because she wasn't very worried for us. She must have been so distracted by the relationship and the unhappiness. I was conscious of a terrible upheaval between them and, overriding everything, my father's righteousness and Christianity and representation he was God on earth.

"When I was just a baby, he used to take me away from my mother and sister and hold me on his lap and say 'God' to me over and over. I was terribly frightened and I remember something happening to me in my mind. I don't know what it was, but at that age the intensity of this man forcing me and the anger in it . . . It was almost as though he was on a mission for this unseen thing; he represented it, and if I didn't understand this, something was going to happen. I got the feeling of imminent danger if I didn't understand. He wasn't forcing me to listen, he was forcing me to understand. He really, literally, put the fear of hell in me.

"I remember being little and reading a comic book and having him come up behind me and shock me, frighten me, because I was concentrating on a comic book at the age of five, and he warned me not to pay my mind on anything but God . . . and after that I never could concentrate on anything for very long, ever in my life.

"He got me to go to Christian Science school, but not Constance, he kept the religious thing on me all the time. I had to go to Sunday school. I remember that I was so humiliated by it that it seemed so deep, dark, horrible, secret, like a room with some awful fetish.

"I remember sitting in a movie and the words came to me, 'God stinks,' and I remember this was the first time I'd ever thought anything blasphemous. I was a little glad brain floating in space until this happened. And the words shot through my head, 'God stinks,' and I remember the appalling panic that I could say such a thing. I never got over this panic."

In the earliest photographs I have of my mother, she looks like an Indian child, with her black hair and frightened animal eyes, the seemingly ancient lines of worry on her brow. Beside her, as though to confirm her story that Contance was spared, is the placid, blond head of her baby sister, here as always seeming to sail painlessly through life. The only good thing my mother remembers about her earliest years is Angel, an erratic presence that comes and goes, there and not there, not always allowed, and never enough to keep her safe from the man who comes out of the dark bedroom to lift her, hold her tight and tell her about God.

On the one occasion I met my grandfather I was fourteen and working as a summer "mother's helper" with a family in Maine. Somehow, mutual friends of his and my employer's had discovered his connection to me and, without warning me what was to happen, invited him to lunch and a swim in their pool. When we were standing around in our suits—and that was part of it, because I was at an age to feel my own physical vulnerability thus exposed, awkward and newly sexually conscious—they produced Vergil out of the shadows, as I remember, with the, to them, delightful line: "Here is your grandfather." But it was not exactly Heidi. I remember the man and his name, both like some broken bit of machinery, a crank, a handle, some hokey and useless bit of Americana, there in Maine in a cracker-barrel check shirt, his eyes oddly oily or brimming, with the trapped, guilty look of a dog who expects to be punished. He was "gentle" now, this white-faced monster of my mother's childhood, a frail and broken man of God. I remember how instantly I despised him. He approached to say, in a soft, quavery voice, that I was beautiful, and I felt a sickening victory, something I didn't understand, something like Susannah with the Elders, simultaneous shame and revulsion and triumph over an old, spying, broken man, someone I could wound simply by being young. Afterward I never replied to any of the notes that followed our meeting, notes that began "My dear little grand-daughter," nor did I acknowledge the crumpled five-dollar bill he once enclosed. And now, all I have left of him, apart from the hell he bequeathed my mother, is his death certificate and a letter as pathetic as he then seemed to me, from a state-run home for old men in Bangor, asking what should be done with his odds and ends, a few pieces of sculpture, a small parcel of clothes.

I have a photograph of my mother with her father. She is the same age I was when I met him. She is feeling shame, too, tall and skinny and wearing a sort of Sunday outfit of hat and coat that makes her look like a refugee, maybe because it's the late thirties and she seems thin, frightened, dressed in other people's clothing. She is very subtly pulling away from him in the picture, while he has a possessive, utterly unnatural daddy arm on her shoulder. There's no power any longer in his expression, nothing to indicate his special commission from God. But perhaps he knew he was on his way out by then, since sometime in this period Emma and he were divorced. Perhaps his awkwardness is only that of the visiting father, his affability that of someone who must make up in the formal photograph for all they've failed to be in real life. My mother looks as though she's waiting for the photographer to get it over with so she doesn't have to stand so close to him or have that hand on her shoulder. And there's something sexually dubious about him even here, something sheepish in his face, good-looking in an unstable way—a weak man's steaminess coming out of him, ready to slip over into viciousness or tears. Maybe I'm imagining this, and maybe no snapshot can be so freighted. The main thing is, it was one of the last. By the time my mother was fourteen or so, Vergil was gone. And Emma, still only thirty-two, could try once again to be free . . . Except for the children, except for Angel. Because with Vergil and God out of the way, Angel was able to come closer, and it was at that moment, bent on reparation, that she began to flood into her grand-children's lives.

If Mirabel's rebellious daughter Emma seemed to bring nothing but trouble on herself by leaving the nest, Mirabel's good daughter Shrimp had apparently reaped only rewards for obedience. A good daughter she remained, and a good student. She had married properly and glamorously after her stint at Columbia, Lars Hamilton, young

star reporter of the New York *Herald*, a man of Hollywood good looks—
Ronald Colman hair, Ramon Novarro eyes—and though for a time she
kept up her writing, with short stories published in *Vanity Fair* and
items in her husband's paper, she was willing enough to surrender her
career for the greater happiness of her marriage.

What marriage was, my great-aunt says, was fun, good filmable fun,
full of the romps and glamour of a thirties comedy, with drawing
rooms the size of hotel lobbies, extravagant clothes and nightclub
orchestras, figures from Harlem and Sardi's and *Mr. Blandings Builds
His Dream House*. Hardly like a depression at all. No, more like a
movie, much too like, for Lars was transferred to Hollywood to cover
the film world, and Shrimp's gay and debonair existence came to a
sudden end when, like a boy from the sticks, he tumbled head over
heels and disappeared with a peroxide starlet. At that point it became
clear to her all over again that she was and had always been merely
Shrimp, Emma's less favored sister, the homely Mirabel's true daughter—and then Shrimp, like her mother, had a nervous breakdown, out
there on the West Coast, hers more properly following divorce rather
than proposal. "A real wingding," she told me, "ECT, the works. I
went to Reno in a wheelchair." She returned home, as though the
whole thing had been a dream, to the shelter and peace of Mama.
And once she'd learned her lesson, it was as though there was no point
trying again. She took a small job and a small apartment and kept
them both, in stoical solitude, for the next fifty years.

With both her daughters home and single again, Mirabel was once
more in her element. Things were almost as they had been before the
marriages—the arguments with Emma, the companionship of
Shrimp—except that now there were two more girls for her to take
care of. Vergil was gone, and Lars was gone, and then Tennessee died
and it seemed to her that there was only herself to provide. At the age
of sixty-two, never having worked a day in her life, Mirabel took over
the running of the Fan Company, beginning a routine she kept up
until the year of her death: going to the office every morning at seven
and coming home twelve hours later to supervise her daughters and
granddaughters, to hold everything together, just as she'd always done
before.

My mother took no pride in Emma's renewed efforts to gain her freedom. Having escaped, finally, from the poisonous domination of her father, the freakish Christian Science that set her apart from her school friends, the fighting and oppressively sexual atmosphere at home which made her always a little anxious and a little ashamed, what she wanted now was some semblance of ordinary life, something she'd been allowed to glimpse on visits to her grandparents.

But it was not to be. The quarreling between Emma and Mirabel seemed only to escalate once Vergil was gone. What made it worse was that the quarrels seemed always to center on the upbringing of her sister and herself. Emma, now determined to set up at long last as an artist and a free woman, expected to take her daughters with her on the adventure. Mirabel's view was that until Emma found her feet in bohemia, the girls had better come and live with her.

For a few years, as young teenagers, Bett and Constance bounced between the mothers, sometimes living in luxury in Angel's apartment on Central Park South, where they were waited on by the Irish maid and sent to school in new clothes and with money in their pockets, sometimes living their mother's precarious life in a series of what were to Bett utterly unromantic pads, having to find their way from school through cat- and musician-ridden Greenwich Village streets, to some cold-water loft where, among the smells of paint and turpentine, clay and plaster, they would do their homework, elbow to elbow with their mother's friends, "weirdos" with odd opinions and odder manners, long-haired foreigners who played harmonicas, one-legged suitors or much-married Romeos, visiting Peruvians and general castoffs, "originals" that Bett and Contance dreaded might one day end up as some kind of second embarrassing Daddy.

Next to the unconditional love and sympathy that seemed endlessly available from Angel, Emma's way of withholding approval was chilling. My mother's cautious gossip about movie stars or school life would be met by a restraining silence, a grim tightening of the mouth, or an abrupt change of subject. The things to be valued in life, as Emma made oppressively clear, were integrity, honor, self-realization, certain kinds of art, and, above all, "a sense of reality," a phrase which could only mean that, once again, Emma did not approve Angel's offerings of money or clothes and was disappointed that her daughters hadn't had enough pride or independence to refuse them. But for my mother it was to be a lifelong confusion: gifts and money were always a sign of love to her, and reality a thing that stuck to you anyway, dragged you down, and had every intention of finishing you off.

So it went on, while Bett and Constance grew older, year after year of dizzying fights, of coming and going between their disapproving mother and the all-accepting Angel, until shortly before my mother's graduation from high school the miracle happened, and Emma greed to let her daughters go. My mother was seventeen and Constance fifteen when they went to live permanently with Angel, in what always seemed in hindsight a kind of paradise.

They were no longer the skinny refugees of the photos taken four years earlier. The knobbly-kneed coltish looks, the frightened Bambi appearances, had been superseded by something that looked like confidence. And no wonder. Whatever else might be said about the girls, everyone agreed they were unusually beautiful, with their mother's long legs and slim figure, her high cheekbones and long elegant nose (Constance's joke was that the noses ran in the family). On the streets (turning heads as they progressed) they made a striking pair: Bett five feet eight with pale skin, dark eyes and hair; Constance two inches taller, blond and blue-eyed. Out with Emma, who was still remembered as 'the most beautiful girl in New York' and who never looked more than a few years older than her daughters, they might all three have passed as the élite of a model agency; with Angel, they looked like someone's precious daughters, out with their small chaperone. For a few years at least they must have been conscious of the power of their looks (their only power); now, at Angel's, they began to use it, triumphantly. From the moment they moved in, it is said, the life of the house was given over to the girls and their "beaux"—the term an enduring piece of family parlance, owing its existence to the otherwise largely unregistered passage of their Tennessee grandfather. Throughout the mid-forties young men dangled from chairs and sofas in the living room, catered to in the daytime by the Irish maid, entertained in the evenings by Angel, as they waited for the girls to appear.

My mother remembers West Point cadets and young lieutenants, stray GIs whom Angel would find on the streets and invite home to meet her girls, as though they and she were just one more service in the war effort. All strictly proper, yet undeniably odd, this picture of the small, homely lady, gossiping, drinking and playing cards with young men lured by her granddaughters. But Angel's reply to those who questioned her hospitality was always indignant and always the same: "I trust my girls." So began for Bett and Constance the life of constant hangovers and late risings, love and parties and nights at the Stork Club, the glorious era of being beautiful and spoiled, welcome and happy and free.

Bett and Constance had been collectively known as "the girls" ever since they became the focus of family dispute following Vergil and Emma's divorce. But their common circumstances—the fear and hatred of their father, their longing for and rejection by their mother, their shared life at Angel's—disguised differences of character which flourished once their common enemies were gone. Like the sisters in the generation before them, Bett and Constance had begun in closeness and matured in opposition. But unlike Shrimp and Emma, they were not content to remain sisterly until life let them go their separate ways. At Angel's their quarreling began in earnest. Having grown up simultaneously motherless and overmothered, and having thus had too shifting a target for rebellion, they found it easiest to define themselves by division, through methodical combat. Since they were both equally courted, it was not a simple case of jealousy—no argument over a common prize; instead, each battled by disdaining the tastes of the other.

Constance's look was a makeupless Grace Kelly affair, which suited her silky, straight blond hair and long, slender frame, together with an air of haughty remoteness, a style into which she'd transformed the gruesome shyness of her gawky, loveless adolescence. Disdain soon became her weapon, along with an early pretense at worldliness. She had a line in repartee, barbed often enough, that would make those around her alternately nervous or flattered to be taken as allies in her wars against the Other. She was fully engaged by the romance of the self and would regale her acquaintance, no matter how recent, with anecdotes of coups by beauty or brilliance, or with amusing accounts of her humiliations of the slow or vulgar.

My mother, on the other hand, went to drama school, hoping one day to join the figures of popular adulation in Hollywood. Her publicity photos show she favored the Rita Hayworth look, windswept hair, moist parted lips and a bosom as full as she could make it. She had her debut on Broadway—a small part, but the title role, significantly enough, as "The Pick-Up Girl." Equally significant, it seems to me, was the way her career came to a sudden end on her first and only night, when her nerves failed her, words failed her, and the curtain dropped. Stage fright was to be my mother's chronic affliction. She always looked the part, and never knew the lines.

They were at Angel's sometime after V-E Day, Bett still memorizing lines, Constance practicing posture in front of a mirror, or both of them, according to Shrimp, "lollygagging" through the afternoon, having slept off the night before, waiting for Mirabel to return from work, when it would be time to go out again—it was sometime then that the girls came across my father.

My father once told me, in his deep, rolling tones, and apropos my going on holiday with a boyfriend—this when I was nineteen and the rest of the world was enjoying the late sixties—that I had a reputation to consider, which, once damaged, "like communism, stays on your record." "There are," he said, entirely seriously, "women you marry and women you take to nightclubs." Nevertheless, it was on a zebra-skin-covered banquette at El Morocco that he first came across Constance, and through her was introduced to Angel and Bett.

My mother's marriage, like Shrimp's, made a good movie, a little faster from beginning to end, and more melodramatic, the plot of which can be given briefly: A beautiful young American bride accompanies her tall, mysterious English husband to postwar London, where innocent love is overwhelmed by the forces of weather, rationing, infidelity and Gothic in-laws. My mother, who loved everything she knew about England—the bobbies and fog, Ascot, Basil Rathbone and Mrs. Miniver—was unprepared for what she got: long days and nights looking after a baby in a damp, heatless basement, while her husband swanned around town in his

Bentley, smoking cigars and looking for capital ventures. There was cold, deprivations of all kinds, sudden and inexplicable loneliness, and the horror of what was expected of a young wife in England: a self-occupation that my mother, on foreign ground, or at least on this foreign ground, this nation of "misshapen and very homely people," where there was "never any sun in the sky" and "nothing in the shops, you had to eat rabbit," was incapable of. As a relief from London, there were terrifying weekends at the huge, also unheated, country seat of her new in-laws, the fierce and brooding Lady Massingham and her remote and silent husband, Sir Edward. My father's decision to marry an "American actress," a "Jewess," as I later heard her called, did not go down well; nor did her real silk stockings, nor her willingness to change the baby's diapers *in the drawing room*—a scandal that burned long enough for me to hear about it sixteen years later.

In the end, they scandalized one another, and less than two years after her wedding Bett was once again in the living room in New York, telling Angel and Shrimp and Constance about the scene at the airport, during which her mother-in-law had grabbed hold of the baby's leg and hissed, "Leave her here with us, you'll never be able to give her what we can." My mother wrenched her child away and ran through her tears toward the plane that was to take us back to the free world. She did, however, stop to accept a handkerchief that Sir Edward held out to her in "the one act of kindness I ever received from them," and for which she retained a soft spot for her former father-in-law in years to come.

With Bett returned, and with a daughter, the family was its complete, exclusively female, self: the widow Mirabel (Angel) and her two daughters, the good daughter Shrimp (officially named Elizabeth after Angel's mother) and her bad daughter Emma; Emma's good daughter Bett (named after Shrimp) and her bad daughter Constance; and now Bett's daughter, named for Constance and later, following an argument with Constance, renamed Helen. Now we were six, four generations of almost mystical Manichaean symmetry and Mendelian simplicity, an unassailable oval, an egg shape of female solitude, thus:

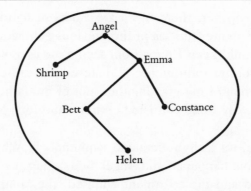

At that time, marriage and changing your mind went fast enough. Divorce took a little longer, and in the case of my parents had to be done in England. My mother, therefore, had to go back and forth somewhat after her dramatic exit in order to negotiate with my father's lawyers and her own. On these occasions I would accompany her on the plane and be parked at the Panda Hotel, an elegant if unusual establishment in Kensington, exclusively for children. The divorce took five years to come through, with a lump settlement of five thousand pounds, proscribing all further claims of support. With this, my mother was at last able to finance the traditional marriage-related nervous breakdown.

Before then, however, my mother had to earn her living and mine somehow, and so while Constance was still at Angel's, conducting her salon and working as a model, Bett began to assist Emma with commercial sculpture projects: modeling mannequin parts, lamp bases, ashtrays and other decorative bric-a-brac, the kinds of things Emma had been making to support her work as a "serious" artist. Unlike acting, this sculpting proved to be something my mother had a talent for, and as long as it was simply work and not "art" that was involved, she could enjoy it. Art, as had been imprinted on her since childhood, was the banner under which Emma had fled from home and abandoned Angel, under which Constance and she had been neglected and for which she had suffered such agonies of embarrassment at school. Like God, Art was for my mother a very dirty word. Furthermore, she was and remained ambivalent toward her own artistic gift, which came, like the commissions, from Emma. I am told that, despite Emma's attempts to help her, there was a great deal of fighting between mother and daughter (just as in the previous generation) and that my mother would keep Emma from seeing me as a way to punish her for her former indifference. Whatever the cause, I have no early recollection of my grandmother, nor of my father or Shrimp or Constance. My world consisted entirely, and for a long time, of my mother.

In any case, we really were alone soon enough. When, in 1951, the unthinkable happened and Angel died, when the family company was sold and the apartment emptied, the family broke up. The company, which had lasted just over seventy-five years, and which had been the support of five generations, was now found to be almost worthless; and Mirabel, who had worked ten hours a day until her last and seventy-third year, proved to have been something less than the brilliant businesswoman everyone assumed her to be, or could have guessed from her eternally cheerful, calm demeanor. It had all been done by mirrors, and Angel, the great provider and fixer and unruffler, had simply and characteristically not wanted to trouble anyone with her problems, or alarm any of her girls in their already complicated lives. And who would there have been to confide in? Not Emma in bohemia, nor Shrimp in her solitude, nor Constance at the Stork Club, least of all "poor, sweet Bett," trekking back and forth from New York to the Panda Hotel. After three-quarters of a century providing for the marital lame ducks and their female offspring, the family milch cow had run dry, and from now on no one was able to keep "a sense of reality" at anything like the desired distance.

When whatever was left was divided among the women, the rebellious daughters departed. Emma went to paint in Spain. Constance went to Madrid, where she met a Spanish anthropologist and accompanied him on an expedition to the Sahara. The good daughters stayed behind: Shrimp in her solitude; and separate from her, Bett, free for the moment of Emma and Constance, bereft of Angel, and, now, all alone with me.

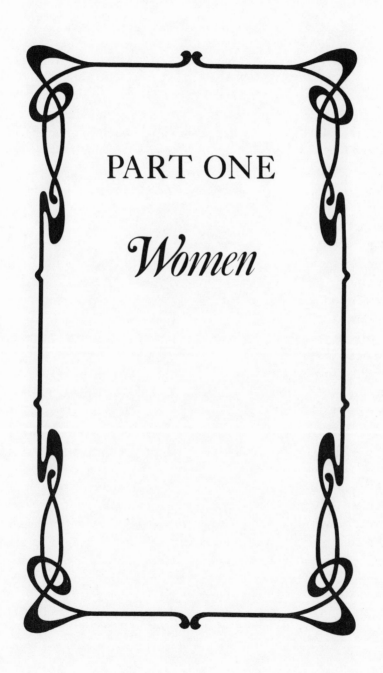

PART ONE

Women

ONE

WHEN I WAS LITTLE I knew nothing of this history of my mother's, and nothing about the others. All I knew was Bett and my rapacious desire for her. It was a state of longing so fierce, because we were so often separated, that I can only compare it to being in love. Not just compare it. Let me state from the beginning that when I was a child I was absolutely and ferociously in love with my mother. My existence, so much of it apart from her, was haunted by her absence, my present soaked through and colored by knowledge of where I was not. I knew two worlds when I was a child, discrete and simultaneous, a world of things that was immediate and sensuous, and alongside that the world of which I was always conscious: this desired other which was she. Only when these two worlds came together, only when she became my concrete, sensuous present, was I ever whole.

I lived this fractured life at a place called Mirrenwood, a small boarding school for girls in New Hampshire. I suspect now the school was chosen because the name reverberated for Bett with some buried reference to her beloved grandmother. Giving up her daughter to some evocation of Mirabel was a repetition—with a double sense of mourning (the loss of both Mirabel and me)—of a renunciation made very differently in an earlier decade by Emma. To me, of course, the school was no haven at all, but a place of exile.

One Sunday in the mid-fifties I sat on wooden steps, fully dressed in my formal navy-blue uniform in the early heat of May. I could feel the sun baking my clothes and smell it on the pale gray paint of the porch where girls with permission to have lunch

39

out with parents were meant to sit. I was there by myself, the other girls having left already, taken off one by one in small explosions as each arriving car removed a daughter from our group. I enjoyed being alone, sitting here and knowing she was on her way. There was a sweet, acrid smell coming off the box hedges in the driveway, mixing with the gasoline wafts from baking tarmac. There were iridescent slicks on the black puddles, from which in spring worms would emerge mysteriously after the rains, and which would dry as the sun grew stronger to a muddy orange, or refuse to dry, remaining deep enough to reflect in ruts and pools moving shadows of the overhanging trees, enormous and centuries old, which arched over the entrance to the school and marked our separation from the world outside.

Since my mother was late, I could hear the noises of the other girls eating lunch inside, the sound of plates and cutlery and the excited voices, impatient for parents who would arrive at three and depart by six, when we would all reassemble for the remote consolation of Walt Disney and Ed Sullivan, and before that, the cartoon smiles of the Dutch-boy-haircutted Campbell twins, who held hands and sang soup songs before and during *Lassie*—a program which began every week with the same long cry of the little boy for his dog, a cry full of desperation, it seemed to me, and which hung on the air long enough to make the embrace, toward which Lassie bounds with all the strength of her maternal body, symbolic of what we had all just communally relinquished.

I had an unusual view from where I was sitting. Normally the school began for us the other side of the house, at the back entrances with the playing fields below and to the right the slate walk to the schoolrooms, with the lawns and orchards beyond. From this side, the outside world was closer and the school foreshortened: only the driveway with its triangular hedges and the big moving trees that today filled the air with odors which crashed like snare drums into the smells of Sunday lunch and somehow erotically teased me with their swaying. Enticed by these, I waited for Bett and the first sight of the local taxi as it would turn, black and shiny as an event, with the heavy, bored face of the driver in front and, in the back, all that I could make out of my mother: a series

40

of small movements, a compression of energy, an instantly identi-
fiable relation of dark eyes to pale skin, and then, more clearly as
the taxi drew up, a mime for me of both excitement and, for the
inevitable lateness, apology. But I was happy enough waiting for
her. I knew that her arrival would alter my life absolutely and that
there would be whole hours before I would begin to dread the
parting, whole hours of not counting, not figuring, not bracing, but
just being, as I could only be when I was with her: outside time
and whole.

I was eight then and I'd been at the school three years. At the
beginning I'd waited politely, writing little notes as instructed each
Wednesday and Saturday afternoon, notes on the children's station-
ery we all had, with colored balloons or dachshunds cavorting down
the margins and pathetic messages penciled in on lines drawn with
a ruler and copied from letters the teacher put on the board: DEAR
MOMMY/DADDY, I AM VERY HAPPY AT SCHOOL. Coached by the
authorities as to contents—some school event, some weather
change—I wrote to Bett. I wrote to my father, too, in my first year,
though I don't remember remembering him. But I still have a
folded square of pink paper with dirty white scalloped edges (paper
which by itself brings back all sorts of sensations) on which large,
childish letters knock into one another like clowns mimicking
drunks: DARLING FATHER, I wrote rather vampishly, I AM FIVE
YEARS OLD. PLEASE COME AND SEE ME. I still have it, because it
was never sent. I suppose the school tactfully addressed the
envelope to Bett. I'm not sure why she would have kept it all these
years, among the piles of relics of her precious child. It strikes me
now as a message of restrained irritation: Five years old already,
Dad, let's please hurry it up. Maybe just an early realization that
my eventual deliverance would lie in hands other than hers.

Coming here was, like all her betrayals, accidental: haphazard
and final, without warning and seamless. I can remember sitting
next to her and a man, not my father, in the back of a car with
leather seats, driving under trees so that the sunlight struck our
faces in a series of slaps. I can remember standing on grass and
being polite to a large, falsely friendly woman who took us on a
tour of the school. I can remember feeling increasingly anxious to

leave. My mother seemed to me oddly remote, smiling, watching distractedly as the large woman loomed and bent over me, telling me that there were no children yet because it was still summer, that they would be coming in the fall. It was hard to pay attention to her and not my mother, and I certainly didn't care who was coming. *Can we go now?* I remember my mother getting into the car again, but not with me. I was on the grass with the woman, watching the car slowly back out of the driveway, and then slowly I understood what I must suppose I had been told that afternoon. I remember a terrible panic as the car began to disappear under the trees and then suddenly was gone. I remember neither crying nor whimpering but opening my mouth like the black opening in the trees and letting out a sound I didn't think I could stop, frightening myself with it, one long howl of outrage and devastation, so loud it shattered and displaced everything around me. And then everything returned and I was quiet, standing on the grass with my hand in the woman's hand.

But it is three years later, and I have been trained in waiting. I barely ask anymore about the jobs, or men, or any of the things that were always around the corner and would mean that I could come home and live with her. I did come home. I came home on vacations and, after that first summer, whole summers. It was always where I wanted most to be, but, as I gradually came to understand, it was somehow not the same as real life. Real life went on in this peculiar place and was absurd, orderly and inevitable.

They showed movies about strange and miserable children at that school. *The Boy with Green Hair* was one. And then they showed big sentimental films about family life: *Cheaper by the Dozen, Life with Father*, films they played so often that the pictures were scratched or burnt and the tapes would snap, so they'd have to put the lights on again and we'd wait, blinking. They seemed to like those films more than we did or they thought we should. It was like the Sunday TV we watched, by which they'd plug us in to consoling images of healthy family life: fathers, mothers, siblings, puppies and bicycles, precisely everything none of us had. We were all there for the same reason: some failure of ideal American life—divorces, breakdowns, deaths. You used to see the parents arriving, daddies alternating with mommies, or even when they came together, looking a little embarrassed about having left their children in such a place, about having failed as a family, as citizens. Mirrenwood was not the kind of school you'd send anyone to for social or educational advantages. There were about fifty girls in eight grades and only four teachers, who had to double up classes. It was more of a boardinghouse than a school, a kind of depository for the strays and detritus of misfired adult lives. I remember one night in the dormitory discussing this and the issue of money. I remember someone saying we were all waiting for parents to organize their lives (finalize a divorce and remarry, or get back together, or move East), but how there must have been money at least or we wouldn't have been there. And I said, because it was true, that I was there because there wasn't enough money. (Even with problems, if there were money, we'd be in a real school, I said.) "I suppose you're poor," an older girl said sarcastically. I took a tin basin from the bathroom, put a towel on my head and walked around the beds, making up a song about being poor and having to beg for money. It should have been filmed, like *Oliver!* (or *Gandhi*), with all the waifs bouncing on their bunks and doing the chorus. Only no one bounced or sang, because they thought they were rich and I thought we were all poor. As soon as Bett got hold of a real job or a man with money I'd be gone, I knew that. I thought it was the same for all of us.

There was no caste system at Mirrenwood, nothing like what I have heard about life at English prep and public schools. Except for those days on which we were visited by our families, except for the private and never-spoken-of interruptions of the school year— four weeks at Christmas and Easter, three months in the summer— we were all made equals by deprivation, fellow orphans and solitaries linked as linearly and randomly as colored beads on a necklace. We were little girls with secrets, our own codes of honor and bravery; we made and broke alliances with fierce infantile passions. To ourselves we were not children in a world of grown-ups but, rather, unique and whole beings in a universe that was part captivity and part natural paradise. All our intelligence and cunning directed itself toward evasion of the tangent points and boundaries of our confinement. Whenever possible we escaped from school a few hours at a time, or else conformed with regulations simply to avoid contact with the women who controlled us, in order to experience ourselves as the free creatures we were not. We took life in the gaps of regulated existence, looked for cracks in the schedules and the watch of our guards, communicated in subtexts and privately dreamed of rescue.

But as with Mirabel at the moment she understood the gulf that separated her small, homely self from her surroundings, there was for all of us at Mirrenwood a similar sense of divide. Outside and around us and in the margins of our awareness was the ceaselessly pumping opulence of our environment, inside of which we dwelt in dank, regimented loneliness. Abandoned in this natural paradise, we waited for reprieve from parents on whom we projected all the fierceness of our desires for salvation. Our universe was pristinely Manichean, and we invented the absent (future) parent as counterweight to the hideous, to us barely human, figures that ruled our present. Nature was a neutral entity, neither benign nor welcoming, but seductive, impartial, and containing evidence of a richness and energy that surely existed in the universe though from us withheld. Virtue, the longed-for radiant face of the Good, was projected over this dark unhappy place into a notion of home and mother, home and father. "What is away like?" we, too, would have asked, had we not known ourselves at every moment to be in exile.

For myself in regard to Bett, it was a long time before the flaws in the deity appeared. Signs of her weakness, indications of something other than omnipotence, gradually pierced the waves of devotion that had surrounded and protected me in thinking about her. Latenesses, failures to show, to provide, to protect and ultimately, as it finally dawned on me, to rescue, grew as cracks in the monument. Waiting for her at Mirrenwood, year after year, I knew myself to be helpless. But what began now to be clear and no less than terrifying was my growing understanding that she was as helpless as I.

But I am waiting for her, sitting in the sun on the gray, peeling porch from which the others have gone. I am eight years old and it is time now for me to bring my mother, late as she is, into the driveway by the black taxi.

And all at once she's there, opening the taxi door, which hits the sun so light smites like a hero's sword on the windowpane and on her, sunlight and shining blackness breaking into the swaying greenery as she gets out and crouches and opens her arms. I walk and then run, colliding with her and taking in the feel of her cool cheeks and warm dress, of her glossy dark hair, her mouth and neck, warm and damp and scented faintly with Blue Grass. And she, in her ritual of repossession, removes from me this warm May day my beret, my sweater, my bloomers ("Why are you so bundled up?"), my shoes and socks if she could. But she stops there and holds my clothes in one hand and me in the other as we get back in the taxi together. She smells the top of my head like a mother cat, brushes my hair out with her fingers, tousles me, unpins me, unbuttons me as far as she can and then, only then, she says, "Where shall we go?"

We go into town, where we can spend the afternoon without a car. We have lunch at one of the places near the center. Other parents go to the fancy Red Lion further out of town, which has a parking lot with trimmed hedges and wrought-iron lampposts, where there is a red carpet and a tasseled menu and dark wood paneling. We have been there before with one of the other parents. But we prefer to be alone and we don't have a car. Going into town is the best idea. We can spend the afternoon walking about like the pedestrians, city folk, we are.

Sometimes, if Bett got a lift from the station with another group, we'd have no choice but to walk around the school and out by the back way, along the main road, her in her stilettos and New York clothes, me in my unpinned uniform, walk miles, it seemed, to the nearest place, a roadside house where they served greasy hamburgers and home fries in a dark room at the back, where we'd have to walk first through a front bar of sullen, heavyset men in shirt sleeves, smoking and drinking beer and listening to baseball. They'd eye us and pass looks among one another, then return to their drinks, and you'd hear, in the lugubrious male silence, the (to me then infinitely depressing) tones of some rural voice coming regularly through the radio above the bar: ". . . a hiiigh fly to left field, Johnson's got it and the inning is O-ver." In this alien corner we would sit leaning toward each other over a ketchup-sticky shellacked redwood table and we'd know we have to draw it out because there was nowhere else to go but back to school. And so we'd talk as the screen door banged and the men up front greeted each other and the tired male voice said over and over with meaningless fortitude: "fowel baw," or "bawl fore," or "Wilson fowels it off."

Today we are in town, the only customers in a restaurant with a ceiling fan and tea-stained menus, but where we can have lobster salad sandwiches and Coca-Cola and still go to the three o'clock movie across the street, where they are playing *Farewell to Arms* with Rock Hudson and Jennifer Jones. Sitting at the big plate-glass window overlooking the patch of lawn in the town square, I can have her all to myself, this beautiful mother, with her Italian haircut and dark penciled eyes and red lipstick. She always dresses like this, stylishly, sexily, beautifully groomed and made up, and it's all for me. There are no men here and nothing to feel anxious about. (My mother's looks are so unprotected.) I am aware all the time how men look at her. Sometimes I am a little confused, if she is, say, in a group at school. She is by far the most beautiful mother and I don't have to take my word for it, I can see the fathers casting sidelong glances and getting shy and excited. And I can see what other mothers look like, about a hundred years older and a hundred pounds heavier, as though life had been over for a long time and they are buried, stranded, inside. But her life is so clearly, radiantly beginning, beginning even more than mine. There is something so fresh and also vulnerable about her youth and beauty that I sometimes worry for her and feel helpless because I am not always with her. She comes up alone, unescorted, and she goes home alone, feeds the cat, unplugs the iron and puts the board away, thinks of me and is sad. She knows she has to get up early to work or find work and who knows when she'll be able to get up again? And then there's the summer, she's got to get ready for that, job, money, place. She's alone in New York, beauty doesn't help, it's just another thing to take care of, another imperiled part of her.

I am used to her life in New York, the way we keep moving. There are times when I never spend a vacation with her in the same place. When she comes to get me at the start of our holidays I never know where we are going. We have lived in apartments on East Seventy-second Street near Fifth and in a town house on Eighty-third with a bathroom in the hall, over a bar on Lexington, where I had my own room, and once, for two whole months, at a hotel in a little room, eight by twelve, with a hot plate and a wheel-in cot. My mother likes the elegant neighborhoods of the Upper East Side; it makes things seem a little better when you can go out of your door and see well-dressed, happy people. She "loathes" the West Side, where she grew up, she says. Broadway in particular depresses her, most of all Greenwich Village, where she was "forced" to live as a child. Her jobs tend to be this side of town, too. She is Gal Friday at a model agency, or once a dress designer at Helena Rubinstein or a "temp" at lots of places where she doesn't have to type but simply "look great" and answer the phone. Her bosses always seem to like her and welcome me, but there's something sad about it, even I can feel them thinking: This woman shouldn't have to be here, someone should take care of her.

She has boyfriends. They are charming and dapper, sometimes between marriages or jobs, and they never seem to work out. There are older men who adore her, bring her flowers and presents and take her to the theater and sometimes want to marry her, but she is never in love with them. She falls, she tells me later, for the "heels," the good-looking ones who make her cry hour after hour into a towel in the bathroom.

But I only get her life in bits and pieces and my interests are fiercely egotistical. I want her to be happy but I don't really want to share her, and what she does when we aren't together, like what I do at school, is nothing compared to this radiant common ground. I am, she tells me, and I know it's true—despite Mirrenwood—I know and have always known and always will that I am the most important thing in her life. I am the very center of her world. I must grow well and be strong because I am all she has.

Last time we went to the movies we saw *Bambi*, and we both cried at the death of Bambi's mother. Nothing could be worse than such a devastation, we both knew that. Men can make you cry but men don't matter next to this kind of thing. This is the real love, the real connection, all the rest is a weak reflection. Or at least I think so. Once I asked her about someone she seemed to be seeing a lot of, someone who even came up with her to see me at school, someone with whom I went with her to spend my Christmas vacation in a house in a suburb where I had to play games of Monopoly with his motherless little girl (who didn't much relish the prospect of having me and Bett to live with). I asked Bett if she loved him more than me and she said it was a different kind of love, an answer which didn't satisfy me at all, so she said, looking seriously at me, never, never, never, never, you are my great love. And so I was.

We had seen *Bambi* and now we saw *Farewell to Arms*, and again we cried, because "Cat" had died in the last scene and the music was going. We had to wait to leave our seats till our faces were dry. Walking back across the center of town, I kept hearing Rock Hudson's words as he walks away from the hospital, as dazed as we were: "That's what you get for loving a woman." But Cat had died in childbirth and somehow the message of that film was not that love was fatal but that having a child was. I think then I had the first inkling I would be the death of my mother.

In the meantime, she was nearly the death of me. We were standing waiting to cross on the green, and then we did cross and were getting to the other side when we were halted by the full blare of an ambulance bearing down on us. And, this was the terrible part, he caught us at a fork in the road, facing him, so that we couldn't tell if he was going to turn left or right or where we should stand, and as the ambulance slowed and loomed we could see the hard red face of the driver twisted and shouting at us inside, the lights on the van swirling red and hitting us in the face and the noise deafening, and I looked up at my mother and gave her my hand so she should take us to safety, but she couldn't move. Then, with me in tow, she went forward one way and froze and crossed back and started to move again and halted. I was still too young to take *her* to safety and we stood there paralyzed and stupid on the middle of the road until the driver went around us, swearing.

When we were in New York together I used to love the absolute glamour of being with Bett, watching her dress for dates, after I was bathed and in my nightgown and meant to be reading quietly with my babysitter. But far more interesting than reading quietly was watching my mother prepare for assault. She would stride in and out of the bathroom wrapped in a towel or robe at various stages of dress, wafting the odor of Yardley's lavender soap or Blue Grass cologne, searching for unsnagged stockings (reprimanding the cat), looking for an earring or a pair of shoes. The makeup and hair by itself would take hours (and I can feel all this now as a link with her life—then not that long ago, ten, twelve years—at Central Park South with Angel, when she and Constance were the most beautiful girls in New York, before the English misadventure): skin scrub and moisturizer, plucked brows, pancake, mascara, eyestick and lipstick and later Erase for dark circles—but in those days there were no dark circles, it was all light. With five minutes to go she would appear, made up, in stockings and high heels, and begin to search through the closet for whatever she was wearing—black always, it seemed to me—with which she would set out like a beautiful boat with strong nets, a fisher of men, to catch her catch. And they would come and call for her, these tall, handsome, glossy men, and have to be polite to the sitter and me and wait and wait (as we all did) for Bett, as she called her apologies gaily from the bathroom and finally came in, lighting up their lives like a search-light and bringing them to life like marionettes. And she would kiss me good night and give instructions (entirely unnecessary to my well-practiced sitters) and be off on her date, which was my adventure, too, because I could hear about it in the morning. I loved my mother the most then, in this glamorous sailing move-ment, perfumed and happy and full of confidence and as unop-pressed as ever I knew her.

My life with my mother and my life at school remained utterly separate, except insofar as the chaos of one prescribed the constraints of the other. Apart from the stir of unease created in other parents by her unshackled sexual beauty, her existence in New York barely affected my life at school, and it was all the more potent and mysterious that way. I used to think that if only I could get to her where she was courted, appreciated, happy, as I told myself, I too would be saved. But increasingly, and while still at school, I would feel the beginnings of doubt about this salvation. I began to register little things—the latenesses, the weeks without visits, the constant change of jobs and men and addresses, and then little inadequacies, barely noticeable except in the context of school, and really, even at the time, rather touching. There was the Halloween party costume, which I told her about at the beginning of term and reminded her of for weeks, and waited for, and which, when it finally came on the morning of the party, dramatically handed over by our headmistress, the preposterously named Miss de Vine, and unwrapped under the eyes of the whole school, was no more than a sheet (desperately taken from her own bed at the last minute, I'm now sure), with eyeholes cut and blackened in her own hand, the shaping of the black eyes done, as I recognized even at the instant of crushing disappointment, with as much love and flourish as possible within the limitations of the form. Or her contribution to the communal Christmas project, the Mirrenwood Cookbook, which was to be culled from favorite family recipes and printed and bound in red and green. Among the elaborate entries for cakes and casseroles, soufflés and gumbos, pâtés and marinades—all those good recipes from good mothers— was Bett's offering, rather small on the allotted page: "Take a steak. Sprinkle both sides with salt and pepper. Grill each side till done. About ten minutes under medium heat."

In such hardly noticeable ways my mother's fallibility began to suggest itself to me when I was at Mirrenwood, sweet indications that lay among the more obvious signs I chose and needed to ignore: because if the solid, unshakable force of good and love were not wherever she was, then it was nowhere, and there was to be no alternative to the malevolent and stupid existence I endured at school. And not able to bear such doubt in my universe, I therefore continued to worship my goddess and dream of our future life together, of the time when all that was wrong would be well.

But there *were* doubts, even during my holidays, holidays which I re-created for myself at night at school. Among the iron beds of little girls trembling for love of home, I was one, playing my lantern slides: of my mother concentrating tenderly as she hands me my kitten while it still sleeps, or the soft, protective position of her body as she reads to me. Even on these holidays there were things that must have seemed to my idealizing, re-creating brain less than perfect and not quite safe. At that same apartment where Bett read to me and I had my kitten, I was often locked out by my forgetful mother. I remember once having to pee on the sidewalk, squatting in what privacy there was on the bright, busy afternoon and watching the stream roll down the slanting pavement, glinting in the sun. Or on that same sidewalk in front of our building finding a razor blade and taking it with me into the darkness of the bar beneath our apartment, which reeked of sour beer and middle-aged men, where I looked at the jukebox and came out again into the blinding sun, miraculously covered in blood, my white shirt red with it, because with no awareness or pain I had sliced the nail off my thumb, and then standing there in my bloody shirt while people passed and turned back to look at me and I waited for Bett to come home. Or on afternoons when she was at work, being locked in rather than out, I remember hours and hours of boredom, and how I would lean over the windowsill and watch the ferocious German shepherd in the super's yard and one by one throw my toys at him: my stuffed rabbit, my clown, my corduroy elephant, my puppets, my dolls and balls, hurling these missiles at him until my room was empty, while he rushed his chains and ran toward me barking, snapping, unhinged. At six my mother would return from work, groceries in one arm, my dirty toys in the other, sadly handed to her every evening by the young Polish superintendent, who like everyone else in those days was a little in love with her, proud and infinitely respectful of so much beauty overhead, and therefore never very angry with her or me.

I was at this period of my life that I had the recurrent dream from which I always awoke afraid and depressed and which, it now seems to me, must have expressed my sense of uselessness to Bett, my abandonment at Mirrenwood and my fear of what was coming for me in the world beyond school. This is the dream that came in exactly the same form week after week for a few years: I am in a large white room; I shut the door and pull down the shades so the sun enters in cracks, frames of light at the windows; the sun is shut out but the room is still white, and in the tense silence I begin to scream, like a dog barking at something that is there. But I do not know yet what's there. There is a kind of rubber track in this room and I begin to run on it, at first slowly and then with increasing speed, running and screaming and working myself into a frenzy of fear in this closed-off room, around and around until I see what is pursuing me at lumbering, mechanical speed along the rubber track: a huge, all-white truck, at first like the ambulance that bore down on us that day of the film and then, as it gets closer, the great, white, grinding, groaning machine becomes a sanitation truck, its jaws in front, not behind, and the garbage to be disposed of being me—as though I am the blot in this pristine white room—and it comes after me, swallowing, crunching the air in front of it, pursuing me doggedly, evenly, and there is no doubt that it will catch up with me, run as I can, scream as I can, and then I wake.

In the year I was nine, I had a strange illness at school, with high fevers and hallucinations. As I lay in the sickroom one afternoon with the fevers and nausea behind me, but drowsily gazing at the light through slowly blinking bubbles of warm ginger ale, I saw on the mold-stained wallpaper among the pattern of blue-and-white shepherdesses, loitering under willow trees with crooks and lambs, a ginger-ale-hued vision of my mother as I had never seen her in life. She appeared to me, standing mournfully by the door of the kitchen in our most recent apartment, a broom in her hand. And as she bent to sweep, her features began to change, so that in place of her usual sweet expression, I saw dark tension and anger. And then I watched as my beautiful young mother slowly disintegrated in this anger and became a bent and fearful crone. I was overcome by a terrible sense of loss and I wept to see how easily the magic protection could leave her, to see her grow old and be devoured by something so black and dark and terrible. I don't know how long I had this grim premonition of Bett among the shepherdesses, but I remember crying that afternoon, long and disconsolately, exactly the way I was to see my mother cry, and for the same reason, many years later.

If I had no inkling, then, of the dark depressions that were so to transform my mother—and that sickroom vision is all that I can remember, despite the fact that her breakdown was the reason I was at Mirrenwood—the other instabilities were coming closer to my dream-infested hiding place: the money problems, for one thing, not just our moves and increasingly erratic Christmases (the yearly measure of just how bad things were), but the years of unpaid bills at school, of which I had been ignorant until now, and which I first learned about when one evening Miss de Vine called me into her room.

It was natural for me to assume I had done something for which I was about to be punished, and I must have looked rather guilty as I stood before her, trying to imagine what she'd discovered. She sat patiently, gazing at me somewhat dolefully over an expanse of orderly, paper-covered desk. An imposing, not very recent photograph of her son Hugh, wearing a naval uniform, stood on the bookcase to her right, an oddly intimate touch in her austere room. From time to time we had heard her refer to this Hugh, but so sparingly that many of us assumed he was dead, and in any case only to emphasize how—unlike any of us—he had been a model child, easy to raise because he was a boy, and very good to his mother. Sighing deeply at the task before her, this suddenly just-plausibly maternal figure, in a tone almost of confidence, said that my mother had not paid my school fees for nearly three years: was I aware of that, and what did I propose to do about it? I said nothing, though I was deeply embarrassed. But I was fiercely loyal to my mother and refused to apologize for her. Miss de Vine sat a few moments, waiting for me to advise her, and then, looking acutely in my eyes, told me I was a "brazen hussy," a phrase which meant nothing to me at all, though it suggested something polished and military. "I don't know what I am going to do about it," she said finally. "Go to bed."

I can only have put the problem out of my head. By then I would have been more worried about adding to Bett's burdens than restoring my honor with the school. I had no idea what my mother's circumstances were, but I might have guessed. I suppose now that I simply decided, for lack of other alternatives, to ride things through until the last moment, which in the event wasn't long coming.

One morning, shortly after the end of Easter vacation, when I had just turned ten, no doubt after many recriminations about unpaid bills, I was finally delivered from my exile. Bett's strange experiment in protecting me from her life was finally over, and I was to see my irregularly descending goddess up close. I was to be out and away from Mirrenwood and free to live my life as I had dreamed of it since I as five: at long last together, alone, and always with Bett.

TWO

FOR A LONG TIME, I could never listen to any piece of classical music without feeling depressed, not just melancholy, but grim and a little dead inside. It was my mother's habit when she was "blue," but "gray" was a better description, to walk about the apartment with collapsed features while from the radio stringed instruments accompanied her with messages of spiritual uplift. But to me, far from suggesting the existence of some higher, better world, the richest harmonies and most soul-searching orchestrations merely emphasized the dire emptiness of ours. My mother's depressions were always followed by the sudden withdrawal of light and energy from our surroundings, and our apartment, so often full of color and movement, would have all the liveliness of the void. Anxiety and dullness settled on me in the vacuum which her black moods created, disguise them though she would. Often she would take herself out of my sight, and hearing as she imagined, and leave me alone with the radio stridently beseeching or pumping with Slavic fatalism. But I knew well enough where she was when the music was going, and what she was doing there, and I would find her on the edge of the bathtub or toilet seat in sobs which she attempted to muffle in a towel, having lost the fight against what she called her "panics." I would knock on the bathroom door and get myself admitted and then stand in front of her, shaking her slightly and demanding to know what was wrong, and she would look up a little dazed, her makeup wet and greasy under her eyes, her nose and cheeks red from the pressure of the towel, the skin around her dark eyes tense; she would smile and say, "It's not you, Puppy, Mommy just gets like this sometimes." I would tell her not to cry, because she had me, which at least in the beginning would make her laugh, hug me and say, "I know, I know, I'm so lucky."

Often I was convinced enough by this myself and would feel glad that indeed, at least, she had me. Yet, though she never failed to absolve me from any connection to her troubles, and always tried to protect me from the sight of herself so fallen, I could never entirely absolve myself. If I was, as she always said, the light of her life, why was it so often so dark? And if she was so lucky to have me, why was it I could never seem to make enough of a difference? Standing right in front of her in the bathroom in New York, I would feel as useless to her as I had shut away at Mirrenwood.

My mother's depressions came and went. And when they had gone, no matter how precarious our existence, we did at least imagine ourselves to be enjoying it. There were many evenings when I was very happy to be caught up in the adventure of my mother's life, or what I took to be its adventure: little candlelit dinners when the electricity was turned off, last-minute Christmases when there were elaborate apologies beforehand because there could be no tree this year, or presents, followed by reassurances on my part that it did not matter: I was not, at nine, ten, eleven, a child anymore that needed presents. But then there it would be, the yearly miracle: the tree, the presents, and my gratitude, I suppose, that it had never been put to the test: my indifference to Christmas, to my mother's ability to pull rabbits out of a hat, in short, to guarantee our survival.

As I grew older, there were wishes she could not grant, humiliations she could not prevent, losses she could not make up, but what we both told each other over and over became true for us: what mattered was that we had one another. Like two heroines on a mountain precipice, we played our little comitragedy clutched in each other's arms, terrified yet certain of rescue. And how could we not be rescued, this adorable pair of dark-haired girls—my mother with her film-star looks and touching sweetness, and her little daughter, looks so like you, and, as I grew older, always the same: you could be sisters.

My mother not only looked like a film star, she experienced her life as though it had been scripted: abandoned by her mother and orphaned by the death of Angel; thrown out into the real world after a disastrous first marriage, a real world that was an enemy from which only her beauty and kind fortune could save her. But fortune could offer her nothing more than survival in life. The pleasure of it, triumph through it, were for her—unlike Constance—possibilities she never hoped for. The early morning panic of oversleeping, the rush to deal with unpressed clothes and ruined stockings, an empty icebox, no cab fare, was followed by "work" in various nine-to-five jobs in which her strategy was simply one of hanging on, not being fired, above all not being propositioned. I don't remember, in all her years in and out of jobs, my mother ever once asking for or getting a raise. It was enough and a sign of overdue disaster that she should remain in a job as long as a year. The joke in this—some joke—was that more often than not she worked at jobs way below or outside of her capacities: a receptionist who couldn't remember to write down messages, a typist who couldn't spell. When, and it happened occasionally, she found herself in situations that suited her talents, as when on and off she worked as a sculptor making medallions or doing children's portraits, she would become "bored" or frightened. Or someone would make a pass, or pride would be hurt, and she would leave.

Sometimes she would invent things: a dishwasher that ran off water from the tap, "topless" sandals that stuck with special tape to the bottoms of bare feet, textured glue-on false nails in tweed and brocade, four-sided "cubist" dresses that she made and wore herself. But beyond the pleasure of invention, and though many similar items were later produced by other people more enterprising or confident than she, these designs never came to anything, and soon gathered dust in the corner of a closet. Much later she taught herself economics, read at night through Marx, Heilbroner, Galbraith, and wrote a 400-page treatise on privatization, which we around her thought not only grimly ironic (Bett's economics!) but sort of mad, yet which one NYU professor to whom she sent it pronounced "a work of genius." But this was long before Reagan and Thatcher, and it was hard, for many reasons, to take her seriously.

Still, none of these things, the designs or the manuscript, all carted around between evictions from one closet to another and piled with photographs and increasingly ancient souvenirs of youth, ever dissuaded her from her lived-out conviction that salvation was something other people did or failed to do for you and, like piling your plate at someone else's table, certainly not something one did for oneself. In this she was very different from both Emma and Constance, who after Angel's death set themselves loose on the world as though it were an orchard. But my mother's life was not much of a banquet to her; instead, increasingly, something simply to endure. She saw others living their lives differently, she wanted me to be able to live my life differently, but for herself, though she never said as much, she felt she had been sidelined from the start. She had her looks and she put up a good show, but that was the feeble best she thought she could do. If anything was going to change her life, it would have to be a piece of random good luck, arriving by mistake and flying in from offside.

I don't know what my mother really wanted for herself, apart from relief from pain and worry. Love, I suppose, to be "in love," though that never seemed to make her happy. Other than that, what she wanted was probably very simple: a few vacations, restaurant dinners, pretty clothes (what she had, of course, when she lived with Angel). I think she was really terribly pleasable and it was that that made her sadness so awful. You always felt the injustice of her unhappiness, and the pettiness, as though fate were simply a meanspirited adult withholding candy from a baby.

Sometimes in the apartment, at different ages in my life, I would glance up from whatever I was doing and see her, engaged in some minor business, changing sheets, feeding the cat, and I would be startled by the look she had of a pretty child, of twelve, say, a child without fears or responsibilities, with the same little glow of blighted innocence you'd see behind the mask of Marilyn Monroe, the same sweet, confused look of a good, kind little girl trapped inside the beautiful bruisable peach flesh. And sometimes it also seemed to me that my mother was sort of frozen in this girlishness of hers, that it was both her charm and a doom, and that like Sleeping Beauty she would only ever get to live her life if somebody came and ended the enchanting spell.

I didn't really "know" any of this when I came back to live with her after Mirrenwood, but in another sense I did begin to understand it. If we were like sisters to the world, it was because we were both children, and it seemed to me more and more that I was going to have to be the one to grow up if either of us was going to survive. I was bent then on our doing that, and I still believed it could be done. Of course, part of me still expected Bett to do it for us, only the more I observed, the more I could see that we were one mother short and that it was going to have to be me that looked for the bread crumbs and led us both from the forest.

Meanwhile, I was not, at ten, very heroic material. When I arrived at school in the city, I had very little of the knowledge I needed for myself, let alone for both of us. After six years at Mirrenwood I could not even tell the time, and when called upon in class in the most offhand way to do so I would glance at my Cinderella watch, be suddenly overcome with a need to leave the room, stalk a hall monitor and ask him, and, pretending to be adjusting my own merry timepiece, return and deliver his pronouncement to the teacher. It was my own version of my mother's vagueness about hours and lateness. (I would often arrive at school by cab half an hour late, and occasionally call in sick when she had seriously overslept.) Also, though I could read and count perfectly well, I could not "write," at least according to my new school. Printing was not considered writing at the city school, whereas at Mirrenwood "joining letters" had been strictly forbidden almost on moral grounds. Printing was clean American truth-telling, whereas script could hide a cesspit of sensuality, secrecy, sin. Furthermore, after all those years of doubled-up classes, I had come out with no knowledge of science, history or geography, or anything else much, it seemed. But we had IQ tests, and after that the teachers seemed a little, though not a great deal, happier. After the testing the very brightest were put in the IG class, as Intellectually Gifted. At one level below them were the Gs, simply

Gifted, though at what they never said, and that was where they put me. The rest of the school dwelt in unlettered shadows below.

PSL was a gerrymandered public school on Madison Avenue and Eighty-first, at that time a fairly new brick building and already a selling point in New York real estate ads. "Within the PSL district," they said, hoping to lure a tenant with the promise of superior, free education for the children in the price of the apartment. The lines of eligibility were firmly drawn in those days to include the well-off children of the brownstones and co-ops of the Seventies, Eighties and Nineties from, I think, Third Avenue to Central Park. As far as it could, in this "liberal" section of town, the catchment excluded the poor Irish and Italian children east of Third and the blacks and Spanish to the north. The private schools were also in the area, so that the whole neighborhood was given over, in its shops and playgrounds, to an atmosphere of prosperous family living, and unlike in the rest of Manhattan, it was a common sight to see school-uniformed children, fancifully clothed and nanny-attended babies—expensive infant flesh, in other words, a rare softening touch that in other parts of town seemed to have been passed over in favor of poodles, Dobermans and Akitas of Distinction.

To get me to this elite island of children and to PSL in particular, my mother had moved us into a room at a seedy white elephant of a hotel on the upper reaches of Madison Avenue, the outer fringes of respectability, near the point where the flat earth of "acceptable" Manhattan falls off into the sea of dark faces. For many weeks, while my mother looked for somewhere more permanent (or less temporary) in that expensive neighborhood, we lived at the hotel, sharing a bed and a gas ring in a small room, almost slippery from the grease of the twenty-four-hour coffee shop downstairs and infested with unbelievable numbers of cockroaches, which my mother called *cucarachas* in a futile effort to endear them to me. With uncharacteristic calculation, and somewhat shamefacedly, she told me not to let the school know we were living at the hotel but to give its address on Madison, a deception that my unjoined printing accommodated perfectly well on the registration forms. For a time I lived in dread of imminent investigation of the suspiciously high and unresidential number. Anyone checking would have been stopped in the lobby by the manager, who sat in a black toupee, well lit by the pink neon ring above his head, lethargically bookkeeping next to a vase of dusty plastic flowers, hunching and muttering at residents from beneath the shoulders of his cheap, patterned jacket, lavender with age and impregnated with the reek of the kitchen and the stench of his spit-drenched cigar.

After the hotel, we lived for a while in a tenement building off Third, in the home of a single mother and her frail, bespectacled daughter Kate, who was my age. They had a back apartment, dreary day and night, and its regular occupants seemed strangely miserable, very busy with their misery, and resolutely hostile. There were posted stipulations everywhere about what we were and were not entitled to for our share of the rent, and a constant air of barely suppressed rage that they had to share their apartment at all. Perhaps they disliked us because our existence made theirs seem all the more hopeless. We were their down-and-out mirror images, though they seemed fairly down-and-out themselves; but our homelessness was evidence there might be further for them to fall, and our presence a reminder of the numbers there were of us: children without fathers and women without men.

But I didn't really feel we were in the same boat at all. No one as exceptionally beautiful as my mother, it seemed to me, could be called impoverished; and apart from the bathroom depressions, she was always too childlike and high-spirited ever to seem resigned to misfortune. Despair and rage, which I saw on the faces of Kate and her mother, were not then among our expressions, and we would and did greet the world for the most part cheerfully, if ineptly. Besides, it still seemed, as I say, that our precarious finances were only temporary (as indeed they always were) and that Bett was bound to find her familiar footing and just redemption. My mother's situation was really a version of Mirabel's, though a negative of it, since Mirabel's only lack had been beauty, which was my mother's only wealth; but her beauty did, then, seem a kind of wealth to me, and I was always very proud of it and her. It was the kind of thing teachers, particularly male teachers, would always mention to me after any parents' day, and for which they treated me with a new respect, I thought, at least for a few days afterward, though one of them once added to his compliments that my mother always looked "a little sad." But though Bett's beauty honored me at one remove, at least with the teachers, it was a mark of distinction I did not share, and though it unfailingly protected her from any shabbiness which our finances involved (though she would have disagreed), it did not protect me. At ten, suddenly outside the leveling invisibility of Mirrenwood, I felt exposed by a sense of drabness I could never ascribe to her.

I had not felt this at the beginning of my city school life. The use of uniforms at Mirrenwood had not only shielded us from the invidious distinctions children make as to the cost and variety of their belongings, but it had also deprived us of any sophistication with regard to clothes codes. I simply didn't notice in the first weeks at PSL what kinds of clothes were being worn around me. Clothes that for so long had had no importance whatever and were distinguished only by a name tape or tear now became immensely complicated. Not only was there a limited variety of dress styles it was all right to wear, but each element had to be correct: not only clean and pressed but from the right shops and in accordance with the prevailing codes. Everything was noted. As with the Prince of Wales at Ascot, innovations could be made only by agreed-upon sartorial leaders, and then everyone immediately conformed. Any divergences from what was correct, and particularly any poverty-emanating lacks or improvisations, were greeted with the piteous turning of the eyes English dowagers reserve for the errors of the nouveau riche. Into this highly sophisticated fashion world, as precisely restrictive as the In/Out columns of *Women's Wear Daily*, as steeped in money and ambitious mamas as the turn-of-the-century American set on their European tours, I strayed with my wearable pieces of Mirrenwood uniform, my frayed-at-the-edges acquisitions from the children's secondhand-clothing shop on Madison Avenue (the shop is still there, discreetly hidden from street view on the second floor, and I can't pass it even now without a pang of humiliation; my greatest terror was not just of being seen by some classmate entering or leaving, but of someone recognizing on me, and, of course, announcing it, her own discarded clothes from the previous "season") and my occasional new (invariably wrong) purchases, on which I would load all my sad hopes of acceptance into this world of new outfits for every day, everything laundered and pressed by Janine or Sally or Lila, whoever it was who slept in the room off the kitchen—a world from which I had already been warned of my exclusion with the sweetly voiced, genuinely curious question my third week at school, "Why do you wear the same dress every single day?"

After the tolerance and familiarity of life at Mirrenwood, at PSL what was immediately clear was the impossibility of unmanipulated social life. As with clocks and watches, I couldn't read the signs for social maneuvering, the very subtle indications to join a group or stay away. I remember the shock of rebuffed overtures and gruesome solitary lunches on the benches in the playground when all around were twittering arm in arm. But it wasn't just the loneliness that was new to me after boarding school, it was the huge, slippery sensation of shame, oppressive as bad weather, dislocating, hateful and—what with the concealment of our address, the daily mortification about clothes and my ignorance about how to make friends when before I never had to "make" them, they were just there— overwhelming.

After our uncomfortable stay with Kate and her mother, Bett and I moved to a studio apartment in a newly brick-fronted building on Lexington Avenue near Ninety-second Street, across from the monstrously ugly YMHA. In the past, wherever Bett and I had lived had been characterized by something which appealed to her need for elegance, and it had always been all right. This was the first apartment which just wasn't all right, to either of us. It faced front just below street level, and all day and night you could hear the noise of people passing, constantly, it seemed to me, clearing their throats, and, following an endless, thorough-searching, catarrhous cough, a well-aimed and all too easily visualized "oyster" would land outside very close to where I slept, on a raised platform under the iron-gridded window, the sole source for the flat of air and daylight. The rest of the studio, apart from this four-by-twelve-foot platform on which my Castro convertible chair-bed was, was no more than perhaps eighteen by twelve. There was a brief wall of kitchenette that you walked into when you entered the apartment, and off that a small, ugly, turquoise-tiled bathroom. My mother slept on a studio couch in the lower part, where there was also an oval table and two chairs. Even Bett couldn't pretend it was any better than awful, but we would move, she promised, as soon as we could.

This was the setting into which I would have to bring any playmates I could entice, and for a while I was grateful there weren't going to be any. But one day there arrived on roller skates a cheerful, freckled girl I recognized from the playground at school. She had braids and ribbons, braces on her teeth and sparkling blue eyes, and she was bubbling with friendliness. It seemed she lived around the corner; it seemed she hoped she'd see me again in the neighborhood; she waved goodbye as she revved up on her roller skates and disappeared. When I saw her the next time, she invited me to her house and I accepted.

Shame is the beginning of deceit and calculation, and around this time these gruesome strays accompanied me everywhere and I couldn't shake them. After I had been a couple of times to Rita's house, had milk and cookies in her big kitchen, become familiar to her maid, been shown her perfect little pink-and-white girl's room, with its perfect little girl's furniture—a suite in the Early American style, not only impressively antique but unmistakably brand new—played with her games on her pink pile carpet, I felt obliged to invite her back.

I thought that the studio might just pass as an eccentrically furnished living room; as the whole thing for two people I knew it was hopeless. Yet I brought her home and she sat on the daybed, politely looking around. "This is the stage where we put on productions," I said, pointing to the raised area under the window. (She had a singing group, the Little Angels, that tried out for radio shows; I thought having a stage might impress her.) But soon enough she had seen and, getting quieter all the time, carefully noted all there was. Defeat, embarrassment, threatened to settle, when I attempted to postpone them. "I'm just going to get something from my room," I said, opening the closet, squeezing narrowly past the door and pulling it tightly behind me. I simply willed her to believe that the door behind which I was standing and holding very still was the door of a corridor, off which were who knows how many rooms, perhaps not only a child's room but a mother's room, perhaps a guest room and a maid's room, and in these rooms which I wished her to imagine there were all the things she took for granted: a television, phonograph, books, pictures, rugs, mirrors, possessions strewn and possessions straightened, a whole second apartment here behind my mother's raincoat and shoe boxes and slender, dangling wardrobe.

After two minutes I opened the door, again holding it close to my body and shutting it quickly behind me. She was in the place I had left her, looking at me. "There's no bedroom there," she said flatly. "That's a closet." I saw that I couldn't very well insist. We changed the subject. I didn't see her for a while, and then about two weeks later she invited me over. We never went to my house again.

Thus began a long and consuming friendship, my first discovery in myself of the intoxications of masochism, my first participation in a peculiar corruption. I spent many evenings at Rita's house. They would start normally enough in the kitchen having supper, talking about school or films or listening to the shouting between Rita's little brother and the maid. Her parents were often out, and after supper we would walk through the darkened apartment, putting on lights and examining the rooms like interior designers on assignment. Invariably we did the whole tour, beginning with her brother's room on some pretext until he screamed for us to get out, then crossing the hall, where we stopped to admire the botanical prints, and entering the thickly carpeted living room, large and imposing in the first darkness, with little green lights from the giant TV screen and elaborate stereo system glimmering softly on the black leather chairs and sofas, the gilt frames of mirrors and photographs, the polished bindings of encyclopedias along the "library wall," and on the cellophane-wrapped candies that sat untouched in their crystal goblet on the black coffee table. We walked through this room slowly, running our hands over leather and lacquer surfaces, dragging our stockinged feet in the thick carpet, as sensual as matrons in this material splendor. Rita led me with excitement, as though she'd never been here before, enticing me into her world of objects in a kind of foreplay for seduction and abandonment, our ritual of ravishment and betrayal, a drama accomplished without anyone laying a finger on anyone else. Dizzily we wandered down the corridor, trailing our hands over embossed wallpaper, in and out of her father's "den," into her parents' plush and pastel bedroom, where Rita would pause and look around. "Powder blue," she would say, as though just remarking it, and I would always answer, "Beautiful." We would look at the bathroom with its porcelain jars of little soaps, potpourri, its vat of Chanel No. 5, its blue lacy toilet-seat cover. We would return by way of the austere dining room: "Spanish Colonial," Rita would say, "Beautiful," I would say, and we'd continue, back to the kitchen, stopping to look in at the maid's room, where the maid watched her own television next to her own bathroom. And then we would be ready to approach the Chamber of Horrors, Rita's own bedroom.

It was very large and bright, decorated in pink and white ruffles, with an endless wall of matching furniture and a huge canopy bed. There were dozens of stuffed animals and expensive dolls displayed in casual wreckage along the floor and on the bed. On the bureau, next to her matching desk with its leather writing set and locked "My Diary" (in which no doubt all our evenings were confided), was Rita's own stereo and television, which we would watch until Rita suddenly turned it off with a snap and suggested we do something else. The something else we invariably did was to open her closets along the far wall. I would sit quietly, nervously, among the lacy eyelet pillows and dolls on her bed, leafing through comic books while one by one Rita took out her clothes, held up each garment and dismissed it with a disparaging remark. "This one's so old, I've had it since last year," or "I got this for my birthday but I'm never going to wear it," or "This one's so horrible, my mother must be crazy." Always she would offer to give me things and then think better of it: "I guess I really shouldn't, Mommy wouldn't like it." If I resisted, she would draw me in with a question: "What do you think, would you like something like this?" Or "Don't you think this would look nice on you?" She might insist that I put these clothes on. Together we would dress up, putting on makeup and jewelry in a frenzy of sharing until it would be time for me to undress and go home. Putting on my own clothes, it would always come as a mysterious symptom, like a sudden headache, that I was feeling utterly depressed. I would fall silent, stricken, and Rita, her blue eyes friendly and innocent as ever, would always ask, "What's the matter? Did I do something?" I would shake my head and sort of shuffle to the door, the other side of which I would feel such sharp desolation that I would often begin to weep in the elevator, in front of the doorman and running across the street to where, in my own bed, I could let go and sob passionately, unconsolable and incommunicative to my alarmed and baffled mother.

It took months before I understood the mechanics of my evenings with my blue-eyed friend. In the middle of it, it always seemed entirely innocent and the pain always took me by surprise. I didn't really admire the contents of Rita's apartment, though I always obediently responded. I think even then I had a sense of the excess and banality of her surroundings. Yet the mere existence of such excess in the home of someone my age was exciting to me, and devastating. I never consciously blamed my mother for her inability to provide us with any of it (not even *one* television, as I was taunted about for a week when I made the mistake of admitting it at school), just as I very rarely complained, because I knew she suffered from the lack of things as much as I—we were "sisters"—and was doing all she could to keep us afloat. But after visits to Rita's house I had private bouts of envy and self-pity and they were novel and irresistible sensations. And perhaps I put myself through them by way of punishment, a ritual flagellation, for everything Bett and I lacked. Later, as I got used to how things were, I was more careful with myself; and I learned fast enough how to pass near other people's lives without getting scorched.

I soon became aware of other ways of responding to the situation in which Bett and I found ourselves than the self-torture I engaged in with Rita. Around the same time as this friendship Bett and I became attached to another single mother and daughter who seemed the very models of dignified forbearance and virtuous self-denial.

My mother had met Claudia Mieli at a cocktail party and they had liked each other immediately. She was a tall, elegant woman in her early fifties, with prematurely white hair which she wore in short, pretty waves and which set off the cold blue of her eyes. She seemed to me rather grand and formal, carrying herself with an aristocratic stiffness, as though always bearing the secret burden of some ancient wrong. She had a daughter, Antonia, whom she adored, who was two years older than I, and with whom, under my mother's influence, I became friendly. For a while we were all four of us very close, and I began to find out about their lives, like ours, without money or men.

There was a proudly spartan quality to the Mielis' apartment, with its faded, patched and starched linen coverlets, its bare, clean-swept floors, dappled by a few patches of sun, and a terrible finality to Antonia's white bedroom, decorated with pictures of saints, and the reprovingly empty, somber chamber of her mother. For me, there was also something frightening about Antonia's room, with its devotional books and objects, crucifix and porcelain Sacred Heart. She attended a private Catholic school in the area, whose uniform she wore, and she seemed, like her mother, some-what rigid and correct. She did her homework hour after hour on the kitchen table, and she simply adored her mama. Mother and daughter spent many hours together, kissing, petting, sharing secret words and jokes, and Antonia often spoke about Claudia as though she were a princess. Nothing in the world mattered to her as much as her mama, not even the other Madonna and the saints, whose lives she gave me to read until I had nightmares of black-hooded nuns in white halls, thorn-scratched Christs who would turn slowly into the light and point to their open chest cavities to reveal their luminous, still gory, still pumping, Sacred Hearts.

For a time I tried to emulate Antonia's expressions of devotion to her mother. In the manner of a lovesick gallant, I, too, would stop on my way home from school to buy with my lunch money a cake of my mother's favorite soap or a single rose, or I would sell my books at the secondhand shop to buy a special ingredient for supper, or I would write her poems about her virtues. Our normal relationship was thus transformed into something nobler, a kind of courtship, as though our enforced closeness and isolation were expressions of a preference, a passion, blind and superior to the run-of-the-mill dealings of other parents and children. And for a time Claudia's baronial dignity and little Antonia's docile devotion did seem an idealization of something in my relationship with Bett, turning our solitude into a form of renunciation and seeming to offer a legitimate model for a way of living without rescue. But my mother was nowhere near fifty, did not have white hair, and I was not a little saint or courtier. I impersonated Antonia's manner and contented humility only for a time, and then rebelled in my heart against it. It seemed to me to be still too soon for stoicism; and I was unwilling to surrender my hope that some event or person would arrive to take my mother and me back to the world of the living, happy and loved, the place where I knew normal life went on, men together with women, and where I still believed we were both meant to shine.

It was a confusing time for both of us. At thirty-three, my mother was beginning to realize how little mileage was left for her as one of the girls at Angel's. Constance was in and out of New York, leading an enterprising single life here, and in Madrid, or off in the desert, while Bett's was seemingly standing still and seeping away. There was always pressure on her to remarry, though she preferred the impracticalities of being in love, about which she was regularly lectured whenever we went to visit and report to my "aunt" Veronica.

Veronica was a wonderful, breathless, full-figured and kimono-wrapped friend of my great-aunt Shrimp, whom she absolutely worshipped as the fount of all sensible advice, on matters from Bett and me to Scrabble and taxes. She had been married when she was forty (and still a virgin, as she later admitted with horror), following a brief career as an entertainer. Daniel, a distant cousin of Mirabel's and a mild-mannered army colonel, had fallen in love with Veronica when she was a background hoofer for the troops with the USO, and sometime after their marriage, when Bett and

Constance were still living with Angel, Daniel had taken Veronica to meet his cousin. Through her, she had met Shrimp and Emma and become embroiled in "the adventures of the girls." When Daniel suddenly died of a heart attack, leaving her childless after six years of marriage, Veronica became a kind of permanent widow. She went into business, unable to type or spell but determined and destined to succeed. When I first knew her, she was in her late fifties, prematurely white-haired and already referring to herself as an "old lady." She lived where old ladies lived, on Central Park South, two blocks down from Mirabel's former apartment, and dined regularly in elderly company at Rumpelmayer's. While Constance was still in North Africa and Emma still painting in Spain, Veronica, together with Shrimp, whom we saw less frequently, and Mirabel's retired maid, to whom we paid yearly visits in the Bronx (she sent *us* money at Christmas), made up the entirety of our family.

About once a month, Veronica would invite us to visit and we would dine with her at Rumpelmayer's or at her home, where we were served course after simple course (she was forever on a diet) by her small and anxious cook, whom Veronica would summon from behind the swinging door of the kitchen, though it was barely two feet from where we sat, by a little silver bell, shaped as a long-torsoed shepherdess.

Over dry wafers of Swedish rye and bowls of consommé, on which floated a desultory sprig of parsley, Veronica would interrogate Bett on the progress of her search for marital and financial stability. "Now, Bett," she would say, once the niceties of the first exchanges were swept through, "who's the latest?"—her girlish, gossipy manner not always able to hide the increasing despair behind her question.

Everything in Veronica's world was both simple and extreme. No one was merely attractive if they could be beautiful, no one simply bright if there was any chance they might be a genius. To Veronica, Shrimp was "a genius," my mother and Constance "stunning." To her, ours was a fascinating family, whose ups and downs, she thought, could make a book (and perhaps a musical), for which she proposed the title *Never a Dull Moment*. All this enthusiasm I attributed to the fact that Veronica was a theatrical agent, an occupation to which I also ascribed her indiscriminate and peculiar pronunciation of the word "dahling," her long-armed door greetings, her manner of stretching her slippered feet onto an ottoman and taking her phone calls with one hand resting on her Burmese cat, or dipping in and out of the bonbon dish by her side. Her dramatic sense of life was such that I came away from our visits always feeling that anything was still possible for us and that we were destined for the extraordinary, that perhaps our grim existence below street level might indeed make some musical comedy called *Never a Dull Moment,* though for me there were often stretches of no other kind. Veronica believed in Bett's ability to succeed eventually, just as she believed in America and, above all, in the power of Sex. She knew that Bett, whatever her blind spots and limitations, had Sex Appeal and that with it there would always be a ticket to Destiny. She believed that Science backed her up in her observations and would keep little news clippings, which she'd show us, reporting studies in which laboratory animals had been willing to give up food, water and sleep in certain circumstances, but had surrendered "the Sex Drive" only on pain of death. Their last gasps would be love calls, Veronica said, which was the Way of the World. Sex was a force like atomic power, she said: it could not be stopped, but it could be harnessed.

Veronica, having known Bett and Constance when they were young girls, felt entitled to repeat the conventional wisdom that they had been spoiled by Mirabel when they were teenagers and that was why they were unable to deal with the Realities of Life now. Constance, who was not so incapable, but whose life seemed to Veronica bound to end badly, was dismissed as impractically exotic, while my mother was "loveliness itself" and would be reproachless if only she could be a bit brighter about landing a man. Veronica could not understand why this should be taking as long as it was, since my mother clearly possessed the two necessary attributes (apart from Sexual Attractiveness) for successful partnering: Beauty and Sweetness. "Sweetness" was sometimes said as though it meant naïveté (this when Veronica was cross), sometimes (when there was a glimmer of hope) deservingness, affability or that quality necessary to please men and keep them, something like docility.

Veronica was not the least self-conscious about her inquiries. If my mother admitted she was seeing someone, Veronica would immediately perk up and ask, not the subtler "What does he do?" but "Now, Bett, does he have any money?" If, as was probable, my mother replied that she had no idea, Veronica would tell her sharply, "Of course you do." Or "Where does he work?" she would say, and their conversation would stumble along like this:

"In an advertising agency, I think. I don't remember which one."

"Never mind. What's his position there?"

"I don't think he said. Executive something or other."

"Good. Now, Bett, does he have any children from previous marriages?"

"I think he's still married."

Veronica, shocked, "What, living together?"

"No, no, not really, they've separated."

"And when is the divorce?"

"I haven't asked him, Veronica. I don't think it's any of my business."

And Veronica, leaning back in her chair, would sigh and pronounce, "Really, Bett, you are not very Sensible about life. You're awful Sweet, but not Sensible. Do you love this man?"

Silence, or Thoughtful Silence.

"Well, is he"—here, a look at me, and then an expression of determination not to mince words, Life was Life, after all—"any good in bed?"

My mother, of course, would refuse to answer any further, and Veronica would repeat, "Now, Bett, I want you to try to be bright about things. Use those great looks of yours to some purpose. They won't last forever. You must go out and land this one."

After this exchange, which was really the purpose of our visit, we would all three play Scrabble, my mother forgetting her turn when it came around, Veronica taking forever with her word and then misspelling it, after which I'd correct her. "I see you've got the brains in the family," she would say (forgetting Shrimp for the moment), or "Your father's brains, your mother's looks," and then, inevitably, "Thank God it wasn't the other way around."

Veronica's strictures on my mother's incompetence in matters of mating always seemed to me, as they must have seemed to Bett, endearingly old-fashioned but nonetheless faintly immoral, as though what was being proposed was a frank and simple exchange of looks for cash. It was rather European and courtesan of her, though I have since heard women (European, of course) of otherwise peerless propriety ask with incredulity why it was my mother never married again "while she still had the chance," as though feelings, passions, chances, run out after a while like eggs from an icebox. But as for what Veronica vulgarly called Bett's "assets," these had a baffling way, no matter how arduous my mother's existence, of hanging on, and despite her own fears for their erosion, she never, ever, even when I was myself in my thirties, looked more than ten years older than I, a fact which was often troublesome to me in my most self-conscious years, when I was certain I would be taken as the product of an Ozark preteen's shotgun wedding. Around the age of eleven, I began to call my mother by her first name in order to avoid drawing the unwelcome attention that the word "Mommy" uttered in public would provoke. In shops, on buses, strange men and women would approach when I was with her and say, "Excuse me, did you say 'Mommy'? Surely not 'Mommy.' Is that really your mother? Goodness, you two look like sisters, you know that?" And I would say, "Yes, yes, we've heard it before." Even after they knew us, people would continually remark upon it, and it got on my nerves. Chet, for example, one of the men my mother was seeing around that time, could never stop saying it; it seemed to be one of the wonders of the world to him, and he would just burst with it whenever we were together. Chet was to some extent the answer to Veronica's prayers for Bett, and at the height of my Rita-whipped desolation, a time when the radio accompaniment to Bett's depression played most frequently, it seemed he might also be the answer to mine.

In the beginning, Chet's intention was to take us at what he thought was our own evaluation, as two gals in the big city. It wasn't clear whether he was acting as family man or big-time spender when he took us out, both of us, to evenings on the town, dinners often at the Friars Club, where battered, pink-eyed comics I vaguely recognized from low billings on TV went table to table, touching one another on the shoulder, on the back, removing cigars to speak, replacing them to listen. "That's Bernie Kanter," Chet would say, getting excited but keeping calm, and my mother would turn her head to look, and smile back at Chet, graciously but in unrelieved ignorance. I knew more of them than she did, but no one was famous enough to be interesting. The place felt like a men's gym, somewhere we weren't supposed to be, and though the head waiter seemed affable enough with Chet, I was never too secure about his being there either since he wasn't one of the comedians, who anyway didn't bring women with them and certainly not kids my age. Once when I was shivering in one of my mother's sleeveless dresses (I usually wore her clothes when I went out with them) Bett asked Chet if they could turn down the air conditioning. Embarrassed, Chet asked, and they refused, which didn't make any of us look good.

We went to Quo Vadis, too, and other dark men-and-mistresses restaurants. I always felt a little out of place, not so much because I was tagging along, which I really wasn't—I never felt I was interrupting anything or that there was anything to interrupt—but out of place just sitting there in one of my more presentable ten-year-old's dresses, or one of hers where the top sagged on me, and not knowing whether the mistake of bringing me along was Chet's or my mother's. She always looked so pleased with us—what could be nicer than all of us being together in a lovely restaurant—as though it were beyond her to imagine that an evening without her beloved daughter was an evening worth spending. Anyway, Chet always invited me and she always agreed.

So she and I would sit on the banquette, side by side, Bett occasionally squeezing my hand or hugging me if I said anything adorable, and Chet would tell his faintly off-color stories, inquire with great flourish into our dinner preferences, trying to charm me as potential suitor to my mother, trying to charm her as potential dad and pal to her child. Night after night, school nights as well as weekends, we dragged around the New York hot spots, till 2 A.M.

once, I remember, almost the only people there for the last show at the Copacabana, where the kicking girls with sequined bosoms and feathered tails looked down at our table and got unnerved by the sight of me, there in my mother's dress at that hour, and where Joe E. Brown came out and did his bit with a full glass of whiskey in his hand while Bett and I stared at him over our Shirley Temples and Chet watched with his wide expectant grin. But Brown was so bored or so out of it he talked only to the band and the band chortled mournfully back, and Joe E., propped up by the mike, began to slide and crumple and repeat himself, hanging on to the mike now for dear life, and Chet finally said, "Well, where to now?" and my mother said she thought it was time to call it a night.

This was all the year I was ten, and around October Chet's campaign to win this ready-made family stepped up. He'd been laying plans for Bett to come into his furniture business—plans to which Bett kept saying, "We'll see" and "Sounds nice"—and one evening he said we should come out with him to walk on Fifth Avenue. We walked to about Seventy-seventh Street, and then Chet stood back dramatically, opened both his arms about ten feet from the awning of a co-op building and said, "Here it is."

"What?" my mother said.

"Your new apartment. I'm going to sign the papers next month, you wait till you see it."

"New apartment?" my mother repeated.

"Sure," Chet said. "Once we're in business you're going to have plenty of money and no time to look around. I've done it for you. It's just come on the market. Of course, I'll stay where I am, no question," he added, a little pink, looking at me quickly, looking at her, looking back at the awning.

"So, kid," he said, "you want to know what's in the apartment?"

"Sure," I said, no question.

"It's got this sort of staircase, sort of a duplex, you know, two floors, you come down the staircase and there's the door you go out. Or there's the door, you go in, there's the staircase, you go up. Anyway, you're upstairs, there's a room for you and a bathroom and your mommy's room and her bathroom, and I think another room up there, anyway two bathrooms so you girls don't get in each other's way when you're getting ready to go out.'' He grins at us, squeezes Mommy's arm.

"Go on, Chet,'' I say.

"So, there's the bedrooms upstairs. Downstairs what have you got? Let's see, a big hall with a coat closet, oh yeah, big living room, great view of the park, let's see, kitchen. I don't know, lots of space, can't remember it all, you'll see it when I'm back in town. We'll get the key, then we'll know what's what.''

"What floor's it on?'' I say.

"Fifth floor,'' Chet says. "Fifth and sixth. Let's look at the windows.''

So we crossed the street and peered up at the building, counting to where some white curtains blew in a crack of air.

"Old people are still in there, I guess,'' Chet says.

I continued to ask him questions as we walked home. My mother was sort of quiet, as if stunned. Then we said good night to Chet, who was going out of town early in the morning, and when we got back to the studio I asked her, "Is it true?''

"I guess so,'' she said. "I don't know.'' And she seemed pretty vague to me.

In the weeks Chet was away I took a daily detour to pass in front of the building on my way home from school. I was beginning to accustom myself to the doormen and the entrance hall and the nice grillwork on the doors. The duplex staircase had got to be marble by now, and there was an Afghan dog somewhere running up and down. Mommy and I lived there (without Chet, of course, the imagination stopped right there, maybe we'd keep going out with him to sort of humor him). Bett was calling me from downstairs and there was bubble bath coming out of our bathrooms where we were running baths and getting ready for a night out. Furthermore, I was up and down in the elevator with the dog, in sunglasses by now, and with a long arm straight out like Veronica's when she had a guest, because the dog was pulling me to take him to the park. Outside was a group of girls from school who would hear the clank of the elevator gates and go to the park with me and come home afterward, impressed and envious, not just because of the place and all the beautiful furniture (which Chet hadn't mentioned but would no doubt come—we couldn't just put the Castro convertible chair-bed and the studio couch in there; no, we'd get rid of everything and start again, clean, new, elegant), anyway, envious of me, not just because of the co-op but because I was living alone with the Afghan and my beautiful mother, far more beautiful than any of theirs, and we were like sisters, living alone in our "cozy little nest."

November was a time of phone calls from Chet. He was setting things up and had to do one more trip to Florida (we'd received a basket of grapefruit in orange cellophane wrap). He was coming back the first week in December and the move was set for that month: we could be in before Christmas. This year there was no scene about trees and presents, we were busy with better dreams. We bought our cards and sent them. Season's Greetings. We waited.

I came back from school one afternoon wondering if Bett had heard from Chet, and I saw her sitting on her bed, frowning.

"Sweetheart," she said, "there's a problem. It's terrible for him, his son." And then she didn't want to say, it was so awful for Chet, and she always liked to keep me from the grim side of life. "Something about a brain tumor, the son."

"I didn't know he had a son," I said to her.

"I didn't either."

"Well, when's he coming back?"

"Sweetheart, I don't know. He must have so much to think about."

"Well, did he say anything?"

"He'll call us when he can."

Of course, he never could or did. I say "of course" the way Shrimp would say it, and probably did at the time, but for a while I really waited for his call and I was really surprised. Once, much later, I asked my mother what she thought had happened.

"I don't know," was all she ever said.

Bett and I in the neighborhood Saturday morning, doing errands, picking up shoes at the nice old Italian shoemaker, Bett wearing a suit, still chic but worn at the nap. She gives the shoemaker her ticket and he keeps it a few minutes. I'm sort of looking at the polishes and laces on a little display shelf near the door and I hear this:

"Feefty dollars." Sly, low-voiced.

"For what?" says my mother.

"You know." His voice gets lower.

"No," says my mother. She doesn't.

"I geeve you feefty dollars. You say when. You such a beautiful lady."

She freezes, moves back a little from the counter. "Can I have my shoes, please," she says.

He holds out on her a few moments, then shrugs, turns away and gets the brown paper bag that matches the ticket. My mother puts her money on the counter, turns smartly on her heel, in the debonair manner she reserves for awkward occasions, and leaves the shop, while I hang back a little and watch him. He stares after her as she leaves, ignoring me, shrugs his shoulders one more time, gloomy, undeterred, following her with his eyes, seeing no reason to deprive himself, appraising, savoring, the lovely receding view.

THREE

I DON'T REMEMBER THE MONTH she arrived back from Europe—Spain in the last few years—with a shipment of canvases, crates of sculpture and Bill, her new, young husband. My mother's bad mother. You can never tell where rescue is going to come from, or where and in what shape it's going to leave you when it goes away again. I do remember that once she was here everything changed for me, and then changed again when she left. She had the paradoxical substantiality of a vision in a dream, remaining indelible, a presence I carried around inside me for the rest of my life, and she would surface many times in the middle of the night, or when I was alone and unhappy, and tell me how to proceed. Sometimes it was like a real voice I heard, very calm, very direct, the affection nowhere in the body of the voice but prompting it somehow, and the task (of continuing or renouncing or believing or whatever it was) not, once that voice was present to me, really arguable. Sometimes it was just like a thing I could call up, not really a sensuous, physically endowed memory (as I always have with Bett), but a simple fact. A fact of who you are. And without a doubt I am me because of her, still here more because of her than anyone else. So it's all the stranger how little there is to report of the time I knew her.

Later you ask questions of this person, questions that have to do with your adult life—nothing to do with the way you were then and how you were when you were with her, which was heedless, rapacious, oblivious. Yet something adhered. You must have noticed and squirreled away something you had no means of knowing you'd want or recognize decades later. Without seeing, you stole

79

something from the past as you lived it, something you could look at and finger in the future. And you did all this unconscious, a kleptomaniac in your own life.

I remember the way she walked in the loft, and her coloring, the rich black hair, cut short, lovely dark eyes, the pale skin that had its own light, and sometimes a kind of café au lait color, creamy coffee skin. And inside this, bearing it and proclaiming all her fierce containment, were her bones, remarkable bones that structured her loping frame, that sat like bracelets on her wrists and ankles, that created mysterious rising and disappearing islands of hip and shoulder blade, invented the forms on which her clothing lay and rode and which it obeyed. She was a beautiful woman, and her beauty was inside her. You could push against my mother and something would give way, but my grandmother radiated indestructibility.

We sat in her studio loft drinking black coffee and discussing what I should call her. Any version of "Grandma" would have been absurd. She conveyed no quality of "grandmother" I ever knew about. Even to me she looked young, and would have looked younger if it weren't for the complex expressiveness of her face, the layers of intelligence evident with no apparent movement of eyes or brow or mouth, as though everything registered deeply with her and instantaneously. She had the beauty of a solemn, magic animal, not at all like my mother's beauty, not pretty, too severe for that, and not "sexy" in any way that I could read, although Eros was there. She was strong, tall, slender, a lustrous vehicle of dark and light that gave off heat and energy on a constant burn. She was graceful, buoyant as a dancer, and moved differently from other women I had seen, without apology or mincing or defeat. There was purpose and often happiness in the gestures of her body, or not happiness but some secret alliance with life, that rarely surfaced in her face, which had a calm, almost humorless composure. Where my mother was soft, yielding, and conveyed a physical confusion regarding her whereabouts—a kind of whirring blurriness of hesitation and withdrawal, as attractive to men as the panicked swimming of wounded fish to sharks—my grandmother strode and glided in her surroundings with impervious directed-

80

ness. It was as though she had her own arrangement with the world, and it made you always want to be with her, to trail after her because you knew you'd be safe in her wake. Safety was one of the first things I felt about being with her once she accepted me.

For all her youthfulness, my grandmother seemed to me like someone who had been on a long journey and survived. There was a heroic quality to her, immediately apparent but confusing in the light of her evident femininity. In my experience women had been martyrs like Claudia, or broken angels like Bett, or lumps of misery and rectitude like the mothers at school. Heroism had been exclusively for males, and as for power, as far as I knew, it existed in women only in monstrous form, as in the case of Miss de Vine. Power contained inside a female and used as energy rather than rage was new to me and made my grandmother almost supernatural. And whereas I always argued with my mother, and lately more frequently, I would no more have questioned my grandmother or disobeyed her than I would have let go of a branch suspended over crashing water.

Other people must have felt similar things about her. I don't know whether integrity or courage or whatever it was was so obvious, but she was always treated with respect. It was very different from the respect that was accorded Bett, which was more like a quick intake of breath having to do with her looks and which lasted only long enough for the person in question to crack through in order to get somewhere with her. With my grandmother, people left a kind of space around her, and even when they were strangers offered her smiles of recognition and only straightforward conversation. No one ever used, as they frequently did with Bett, the least innuendo, nor was anyone ever rude or in a hurry or short-tempered. Because people treated her this way, she must have had a peculiar sense of the world. It was probably a better place than the one Bett and I inhabited.

The business of finding a name for me to call her lasted only as long as our brief discomfort with one another, our first investigation of whether either of us wanted this relationship at all. For a couple of hours it might have gone either way, at least from her side of things. She was rather formal, though friendly with me, willing only up to a point to be curious. As for me, I may have had some initial wariness about her, given Bett's barely repressed resentments. But our mutual appraisals didn't last very long. I left her studio on that first day completely taken with her, and calling her, at her suggestion, by the name I'd apparently used in the unremembered past, when as a very small child I'd addressed her in choked gutturals as "Gogi."

She never was a grandmother to me. As far as I was concerned it was a brand-new relationship, despite the existence of the infantile designation, which later seemed to suit her and express a quality of energetic forward motion. But though she always introduced me as her granddaughter (a procedure which would provoke the same dazed cries of disbelief as when I called Bett "Mommy" in public) we were never grandmother and grandchild. Rather we were like friends in the kind of fixed and contracted partnership where one is the absolute leader and the other absolutely accepted. Gogi and I got to a point of closeness very quickly, speeding through all the normal stages of acquaintanceship as you do at the beginning of a love affair, as though time is very finite, very precious. I had a strange sense of familiarity with her, not at all as if I'd known her all my life, but as though I'd been expecting her all that time and so wasn't so much surprised, perhaps, as relieved to see her.

In the light of my clear infatuation, my mother withdrew whatever opposition she may have felt about our friendship. In fact, Bett's attitude was typical of her generosity toward me as well as of her habitual sense of her difference from the rest of the world. She wanted me to have a relationship with my grandmother if it was available to me, just as years later she never stood in the way of my meeting my father. Her own troubled dealings with Emma, frightening and crippling as they'd been, were never established as a barrier to mine. If she had been deprived of maternal love, that was simply her own characteristic bad luck, and she wouldn't dream of letting it stand in the way of my getting what she had so passionately wanted. On the other hand, Gogi's love of me never softened my mother's feelings toward her. Though she never said anything to me against her, whenever she brought me to the studio

or picked me up—arrangements which in any case became unnecessary once I was a habitué of my grandmother's life—their exchanges were always mysteriously stiff (on both sides) and un-
friendly. It was the only time—except when men were making
unwelcome passes—I ever saw my mother acting coldly or heard
her use defensive ironies, barbs about as intimidating as the swat
of a kitten's paw, and somehow, at least to me, if not to Emma,
just as touching. Whatever Bett secretly felt, she never made my
seeing Gogi an issue of loyalty between us, and I was grateful to
her for that. Perhaps she was, as she behaved, simply happy for
me.

She was undemonstrative, my grandmother. I can't remember
that she kissed or held me very much. It's clear to me now, though
it didn't occur to me then, how much Bett and Constance must
have suffered from her coldness. But to me, her remoteness was
just an aspect of her wonderful containment, her natural distinction
from the ordinary world. Besides, I always knew—as they never
did—that she loved me, and when I was with her my confidence,
my sense of my own value as a person, soared. My mother's love
didn't give that to me. It was different, unmeasured, a kind of
inertia, something she could not help. Whereas Gogi's love was
something I had to win, and therefore, having it, knew I deserved,
I would never have dreamt of trying to test it.

My grandmother made absolutely no concession to me as a child.
There were no games and no indulgences. No "children's" food,
never any dessert at meals, let alone milk and cookies. I took my
part in her life as though I were simply a small version of her, and
we would sit in the afternoons drinking black coffee and listening
to news on the radio, or else we'd work in her studio, where I had
my own paints and easel and my own sculpting stand. When we
went to the movies they were usually "art films" and when we
went out it was to the bank or the grocer's. No grandmotherly
expeditions to zoo or park or circus. But I was very happy in her
world and never bored, the way I was often bored at home. I loved
the smells of the studio, the oily clay and plaster, turps and oils.
And I loved her loft. It was big and bare, with "nothing" in it
except the work materials and a couple of high gauze screen room

dividers, some studio couches and canvas chairs, and the upended crates where Bill and she kept their books and magazines. But the "nothing" here was very different from the "nothing" at home, which always felt like deprivation. In the loft, without even a kitchen (we washed the dishes in the bathtub), there was an air of inventiveness and originality, superiority to custom. No deprivation: this was clearly just how Gogi wished to live.

It was not quite true that she never indulged me. She would often read to me, when I asked her, from the Edmund Dulac edition of fairy tales, the stories of the Snow Queen and the Emperor and the Nightingale. Or from Lewis Carroll. But these were books she liked as much as I did, and if I had asked her to read something she didn't care for, she would have refused. In any case, soon enough I was happier reading to myself, and indiscriminately consuming all kinds of popular "adult" novels like *Exodus, Marjorie Morningstar, Gone with the Wind*, books which swept me up in gusts of sensational music and which I might read throughout a whole afternoon at the loft, lying with the cats in the corner of the studio among the drab fifties olive, black and turquoise square and triangled cushions, and allowing the sounds of where I was—the cleaning of brushes, sanding of plaster, phone conversations, running water—to enter and mix and solidify with the other lives I was living, on the plantation or kibbutz or in satin-sheeted beds.

Gogi read, I think, less than I did, and I don't associate her with books but, like Bett, with cats and listening to the radio (talk programs mostly, or blues and jazz). But really I associate her with work, the painting and sculpting by which, in its commercial form, she earned her living, and which, unlike my mother's, seemed entirely to engage her. She didn't distinguish work from pleasure the way everybody else did, and that was infectious. For all its apparent austerity, it was really a kind of child's world my grandmother inhabited, something a child would have invented for itself: full of adventures, encounters, eccentrics, pastimes and constructions. Perhaps Emma had this notion of the world as reliably fascinating (when it didn't get too close) because of her happy childhood, and perhaps my mother's sense of it, much like what the poet Ehrenburg said of Modigliani—that his world seemed an enormous kindergarten run by very unkind adults—perhaps her unhappy childishness came from her earliest deprivations. In any case, in *my* childishness I wanted to believe that the universe was more benign than yet I'd found it, that it was interesting as well as good, and it was Gogi's evident conviction of these things as much as her heroic presence that seduced me. Without any of the props with which adults restage childhood for their offspring, without toys or games, Gogi gave me, late but not too late, the solider, happier parts of childhood which she'd retained and which fundamentally connected with her life as an artist (even a commercial artist, as she often was). Her dealings with both work and the world were a form of serious play, and they had serious implications for me about what was "out there," that place which seemed, each succeeding year I lived in New York with my mother, increasingly both brutal and dull.

Gogi's studio was really a kind of intelligent child's paradise. There was not only the desert-island makeshiftness of the place, and a continual "rainy day" activity with paints and paper and clay, but the whole loft building was like a village a child might have constructed, with pop-out characters behind the beveled milk-glass doors all along the gleaming, brass-trimmed corridors. There was a dentist, a watchmaker, a couple of perfume makers in matching jackets and bow ties, a notorious sculptor who had once been married to Gypsy Rose Lee and a Korean painter with a silent, doll-like family. All day long they came in and out of their boxes to gossip and have coffee. Their doors were often open, and open especially to me. The dentist used to show me his collection of remodeled jaws, his little wooden drawers of extracting instruments, each one specifically designed for a specific emergency, and so many kinds of emergency possible. Mr. Marx and Mr. Shelley would give me perfume samples or tiny pastel-bow-tied sachets of potpourri for "your lovely mother" or "your dear grandmother." The reputedly wicked De Diego, who had once in my hearing asked my mother to pose for him ("*Of course* without clothes!" he said, as though her question were ridiculous), made me one Christmas a devil doll of papier-mâché, a sort of plump white owl with peaked eyebrows, a red silk cape and a long forked tail. There was a violinist, too, and a small, lugubrious pianist, sometimes accompanied by a singer doing scales, so that soprano notes and repetitions would channel down the hallways, a vibrant, dunning sound that was both ridiculous and beautiful. I used to ride the elevator up to Gogi's sixth floor, getting progressively intoxicated by the impregnations on old wood of brass polish, oil and turpentine, bounding like a puppy on a leash to see who was in and who wanted to talk and what had happened since last time. Impatient, too, to be back where increasingly I felt at home, or at least where that part of me that was most alive, playful, hopeful, really lived.

Gogi's loft was only a couple of blocks from Carnegie Hall, and the surrounding brownstones and commercial buildings were full of rehearsal studios and cheap accommodation where the musical inhabitants of that neighborhood worked and lived. At any hour of the day you could see pale, foreign-looking symphony players in long, dark coats carrying battered instrument cases, or monolithically bosomed singing instructresses sauntering in moth-eaten furs, addressing tiny dogs in loud, accented voices. In the evenings, these same down-at-heel exotics would hurry to concerts in performers' evening dress, a kind of shiny, baggy, perhaps once elegant version of the real thing of several decades before. The delicatessens along Sixth Avenue would also be full of musicians in those days, nursing single cups of coffee throughout an afternoon (though this was commoner practice in the unsupervised automat nearby) and arguing with the waiters about the freshness of the rolls. I was fascinated and sometimes intimidated by them: their hands were never still, their hair never brushed like anyone else's; they wore elaborate, rumpled, often self-delighted clothes that never matched their serious brows or demeanor. They were to me like circus people, only from a darker, sadder circus (after all, they made the music that Bett listened to when she was unhappy). My grandmother knew some of them, and we would stop and talk from time to time, idling on the streets that were not yet given over to the high rises of Sixth Avenue, but which, like the nearby Museum of Modern Art and its garden, seemed to belong to amateurs and professionals of all the different arts. All those loft buildings, old cinemas, many of the delis and rehearsal studios are gone, and now even the MOMA garden seems an artificial oasis, a kind of harmless corporate gesture to something that died away (and perhaps was dying when I knew it) long ago.

I didn't keep up the painting and sculpture when I was away from my grandmother, and unless I was specifically making a Christmas or birthday present for her I didn't do it at home. It never felt like something she'd given me that I could keep for myself, but rather part of a language I used when I was with her. It was part of the way I *was* with her, the grammar of our conversation, and doing it without her or not with her in mind would have been like speaking a lover's babble to myself. But together we would stand by the huge windows, behind the linen screens that separated the "serious" part of the loft from the sitting and sleeping parts, and I would work by her while she did her rhythmic, barefoot dance, approaching and backing away from her sculpture stand, a tool in her right hand or a piece of oily green clay between thumb and finger, held out at chest height with the tense, slightly shaky attention of a hunting cat. Or she'd mix her paints or sand, with the heavy, ridged iron sanding bar, one of the factory-cast plaster mannequin heads or limbs or torsos. Probably she didn't do any important work while I was there: it's pretty difficult to work freely with someone standing nearby. But I absorbed a sense of her concentration by a kind of unconscious tracking of the movement of her feet as she danced with her work, and by her breathing. I never felt the kind of emotion being with Gogi when she worked that I did when I was with my mother, who had no choice but to concentrate while I was there and whom I was able to watch for hours. Especially when she did portraits of me, I could look directly at her face, which I didn't like to do with my grandmother. When Gogi worked, her expression would some-times get a little grim, her mouth would tighten and she might appear angry, though I think I knew that was simply how it looked. But my mother always had a wonderful sweet seriousness when she sculpted, and a little moving smile in the corners of her mouth and eyes, perhaps by way of apology for keeping me sitting. Maybe it was just the professional thing she had to do when she did portraits, her consciousness moving in and out of the work, solicitous, conciliatory. But even when she was wholly in the work she had a look of tender concentration that I loved very much, and sometimes she even looked happy, reprieved. I don't know—you lose yourself when you're working like that, and perhaps that loss of self was what made her happy. After, when she "came out of it," she'd keep that peaceful look for a while until the habitual anxiety, and sometimes her "panics," would return.

She *said* she didn't like it, making art. That it was all part of Gogi's world and her father's world and reminded her of her terrible early life. Yet she *looked* so contented doing it, and I wish she'd been able to do it more, because she was talented and it seemed to fulfill her. But she'd put off assignments or get some measurement wrong and some of the companies, the medallion company, for example, for whom she made beautiful commemorative medals, eventually dropped her. After that it was always more difficult because she had no confidence at all. And she really hated the rest of Gogi's world, all the trappings of bohemia, that bare, eccentric loft. She was polite, of course, to the other inhabitants of her mother's building, who all liked and asked after her, but it was clear she thought they were sad cases. Still, she could have done the work on her own terms, in her own setting. Maybe it would have given her the pleasure it always seemed to when you watched her sculpting. It makes me sad now to think about it, and to see again the expression she had while she worked. Because rescue was *right there*, where she thought there was nothing. She *was* talented, everybody said so, and she could have carved a way out of her life with her gifts if at every artist's gesture, every whiff of clay or plaster, she had not had to overcome all the associations of a frightening, dreadful childhood.

I haven't said anything about Gogi's husband. For a while I was so astonished by the new female presence in my life that I barely noticed the accompanying male. Men were meant to be wonderful creatures (or else why all the fuss?) and he was less of a surprise to me. Perhaps I knew I needed really to register the startling fact that a woman could possess such virtues as Gogi did, and took my time with him, as though even then I could understand through her something about women that I'd need later.

But I liked him from the beginning. I thought he was very attractive and funny. And I liked the way they were a couple and the way he loved her and made her happy. He was twenty years younger than she was but I didn't notice it, the fact just fell into the general soup of differences between them. He looked a little like pictures of Hemingway in the twenties: tall, dark, big-boned, sort of clumsily physical. He had a mustache like young Hemingway and wore similar clothes, English, maybe Spanish suits of thick tweed with narrow cuffs on the trousers. I remember the suits and jackets seeming very European and scratchily, bulkily masculine, nothing effeminate or Italian. He had real presence to him, and happy blue eyes. And he was far more demonstrative with me than Gogi ever was.

He was a photographer and spent a great deal of time in the darkroom which they'd constructed in the corner of the loft where the kitchen used to be, and which you had to enter when the red light was off if you wanted to make a cup of coffee or use the stove. The sink and the counters were used for developing. It was a pretty strange juggling act but they managed it. The time I didn't spend over by the big windows making sculpture with Gogi, or reading on the couch, I spent with Bill in the dark under the infrared lights, pulling sheets of paper by their top corners with a pair of bamboo tongs from pans of delicious, strong-smelling, slightly yellowish chemicals, putting them flat on their backs into other pans, and watching the images appear giddily from inside the amniotic liquids. Bill taught me many of the photographic procedures: enlarging, reversing and projecting negatives, bleaching, fixing, cutting and carefully handling the razor-edged high-gloss paper on which he printed. He didn't teach me how to take pictures, though, or maybe I was never very interested. I loved the work in the dark, with the red light and the atmosphere of necromancy, the amazing things that light and dark and chemicals could do.

He used to talk a lot about Spain, where he met and married my grandmother, the beautiful solitary foreigner that everyone in the village gossiped about. They had a large house in Málaga where cats and goats wandered in the olive groves and slept on the terraces, where there was pink dust everywhere, the sound of Ray Charles on the radio, and a view of the sea. A maid from the village took care of them, shopped and cooked for them and carried the huge bottles of water up the hill. You could have all that, he said, the big house, the maid and all the red wine you could drink, for twenty-five dollars a month.

Whenever Bill and Gogi had a conversation they didn't want me to understand, they spoke Spanish, but mostly they let me into their lives openly, and I never felt I was in their way. I used to stay overnight sometimes, on one of the studio couches with a screen around it. I saw Bill naked once through the screen, lit up in flashes of neon from the lights across Sixth Avenue. He looked vulnerable, white and exposed like Christ on his cross. But there was strength in his legs and shoulders and I felt him as a mixture of weak and strong, light and dark like his work: the white skin and smooth muscles, the mysterious dark triangle under his narrow hips and white belly.

Being there at night was sometimes frightening. Though I was never frightened in the dark at home, here the green and pink neon from the big hotel sign over the way threw eerie patches onto Gogi's mannequin parts, onto white plaster arms and hands, and the bald and eyeless, swan-necked female head. Among them, on the large worktable where they were arranged, the cats would weave in and out like water snakes, moving both slowly and suddenly in the on/off strobe-like illuminations.

I was comfortable with Bill in a way I never was with any of my mother's suitors. Perhaps the anxieties which I always felt with them, whether they'd stay, whether they'd leave, how soon they'd make my mother cry and turn on the classical music, didn't exist with him, and that made things easier.

We used to go to movies at the Museum of Modern Art or to art and photography exhibitions. We walked in the park, he in his long tweed coat with his cameras banging against his buttons or held in his cold-raw hands. His shoes with their thick soles would sound heavy on the slates by the side of the duck pond, and every footstep would seem solid, male, reliable. His face was lighter than the rest of him, particularly his pale blue eyes and his mustache— perhaps the first and last mustache I never found ridiculous— which smelled of mint mouthwash and Gitanes. I liked him physically. I liked the way he pulled up my collar and his collar when we were out in the cold, the way he handled, rearranged me for his photo sessions. I liked his ease with me, and acceptance. We were friends, or maybe he was the first man I ever loved.

They had a place in the country, near Carmel, where I went in the summer. It was a lakeside community, crowded with little houses on little lots, with scrappy gardens and outhouses. But it was my Shokan, and I ran through other people's woods and gardens, up and down the dirt roads and all through the ribboned lots of unsold acreage as if I were a young heiress on her own estate. I had friends along the road, children of other summer visitors, with whom I rode bicycles, shot bows and arrows, shouted, fought, ran wild. Or quietly, for hours, I sculpted alongside Gogi in the garage she'd converted for her work, both of us barefoot on the cool cement floor, where in the midday heat the mulching odor of wet clay mingled with the smells of sunned-upon rubber hoses, fumes from the cans of gasoline and, from just outside the garage door, the smell of the pale wild tea roses and mint and sage from the herb garden, through which the cats walked with high, careful, nervous steps, like Viennese show horses. Those cats ran less wild than I did in the country, they hung around the buildings, frightened of country noises, alarmed by birds and toads and the sudden sounds of the iron well where we pumped water. They would jump vertically and land on their feet, or scratch and panic their way up the plum and apple trees and lie crouching in cradles of branches, below which the hammock swung and groaned on its ropes and Bill and I would lie reading or laughing, "horsing around." I remember Gogi appeared once when we were doing this, and I can see her still, standing framed by the doorway, looking down at us and suddenly in a chilling voice calling Bill inside. When he came out again, he looked shamefaced, rebuked, unable to meet my eye, as though we'd been caught doing something wrong.

We had our routines. Art in the daytime, catching the thin,

bluish morning light, and the richer, thicker sun of the afternoon. When the light began to bend we would go swimming in the lake, which was muddy, crowded, often teeming with the people we never spoke to. I found my friends and would swim with them under the end of the dock, where there were rumored to be crabs and eels and where you'd see large, bug-eyed white fish bellying their way through the coffee-colored water. We had black rubber tires to float in and bright-patterned bathing suits. Swimming beyond the shore I could hear the parents shrieking for their children to get out of the water, watch them fuss roughly with towels, sometimes slapping them, always whining or hysterical. I knew then I was privileged living with Bill and Gogi, because I had none of that stuff, the family misery.

Sometimes we would drive in what Bill called the "English Ford" to a place further along the rim of the lake, stop the car under a clump of trees and sit talking with the doors open while Gogi swam across the lake. Through the noise of crickets our voices would carry a short way over the water and we would watch the fireflies and the distant headlights of traffic on the other side. An hour or so later, sometimes late into twilight, Gogi would return, glistening, breathing rapidly in the stillness, a figure long, lean and heroic. We were lesser creatures, waiting for her.

They slept together naked on the screened porch that ran around the house. I slept in the attic, which smelled of pitch pine and roofing tar when the sun heated it, and where I could look through a small window into roof branches which shook when the squirrels leapt. There were no real bedrooms in the house. If anyone came to visit they were meant to use the "guesthouse" at the bottom of the little wooded area beyond the lawn. It was a tiny, single-roomed cabin, fixed up like a child's playhouse with a Baby-Belling stove and a shallow sink, a child's table and chair. Under the low slope of the roof was a bed, far too large for the space, from which it seemed to swell like something growing, rotting, gaseous. But no one used this house and it was mine to sit in, though far too stifling in summer heat to remain in very long. I came upon it by accident before I knew what it was, peered in between the branches of the wild rose bushes through the cobwebbed windows, pushed on the rusty doorknob till the door gave way, and I stood inside, watching the beetles scatter and inhaling the thick, musty air and the overpowering smell of baking oilskin from the blue-and-white-checked table cover under the window. On the bed, bloated as a mushroom and covered by a colorless, mildewing quilt, there were two dolls, their eyes open and staring at the ceiling, their cloth arms and legs bent under them like broken limbs. They were not dolls for children, but soft, disintegrating rags attached to cracked, dirty, immaculately rendered porcelain heads. The faces had been delicately sculpted and given haughty, adult features. One had a blond wig and the other was dark. I recognized them immediately as the dolls Bett had once told me about, the ones Gogi had made and given to them when they were children: the Constance doll and the Bett doll. They had been cherished for the gesture, as a rare sign of their mother's affection, but the dolls themselves were never much loved because their expressions were as cold as Emma's and they seemed like cruelly mocking replicas of their own unloved, perhaps unlovable, selves.

My mother came to visit from time to time, and once she asked me, in a private, secret way, if I was happy. It was hard to believe that she didn't know, but I wasn't emphatic because I didn't want to hurt her feelings, "Puppy, if Gogi ever frightens you or makes you unhappy, you must tell me and I'll bring you home." "I'll tell you," I said, and I remembered again the faces of the dolls, the poor, dead girl corpses. I had to love my mother less to go on loving Gogi. And for as long as it was necessary I loved my mother less.

One summer I don't go with Bill and Gogi to Carmel. No one tells me why. I go with Bett to a camp run by Christian Scientists, but still a regular camp with color teams and khaki shorts, whistles, cabins and mosquitoes. To get us there, my mother has taken a job as arts and crafts counselor, just as her father had once when she and Constance were children. (Later it seemed extraordinary that she does this, reconnecting with the enemy, and then later still I understand her trying to catch her childhood again in the face of what is about to happen.) She is twelve or fifteen years older than the other counselors, college boys and girls, but they like her. She writes a musical for the lower camp, songs and lyrics, makes all the costumes. It is a great success, but it is done at a level of professionalism that throws them a little. They treat her like the strange, talented beauty, but outsider, she is. I am rebellious, badly behaved (why am I in this regimented, mindlessly cheerful place, why am I not with Gogi?), but I get away with it because I am her daughter. In this way, they are protective of her, about me. At night I am haunted by a recurrent dream, an abstract dream of pure sensation, a taste and color and wetness. I dream of a bloody, pulpy wound that is like the place in your mouth where a tooth has been extracted, like the feeling of putting your tongue there pushing on the soft, spongy gum, making it hurt, tasting the oxidized gouts of blood, feeling the blackened redness. Then this place in the mouth grows, becomes a whirlpool, sucking me under, spinning downward; airless, soaked, I drown in blood, awake terrified with my sheets cold and wet with urine beneath me.

At camp there is an epidemic of flu. I go to my mother's cabin and watch her looking after her group, the youngest girls, babies sneezing and shivering and reading their Bibles under flashlights: little storm lamps among the cots. The murmuring of childish reading, like belowdecks on some slave ship in the eighteenth century: "And God said," "And be not" and "Oh, my children." And my mother sitting among them, not joining in and not fleeing, and not seeming to react at all.

My mother is in the end-of-summer show. She comes on in a grass skirt and a narrow halter top singing about Tropical Sadie or some such and her heat wave. She sways her hips and arms to the piano music, sweeping out and back in her grass skirt, darting around the stage. In the glow of the footlights the audience, the young men counselors and their dates, stare up at my mother's strange, solitary, sexual performance. She's very good doing it, but it's excruciatingly embarrassing.

I can't wait to get back to Gogi and Bill when the summer's over, but they make me wait. And then one day I go and Bill is strange with me, and takes me behind a screen (the open loft room has closed areas now, and secrets), brings me gently to Gogi, who is lying in bed, looking much older and frighteningly thin. Her forearm is out by her side, held awkwardly as though it belongs to someone else. Her papery flesh lies on her bones as if held there by a tension, a passive argument. Her bones seem to be pushing outward at the wrist, at the elbows. They no longer hold her beauty but seem to have turned against her, to hurt her, hold her captive.

Her cheekbones, of course, are more prominent, and they, too, push against her, making the skin shiny as fruit, but colorless, and creating the effect of pain with every expression. Her eyes are enormous, and reflect a new anxiety, but it is on my behalf. There is a new question in them, about the strength of my love, my wisdom to read beyond appearance, to recognize my beloved in this new, endangered form. There is the slightest element of pleading in them, and humility, and these embarrass me, demand a demonstration of acceptance that has never been necessary before. "Does your grandmother look like a witch?" she asks. And I am ashamed, because she does and I *hate* her apology. She had never had to apologize to me in her life, and it's ugly, wrong. I say no, of course not, and kiss her. Her skin smells bad. I'm already dissembling, abiding by the new terms.

That spring when I was at Carmel I had found a green necklace of hers and said, "Can I have this when you die?" I said it that way because I coveted it and yet did not want to take it from her, and I was saying I would wait. Yet she had heard impatience to possess the beads, and the shocking word "die," of course, and she had answered me sharply, as I thought then, "You can have them now if you want them. But don't ever ask for something out of anyone's death." I think of this exchange as I stand next to her, conscious of her pain then and my former ignorance, and now this new ignorance. We are in this together and we are both fumbling. Even she has no guidelines. I comfort her. I make myself touch her, and after a while I don't have to force myself. But it is a new being I am dizzily, speedily having to learn to love, and she knows that. We hate this, she and I. But we accept the terms because we have no choice.

They say it is cancer, and now she is always in bed, often tired.

I can't ever stay for very long. Sometimes I have to leave her in the middle of a visit. I disappear into the darkroom with Bill, ducking in under the red light to look for the magic, anything that will deny what goes on the other side of the black curtains. Bill and I develop prints while she sleeps. She doesn't work anymore. We do it without her. Something's very wrong and it's not going to get any better. They removed her from us over the summer while the little girls read the Bible and my mother danced in her grass skirt. Bill and I take care of her, bring her soup, answer the phone. The power's gone and she's ashamed. Her shame is the worst part of it. But she never complains, never refers to it. Only, sometimes, apologizes, says she needs to rest.

There's nowhere to flee. I can't talk about this with my mother. I can't talk about this with Bill, who is looking after her all the time, wearing a haunted expression and anxiously, tenderly watching her, feeding her, giving her her injections, sleeping naked next to her in the bed where she is dying. I can't help him either. He's gone somewhere without me, his eyes red-rimmed, his clothes rumpled. One by one he sells the beautiful machines out of the darkroom. There's very little left in there. We only use it anymore to get away.

At school, junior high school now, I am lost, unbalanced, vulnerable. It must be coming across. One of the older boys they keep behind in special classes picks up on this, on me, follows me home, lurks in the hall, corners me one afternoon and shows me his knife. "How you like to be cut up?" "Not particularly," I say out of some British wobble in the DNA. That stops him. He steps aside to let me pass. After that it is as if he has fallen in love. For weeks he follows me, loping, stealthy, his big, dark, Latin eyes heating in his head, his hands twitching. He is anger and adoration both, mixed up crazily and increasingly dangerous. Some way it gets confused with Gogi's waning strength. I'm suddenly vulnerable, to him and more. I won't get through. I will be cut up. One day he fires a gun at a policeman. It makes the papers, and they take him away.

I have friends at school. Jacqueline, who lives in a tenement building with her Italian family. Her father beats her mother and she is ashamed. And Clare, who lives on Park Avenue in a large apartment where everything is covered in plastic, the sofas and the carpets, the candles on the piano. In her parents' gold-and-white "Louis Quinze" boudoir the walls are lined with photos of Clare taken years earlier at children's talent contests: Clare in tiara and tutu, in clown costume, as a princess with a wand, blond hair singed into ringlets, a desperate smile on her baby face. And now, among the crackling protected furniture, she wanders timidly in the strange clothes her mother buys for her in jumble sales, torn sweaters and buttonless coats. Her hair is dirty, sometimes matted, and they feel sorry for her at school. But it is as though she surrendered her physical presence to the whims of her parents long ago, and lives inside her rags with her own fierce, bright spirit, indifferent to the pity and neglect.

We three are a band of angels, stumbling through the given world; we are each other's balance. Each possesses the other's secret, and that makes us close. That and the relief there is for us in one another. Whatever they do out there cannot hurt us while we are together. We are alive somewhere under this confusion, marginality, abuse. We are the only joy going, one for the other, but it keeps the promise of joy sharp and clear for us. Knowing it, we know things can change, that we will outlive our separate bad worlds. Patience, cunning, hope, are what we give each other.

At three o'clock one afternoon I telephone Bill. I know this because I can see now the dirty pale blue leather watch strap on my wrist, and the gold-rimmed arc of the quarter circle that told me the time. I start to tell him a joke I have heard at school. He cannot talk, he says, and his voice is hoarse. I wait but he doesn't call me back. Later in the evening, an older woman comes to visit Bett. They go off into the turquoise bathroom, their only privacy from me, and for an hour I listen to my mother sobbing, keening in an unfamiliar, violent way. Her voice is harsh, deep, barbaric. When they come out my mother's face is so hard and bereft I cannot look at her. It is the other woman I ask: "Did she die?" She nods. "Today at three o'clock," she says, and I am mortified to have set the phone ringing at just that moment, pulling Bill from

97

her. And it feels ugly, strange, that I tried to tell him a joke, when I must have needed to say goodbye to her. And now never shall.

It's summer again. I go with Bill to the house in Carmel. But it's just for the day. We walk together in and out of the house. But it's a dead person now, we can't stay. Bill is with a real estate agent who's telling him how little it's worth and this and that. "I'll take it," Bill says. We leave everything: the canvases in the garage, the bins of clay, the double bed on the sleeping porch, the hammock, the Bett and Constance dolls in the hidden playhouse, lying there with their eyes open looking at the ceiling.

In New York I see him. We meet in Greenwich Village and try to catch up. But he's moving away from me. The pain's too big. He can't hang around. He's going back to Spain, he says, Ray Charles and red wine. He's closed up the loft, left the work, the darkroom, just walked away from all of it. "She left you her money," he says. "But it went long ago and I still owe the hospital. I'm sorry, but you should know what she wanted." We have coffee among the beatniks. He is looking sheepish again, underslept, unshaven. The same shamefaced look he had the day Gogi called him in from the hammock and told him to stop playing with me. He asks if he can borrow five dollars. And I give it to him but I don't like it. She's taken all our strength with her. She made us believe that we had it, too, but neither of us has. Later I get two or three letters from Spain; he's okay, he's working, he has an English girlfriend (like the "English Ford"). I never see him again.

Much later, they tell me that Gogi had cancer all the time. That that was why she came back from Spain. It's very strange. It was the reason I had her at all. She only came back to leave. And if she'd been well I might never have known her, or at least not then, when she was absolutely necessary.

And that was all. Love and the disappearance of love. Someone haphazardly given to me and then as arbitrarily snatched away. A sudden inexplicable life and its removal. A huge promise and a forgetting. Only I never forgot, and I have missed her all my life.

I knew nothing at all about her apart from this; I knew nothing of her as a girl or a sister, never saw her as a mother, a daughter, hardly as a lover or friend. I had only my brief and accidental knowledge and it became everything. But she knew, she fought against the inconsequentiality of our experience by pulling me into her own history when she died, bequeathing me a lineage and a future. She left me this letter:

Helen, dearest,

This is going to be a funny kind of letter, but because we love each other very much I'm sure you'll understand it.

You know I hadn't been feeling well for a while before you left for camp, and since then I've had some very good doctors helping me to feel better and more comfortable. But sometimes even doctors can't make you get well.

But when you've had children and a grandchild ["grand" underlined three times] and friends and a life full of all kinds of interesting work—and besides all that a wonderful husband—then it's not so bad and quite natural for living to be over, sometime.

Anyway, it never really *is* over—because you and Mommy and Constance and I are like branches of the same tree. So long as the tree is growing and blossoming, the whole tree is alive, even the older, sleeping parts.

Ever since you were a small baby, I've thought you were the finest, most all-round wonderful person I'd ever known—and you always will be. I've been happy every minute I've been with you.

I know you'll have a happy life, and all the things you really want most—sooner or later, because you deserve them.

All my love, dearest,
and a million (or two) kisses,
Yours always,
Gogi

Perhaps that is how you say goodbye to a child. There was another side to her, of course, many sides, but I found it later, when I was looking at photographs and what documents I could find, in a letter she wrote to Shrimp during the war, when Shrimp was in pieces, having her nervous breakdown, after the end of her marriage. Gogi writes to her in California:

99

Be glad, dear, that you are not "fortunate," for it would shut you from the world's heart—which is aching badly.

Pack Mother up [Mirabel, I suppose, on a mission of rescue], and yourself. Laugh—be very gay—with the gaiety of one who can no longer lose—and come to New York as quickly as possible. *We have work to do* . . .

FOUR

WE WERE LIKE WHITE MICE among the carnivores at junior high school. We were in the "Special Progress" group, three years' work in two, experimental classes for eleven-to-thirteen-year-olds: poetry full of abstraction and sexual innuendo, prose with swear words. Our young teacher amazed us, stirred us up and rattled us. We watched in breathless love as with theatrically businesslike manner she tacked a melodramatic blue Picasso reproduction onto the blackboard or put onto the crackly player a thick, shiny Shostakovich record and asked us to compose our poems to these inspirations. One morning she read us Freud's essay on *Hamlet* and made us act out scenes that would show the Oedipus complex at work. She prefaced a class on Hemingway by entering suddenly, demanding silence and hurling abuse at us. "Hell," she said. "Damn. Shit. These words may be shocking." She hoped they would be, but it was far too late for that. Each morning, we pale, fragile, stick-boned Special Progress students got to school un-scathed only through cunning, avoiding the streets where the demurely blazered, crucifix-bearing girls of St. Ann's lay waiting in ambush, to rip our clothes and steal our books, break our glasses, noses, teeth. We avoided the big school pens where the enormous boys of ninth grade, on average fifty pounds heavier than we and long gone in puberty, displayed their weaponry, smoked cigarettes and fought over women. We of the Special Progress classes were not men and women yet by any means; to the regulars we were white mice, snake food, and they shoved and jeered at us through the hallways. From time to time whole gangs would disappear from the play yard, having been sent to reformatories out of town, while we, coddled with poetry and offered the delectations of advanced culture, sat indoors and developed our minds.

It was in our first year of my time at this school that Gogi died. We held our graduation ceremonies without her one blazing June afternoon, in an air-conditioned cinema, an overblown rose of a Loews Palace on Eighty-sixth Street. All of us, thugs and mice, rose from orchestra seats in hired red satin to sing "Brotherhood of Man." Three thousand of us, our mortarboards bobbing at ludicrously jaunty angles, filed by in interminable orderliness to collect our antiquely worded, meaninglessly congratulatory scrolls. Robert F. Wagner was there, and in that election year saw fit to electioneer from the podium, while we rustled in our gowns and yawned, caught our parents' eyes and looked down at our first pair of high heels to see how our blisters were doing.

I was going to private school in the autumn. I could have gone to the High School of Music and Art since I'd been offered a place. I could have been an artist then, like Gogi, but instead I was "going to be a lady," as Clare's mother said to me with mixed irony and admiration as we stood in the plastic-covered living room. I had a scholarship, not because of my grades, to be sure (I would have to spend the summer being tutored in almost every subject), but because the headmistress had liked Bett and wanted to help her. When I got there my classmates were going to be two years older than I (thanks to my "special progress") and far better educated.

In the meantime Bett and I were to move from our basement flat near the Y. We were going to live in a pretty one-bedroom apartment in a brownstone on Ninety-fourth off Fifth. It was a five story walk-up, tiny, but elegant in the ways my mother liked, having a fireplace and a small front balcony. I was going to have my own room at last and throw out the convertible chair-bed. We were starting over, better; the school was only three blocks away.

My aunt Constance came to my graduation, wearing the kinds of clothes I used to think, when at PSL, she chose purposely to embarrass me; she would arrive at school plays in raccoon coat and purple stockings, a four-inch-wide gold ankle bracelet above stilettos, outfits I'd have to hear about for weeks afterward. By now, though, I recognized the defiant worldliness as admirable and I was beginning to be proud of her. I was terribly, timidly conventional, having been knocked into it by my humiliations at PSL. But my time with Gogi had confused this in me, and the huge range of styles and real deprivations in my schoolmates at junior high school. Besides, my mother's relative conventionality was beginning to seem a poor defense against humiliation, which was the only part I cared about, whereas Gogi had been a star, bohemian or not. In fact, through her I had begun to believe that honor and maybe even glory might lie in distinguishing oneself from the herd. In any case, if I looked at the herd now, lumbering, shuffling, gum chewing toward the podium, unloved, untended, uncourted even as voters, I didn't think being like everyone else was much of a formula for survival. I was on the verge of being an impoverished outsider once again at the new school, but I had Gogi's self-respect as an example to me, and I knew if I could hang on to that I'd get by. I wasn't going to creep around again apologizing for no clothes, no money, if I could help it. And anyway, thank God, Bett and I were moving. We were going to live in a nice place even if we were only there by our fingernails—but that's how we were anywhere. And something else: private school was far too elegant and well meaning to go in for the kind of persecution I'd had at PSL. We were going to be "ladies" and one thing ladies don't do is talk about money (or TV sets or maids). I'd met some of my future classmates already at a little lunch for new girls. It was all very grown-up, polite and friendly, full of talk of higher things, the chat of roses reared far from the tracks. Maybe, I thought, shame and snobbery was just a phase for kids. I was going to be with older girls now.

Bett's relations with Constance were strained, by inherited animosities periodically renewed. They had a deep connection to one another that surfaced in lengthily spaced, aborted gestures of affection and explosions of mutual outrage. (It was Constance's view that she had often tried to accommodate her sister but Bett's unworldliness made friendship "impossible.") But for extended periods they simply stayed clear of one another, and Constance would often test our friendship with remarks like "You know what your mother's like," to which I would shamelessly nod. Well, I did know. And then Bett would say, "You know what Constance is like," and I'd say yes because I knew that, too. Shrimp would worry that I was falling under Constance's spell and might get into bad habits of mind, like thinking "you could use anybody," sail grandly through life without consequences. But I loved Constance's grand sailing, that was exactly what I loved. And if she was never the unambiguous heroine to me that Gogi was—her sharp tongue could and did easily turn on me as well—I thought she was pretty impressive.

I had a new relation to Bett after Gogi, and when she was gone I knew that I had secretly abandoned my mother as my heroine. I remained fiercely loving, but a little part of my brain was already fixed on betrayal, fluttering anxiously for some way out of the tunnel her life, and mine with her, increasingly seemed to be. I was still too young to move forward; I could only signal needily from the sidelines and present myself as disciple to other women around me. It was in this spirit that I began my friendship with Constance. If there was a way out of the predictable disappointments of my life with Bett, I was, as I had been with Gogi, willing to hear about it. And if I could have got away then with Constance's glamorous indifference to the world, I might have imitated it, spiked and treacherous as it also seemed. However, I would have to wait until I, too, was a six-foot blond ex-model Africa explorer to bring it off. And in the meantime, I had to go to my new school.

I had never encountered girls like these. They *were* ladylike, sort of harnessed in it, well behaved, well groomed, terribly courteous with one another. They were well read, besides, at least they seemed so to me, good at languages and art history as well as math and science. They carried books put out by small presses, volumes of verse in whose margins they wrote urgent, sympathetic remarks. I was comfortable with them because they meant me no harm, at worst ignored me on account of my age and newness at school. And I was comfortable because I recognized in them certain aspects of my mother, her gentleness and femininity, and that virginal quality she never lost (though when she thought it necessary, she sometimes put it aside). If I was uncomfortable, and I often was, it was because I was always behind in classes, wore as ever the wrong clothes and the same ones, and felt in my thirteen-year-old state a different form of humanity from their sleek, lovely fifteen-year-old selves. Adolescence had set up inside me a disturbed housekeeping, not quite upheaving the works, but making things on which I thought I could rely, like gravity and cause and effect, relative and unpredictable. I was both moody and inarticulate, inert and foolish, liable to say what I didn't mean or find myself where I hadn't intended. I wanted to please because I liked those girls, because the school had given my mother and me a chance, but I could never be sure of anything. I didn't even know yet how to camouflage my unsureness. They had passions, those girls, for boys at Yale, for makeup, for certain insipid kinds of music, the intensity of which I could barely understand. It was all pretty simple. They were the other side of puberty and I was not.

It was happening too fast. I'd made "special progress," and I didn't really like it. My new classmates seemed to be hurrying me with them into the jet stream toward a whole new field of athletics, with its own new rules, uniforms, coaches and whistles, the unfenced world of boys, love, college, life. I would have sheltered from it all if I could have, but I'd seen grown-up things early and I couldn't pretend them away. Gogi and Bill both seemed absolutely vanished now, only two years later, and somehow unwearable, like clothes you've grown out of. Even their painting and sculpture had disappeared, and not even Shrimp knew what had happened to them. I wanted often to cry and run away, but the places I ran to were often sharp and hostile, with jagged edges and weird protrusions. The outside world was beginning to feel unsafe in a new way, and where I might have fled for safety the floorboards were no longer sound. Constance was still too fast, too unreal for me, Shrimp too solitary, and Bett in her slowness dangerous. I knew what was waiting for me at the other end of school—not love, college, life, not at all. I knew very well, and had always known and once cherished the idea: life with Bett, looking after Bett, loving Bett as I couldn't help, but if that was all there was going to be, I wished things would slow down.

I'm scared of a lot of things. Scared of not growing up, being left in a puppyhood of confusions. Scared of growing up and getting lost in the traffic like Bett. Scared of going their way and getting buried. Scared of going my way like Gogi and getting punished (she had been punished with cancer, hadn't she, the bad mother?). The good mother fumbles through her life and I fumble along behind her, only without her magic. My mother is still and always a beautiful woman. I'm just a nice little girl, not so little anymore, not so adorable, beginning to be less amenable, but no less helpless.

My mother lives in a daze. Time isn't time to her the way it is to me. I dread what's coming or I long for it. I'm never ready for the next step, can't follow the music, overbalance, fall. But my mother has her own time, a slow-moving water that flows under the other kind of time, the one marked by bills, the exigencies of employment, arrival and departure of men. They are dwindling. More and more the classical music plays on the radio, yearningly, mournfully or with an exuberance that comes nowhere near us. My life has less and less connection with hers. She just goes on in the same few modes every evening. Like weather, I know immediately if she's happy or unhappy. "It's not you, Puppy, Mommy just gets like this sometimes." Neither of us is waiting for the man who will take us away from it all anymore, at least I'm not; I'm carving my own life or it's carving me. It's so hard, she can't know how hard it is. She thinks I'm a busy, successful little girl with adorable problems. She's proud of me, no matter how I do at school. She loves me, no matter what I do. Nothing makes any difference. Nothing. I might as well not exist.

She is still unaccountably young, my mother, less like a good child, except in off-guard moments when consciousness slips, than like a dizzy teenager. When she mixes with other parents at school, there is still a circle of admiration that closes around her. This youthfulness is her achievement, and it's impressive. They didn't have young mommies in those days, or not still, not by "high school." Now the mothers meet to collect their teenage daughters in jeans and punk haircuts, but in those days even young women dressed to look older, in stockings, jewelry and spray-coiffed hair.

The parents treat Bett like a special creature, a valuable bird with soft and strangely colored feathers. Her beauty is not as it was at Mirrenwood, not so challenging in a crowd, it is more like loveliness now. "You have a lovely mother." They wear correct, confining clothes. She is separate from them, by virtue of her dress as much as youth, her manner of someone not quite beholden to their world, not quite there and possibly somewhere better, more innocent, more sunny. But then, she does not attend school events when she is dark: the darkness remains a secret between us. Except for certain kinds of men, on streets, at parties, people are gentle with my mother in response to her gentleness. We both look young when we're in these groups, but my youngness is a kind of absence of characteristics, whereas hers has substance and, still, a sort of light like glory.

The money was bad as usual, but somehow we managed to hang on to the brownstone apartment. They tried to evict us often, and the owner would scream down the telephone like a madwoman. The lights would get turned off and stay off, and I would do my homework in the further obscurity of candlelight. Or the phone would go off, but then at least we didn't get the abuse of the landlady anymore, only the summonses. We'd resort to Shrimp again, which kept her away from us, made her ironic and self-protective, so that Bett, once she had the check in her hand, would be indignant toward her. There's not much gratitude possible when one is always asking and the other always resisting, doling out, remaining unthanked.

I had made money babysitting since I was eleven. Those first jobs were bizarre, sitting in tenements with five-week-old babies while the parents stayed out till 3 A.M., when, nodding off myself, I'd get my mother over to babysit for both of us, though that was bad because she always lectured them when they came home. Or I'd sit for rich people who wanted me to wash the floors. Or rich people whose closets I went through and records I played, whose two-year-old I once slammed against the padded table when he wouldn't stop screaming, the child I'd changed, fed, cuddled, rocked, sung to, and who still wouldn't stop crying, so I shook him as violently as those toys with a bleating box inside you want to break; and then we both stopped, him screaming, me shaking him, both of us horrified at where this was going.

I made good money: a dollar an hour, much of which I gave to Bett. But when I was thirteen and fourteen at Wickhurst I used to babysit for other reasons than cash, because I used very much to want to be part of other people's families. There was one that was just like a novel I had written when I was ten, when I made a consoling fiction for myself of sisters and brothers, whom I tenderly named and dressed and made interconnect and have adventures. They always sat around a big lamplit farmhouse table and expostulated like ghetto Italians, but they were children's book Wasps. These real-life children were the daughters and son of Mr. and Mrs. Norris, and they too had storybook names and natures: Lucia, sensible schoolgirl, eldest sister; Celia, pretty and flamboyant; Flavia, hesitant, musical, shy; little Sophia, lisping, blond, shoeless. One or the other is always picking up and carrying or setting down on stair or landing or laundry basket the two-year-old Colin, male already, broad-torsoed, spoiled, indignant when toppled, his sisters' doll. Their mother, harassed, late for work, half zipped, sweet-faced, kisses them goodbye, wipes cookie crumbs off her face from Colin, leaves us alone: to games in the garden or schoolwork, piano lessons or bedtime reading. There are so many of us it is hard to tell who belongs and who is paid to come.

We go to the park, five half-dressed, half-combed little girls pushing Colin in his stroller. We have the heavy iron key to the little subscription garden behind Carnegie's mansion on Ninety-first Street. Behind the iron grillwork, like in a Paris park, we sit on benches, stay off the grass, upend buckets in the sandbox, play jacks on slate paths, don't talk to white-uniformed nurses or men, do talk to kindly grandmothers. We wander into Carnegie's arched, mahogany-veined and mirrored conservatory, say "Hush, Sophia, stay behind the rope." Lucia reminds us when to leave, she is always the responsible one.

Once walking with Bill, he said, "What do you want for your birthday?" I said I didn't want anything. He said, "There must be one thing you want more than anything else." And when I couldn't think, he said, "I think what you really want, and always have, is a family." "Do you think so?" I said, it seems a strange idea. He said, "I think that's your secret."

My classmates seemed lost in the paraphernalia of maidenhood: letters, calls, dates. They told secrets and blushed and stared into each other's faces after college weekends because "you can always tell after it's happened." The year before, the President was shot and the Beatles came to Carnegie Hall. I felt mostly bored, sort of adrift in inert girlhood, a sort of low-swelling sea, slightly dislocated, a little nauseated, too far from childhood and too distant from the glamorous shore. When that time was over I was someone I didn't know. It was like coming out of an illness, a delirious tedium or tedious delirium, coming through as someone else, having let go of, or lost in the confusion, the person before. Occasionally I mourned this person, my ten/eleven/twelve-year-old self, the child that Gogi loved, with all her hopes and certainties. But I did come out of it. By the end of my fifteenth year, when the Fab Four sang "Twist and Shout" and everyone in the orchestra rushed the stage, even though a few of us sat alone in our seats and made sarcastic remarks about our screaming classmates, I was already over, just docking on the other side.

When I was fourteen I had no boyfriends. The boys I met through school were as snobbish as I was, and as insecure. Understandably, they went for the blondes in twin sets and pearls when they could get them, and they mostly could. This lack was no problem until the school dance that year, when I was obliged to come up with a partner. My mother grasped the problem, understood that the boy was to be chosen not for companionship but to put out the eyes of the other girls. She knew from memories of her own scheming girlhood that I was up against sophisticates with years of experience applying makeup, attending mixers and charity events, against sixteen-year-olds, in fact. We had a neighbor on the third floor that my mother would occasionally play cards with. He was flirtatious with her and polite to me, a very good-looking twenty-five-year-old part-time actor and man-about-town. One evening my mother won him in a poker game. He was going to be my date at Wickhurst.

Did I ever believe it? I tried to imagine it the way she would have. Only if it had been her, she would have been looking amazing, too; in this case he would have to do the work for both of us. I just had to bring him in on my arm, this movie-star-good-looking man, wearing a suit and being very kind to me—this is just our little understanding, you, me and your mother. He'd perform the scene with me, dance every dance, so that on Monday morning my life would be utterly changed. Those girls were going to suffer and hate themselves, and then hate me, and respect me with this new hatred forever. Just flashing this man on my arm at school was going to make me someone to contend with. This must have been my mother's fantasy, dredged up from some teenage moment of her own, but of course it never happened. Gary claimed he had the measles (of all things, a childhood illness to avoid an obligation to a child). I never believed those measles, but I could easily imagine the horror with which he had sat downstairs the hung-over morning after his promise, contemplating, head in hands, an evening of pretense with a fourteen-year-old whose mother he thought was quite cute—a whole evening at a girls' school dance.

At the last minute Claudia Mieli found me someone, from her mothers' list for events at good Catholic girls' schools. He showed up, two (rather than eleven) years older than me, better than I dared hope, but a little stiff, and I was sure I was a disappointment to him. Only he behaved as though he did these things (showing up for dances) almost like a job (a job he was lucky to get), with a kind of humble and official cheerfulness to him. I took him and we danced; it was all right. Then, afterward, we went for dinner somewhere, and his childishness and mine became annoying. He couldn't find a cab, didn't know which restaurant. He was pretty helpless, and it was such a charade anyway, I had to help him out, even though I knew I wasn't supposed to. I was impatient: I didn't know how to be a "girl" yet; I dropped all that as soon as we left the school, after Lester Lanin played his last unmemorable tune, when the older girls were already lighting up cigarettes inside their waiting cars, their black-stockinged legs disappearing in a sexual slither inside the darkness of cabs. Duncan and I went out onto the cold streets, looking for, not finding, a taxi, and I thought it was all pretty hopeless and we might as well go home. But we went on instead, and what I dropped was not the evening or him but the pretense that this was boy/girl stuff; it was just two kids, myself being the more competent one. I got us to the cafeteria while he sulked because that was what he was meant to do, and he didn't like my attitude, and I didn't like his whininess. After the politeness, tension, pretense dropped, we talked to one another, more or less simply.

He couldn't *be* simple. He had an idea of himself that, once the deb's escort number crumbled, he produced. Himself as a rebel, late-night bar crawls with his Jesuit teachers, his outlaw behavior at school. He knew huge chunks of advanced poetry by heart, and wrote his own. I noticed he had dark hair and eyes, pale, temperamental skin—black Irish looks, he said—and an intense, damned-poet manner. Later he gave me a copy of *Portrait of the Artist as a Young Man* and said it was about him. I thought it was the most beautiful book I'd ever read, and if that was him, I would listen. Months later we went to Greenwich Village, where he taught me to drink certain drinks and smoke and stay out late. He took me over some hurdle into Manhattan nighttime, where we played at worldliness and tormented virginity. For a while I was an attentive audience for him, which was all he really wanted, though he was still impatient with me about my ignorance of important books, and my lack of decadence. He was sure he was going to die young, and he had to experience everything now (everything except sex, which I think still frightened him), and he challenged me to speed through it all with him. He talked a lot about freedom and loneliness and how you couldn't have the one without the other—it seemed a kind of career thing to him, freedom, though I really heard and responded to the loneliness. We went to Greenwich Village a lot and sometimes I cut classes the next day at school. Many months later he stopped thinking he was alone when he was with me, and I thought I loved him.

By the time I was fifteen my mother couldn't control me. I was approaching the end of my junior year at Wickhurst and I was supposed to think about college. But I knew there wouldn't be any money, and that I was going nowhere after school. It was so clear,

Bett and I didn't even discuss it. If I had been great at school I might have thought about getting one of the few complete scholarships that the major colleges gave, but I was still pretty erratic, getting a few A's and many C's. I was not scholarship material. This was way before Open Admissions. You had to be very, very special not to pay. It didn't even occur to Bett or that school that I could go to City College or any of those places. I guess no one thought much about it at all. My mother was still dealing with the rent every month, that was as far ahead as she could plan, and Wickhurst had probably never had that problem before. I applied for colleges along with the other girls, but we all knew that even if I got in I couldn't go. I felt I was heading for a thick wall, a life of jobs selling handbags at Macy's or full-time babysitting. I would live with Bett or get married, that was the full opening-out panorama of it. Duncan thought he was going to die young; somewhere in my mind I thought my life was going to end, too, or at least this form of it. Together we hung out in the Village, drinking black coffee and red wine, pretending we were extraordinary while fending off the terror of getting swallowed up in the world.

Bett lost a lot of jobs that year. She was having a difficult time and our rent was almost always late. In the spring we were nearly evicted twice and we now owed two months' rent to an apoplectic landlady. I went to Shrimp to borrow the money, promising to earn it myself in the summer, so she would be paid back this time. We both knew this was a special case, because I'd never personally had these dealings with her before and she was kind of testing me to see what I was made of. (All these transactions hurt her, she would have chosen a different relationship to us if she could have; the one we offered her was very unfair.) She gave me the check and I got the job, as mother's helper in the Hamptons. There was no question but I would pay her back.

I had got the job through Wickhurst and had to lie about my reasons for wanting it, saying I was saving money for extra expenses at college. It had to be as genteel as possible, and I was canny enough to know that saying I was taking a job to pay my mother's and my rent would have got me nowhere. I impersonated a nice young Wickhurst girl saving money for extra expenses and went off to the Hamptons. Molly McCabe and I became friends, and on those weekday nights when her husband (a real black Irishman, very handsome and short-tempered) was working in the city, she and I talked. I never told her where her weekly checks were going, but she did get the general picture of my future collegelessness, and she wanted to know if there was anyone in my life who could help me. I said I didn't think there was, but that I was prepared to take on a bank loan. In fact, I was *not* very willing; I didn't know much about bank loans, but to borrow a sum of ten thousand dollars at fifteen, with an earning capacity of thirty-five dollars a week, seemed terrifying to me, and I thought I'd be saddled with debt all my life. I'd seen enough of Bett's debts to want to avoid this. I could wait tables at college, but what kind of dent would that make, and anyway, what college? I was not likely to get in anywhere I wanted to go. Besides, I was tired of being the poor one at a rich school, tired of the burdens of pretense, keeping up, tired of the hopelessness of it. In my tiredness at it all, I thought I would hang out in Greenwich Village for a while, and if necessary spend my life behind a shop counter.

It was Molly who invented my father. She conjured him out of nothingness, for I had no sense of him as anything more than a random biological moment in my life. My mother never mentioned him, nor had anyone else very much. I knew he lived in England, in a place my mother said was just outside London, called Norfolk. I knew his name and could guess his age, but I had no clear image of him. Yet when Molly proposed that we should write to him and ask if I could visit, I went along with the plan. I had seen a few films about England—*The Loneliness of the Long Distance Runner*, *This Sporting Life*, *Room at the Top*—and, unlike my father, the place had some reality to me. Since I wasn't going to college anyway, perhaps after graduation next June I would visit the home of the Beatles.

Molly seized on this reunion with all the ardor of her rather romantic twenty-six-year-old self, and all the pent-up boredom of a long, mostly husband-abandoned summer by the beach. She drafted us a letter she thought appropriate. I was to put it in my own handwriting when I returned to New York after Labor Day and found his address. "My Dear Father," it began. "Many years have separated us . . ." and it went on from one florid locution to the next, as though I were already English, and had been so for a hundred years. Proposing a meeting between his undoubtedly eager and my charming, accomplished self, it hinted that this encounter would be a momentous thing for both of us, involving no obligations or extended visits. I was inviting myself to meet him, that was all. Molly and I thought the letter romantic and touching and that writing it was rather an exciting, adventurous thing to do. She kept the letter a secret from her husband, and I promised I would send it off.

In New York, I looked up my father's name in the phone books they have at the Forty-second Street Public Library for all the countries in the world. I found him in Norfolk and sent the letter. In September and all of October and November I waited for an answer, the airmail envelope that would change my life and save me from Macy's. By Thanksgiving, when I had still had no response, I stopped hoping. And in my hopelessness, things got very bad, both at home and at school.

She loves me, my mother. She loves me as much as ever. It is the one certainty in her uncertain life. She will not see that she is losing me, that there is a world out there I am scanning for clues. It seems exciting to me often, and her habitual flinch against it seems unimaginative and dull. Defeat is dull. I cannot recognize that my new rushing around is a fear of her defeatedness. I am only asking questions. There is rashness in me, and a new cynical humor that makes the other girls suddenly look and begin to listen. At first it is marginal amusement at this formerly invisible creature, suddenly there, being quite eccentric and really quite funny, reliably witty in class. Some of them come with me to meet Constance, or I give them books, different versions of those small-press paperbacks they've been carrying for years. I know this and that now, and it is interesting. The thing is, I've stopped apologizing. Only this is just a new form of contract: my unconventionality as a way in, my wildness so they will tame me. I go to their houses and we speak the same language, of boys and suffering and poetry.

It doesn't matter to them that my background is different—different is suddenly good to them, better. I am interesting and that is suddenly, the last year at Wickhurst, worth something. What makes me interesting is my recklessness. To them it looks like bravado. To me it is only because I think there is nothing to lose. In the afternoons when they go to art history classes, I am often in the coffee shops, drinking black coffee, reading verse, smoking, waiting for them to arrive, so they can see me and how little I care. Sometimes one of the teachers passes through and they worry that I will be reported. But to me these gestures are worth nothing if they're not public.

Naturally my grades suffer. The headmistress calls my mother, and afterward Bett and I fight, long heartless fighting that she hasn't ever got the energy to win. School business was never her forte. Boys she understands, dates, and so she is basically in sympathy with what she assumes are my choices. On the other hand, someone is asking her to curb me and it's a challenge to her. I have been going out on weekends and staying out till one or two. My mother trusts me utterly, but now there are restrictions because of school. Which I ignore. I am a provocative, rude, willful creature she cannot recognize. Sometimes our fights are violent; she hits me and I hit back. Her helplessness with me frightens her. The sound and look of my contempt. What, you, too? You, too, are turning? Things are slipping from her, hope, looks (she thinks), youth, and now this young hopeful child of hers seems to be slipping, too. She has to hold on to me, to hold on to those things in herself without which she believes she is nothing. She is to herself nearly nothing anyway, and without that . . . She cries often these days, not over lost men (where were they?), but over lost self. She is only thirty-eight but she is in mourning for her youth. She cannot hold to jobs. They fire her now regularly. She cannot concentrate and she is, she says, no longer pretty enough to get by on looks alone. She is, she feels, brainless—birdbrain, dizzy, worthless; she had been a fraud all her life, an exquisitely packaged fraud, and now all the packaging is coming apart. She felt safe when I was there, loving, sympathetic, helping with the rent, sisterly, and now I'm suddenly a monster she's never seen before: good daughter into bad. "How sharper than a serpent's tooth," she quotes at me.

I cannot help it, or her. Her love is valueless to me now, I'm running. To her it is the great thing in her life, her "achievement," and it is destroying her to see me spurn it. Under threat of this destruction, she lashes out, and so we fight, long unseemly domestic brawls, nauseating, exhausting, stoked and recharged and violent. She locks me out. I run away from home.

Where do I run to? I run to Veronica, and she takes to the appointed task with exuberance and a theatrical sense of responsibility. "As you know," she says, "I am very fond of you. You are a charming, *extremely* gifted young girl and I am delighted to have your company. But there are going to be some rules.

"Now, I was never much of a student myself. Nevertheless, since you are, or are going to be, there will be no more cutting of classes or you will not graduate. That is what they have told me as you well know. That school did not give you a scholarship so you could go out every evening with boys.

"I know boys are wonderful, and it is very exciting, but you are fifteen and you are going to work now and graduate in June. There will be no boys on school nights and no staying out after midnight on weekends. The boys will have to come here first and I will meet them. They will bring you home before twelve.

"Also, you have to show me your homework, not, of course, that I will understand a word of your homework, but I am in charge at the moment and this is what we shall do. Do you agree to the terms?"

"Yes, Veronica."

"Leave the boys alone."

"Yes, Veronica."

"Good. Now, I know you are a Sensible person. Come and give me a kiss. I'm delighted to have you here."

And I was delighted to be with her.

My mother capitulated to the arrangement and we met once a week or so for dinner. It was just like meeting for dinner with her own mother when she and Constance were at Angel's, so it didn't seem that odd to her. She understood I was having trouble at school, she tried not to take it personally. Of course, she had no choice. We were getting along very badly and that was an unbearable notion to her, trouble at school was easier. "Darling, I understand," she would say. But I didn't really believe her, since I didn't understand myself. Anyway, it was all temporary. Veronica was retiring and leaving for California in June. I'd be back then, we both said.

Of course, there were no "boys," just nights out with Duncan and pretending to be bad. Whatever Veronica imagined, sex was as far, I think, from his mind as from mine, although he enjoyed hinting darkly at what he got up to when we weren't together. But he was intensely romantic about women; it was part of his Catholic sense of things, scrambled as that was. It wasn't the female body he worshipped, though his poems declared a long and bitter experience with it in many forms; it was virginity. I was, in my virginity, the scourge of his own desires, the light and goad to his sinful self.

On the surface of things I was enjoying life. I loved Veronica and I loved her old-fashioned guardianship. As long as I wasn't living with Bett I got along with her. I saw Constance (though Veronica didn't approve of her), I saw Shrimp and, on weekends, Duncan and certain friends from school. On weekdays I was in bed by eleven, and I did my homework. Though the last-minute dedication seemed an empty gesture in the face of a blank and increasingly close, collegeless future, Veronica, Shrimp and I kept up the pretense of my getting a scholarship somewhere to keep us going. But panic is always close, and the need to run, to be happy *now*. The future presses, sometimes lit like a beautiful cityscape, so unbearably exciting my throat feels constricted and my heart beats erratically, sometimes dark and dull and limitlessly final, like drowning at night in an open sea. There is running and there is Bett, and it's only ever those two things. When I smoke cigarettes and do my homework late in my little room at Veronica's, there is a Peeping Tom behind venetian blinds across the shaftway, a pair of eyes that flash suddenly with a crack of light and scare me, like Gatsby's eye of God. "Love Me Do" plays at twenty-minute intervals on the radio, Christmas comes and goes. And then I get a letter from England.

It is a thin blue airmail-weight letter, typed, with a typed signature, like a business letter. There are ten points, numbered 1 to 10, as to why I may not want to visit. They are all stated with "humor" but I can read the resistance. One of the points is: "Although we are not peasants, we live in the country. You as a city child may find it hard to adjust to our ways." Another: "Although Americans are no longer the savages they once were, American civilization has many decades to go before it can be considered on equal footing with that of Western Europe. You should be prepared for the fact that we shall hardly speak the same language." These were nos. 4 and 5. By no. 10, the message is loud and clear, despite the close, which says: "If in the face of these obstacles you still wish to pay us a visit we should of course be pleased to see you." It is signed with a flourish, to which I attach as much personality, a generous, affection-capable personality, as I can, not "your father" but the full, sonorous Francis Lowell, a signature which is then typed out (lest there be any mistake) underneath.

So this is our first exchange: the fake, florid, Victorian bouquet, joint production from one bored Hamptons summer; and one "witty," sardonic, but terror-filled blue business letter. And on this construction was built . . . but what was built comes later. That letter was designed to give me pause, and pause I did. Until three weeks later, when his wife, who must have come across my letter herself, or to whom Francis must have turned in some struggle of conscience ("I'm afraid it's happened, she's written to me at last"), took up the lead of this awkward seduction and rejection with unambiguous, clearly expressed delight, and said, come, please, come and meet your father and me and three half brothers, we can't wait, here are photos, come and visit, come and stay as long as you like, we would love to see you. And she signed "with love," in the same welcoming, huge, exuberant, often unreadable (but how easily I deciphered it) hand: Harriet.

So now there were photos of a strange middle-aged couple and three little boys with English haircuts and some English landscape with a cottage and garden in the foreground. And if it wasn't quite real, yet it was at least at last an option, an alternative, somewhere else, a place to move forward or sideways, but move from where I was. And then Veronica and Harriet wrote to one another, and Harriet and I wrote to one another, and I and Francis never wrote to one another, and the months passed and my grades got better, and Veronica never told me how surprised she was, which I guessed only later, when I came across her own letter to Francis, sent out three years earlier, and to which she received no reply.

But now I had my answer. Veronica was going to retire in California that June, and that June I was going to graduate and then take (my present from Shrimp) an airplane to England to meet my father, where everyone, Shrimp, Veronica, even Constance, although Constance had dubious things to say about Francis, hoped and prayed there was going to be some happy ending.

And now it is the end of March. I have been living with Veronica for three and a half months. And tonight it is my birthday. I would like to spend it with Duncan, but Bett has plans for me.

I am abandoning my mother. She knows this. It is not just school anymore, this is getting serious. She is happy for me. "My puppy in Europe," she says, but sometimes she says, "I can't believe you are just going to leave." "I'll be back," I say, just a visit, just a summer. She feels something else is happening. If I say, tell me about my father, all she says is that his ears stuck out and they didn't get along, that his parents weren't kind. But she will never say, don't go, it's a mistake, stay with Mommy. We are still fighting, the subtext is darker now, this abandonment, my baby is grown up. For this reason perhaps she has bought us tickets to the circus for my sixteenth birthday, I who dress in black and smoke and drink black coffee. We are going to do a lovely sentimental mother-and-child thing again, like those "Love Breakfasts" we used to have periodically throughout my childhood, and which we still have now from time to time so she will know I still love her (I still love her). We have boiled eggs, which she paints with our faces or with rabbits, there is chocolate, jelly beans, a present from her to me. From me she always gets the same ritualized things: a bar of Yardley's lavender, some freesias, her favorite flower, or Blue Grass cologne. She doesn't smoke or drink, my mother, doesn't really read much, doesn't listen to records, so it is soap or perfume or flowers. We crack the faces of our eggs and eat our candy and renew our vows.

And likewise, we go to the circus on my sixteenth birthday; it has been hard for her to save the money. On her birthday I always take her to a Broadway musical (it is hard for me to save the money), but these are our rituals. But this year, birthday or not, I am not an easy child. We start off well enough, but the Freak Show has been cleaned up and the clowns are boring and I know I'm going to see Duncan after midnight (Veronica's special dispensation), so I am restless and she keeps trying to squeeze my hand through the endless unicycle, elephant, cannonball, bareback acts, and I am dying, inhaling the sawdust and refusing the cotton candy which she eats alone next to me, smiling as though she's happy, but she's not happy. "My baby's going." "Oh for Christsake, Mommy, I'm not going yet, watch the fucking show." "Don't talk to me like that," and I apologize and settle down and shift in my seat again and run down to pee and have a cigarette and stand among all the crying, laughing, party-dressed little girls and their mommies in the bathroom, and impatience is so high in me that I have to leave. But I come back to my seat and in twenty more minutes I tell her, "I can't stand this, let's go." "Go?" she says, bewildered, crushed. "But the tigers . . ." So what, I say.

I wish I had sat there, closed my eyes and just remembered the birthday eight years earlier, home from Mirrenwood, above the bar, when my mother pulled everything together and invited a group of my friends from school and the neighborhood, and bought them and me hats and cake and party favors, and my presents, hundreds of them, it seemed, that one miracle year, in huge, beautiful, shiny, bowed and balloon-decorated boxes, oblong and square and monstrous, all in a pile in my room. I had said, "Now, Mommy, now can I open them?" and she had said, "Wait till after the cake and ice cream." And I waited and said again, "Now, Mommy?" and my mother had said even then on that one birthday when she had made the miracle-perfect birthday party, "Sweetheart, why don't we wait until all the other children have gone home? We'll open your presents just the two of us. Because it's not their birthday and they may be sad because they don't have any. We don't want them to feel bad, so let's wait." And she was right. My mother's sweetness takes in the whole world, and I knew that even then.

And so I wait through the tigers and endure the Ringling Orchestra and the drumrolls and explosions, and then I explode and I say, "I'm leaving." And I do, I walk out, out of the circus, and leave Bett in her seat trying to find her coat and bag and follow me out. When she catches up with me she says, "What's the matter with you?" And I don't know, I only know I must go, and I go, leaving her standing in the street, openmouthed, trailing her coat and holding on to her circus program.

In June, she and Constance, Shrimp and Veronica all come to my graduation, where I am one among fourteen ladies on their way into the ladylike world. I have my graduation presents, my type-writer, my camera, my plane ticket. My mother gives me, in addition to my portable typewriter, as requested, a set of black lacy underwear, which Veronica finds me the next week packing in my suitcase. "You are not going to arrive at the Lowells' with black underwear," she says, and so I have to leave them. Then we are at the airport, kissing goodbye: Veronica, Shrimp, Constance, Duncan and Bett. "Goodbye, I will write. Goodbye, I will be back soon. Don't cry, Mommy."

"My baby, going on a plane." I raise my eyebrows and I turn my back, but I turn once more and come back to kiss her again, and then I am gone and she waves as long as she can until her hand, her face, her body, disappear and get lost among all the people on the ground watching the plane roar and rise and go, as I imagine I am leaving home.

PART TWO

Men

FIVE

I AM GOING DOWN the moving stairs to the meeting area and I am in self-presentation mode. To some degree I am impersonating the nice Wickhurst girl, but it is more than impersonation, it is how I wish to be *for them*, the most palatable, *recognizable* form of myself, and I wish to be accepted, swallowed without resistance. At the same time, it is how I wish to be for myself and I feel that I can be anything—this is all new, the new life—I can be a good, sweet, well-brought-up sixteen-year-old *because no one knows me.* To some extent I have prepared my greeting: I shall kiss them both on the cheek when I meet them. I shall be modest, as controlled as a beautifully trained horse, and it will all begin. I see Harriet, his wife, it is coming closer. I step forward and we exchange kisses, according to my own script, and then I see my father, looming, four feet away, sort of disturbing the air around him with his massive size and evident, terrible self-consciousness. My prepared kiss stops before I can step forward, and I freeze, stay where I am. And he, too, pulls back and retreats into what I know is embar-rassed mode but which is here simply an unbalancing tactic. "Why," he booms (since I have taken a Pan Am flight), "are you carrying a KLM bag?" Bag? I am immediately in the wrong, suspected of conveying misleading information; I am immediately a gauche traveler. He *means* to say, his powers of observation never sleep, that he is Intellectually Curious and Notices Everything. But I hear: Wrong, You are in the Wrong. And Harriet hears and sees, the girl is afraid of him. She has hurt him, kissing me and not kissing him; he is afraid of her and he is scaring her to death. Oh my God, they *are* related. And why can't people be simple?

We get in the car, an old beat-up Bentley with cracked leather seats, and I wonder, does this mean they are rich or they are poor? We begin to drive. Despite what Bett has told me about Norfolk, it is not just outside London, it is over a hundred miles away. My flight got in at nine; what with Customs, etc., we will not be home before 1 A.M., both ways a six-hour drive for them. Mistake no. 2. I should have researched this. Harriet is wearing a strangely old-fashioned, rather matronly, large-flowered, sleeveless dress. Her arms are heavy and her hands rough and scratched from farm living. Is she like a peasant, I wonder, a country person? I cannot make it out. My father retreats (later I know that this is where he absolutely stays, lives, shelters) into observations, about the out-skirts of London compared with the outskirts of American cities. As he drives, he lectures; from time to time Harriet asks me if I'm warm enough, carsick, hungry, etc. What I am is utterly exhausted and sitting bolt upright in a glow of nervous tension. Nothing I say is natural, not only because I am still the Wickhurst girl (you must *get* me as easily and quickly as you can so we can pass beyond this nervousness of ours) but because no one is giving me any role I can breathe with. Already I am simply accommodating, ingratiat-ing, dancing backward, because they have the lead; I am taking back every shred of selfhood I might have arrived with. Like the KLM bag, I don't want it to stick out, get in the way. Harriet offers me a "biscuit." Before I can eat it, we have to go through the business of "You say 'cookie' don't you?"—"Yes" (in a tone of mutual amusement), and from there to all the other differences transatlantic people who are afraid of one another always recite—lift/elevator, all that crap. Halfway to Norfolk my father stops the car, gets out to pee on the road, and suddenly at last something is real. Strange, but real, the splash on roadside greenery in cold air, the heavy (God, how heavy) sound of his steps, some puffing and laborious groaning, an unhappy-soul noise, as he climbs back into the car. Harriet says again and again, as often as the conversation will bear, "your father," as though to insist on it, bind us together in a way we cannot bind ourselves, as I shrink inwardly, though my spine is rigid in the back seat, and Francis goes on with his factual observations, which is as close to "being pleasant" as he can manage. And meanwhile, burning its way deep inside him and turning hard, is, I am sure, my inability to kiss him, my clear horror, undisguisable because of the very innocence I think I have to fabricate. Give me another chance, I want to say, but I'm not sure I've the stomach for it. And the black car is moving fast through space, deep into the night; it is real, it is real, and too late to turn back. We have still to meet, he and I, or make some pact—and then there is Harriet, watching our mutual terror, torn between pain on his behalf and fear for me of its consequences, and talking nonstop into the abyss.

It is late. We are in the kitchen. I can't see anything through my terror and the neon overhead lights make everything loud, shiny, white, high, high gloss like a hospital. I register farmlike smells and cracked linoleum, bare cold walls, cold air. We have mugs of hot chocolate in our hands, and in the icy lighting we are doing the presents. I have presents for them: a gift box of some Elizabeth Arden thing for Harriet, a book of Robert Frost for Francis. Why these? They strike me now as utterly absurd, the poetry as bland and innocuous as the perfume, and I myself care for neither. Later it will seem worse, when I know that Francis never reads poetry and Harriet only uses Hermès. They are sort of stunned, polite. My father's giant paws rip through the careful Doubleday gift wrapping looking for the honey, coming to a halt, there's nowhere else for him to go now physically with this object, the hands must hold still around the narrow, featherweight volume. He stares at the photographed face of R. Frost on the cover, saying nothing. "Do you like poetry?" I venture. (Is this too personal a question?) He grunts. Harriet, meanwhile, is in raptures about her present. Harriet is so busy filling the voids and disguising the content of Francis's and my exchanges that she is like someone in a different movie, or a 33 r.p.m. record played at 78. I am exhausted for both of them and for myself. My father says they have bought a crate of Coca-Cola and he shows me where it is. I don't know what to say. I don't drink Coca-Cola. Harriet offers to show me my room.

I can't get the house. It's sort of shabby and bare, yet there are all these watercolors, antiques, bits of silver. I can't get anything

127

tonight. I'll sleep on it, sleep on it in a tiny, high-gloss white room with a horsehair mattress that sags in the middle, and a torn, faded, handmade quilt. They have put out books for me on the bedside table, next to a water jug and glass. When Harriet is gone and I have discovered the one source of heat in this frigid room, the square foot of hot-water-bottle-heated bedding otherwise seemingly soaking wet in this damp (and it is June, already air-conditioning weather in New York), I look at what has been chosen. Nancy Mitford (whom I have never heard of), a book called *Love in a Cold Climate* (how appropriate). Something called *Story of an African Farm* and *Uncle Tom's Cabin* (do they think I am a racist?). A volume of Churchill (okay, both light and heavy). I like it. I like my room. My father scares me. I'll sleep. Oh, Mommy.

I sleep. I sleep sixteen hours and for the next three days twelve hours a night. I can't eat anything (I'm not like this). Harriet says, "You look a little green." My father is still taking my foodlessness and oversleeping as a reflection on his awfulness (in the religious sense) and he is right. I am struggling, unsuccessfully, to stay awake and hide that I cannot make it, I'm failing my reunion. The good little Wickhurst girl is disintegrating all too apparently. My father's defenses are coming out, scaring me further into sleep. He remarks on my sleeping, and my Americanness. ("Only savages hold their forks in their right hand and park their knives. If you're going to stay any time in England, you'd better learn to eat like civilized people.") My response at this stage is to numb out, nod off, till Harriet suggests a nap. There is a comitragic business here of my father getting his hits in while I'm still conscious, hits which even he must know in some part have to do with my choice of unconsciousness. But no choice, really, my sleepiness is so embarrassing. My body simply can't get used to this, not just jet lag, but I'm so cold, I wear two sweaters all day in the June sunshine, I shiver through dinner in my summer clothes. They discuss and reject the idea of having a fire in the living room. "In bloody June!" says Francis, and, to me, "Stop shivering like a bloody dog, will you, it's pure self-indulgence," and bang, my chin falls on my chest and Harriet excuses me.

By the fifth day I am adjusted: a meek, sober, pathetic creature

who is desperate not to be attacked and so will agree to anything.
I am eating English style now (fork in left hand, etc.), and I am
eating. After five days' fast, I eat everything on my plate, pleasing
them no end (a form of acceptance, after all). My father senses he
has me, and the gibes and furious comments continue. If I answer
back in witty kind, his brow furrows and he grows dark, purple,
and Harriet says something quickly. But this is just between the
two of us now, by July it is almost open war, and many evenings,
after some rough passages ("You're a bloody fool . . . All Americans
suffer from . . . Do you know the proper meaning of sophisticated?
Adulterated, like a cheap wine . . . Don't make me laugh, you've
never had a decent apple in your life, all American fruit is . . . Your
bloody country . . . Helen, if you are going to stay . . ."), the tears
break. Is Helen going to stay? She is in a trance, she cries at night
and in the evenings she writes letters home: "Darling Mommy/
Shrimp/Veronica. I am very happy here. Today we . . ."; or "My
new family is wonderful"; or "I am so happy the way things have
worked out"; or "I love my new family and they love me."

But neither love the other yet. Not at all, and we skirt warily or
bump and retreat like blind mice, mechanical toys. We have
outings, Harriet's England: agricultural shows, horse shows, teas
with neighbors and relatives, the old family laundress who lives
down a muddy lane and remembers "your beautiful mother, and
you as a baby," and Harriet doesn't like that and tries to talk
instead about Charles and George, two of the boys still at school,
and very shortly we take our leave. The other boy is at home, aged
two, with a nanny two years older than I, a country girl with a
difficult accent who suspects in me an ally against " 'em" but
doesn't quite trust it since I am on the verge of becoming one of
" 'em" myself; and in tense, empty, polite fogs of silence in the
cold, neon-white kitchen we have tea, and always cakes. Here,
they eat all the time, huge, elaborate hot breakfasts, three-course
lunches, teas with bread, butter and cakes, five-course dinners. It
is the only comfort going and they cling to it, and to the rituals and
conversation food permits ("It needs more seasoning . . . No,
I don't think so, perfect . . . This is local cheese, of course
in America you don't have real bread/cheese/butter/fruit,

of course . . ."), and throughout July it is every other night that I am excused from the table, in tears, having eaten, eaten all day to be with them, to partake with them, become of them—with this bread, I, with this wine—but the transmutation of the flesh is not evident yet, so that all of July it is "Don't bloody start to snivel," and Harriet: "Let her go, Francis," and clutching the banisters, I am gone. Yes, I have seen *My Fair Lady,* but this is not Henry Higgins with his guttersnipe, this is a man tortured by the sight of his retribution, and exploding nightly.

A dinner-party exchange, all going smoothly, the guests complimentary on my "grown-upness" and asking about New York and not paying enough attention to Francis, sometimes casting me sympathetic looks, which Harriet sees and Francis does not. And I, attempting to hold up my end of this vaudeville act, this gathering of the superior and charming family, help Francis out with his anecdotes, feign amusement, amazement at all his knowledge (while they have been browbeaten with this for years and some of them, as they later confide, come only to see Harriet). So my father, on and on about international attitudes toward fish, now says, "Of course, for the Japanese, the devil takes the form of a crab," and I make a joke about "deviled crab" and the others laugh gaily (oh, with what effort does the gaiety lift over the dark red wine and bread knife and the groaning table, groaning under the heavy food and Francis's laborious, chastising hospitality). But their gaiety is wrong, and Francis tells them so via me; he says (waiting for silence), "That was a cheap and stupid remark, utterly unworthy of you or anyone else." I am not used to this (to be sure) and further feel betrayed, since I thought I was helping him out of his ponderous imprisoning of his guests, his ignorance of how they longed to lift their spirits, break out and run away; and the injustice is too heavy, it bangs on my chest like a rock, and here we go, throat, heat, tears. Francis, as I rise: "Don't be so damned emotional, Helen," and some lone, brave guest: "For God's sake, Francis, she's only a child," and then looks and chaos. Harriet's dinner wrecked (they think to themselves) and Francis too heavy-handed as usual, and that poor girl who will never survive, but

still, one's loyalties . . . and so the subject is changed and the
remarks are addressed to Harriet, whose laughter and chitchat fills
in the silences and the dark, gloomy seas where Captain Francis
plows his bark alone. And Harriet through her chitter-chatter feels
the other injustice: no one understands what he is going through,
my brilliant, tormented husband, with the arrival of this girl. We
didn't have to take her. Why are they so unfair?

And outside the dining room, some other nightmare occasion
(but I am learning silence now, and continence), I stop him. I will
beard the monster in his den, I will touch him, and I do, near the
door my arm reaches his and he pulls back (what's this?), and I say
with all the bravery I can collect, "Why do you attack me like this,
surely you, too, have feelings, you are sensitive?" I say it slowly,
and I see the habitual scowl break for an instant, see his temptation
to admit that he, too, is sensitive, that we are connected in this
appalling way. But the vulnerable, willing, confidential face disappears and the scowl returns. He says, "Of course I bloody am, but
the world is not, and what you don't learn here, you'll learn more
harshly later." Well, I'd rather have it later.

One evening he comes to my room with a peace offering, a
paperback of *Rebecca* by Daphne Du Maurier. "An emotional infant
like you," he says with a smile, "a romantic." And that's the end
of it. Except for the refrain: "Don't be so bloody self-indulgent,
emotional. Don't bloody sigh all the time," and once: "You mustn't
become an emotional burden to people." Certainly, it must have
been awful to be around me, foundering so visibly in my hell,
which is only them, and so spinelessly eager to be loved.

So we are eating, and by August my body is changing with the
effort to disappear into their world. In one summer (aged sixteen)
I grow nearly two inches and gain thirty pounds. "Look," I am
saying to my six-foot-six father, "I am one of you, I am kindred."
And I quack, too, to this other duck in his accents: I am speaking
Briddish to him and swallowing my words so that he will hear
them, so he won't keep saying I am other, alien, outsider, out,
out, go. But it is not enough that I have risen and widened and
changed my voice, he doesn't understand the gesture. That Sep-

tember he even says, "It's a pity you lost your accent." But I am tired of repeating everything I say, explaining myself, I long for this to flow. The family body keeps casting me out like a cheap transplant, when I wish only to adjust correctly and so be taken in. The crying has stopped, the pain continues, and the letters home: "I am very happy here, this week we . . ." and appallingly when much later I read these things: "Dearest Mommy/Shrimp/Veronica . . . forgive me for being so emotional . . . so romantic . . . so self-indulgent." All their words. They have not swallowed me, but I have swallowed them, or swallowed myself on their behalf. Physically huge, at least to myself, and grotesquely mimicking their sounds, their movements, I have collaborated as far as my body will let me. And soon it is decided that I am to go to school that autumn and become, as I am all too clearly willing to become, an English girl.

Was I protecting my mother with these happy letters, was I protecting myself from her demands that I come home? Was I feeling too foolish to admit to Shrimp that I had made a terrible mistake, did I not want to trouble Veronica in retirement? Or was I simply humming to myself? The school doctor put me on antidepressants those first months at Northton—surely I knew I was more unhappy than I ever dreamed possible. But I denied it in my letters again and again. I spoke in English accents about amusing encounters and the lovely landscape, and never to anyone confided the truth. Is that true? No, I did try to talk to others in this new family, the kind and affectionate aunts who feared for me with Francis ("a difficult man"), but their reports came back to me one week: "Harriet has received seven calls from members of the family saying that you are unhappy here. Now, I don't give a damn what you say to anyone, but Harriet minds and she's done a lot for you. Do you want to go home now?"—silence—"Well, if you're going to stay, you'd better make the best of it, as we all have to."

Why did I stay? Was Bett and the prospect of Bett so much worse? Between the lines of these enthusiastic letters home I can read my relief at not being there with her. I even used their appalling language to lecture her, too, heartlessly: "Mommy, you mustn't be so emotional about this, I am only here for the year before I reapply to college. The separation will be good for us . . . You are too emotionally dependent on me . . . Of course you're not 'losing a daughter' . . ." But, of course, she was, and she knew it and I knew it; I was selling out as fast as I could, even without a buyer, and using the buyer's language. I went through my terrible days and nights because the alternative seemed so much worse. Imagine, then, if I'd let my mother know how awful what I was preferring to her really was. That must have been the explanation of my ecstatic postcards home, my long, loving, "but let me have this nice time away" letters to New York. Protecting her from my unhappiness, but really protecting me from hers. Escape at any price was what I must have thought, even this price, just to be away. And then, too, I always hoped, always, that my father would one day see the light and love me. And I turned any tiny sign, any quiet aside, any kind tone of voice into a message of hope, and lived on that, the tiniest crack in the dark. And it was always true, he might have loved me, but I never knew how to make it happen. Clumsily, unconsciously (I had not "intended" to grow two inches, nor to speak Briddish), I tried to make him accept me. I always knew it wouldn't take that much, whatever it was, but I never got it, never found out, and always, despite the appearance of despair in this matter, lived in secret hope. It didn't make sense to me. I was a gift, after all, I was bright and pretty and grown-up ("Sophisticated is adulterated like cheap wine"), and most of the work had been done already. But to him I was judgment, the observer, come to stare at his shortcomings, his pain. He made me into some kind of eye of God and couldn't help wincing at the scrutiny. And so he struck out, blind and helpless, but with all the huge mental and physical force he had.

Harriet. In the beginning she said, "I always wanted a daughter." Now she says, "Why are you late?" or "Your father wants to see you," or "You must take us as you find us. We're not going to change, so you will have to." I do farm work with her and watch how hard she works. I have seen her lift and carry large calves down hills, mend fences, drive a Land-Rover to follow a hunt. I've seen her cook for twelve and play bridge and dress up for church, her hands cut from barbed wire or chapped with cold. I am exotic to her, "an intellectual" like Francis, only not like Francis because a girl, "emotional." It pains her to see how rough Francis is with me, but she tells me from time to time that her own father was "strict" with her and that's just how it is with English fathers of a certain class and generation. She tells me what shoes to wear to point-to-points and horse trials; these things matter to her very much, they keep her straight. She says "It just isn't done" a lot and I know not to ask why. She means well by me, but to protect me adequately she would have to say what she can't, that this man for whom she does everything (and she does, running the farm, the house, the family) is unhappy, despairing. Were she to admit that to me, all would crack, crumble and disappear. She was lucky, she tells me, to be married when she was twenty-six, already a spinster according to local lights, and to an intellectual from a well-respected family, though a divorcé, which did not make things at all easy, and she looks at me, and we know whose fault that first blot of divorce must be. They never mention my mother; what does come out little by little is the notion that she is not quite right, Helen's mother, a bit unstable (and from someone else: that must be why she sent the daughter over, couldn't manage anymore herself), no real home life provided, which is why they must provide it whether they like it or not. We know she's not very happy, but she will settle down; we're doing all we can.

Harriet at her dressing table, her face over the protective pane of glass, under which the family photos, on which the silver boxes and brushes. The room is chilly, and there's a dinner party to get down for or go off to (though there weren't so many of these). Her heavy, weathered arms move over the glass, she brushes out her hair, and we may be talking in this unusually gentle atmosphere (before the next instructions, reprimands), one to one like this, woman to girl. It is all easy, intimate, I can begin to love her and she me. This is not the men's world or the farm world or the world of what is done; this is the very fragile world of women and intimacy: face powder, lipstick, despair and propriety; girdle, hem length, fabric, color, what is intended to go with what. Just for such moments, when she is at rest, in the hiatus held by mirrors, we are easy with one another, and again I wish it could be all right. We could nearly escape together (as if it were all so simple), leave them, the men and boys, labor of the farm and duties to the community, to look after themselves, just for a few hours. Just like that, one to one, her to me, just like me and Bett.

Monday to Friday I am a schoolgirl. I wear an ugly gray shirt and maroon tie, elephantine shoes and maroon uniform. In my new bigness I lumber around having to go through adolescence all over again, the storm of hormones (and now antidepressants), feeling cold always, and slight nausea from the strange, greasy-watery English school food. Sometimes I get letters from Duncan or his friend Gerry—tight, knowing, ironic city letters. Sometimes I tell these country girls about Greenwich Village, the cafés with folk-singers, all-night drinking. They don't believe much of it—I hardly believe it myself anymore. In just four months I've disconnected myself and not yet reattached. I'm swaying, as swollen as a bruise, in this sea of failed accommodation. There's a huge portrait of Francis's grandfather in the entrance hall. He founded the school for farm laborers' children, and the girls here still come from poor local families. I'm attacked on two counts therefore, as a member of the establishment family and as a Yank. There's a Nigerian princess here, on some missionary-type exchange, and the Norfolk girls form circles around her, calling her "Jungle Jane" and trying to "make her eyes roll." You're talking to someone who can quote Martin Luther King, knows all the songs, and I just don't get it. It isn't the Deep South, is it? And they *hate* Americans, money they say, cigars, vulgar they say, and dumb. But these girls hate Londoners, for God's sake, and they've never even heard of Bob Dylan, barely heard of Goldwater, though of course when they have that's embarrassing and hard to explain. And Lowells—when I have to buy anything in the local shops, they put it on a bill and say, "That's quite all right, Miss Lowell, it will be taken care of," and the girls look and snigger, as they do when any of "my" family show up, and they are always showing up, for school functions.

Therefore, a Lowell *and* a Yank. And then there's just the way we have to live, sleep in iron beds all in one room, no heat, no meat, splintering desks and eternal hymns and cups of tea. I think of my city streets and look out of the window a lot, where it is always bright green under the pearl and ink-stain gray, with cloudbursts, sunbursts and sheep. And at least it's not Sparrow House, where the black-browed father, the oh so unwilling trapped bear, and his protective wife live. I'm glad Monday to Friday when I'm in the school, wearing my elephant shoes and my tie, fending off attacks on Yanks and waiting for letters—I'm glad at least I'm not there, where they really don't want me, but they make their dutiful best of things. If it weren't for the landscape here, what would there be? Antidepressants, the image of home, the reconstituted image of Bett. As at Mirrenwood, I make Bett everything, and my letters home get more and more loving, and my insistence that I'm happy. I need the goddess again, but now I need to have her safe at a distance. Photos, send photos—and when the letters are opened in those bare, unheated, unaired schoolrooms, her face falls out of envelopes and people look and believe me. I read her letters to a chosen few and they are amazed, so young, so lovely, so loving, you must miss her very much, and one of the girls even writes to her, and she writes back.

There is a wonderful English teacher there, mother of one of the day girls who is my friend. Mrs. Roderick and her daughter Delia. If not for them and Angie, a city girl (well, Norwich, but at least she knows about pavements) . . . On weekends Angie, Delia and I ride Harriet's ponies (fairly old, lumbering ponies, but sweet enough) through the gray streets of the nearby medieval town, high above the little groups of local schoolboys that crowd round and admire us. The horses' hooves clop against the stones, echo between the stone buildings, shops, churches and almshouses, and the pale, lonely boys hail us, give us cigarettes, stand us drinks at the pub, while we sit in our saddles above them, smelling of horse sweat, leather and cheap shampoo, drinking our gin and bitter lemons on our horses in the car park. Then twilight coming on, taking the tints from the mud everywhere and the children's-painting green, the horses eager to be home where they can be lazy and warm, me holding mine back, dreading the return but fearing the consequences of being late, just like at Mirrenwood, hating to go inside, to supper with Harriet and Francis and all the hours between sunset and bed, then waiting for the weekend to be over when school may begin again.

At Sparrow House I do a lot of housework and farm work, but I'm excused if I've got studying to do, therefore I now do a great deal of that, reading for hours—languages, history, English literature— as I never did at Wickhurst. Since work buys me privacy, I am working, and beginning to learn something. My marks are always high, though it's difficult to tell what that means, and soon the school gives me my own grading system, so I don't get automatic A's. Francis is all for these intellectual efforts and he gives me his own assignments, though that is just part of their system. For example, if I don't want to go to church with them, Francis makes me write a theological treatise on my objections. He is a serious churchgoer himself (another father with private ownership of the deity, another attempt to clobber the girl-child with a male, orderly, just God), and he and Harriet don't like this antichurch business of mine; they send me to the local vicar on Saturday mornings to be indoctrinated. He is eighty-five, the vicar, Mr. Harwood, and we get on well. He is a pagan at heart and an eccentric. He hates the thick, tame, hymn-singing locals, loves anything High Church, above all loves the ancient Greeks and their homophile culture. My way in to him is homophilia New York style; I give him my James Baldwin and we talk, after a while, about anything we like. In a way I am bribing, corrupting him into this friendship, but he is quite bored and willing to be bribed. Basically, he doesn't care whether I'm Christian or not as long as I'm open-minded. That I can do. Saturday mornings I escape Sparrow House with him, we drive through the countryside looking at old churches and talking about Greece. He is my shelter and my rock.

"This will be your first English Christmas, won't it?" The fat, rosy underheadmistress, beams at me (fortunate child). I am like the

Nigerian to her, deprived of the amenities, about to see history, love, culture, in action, something I'll never forget. At rehearsals for Christmas carols she searches my face, feeling how moved I must be. Imagine the thrill, she croons to herself, England!— grinning at the little Yank orphan, up to her eyeballs in antidepressants. Where's the snow, I think, and Bett: how will she be?

Coming back with Harriet from a trip to town to see the lights (a pretty string of bulbs next to the traffic signal in the otherwise darkened streets), I am told how all this begins for her in August, otherwise she'd never get through; there are the farm families to buy for, and local people, not to mention nieces, nephews, godchildren. She has her lists and even so, she says, she's only just remembered her secretary, the dear Miss Wilson (one of my sweet sympathizers, casts me looks for courage at tea on Tuesdays and Fridays from under her bobbed white ringlets). "What did you get her?" I ask. "A green umbrella," Harriet says. "Isn't that a little impersonal?" I say, and Harriet turns a defensive gaze, ice-cold blue eyes. "It's a jolly useful present," she says, and we drive on.

The house is in an uproar. There is bellowing and cooking and Midnight Mass (Harwood among the Philistines). In the morning there are stuffed stockings for the boys unwrapped in swoops in Francis and Harriet's bedroom. At eleven the nursery doors are unlocked and we go in where the tree is, and the presents, in five presorted piles set out with pencil and sheet of paper. This, says Francis, explaining the pencil and paper, is to write down who and what as you go along, all letters to be written and checked by me this afternoon. All right, the boys are used to it, they fall on their packages and throw paper around while Francis tries to discipline and Harriet hovers, refolding wrapping and overseeing lists. My father has given me a watch. "Not a very good watch," he says when I thank him, "since you're bound to lose it." I turn it over and read the inscription, as he bids me. *Tempus fugit*, it says, a message which I scrutinize for secret affection. I unwrap Harriet's present. It is a green umbrella. There are lots of other presents: stockings and handkerchiefs and book tokens, dozens of remembrances from the list-making members of this huge "new family." Bett's present is late, but we will speak by phone. We are both fine, we will say, sorry to be apart. After that it is Christmas lunch, set out with candles and silver and crystal. There are, for the seven of us, wine and fruit squash, turkey, sausage, chestnuts, Stilton, nuts, dates, plum pudding and brandy butter, Christmas crackers, and silence while everyone eats themselves silly, and then we go and watch the Queen on television and Billy Smart's Circus, do the letters, have more plum pudding with tea and go to bed early. "Did you enjoy your Christmas?" my father asks me sternly that night. "Yes," I say, "thank you so much, and for having me here." "That's all right," he says, and stoops to offer me his cheek to kiss, so I can go to bed happy.

In January, Harriet and the boys and I join a school party for skiing in Switzerland. Twelve seniors from the local boys' school, two masters and us, sitting upright, polite and overexcited on the twenty-four-hour train trip through Europe: a wintery seasick crossing which Harriet deals with by eating (with me and the boys) the four-course sit-down meal, while plates fly and guests thin out; rest rooms overspill in the churn and toss of the sea, salt water and vomit everywhere and Harriet's war-spirit instructions. Then, green, we go to Paris, or at least the station name in the dark, and little one-story towns with foreign advertisements on sides of the buildings, streets as from Second World War movies, and the next day Zermatt and from there to Saas-Fee, a toy village to drink hot chocolate in, bars of Swiss chocolate in the zipped pockets of borrowed ski-clothes, comical Germans to instruct us, nights under snowdrift eiderdowns and wood and cuckoo clocks everywhere. At night, dancing at the Sans Souci, me and twelve boys who have no one else English-speaking to fall in love with, and twice a day skiing lessons and more chocolate, baths if you pay for them once a week, and once in a while reading the Churchill books my father has sent with me, to be reported on so I don't "fritter" away all this time, and everyone becoming athletic and pink-cheeked and laughing over and up against and into the slopes. And dancing at the San Souci so often that when we come in the German band automatically plays the favorite song, "You Really Got Me" by the Kinks, and at the end of my stay the umpah-German instructor laughs (finally) after a spill on a jump and says, "At least you are quite a dancer, I hear, if not skier ever, missy."

Back at school, two of the twelve send me love notes. And at school with the others you wait for the go-betweens to come back before tea with the rain-spotted, mud-spattered, folded or sealed, pocket-secreted little lined notebook-paper notes on which is written: I am thinking of you, mad about you, will you come to the play, sit in fifth row far left, can I meet you after church Sunday, will you wear my rugger shirt; and if it's not Greenwich Village at least it's something close to the outside world where fathers are not and mothers are not and where one may fly without apology with what feathers one has, which may be feathers enough. (Oh, Veronica, boys will save you every time, or so I think then.) And then, soon, the boys'-school catch has left the girls'-school catch and is asking me to meet him in the fifth row far left at the school play, where Othello in blackface leaves a smudge of blacking on the nose of Desdemona, and we whisper whether he is certain he wishes to make this change, and he says X was once the "catch" of Northton, but now you are, and as such I am caught. And therefore I return one lesser rugger shirt and am given one greater rugger shirt, mud- and sweat-stiffened, and the notes go forth, and on walks we share Swan Vestas and Woodbines under dripping branches, both in steaming uniforms as sheets of mist drift over the hills, and cows cough like old men behind the hedges. And he is my new English god, not like those movies I saw in New York, *Room at the Top, The Loneliness of the Long Distance Runner,* but that other movie, *Tom Jones,* with his hero's head and torso set against the West Country hills, his jacket hung like a cape about his shoulders and his boots muddy and high. And it is very easy to fall in love the way they do in the film—to roll in hay barns, kiss and smoke and talk each time about our feelings, which are only this talk, these notes, these movie images, these visits to tea shops where we sit behind lace curtains smoking and drawing hearts on the fogged-up glass, drinking bitter, milky tea and watching the time, dreading, and feeling the thrill of such dreading, the return to the heatless, ugly school or the doom and thunder of Sparrow House.

But it is getting better. Even if my father doesn't, there are boys who think I'm smart and pretty and not "too emotional." Mrs. Rivers wants me to take exams for Oxford (Oxford, not Macy's), and this summer I am going to be in New York again with Bett and Veronica and Duncan, with my skyline and city heat, with windows open and music coming from Central Park or from the open windows across the street where our neighbor Vladimir Horowitz practices. I am going to be myself again. If I can just hang on here everything will be all right—if I can just get through these weekends left from February to June, with Tom Jones, Delia and Angie; only four months of weekends of shouting and gloom, and it's okay if they don't really want me here, I'm not really here, just weekends, farm work, housework, reading in my room upstairs waiting for Francis to stand under my window, his heavy footsteps grinding up the gravel, his shout smashing my Chaucer, Shakespeare, D. H. Lawrence, shattering with the two syllables of my first name, separated and boomed from the depth of his diaphragm as though I were miles away, through his huge lungs, gathering all the rage and blackness that being in the world produces. And me, hearing the sound of my name, as though there were fogs and ice floes between us, hear how at that moment of shouting I am everything wrong with the world, the very reason he storms and rages. He bellows my name until I think the glass will break and I go down to his office trying not to tremble and enrage him further, to hear what it is I have done or failed to do. Sometimes I feel that if Harriet weren't there he would go too far, smash me with his giant fist.

He simply didn't know how to treat me, just as I never knew what to call him and so never used any name at all. To him I was always an inferior, nonproductive version of Harriet or a peculiar form of his boys, and he would treat us all to the same Captain Francis bellowing, as if we were a single, mutinous, laggardly crowd. Perhaps these were the only alternatives he could find to what I might otherwise have been, the embarrassing though legitimate "love child" from New York, evidence of whim and stupidity, above all failure, seventeen years before. In any case, I don't think he ever believed he had a daughter.

I had retaken my American College Entrance exams, and in the spring all the places that had refused me the year before accepted me. True, my exam results were better from all that reading and hiding in my room, and I was now seventeen instead of sixteen, but it was something else because those places not only accepted me, they offered to give me sophomore status immediately, as though my year in England had jumped me over everyone's head. Of course, an "English" education makes all the difference. Never mind that it was a charity school in the countryside I'd been attending, from which not one girl had gone on to university in twenty years, or that I, bad Wickhurst student, just barely a high school graduate, had to have a special marking system—it was England, wasn't it, and therefore superior.

I take my English A-levels, and though I answer one of the general questions, "Why be moral? Discuss," with the words "Why indeed?" and thereby upset Mrs. Rivers, my results when they come are good, are fine. I can go, I can try for Oxford and Cambridge, and I am already accepted at Sussex. Accepted, and it is free (they want me, they invite me). And knowing this, it feels as if my year has been a success, an Alma Mater if not a father, I have something that feels like a future now, so that safely I can go back to Bett and explain my plans to her. And if I can't quite tell her all of how it's been, at least I can tell her the good parts. And in June I fly back to tell her these.

"Puppy," she said on my second night home, "there's something you should know."

"Puppy, you're so tall," she had said the first night, and "What's with the British accent?" But her surprise for me is bigger.

"Puppy," she says, "there's someone new in Mommy's life," and she explains, so embarrassed I have to keep reassuring her. But it's pretty strange. If I betrayed my mother with my Englishness, and my height, and affiliation, or so she thinks, to (her former enemy) my father, she does me one better. She has replaced her seventeen-year-old daughter with an eighteen-year-old lover. Not that she uses that word, and she says "man," not "boy," and she's bashful, above all about the circumstances, which I, fresh from England, where these things matter, ask about. No, not at a dinner party, not at a hunt ball, actually Mommy met Hal when he was delivering groceries. Great, I think, fine, this is New York, haven't I been saying so all this time? But eighteen, Mommy? He's a wonderful person, she says. And I meet him that night. We're both shy. He doesn't understand my BBC/county English (well, Mommy doesn't always understand it either) and I can't make out his thick-tongued Bronx. To me, he's not even cute, though he has what he later tells me is "a great build." But he's a kid, even more than I'm a kid. The thing is not to seem to judge either of them, and I don't, but I haven't a clue what he's saying when he talks, so we speak around each other, as polite and deaf as dowagers in the ladies' room of a posh hotel.

This is a version of the story she tells me. Bett met Hal one day over a year ago, while I was cutting classes at Wickhurst or staying at Veronica's, sometime, as I date these things, between "Twist and Shout" at Carnegie Hall and "Love Me Do" in my little room at Veronica's. This is pretty bad, because I was sixteen and Hal seventeen then, and Bett a cool, sexy thirty-nine, but still thirty-nine, and even Duncan's older than Hal. Anyway, sometime that spring, and clinched no doubt after our abortive excursion to the circus (decades ago, it now seems to my five-foot-ten James Bond-talking self), Hal used to bring brown bags up the five flights of stairs, get tipped and register the tipper. And someone hovered or he hung about on the doorstep while she (unprepared as always) was scratching around in the bottom of her bag for change, and probably took it all in, waiting there for the pretty lady: the cats and the daybed and the little balcony, and something that seemed gentle, lovely and good to his Bronx-orphanage self. Oh, what parallels and perpendiculars between us: Hal saw a way out in her just as I saw the brick wall; Hal entered where I bolted, saw peace and beauty where I saw claustrophobia. And perhaps sometime he said, 'Forget about it, next time,' just that pause of body and defense you need to embed the image, so that the next time Bett ordered her cat food and Ajax she wondered whether the boy would come, and the boy probably made sure it was him, cycling with the bags the three blocks from the store, where the pale, paunchy Irishman kept waiting for him to make a mistake but eventually got to trust him and believe that he wanted to make good, pull himself out of his poor-Bronx life, deliver himself with the groceries and bicycle his way out.

So sometime when I was pulling apart from Bett, he was pulling toward, and sometime then they sat down and talked, had coffee. Bett would need more and more things from the store, and he would bring them and talk, and something in her, some rejected mothering part of her, came back to life with this boy. The fearful, men-controlled part of her could be at peace in this new friendship, because she could be the one who gave, she could help, and she could love more fearlessly because he was only a boy after all. They became friends, then lovers. And Bett was brave enough, honest enough, to be grateful, to take love and happiness where it offered itself and not where the world said she had to find it—from lewd bosses, men at parties, all those worldly men, too worldly for love.

He couldn't read, Hal, he could barely speak, so she gave him brushes and canvases, took him to museums, gave Gogi's gift, which had been useless to her, to him. By the time I got there, there were photos of the work, primitive realist pictures, and then abstractions of which he was proud and shy and had some art-world jargon. "Geometric," he'd say, or "hard-edged," and he'd show me these, as if to say forget about it, this is who I am. So Bett gave him his new identity just as I was trading in mine. Somehow the balance was righted among us and we were friends. Bett had this new child, I could be less guilty, she less bitter. And Hal? Hal, caught in the middle, was happy enough, busy enough being saved, becoming an artist, just like Gogi as a young girl, saving himself, reinventing himself through paint, and, not like Gogi, through the sight of the Self reflected in Bett's eyes.

It was too surprising to be anything other than fine. I just couldn't stay there, that was all. Hal had moved in and was painting in my old room. I went back to Veronica's, got a job selling Mexican pottery to tourists. I'd work the cash machines, go out with my friends from the shop, then back to New York nights, music, drink and the chaste ardors of Duncan. But everything was okay, New York and my speaking British and dinners with Bett and Hal. It was all suddenly okay. England was my armor against New York, and New York, which I was soaking in with every touch of July–August heat on skin, Duncan on skin, sand and salt water on skin, dinner on Broadway and blues and rock downtown and going to the beach with Gerry and smoking marijuana and hearing for the first time about kids in Vietnam—New York was becoming my armor against Norfolk. It wasn't that I had to choose, it was that suddenly I could have both, a double life of there and here: here was love and happiness and the seductions of the present; there was order, "safety" and, apparently, a future.

So that on the boat in September, although I am weeping my heart out at drifting away from my skyline harbor, from Veronica and Duncan and Mommy and Hal, heading back to the fortress of Mandalay, I am crying really because it is wonderful to have so much and be so alive and have my heart broken in parting from my boyfriend, and crying because I have to sit my papers for Oxford when I get back, and my father is meeting me in Southampton, and I have only five days left—how will I get through, bind up my wounds, make scars over my happiness in time to be English again?—five days to do all the work of burying the happy self inside the how-things-are-done self, but meanwhile, crying dramatically over the ship rails and then going to sit, tear-and-mascara-stained, at a little table in the bar.

I took my Oxford exams in November, had an interview and was admitted to read Philosophy and Psychology as I had asked. My acceptance was announced in the traditional way by an official congratulatory telegram. Flapping this, and rushing into the sitting room (a room I only ever approached with the caution of an advance party in a minefield), I was shouted out by my father. I was making an idiotic spectacle of myself, he thundered. There wasn't any reason for surprise or delight. All that had happened was a result of genes (no credit to me) and submission to discipline (credit to him). I should take myself and my telegram upstairs to cool off.

SIX

ET IN ARCADIA EGO. Oxford. They say it is the kingdom of heaven. They say we are on the brink of joy and will be changed forever. We feel we are the hand-chosen, infinitely blessed acolytes of wisdom and beauty, led here by hard work and talent, but above all by a smiling good fortune. It is a utopia, governed by the wise and good, populated by the young, bright and beautiful. Enticed by centuries of rapt description of the place, and particularly by certain writings of Thomas Hardy, Evelyn Waugh and Max Beerbohm, we know exactly what Oxford will be: unearthly bliss in the moment, and the object of sweet, aching nostalgia ever after.

But I also know this town. My Oxford acceptance had been conditional on my getting a certificate of proficiency in Latin, and I was sent to a cramming college here to do it. I stayed with a few foreign students in a damp boardinghouse on the edge of town and rode the buses in three times a week to read Cicero and Caesar. The rest of the time I starved (I had been given very little money) and lived once again on National Health antidepressants. Oxford seemed to me dark and utterly cheerless when, speedy, dazed, hungry, perpetually cold from icy January through to rainy May, I took those long rides on groaning buses in through the drab outskirts to lay siege to the impenetrable fortress of Latin, the sheer walls of words that had to be deciphered front and back, words which cohabited promiscuously, it seemed to me, inside their sentences, words that flew the banner of logic, precision, clarity, but whose meanings shifted and slithered like rotting leaves underfoot, teeming, protean walls that somehow and in some dream state I'd managed to scale in time for this my glorious entry to the university.

I'd spent the summer again with Bett and Hal and Veronica. I saw Duncan, who was getting married (pretty reluctantly), and we finally, and unmemorably, went to bed. I went to bed with Gerry, and with Gerry's elder brother. I learned about callousness and shame by doing it. That was how you learned your limits, like a mechanical toy hitting walls.

And now here I am again, only now inside the very gates of this paradise, in a Victorian brick and buttressed women's college, whose halls are lined with photographs of suffragettes and crowded with chattering good girls and serious students. Still tanned from New York, I wear my black academic gown, as required, over sweater and jeans, carry, nervously folded, my assignment sheets, reading lists, tutorial appointment card and booklet of college regulations. I wear my *tempus fugit* watch like a sign of good intentions and feel only dread inside me, together with a kind of stunned-bird relief that the summer at last is over.

It is another institution, bathed in sheets of rain and run by thin, unmarried women with mimeograph machines. It is located some distance from the picturesque, medieval center of town, access to which is by muddy paths through the Parks or by deep-puddled side streets, down which nervous youths on bicycles, heads bent and water dripping from their noses, ride furiously, like myself late for lectures and looking as though they feel themselves to be as fraudulently here as I do, and as convinced of failure.

I am about to begin my three-year course in Philosophy and Psychology. After the summer, my interest is hardly academic. In the most practical way I want to find out how to live, who other people are, who I am and how we can coexist. I want to know what is good and right and I imagine I can sit at someone's feet for this, or at least in some corner of the library. I want the dignified shortcut, enlightenment in a less psychically, not to say physically, bruising form. Perhaps I want to know things with my head, and for the moment put on hold my "infantile emotionalism" and the body that seems inevitably, for all my recent attempts at dismantling, to be wired to it.

But what they are offering me seems crushingly remote and too much like the dullest kind of mathematics: equations and propositions of logic in the Philosophy department, a full course in statistics for Psychology. Measurement without weight. No Freud or Jung, but charts and numbers, together with cages of pigeons, burnt and bleached teaching films on the mating habits of stickle-backs and timberwolves. And where I'd hoped for Heraclitus, Aristotle, Heidegger, I am offered expensively printed pages of symbols, or texts consisting of laborious, quibbling, hairsplitting, teeth-grindingly slow wordplay, as dull to me in my current search as underwater farce. Though I am told that these wolves and fish and pigeons have mighty things to say about man's condition and that the so-called wordplay is precisely what is meant by the universally esteemed "Oxford Philosophy," I am too impatient for so slow a buildup of information in the face of the imminent, looming forces of Life and Error. If it's the ideas themselves I want, they say (with barely disguised impatience), I should try the Classics department, where of course I'll have to be able to read the original Greek texts. On the other hand, if all I want are some general notions about the meaning of life (suppressed derision), why not try the Eng. Lit. department; I'll get some amateur versions over there.

"We do not generally hold a very high opinion of American education," she says when I present myself for consideration at the school of English Literature. She sits before me like some mythological monster, her lower half slithering as she crosses and uncrosses her sinuous, stockinged legs, her upper body stiff with elderly disapproval, and the soft, gray, furrowed field of her face fixed in hostility, except for the black eyes that dart, startled with dislike of what she sees. The seventy-year-old vice-principal and head of English studies is dismayed that I cannot name five poets between Chaucer and Spenser, is horrified that almost all my education is American, looks with disapproval at both my suntan and my jeans, is without much hope for my progress in her department, which she believes to be the *crème de la crème* of the college and which can only be corrupted by such foreign matter. Nevertheless, she agrees—almost, one would think, in order to experience the thrill of her own contempt, the secret schaden-freude of those in authority—to take me on, on condition I study with her and submit to her private and decisive examinations at the end of one term. If I fail these, she says, I will have to leave the university and reapply next year. She wishes me to expect very little and I tell her I shall. Her cheerlessness is infectious, but it is too late now to return to the harmless pleasures of birds and signs and numbers. As the days shorten and swill around in the unending autumn storms, I read my texts for the first part of the English course: the doom-laden, stoical poems of the Dark Ages (which tell me in drumroll meter that life is a meaningless fast ride to the grave) and the works of Milton, the great blind poet of darkness and exile, with particular attention to the work called *Paradise Lost*.

Light and enlightenment *are* at Oxford, but they are not where I am seeking them—at least, not then in the books or courses or goodwill of tutors, but in the person of a person, which, had I not been so unenlightened, is where I would have known it to be. Redemption also comes on cat's feet, very quietly (I had my own fog). There was no suddenness, no announcement, no timpani or cloudburst, only some kind of cellular attention that finally grew insistent enough to reach my consciousness. In retrospect this fact seems peculiar (partly because Hugh was so handsome), and contrary to what we are led to believe about the beginnings of great love. But his first manifestation was muted; he seemed contained, gentle, solid, behind a veil of impeccable manners. I met him on the day I met Michael, his best friend, a guitar-playing Americo-mane with a line in Elvis Presley imitations, polished to nightmarish perfection from the depths of his Stoke-on-Trent boyhood. Perhaps it was Michael's flamboyant and generalized courtship, his continuous performance of song, verse and talk, and his abrupt physicality—his sudden standing, sitting, bounding, crouching, every movement simultaneously graceful and excessive—and his energy wired to his need to demonstrate it, that made Hugh initially so much less visible. Or audible. Even in the middle of singing, Michael would suddenly abandon his guitar, cross the room to a pile of books, pick out a volume and begin to speak with manic intensity about what he was reading. Everything he did could remind him of something he had done or read before, and the day moved for him in loops of association on a continuum that conveyed his intoxication with his own existence. Both Michael and Hugh had tutorials with one of the reputedly brilliant Eng. Lit. professors, a youngish don who inspired in them a discriminating connoisseurship in what they read and a surgeon's passion for the bodies of texts. They were third-year students, due to take final exams at the end of the year, and they infected me with their excitement, their possession of and by literature. Listening to them talk, rapt, reverent, hilarious, I began to see how English studies might become a delight and entanglement, rather than, as I was getting the message from my own muffin-faced tutor, a lugubrious mystery to which only the dogged and respectfully dressed had any hope of access.

But their anomalous, violent bookishness was only an aspect of their high spirits, and it was them and not their academic passions that enraged me. Initially, it was beyond me to distinguish the two of them, since the phenomenon of Michael/Hugh appeared as a unit. They were physically similar, both tall, good-looking, dark-eyed blonds, but whereas Michael was wiry, sharp and demoniacally bearded, Hugh was broader, with a softer skin and bearing, and his movements were purposeful and measured. He was half German, and there was a hint of ploddingness to his dignity, though he was athletic enough so that the weight of resistance was barely evident. He tried to be as silly and impulsive as Michael, but it was a labor of love. Really, he was a romantic, with all the gravity (in all senses) that involves a Tonio Kröger where Michael was Ariel: a phenomenon of spirit and energy, better suited to flirtation than love. Michael would have been an exasperating lover; he had no shadow to him and his attention span was too short.

Hugh was the son of a German ambassador who had married an American. His American side was Californian, and authentic therefore, not a convert's affectation like Michael's. Outwardly, it confined itself to the wearing of jeans and Double Ringer blue denim shirts (we three dressed pretty much alike). His accent, though, like mine, was British, and the result of British schooling. He had a large, rusty American car with pictures of a blond Californian fiancée in the dashboard pocket. At first I was sort of unspokenly destined to be Michael's girl, while Hugh played the chaste widower, though the fiancée's name never came up and we successfully ignored her existence. Dressed like them, reading English Literature like (and often with) them, having both American and English credentials, I eased into their exclusive friendship, and for a while we formed an anxiety-free threesome, itself the object of our expressed awe and mutual congratulation. Perhaps to protect our self-baffling and absolute harmony, them with each other, myself with each of them, sex, beyond jokes and flirtation, lay like a well-trained hound at our feet, and at least for a while stayed put. Though we were physically demonstrative, though we leaned into one another, kissed, traveled arm in arm or crowded together into Hugh's front seat, though we even slept together on occasion, half clothed, the dog lay low. We experienced ourselves as a mystical triad in blue angelic form, and, as we knew from *Paradise Lost*, angels didn't mate. High without drugs, on constant cups of tea and sleepless nights, we were chaste and ecstatic, and always astounded by the peculiarity and brilliance of our condition.

We conversed in riddles, puns and lines from sixteenth-, seventeenth-, nineteenth-century poetry, and were enraptured by our combined cleverness and beauty. The aura of mutual admiration made us generous, made us good, and we lived off our radiance like bees, buzzing and soaring in our private garden. We were aware that we had created some kind of Eden, but we anticipated no expulsion. There was stasis in this perfection: angelic beings want for nothing but continuance. But we were confident; since almost nothing in the outer world even touched us, we had little fear that it could ever pull us apart.

But then one afternoon in Hugh's room, as I was lying between the two of them reading, and in the usual peace and contentment, I began to notice myself dividing, and that while the side of me adjacent to Michael remained dead and placid in friendship, the side in contact with Hugh was growing disturbed and alive. Once I was aware of this difference, the phenomenon seemed to repeat itself on each similar occasion, and not long afterward Hugh and I became lovers. We arrived one morning on Michael's doorstep prepared to announce and explain, but he stopped us, indicating that words were unnecessary (the only time he ever thought so). And thus rebalanced, the three of us resumed our friendship.

I was now, as I felt, in love for the first time, completely and with my entire will. Sex was therefore an expression of what had already happened between Hugh and me, a response to a fact, and not the barren fact itself. What followed was so entirely different from my previous experience that it seemed to absolve me from everything that went before. I distanced myself from my affair with Duncan as though it had been nothing more than an ancient, sordid, infantile episode. That summer in New York had taught me, or I had taught myself, to be an observer at my own dismemberment, a herbivore at the feast. Disembodied, aware only that sex was taking place in the same room as myself, at most involving a detachable part of me, I imagined I could simply take up the pieces of myself and go home. I'd learned a dangerous skill, a ready access to dissociation. Imagining I was not engaged by it, I was nevertheless harmed, and it was Hugh who put me back together.

We were hardly casual about it, and whereas we spun in talk and noise and music when we were with Michael, alone we were struck dumb. Like two hippies on drugs and religion, we were held in light. Even to us then the experience had an unfamiliar religious quality, and there would be a reliable descent of the Holy Ghost when we were together. Lying side by side, we would sense it approaching and would say, amazed and irreverent, "Here it comes again." In our dumbness we had no ready language for what was happening to us. It was a mystery for which we needed ancient and poetic explanation. *Haelsgebedda* we called each other, after endearments in *Beowulf,* or, plundering Milton, "flesh of my flesh, bone of my bone." Or, giving up, we used our own unbelieving English; "the third person," we said again and again, as the alien spirit, sensational cloud-form, dropped like a theater prop on invisible ropes.

So Michael ceased to be our third person and Hugh and I found our own. We went around Oxford so much in love we were beyond ridicule. Such physical harmony, such proof of the possibility of happiness, creates its own respectful audience, and we had ours.

We were an Oxford love story, two radiant, triumphant children. While the rest of the university worked for tutorials, measured their time by achievements, Hugh and I took as few hours away from our ecstatic coexistence as we could get away with. He nearly failed his exams that year, and so did I. But we didn't—we were under divine protection.

If my account of Hugh seems vague and metaphysical, it was only a side effect of the intimacy. Love, it seems to me, does result, but not begin, in blindness, a kind of TV snowstorm of sensation and acceptance, perhaps a kind of magic in which each lover makes the other disappear. I was as undetached and unseeing with Hugh as I had been distant and observant with Duncan. It was a trusting, infantile blindness, a response to a different kind of sign system in which knowing replaced seeing. I could never, after our initial meetings, view him whole or from a distance. I registered blondness, softness, goodness of heart. I was so utterly accepting of his entire being that physical details—the erotic specificity of most love objects, even aspects of personality and self-presentation, how he appeared in the world—burned out like mist in the heat of my love for him. There ceased to be boundaries between us, and I lost my sight along with my sense of separation.

The future didn't exist for us, or the past; everything felt new. There was no weight of expectation, very little means of comparison and therefore everything could be ventured. We sailed off our ramp into unknown airstreams without fear or scruple, and the more we sailed, the braver, stronger, more exalted we felt. We were conscious of the privilege of our situation but we entered it recklessly as if nothing bad had ever happened to us before. Ruthlessly we obliterated everything that had preceded our being together, because of our certainty, beyond any act or declaration of faith, of the significance of our present life. Our moments accorded with some ancient expectation of happiness, some buried, infant memory. That was the past we connected with, and everything else that had ever happened seemed now to have been just a distraction during the long wait for return to that first state. And everything changed once we understood we were meant to be happy.

Oxford changed. Where before everything had seemed dark and vaguely menacing, now it was luminous, and the light seemed hardly remarkable at all but the given condition of consciousness. Oxford itself broke open like a casket and became the perfect setting for our life of sensations. What had at the beginning seemed the stern heart of the place—the figures of authority, the gate porters, tutors, lecturers, regulations, the work itself—soon seemed barely a marginal nuisance by the side of uninhibited pleasures: of the river, the air—damp and gray or moted and green—of mud, grass, trees, old stone and streets, of reading, of long nighttime conversation with friends, of getting drunk, dancing, of being young, being there.

My father could not reasonably object to my spending a week with the Grunwalds at the end of the year, and I went to stay with them at their cottage in Hampshire. As a family, their impact was spectacular. They were as close to an imagined ideal as I was ever to come across, and far superior to whatever I had been able to fantasize for myself in the wistful little novels of my childhood. They had a kind of solidity and glow to them, a hint of plumpness, really moral as much as physical, that gave them a benign finish, as though they really had come from some realm of invention. The father was somewhat stiff, as befitted his diplomatic profession, with the air of someone used to smoothing things out as he passed, with just a hint of the Hussar threat. He was scrupulously elegant, buttoned, observant and well mannered. His jokes, a little laborious, were always carried at the last minute by a courtly deftness, a sudden charm. Next to such comported stiffness, Hugh's mother seemed stubbornly to inhabit a more instinctive universe, and a little lazily, almost in the Californian manner. There was a handsome, gawky younger brother who adored him, and a very young sister, exceptionally pretty in a European fashion, cool and delicate of feature. They also hung on to Hugh's words, arms, expressions, needed to be close to him, as though his existence gave theirs as much purpose as it gave mine. We were all, it seemed, in love with him, and that made us friends. In the flower-bordered garden and under the thatched cottage roof I lived my picture-book week with them, took walks with them on the Hampshire downs, cooked and ate with them, learned their private jokes and rituals. They were generous with me, they let me inside, they were willing to share the family hero.

And then Hugh and I separated, and I, with four whole months of Long Vacation ahead of me, without money to go to New York or permission to stay in London, went back to Sparrow House, to resume my ancient routine of homework and farm work and lying low inside that rumbling, dark castle. There were tennis parties with the county deb-and-lad locals, horse shows and village teas. It was unending.

And it was Hugh, not I, who went to New York that summer and got to see Bett. At the restaurant where they had dinner, as both wrote in letters I read in envious exile (imagining the sensuous New York heat, the city nighttime sounds and smells, and painfully missing them both), the owner presented them with a bottle of wine, because they made, he said, such a beautiful couple.

So the families closed around us, gave us their benediction. Even Francis and Harriet, when Hugh came to stay late in August, made adjustments for the sweetness of it all, treating us as though we were engaged, offering us now as a public couple at those rural fetes and dances. It elevated me with them, I could see, that Hugh loved me. Even my father, at least in Hugh's presence, spoke more softly to me, almost as though with a measure of respect.

In September, Hugh left to take up his teaching post in Germany. That term I escaped from college twice to meet him for the weekend, making the twelve-hour journey by train and boat to Ostend, where he had driven six hours to meet me. Such exhaustions, transgressions, in the cause of romance, pitched our love at a new angle where desperation, danger, entered in and caused new fevers. And a new urgency. I was indifferent to the peril of being caught so far off campus either by my father or by the college, to the risk of inevitable suspension. Nothing in England mattered to me anything like as much as Hugh, and I felt that, if hindered, I was prepared to run away forever.

Long, passionate letters came and went between us, written and received daily in a state of Victorian rapture. Everything that happened happened at one remove, and only that it might be recounted to the beloved, in the language of the beloved. Every thought and sensation had merit only if it could be shared. Counting the days between our infrequent reunions, living through our separations as though they were simply voids, we suspended our lives, held our breaths, until we could be—he, I and the third person—reunited. The pain was engulfing, and irresistible. We were rocked in a rhythm of wrenching apart and growing numb, of agitation and coming together, like the roll of the sea. We were drunk on it, and our letters were boasts of our excesses. To me, it was also nightmarishly familiar: the sickening lurches of loss and renewal which I had felt waiting for Bett at Mirrenwood, speeded up now and made conscious. I was alive when I was with Hugh; when I was not, I was simply an organism designed for pain.

We lived a life of suspension and return, with the momentum of an orchard swing. It was a regulated manic-depression, in which burning up, growing cool, numb, was how you loved. To be happy alone was simply against the chemical law of such dependency. Alone, you endured, lay low, buried the spirit so that daily life became once again only a wait, a cold, insensible hibernation. Where once the future did not exist, or the past, now they were all that was. The present was a gray dormancy. Soon even the reunions began to lose any quality other than the relief of pain. So love became a torturer's cycle: the simple current of pain and the relief of pain. Worst of all, in cruel paradox, the beloved soon became only a version of the self: a negation of the self-as-pain or a restoration of the self-as-happiness. And even in the moments of happiness there was softness, rottenness, a sickening dependency. Each time I was apart from Hugh I had slowly to grow a shell, and each time we were together I let it crack by increments as I came closer, reattached, surrendered, and each time accepted the future terms of my temporary well-being.

Such fearful necessity became terrifying. Gradually I was so reduced by Hugh's absence that I ceased to function, even outwardly. Now I literally began to hibernate, to doze through my days like a creature fending off cold and starvation. As the strange winter of separation deepened, I lived like someone under a spell.

Waking at one or two in the afternoon after fifteen hours' sleep, I would stumble down for coffee and cigarettes, nod off again two hours later. Waking in the late afternoon in time for a tutorial, I would sit through it dopey, sleep-swollen. My condition was alarming, and as it continued I was sent to various doctors. When their amphetamines and antidepressants failed, they asked me to move to the local bin so they might observe the narcolepsy. They prescribed strychnine in small doses. Isn't that a cumulative poison? I asked. They admitted it was but assured me they would take me off before there was danger. And what if they didn't? I knew what I needed, and it wasn't pills or poison. It was Hugh, and if not that, then it was life, to be once more in the world, to have Hugh's permission to live.

Things happened fast at Oxford, life happened fast. We measured time in weeks of term, parties, meetings. And we were learning so fast, speeding through the centuries poem by poem, text by text. We did medieval literature in two terms, from the Dark Ages to the Renaissance. It was the reverse of Marvell's "An age at least to every part / And the last age should show your heart'; ages went by with the seasons, and in that speeding of eras and sensibilities, our emotions sped, too. There were "men" around us constantly, at teas and in lecture halls, sauntering in the park, leaving notes in pigeonholes, confiding through go-betweens. The pressure to fall in love, to let go and move on, was the pressure to exist, and you denied the one at the cost of breathing itself, it seemed; you lay low and let the love and tears storm in the hallways and rooms around you; you read your poetry and novels about love; you took your tea alone in your room absolutely aware that there was ill-health in this, and the danger of dying. It was breath-holding to resist, a kind of submersion in the water of noble intentions. You believed in love and eternity but you watched the feelings slip and alter poem to poem and friend to friend. It was a Heraclitean world and there was fire everywhere. If you didn't let yourself burn, you'd die of the cold.

I met them, I saw them, harmlessly. Once, twice, I came close and ran away, because I could not be this bad person, could not

157

betray, even by thought, my love for Hugh. I wrote my letters—intense, more passionate than ever, as though the words were flesh, as though I could press myself into them, send myself inside the airmail envelope to where I would be safe.

But then, halfway between the end of the Summer of Love and the Events of May 1968, I attend my friend Marianne's birthday party, a sedate and elegant affair: music students and lit. students dining by candlelight in a vast room in Chester Square. For her birthday, Marianne's father has got us all standing-room tickets at Covent Garden to see *The Magic Flute*. The only opera I have ever seen is *Electra*, to which Constance took us when I was fourteen and unable to get past the unbelievableness of the hulking form that raced back and forth across the stage, bosoms flying, cavern mouth wide and wailing. Mozart will be different, and everyone here is knowledgeable. Most have librettos and that tight, cheerful, expectant manner of the well-brought-up guest. Next to Marianne is a dark, handsome boy from whom pent-up energy rises almost dangerously. There's defiance in him somewhere, against this setting, this gentility. But he, too, is well brought up, a familiar of London opera life. He is talking to her in a low voice, but fiercely, and everything he says swings from affability to spikes. Among the girlish, pleasing, castratedly polite young men, he is the only interesting presence here, it seems to me, someone angered by something. His head and torso twist toward and away from his hostess. His body bangs backward into the expensive seating, he can barely control his long arms. It might be odder if his eyes didn't burn so, if he didn't express such intensity, such discomfort, like something caught, straining at its chains, then remembering its training and tricks. When he speaks to me, the arrogance, posing, suddenly yield, and then rise again as I offer to join his game. We perform a duet of mutual self-distinction from this group, an intricate and imbecilic dance of denouncement. "Everyone knows opera is just a form of necrophilia." "Of course, it's all mortuary stuff: ballet, the novel, the easel painting." "Symphonies, plays, poetry." We are high on the suppressed outrage of the other guests, and courting each other publicly, the content of the wooing ironic given the way we were to live later, but it didn't matter, it was all Oxford bird talk: "Pa, pa, pa, pa . . . papagena. Pa, pa, pa, pa . . . papageno." We delight ourselves at least, and though we stand with as much attention and respect through the opera as everyone else, we are privately pleased that we have pulled down the red drapes, or so we think, around us.

Edward knows I am "engaged" to Hugh. "Everyone" knows this, and at first our courtship proceeds along the lines of our first meeting. We talk books, and tastes. He comes to my room accompanied by volumes of verse, chats films and takes tea. Everyone knows everything at Oxford and everyone has some reputation for charm or brilliance or bad behavior. I am tritely still the foreigner (despite my English vowels), the rebel, exotic and so on. He is the brilliant Etonian, an Eng. Lit. Scholar destined to get a Brilliant First. He is so tightly wound, his brilliance, sensitivity, nearly strangle him. His body twists against his clothes, chairs, walls, space. Silent when a stranger is present, in groups as brooding and dark as any malcontent, he is alarming and touching in turns, impossibly thin, with burning eyes and black, black hair that flops across his pale brow. To me he is poet, awkward adolescent, brilliant talker and catatonic all at once. When he tries to kiss me it is as though his life depends upon it. His urgency, his ferocious neediness, his explosive presence, draw me to him. I am no longer interested in the premise of book chat, it's the starvation I respond to. Edward was the given (and relinquished and taken away) of my life for so long that it's surprising to remember how young he was then, how unknown and amazing to me, and how I fell in love with him, the newness we had for each other, the intoxication of it, before we lived it out.

How he dressed then, long, long before the Armani. He had an ancient blue-black military jacket which he wore all the time in that era of Sergeant Pepper and which gave him a romantic aura, set off his pale skin, black eyes and hair, hinted at future death in battle, broadened his shoulders and flattered his tall, slender frame. He had very few other clothes, in fact, and his apparent pennilessness added to the sense I had of the poetic nature of his universe, its unworldiness and virtue. Add to this the peculiar odor, strong but not unpleasant, which I'd come to associate with

Etonians (the smell of infrequently washed adolescents in formal clothes), and that bare modern college room with the two beautiful blue china plates and the seventeenth-century leather books, but nothing else. How all that told who he was, what his priorities were. How the way he moved, the checked speed and intensity, the hectic flushes and the sudden gestures expressed him: rapt, feverish, intellectual, nothing vulgar, nothing shabby (except, of course, the clothes, threadbare, spartan and redolent, among other things, of virtue). He was also very beautiful, Edward, for all his strangeness and awkwardness of movement, and there was a wonderful purity, even prettiness, to his face in repose or in photographs.

I am the first girl he's made love to. In the great traditions of his class, what he knows so far are the expensively procured abuses of public school, the brute assault of the elders. The idealization (and fear) of the off-limits female world outside. It is strange that now I am the one who knows what to do. Despite the irony, I am aware that it is Hugh's gift I pass on: sex undivorced from love. This is the way the chain works, the recycling of love. Duncan gave me nothing I could hand on, only something I had to unlearn, but Hugh, restoring me, lets me (even in betrayal) restore another. Hugh gives to Edward the way, one day, Edward will give to someone else: this is the lover's ecosystem, red in tooth and claw.

Slowly, that summer term, Edward uncoiled with me, toward me, grew safer, grew sociable, and slowly I uncoiled from the frozen postures of my long-distance perfect love. I stopped feeling guilty once it was happening for real, and Hugh became more of an abstraction. I didn't make comparisons either, because I was lost again in the present. There was no third person when Edward and I went to bed (in fact, there has never been such a phenomenon ever again), but there was passion that was first simply Edward's rapaciousness and my willingness to feed it. And if, leaving Hugh, I fell from grace, the fall did not then seem so terrible.

"Never trade something wonderful, that makes you happy, for something you *think* might be better," Mommy says to me on the phone about all of this. But it was too late, the trade was made:

160

the foreign-dwelling, erratically reappearing lover for one here on the ground, right in front of me, in the flesh. And the trade seemed a good one until the remanifestation in wounded, sobbing flesh of the first, suddenly not-so-phantom lover.

I had never seen a grown man cry like that. He kept crumpling, holding his solar plexus, doubling over as though he'd been shot. The tears seemed to come from this part, the chest wound, surge through the throat and spill from whatever access Hugh gave them—his eyes when they opened between clenches, from his nostrils, from his mouth. He was swollen in grief, turning, tossing like a hospital patient coming to consciousness after surgery. He was oblivious of me, the ostensible cause of his suffering. I tried to hold the flailing parts of him, take his hand when it came out of the fist shapes, stopped pushing against the bed, tried to hold him still with my body where his torso was buckling and writhing, tried to throw myself over him like a widow over a coffin. I should have been wailing and keening, but I had no role to play in this, the legitimate grief was all Hugh's and I had caused it.

From time to time a kind of self-consciousness would return to him, and he'd push himself up in the bed, wipe his nose and eyes with his sleeve or handkerchief or the roll of toilet paper I held out for him, sitting with the roll on my knees like a bedside visitor (miming helpfulness, goodwill) with a lapful of grapes. Then he'd look at me for a second through the blur, laugh Britishly at himself and his excesses, but, dwelling a moment too long on his audience, realize what he was looking at and begin to crumple again. And I, distraught both by his distress and by my utter uselessness to alleviate it, saw with awful clarity that I could never again be the comfort or ally to Hugh that I needed to be, but, instead, the thing he must now get over, eradicate from his life. He felt cheated, moreover, because he'd been willingly paying out for what he believed he would get, enduring months of drabness in Bonn, months of teaching in German, months of lonely nights relieved only by occasional visits and letters to and from that single radiance in his universe, that far-off brightness that was eternal or it was nothing. Months of saving and enduring the poverty of existence, the dark, the bad, in assurance of soon enough enjoying the prosperity, the wealth, of our being together. And I had swindled him, bankrupted our joint holdings. I was criminal on all grounds, not only grievous bodily harm but embezzlement, theft, fraud.

Suddenly I didn't want Edward any longer. I wanted my innocence back. I was sickened by the sight of Hugh's pain and by my role in it. I felt physically sick, and so, needing to undo what I had done, to go back to the before when Hugh trusted, loved and counted on me and when he was all that I needed, I begged him to let me come back, as though I could rearrange all this in some abstract world in which Hugh could agree to forget and Edward would feel nothing of this second betrayal.

"You will just go from one affair to another, destroying people," Hugh said to me at one point between tears. It seemed more than a prediction or a reasonable guess; it seemed a life sentence, a kind of curse. It was a bleak and lonely rather than a romantic image, and I certainly didn't know then enough to contradict him.

At the end of that weekend, Hugh presented himself at his enemy's rooms in the tradition of the Oxford duel. He was fiercely angry, but his challenge was simple—and, on the face of it, compassionate. "Do you love her?" and Edward said, perhaps because he would have felt foolish and unmanly saying anything else (but mainly foolish, since how could he have caused so much upheaval unless there were this reason): "Yes," with a little counter-response of anger, indignation, whatever the wronging party needs to accept the confrontation. Then they spoke in shorter and faster phrases, the angers rising and subsiding, the tears welling again, until Hugh broke from the conference and ran, leaving Edward to look at the open doorway and perhaps wonder what he had got himself into and whether he'd really meant what he said.

We were stuck with each other now, as though conspirators in a murder, as though we had come together over Hugh's stricken body. Having caused so much pain, it seemed we had to justify it, do it for real now, learn how to love one another, and, in our last year at university, learn how to live together. There was a flurry of nest building in the last terms before final exams, a kind of battening down for the final conflagration, with people coupling like storm-crazed rodents all around us. For our final year we were allowed to live out of college. I took an ostensible share in a tutor-supervised house with Marianne. In reality, Edward and I planned to cohabit in his new "digs."

We fell into domesticity fairly easily. We had the same simple and impossible desires, work and love; the same studies to pursue; even now the same tutor, as I had been allowed—as a concession to the liberality of the times, or perhaps because Miss Hope liked me as little as I liked her—to go out of college for my English tutor, even to have a male tutor, at that time an unheard-of request but one which soon became routine, particularly at my college, once the wall was breached.

Now, instead of disapproving glances and an occasional communal glass of sherry, I was treated to neat malt whiskey at noon, inquiries into the progress of my emotional/sexual life and a level of exchange on Eng. Lit. subjects I had previously heard about only from luckier, invariably male, undergraduates. While I'd been trembling on the brink of dismissal the previous year I was in no position to question anything that emanated from the heart and mind of my elderly tutor, but since then it seemed a terrible waste to have to listen to it. I think the last indignity was Miss Hope's insistence that Marlowe's passionate description of certain relationships between men was an expression of his orthodox Christian views on brotherly love (the play *Edward II* and his own reputation notwithstanding). Indeed, all of English literature seemed to Miss Hope to express something of her own interest in theology, her own uprightness and right thinking, and she was intolerant of any divergence from her views. With David, on the other hand, there was almost no opinion, however nonsensical, that wasn't tolerated, at least for long enough for it to be delivered. But it wasn't just this, nor his charm and eccentricity, his sometimes slovenly, sometimes stunning intelligence, that made him so attractive a tutor; it was the utterly unfamiliar sensation one got, as a student, of his respect for, or at least well-performed interest in, what one thought. He agreed to take me on, he said (though he did tend to say such things), because he thought I might get a First (an incentive for him in that prize-collecting institution), just as Miss Hope's assumption I would fail was incentive for her to let me go.

David's optimism was an encouragement all by itself, but it was Edward who taught me in that final year how to work, what it looked like and involved. For the past two years I had got through on instinct and luck, finding time to work when the demands of my emotional life allowed. It would have confirmed my father's worst misogynist views to know how much Oxford had been virtually undistractably about love for me—being in it, dealing with its varying tempos, waiting for its resumption, keeping it warm, putting it on ice, breaking it off, replanting elsewhere. It had been full-time work, and that had seemed to me entirely as it should be. Furthermore, those texts I read with similarly erratic passion appeared merely to confirm this view of a universe in which love and its pains were the noble center: Shakespeare, seventeenth-century poetry, nineteenth-century poetry, the Novel, were as love-centered as the rock and roll that filled every crack of silence in that era. Literature shared my perspective and priorities, I would have said; it disdained most other things (a little religion, a little history, a little nature excepted) as insignificant or, worse, as the blind or venal concerns of the uninitiated.

With Edward this center didn't change, but the peripheries got bigger, and the universe. There was, in addition to loving, thinking: reading, ideas, discussion. In the past book talk had been largely a form of play. I was often, it seems now to me, a maddening partner in conversation, willful, ignorant, overpassionate. Now I began to learn to ask questions to which I was interested in the answers. And if Edward did not exactly make me an intellectual, he did at least give the term some distinction for me, and reality.

We worked together not only in the damp room of the millhouse where we lived (and where dead water rats sometimes floated past the kitchen window when the river was high, and the smell and stains of must sank into every book, paper and item of clothing brought there) but at Lavender House, his parents' farmhouse in the nearby countryside, to which we were allowed to go, often with

other friends, on weekends when they were not using it themselves.

Unlike Hugh, Edward did not come attached to a family—at
least not to anything resembling the golden circle of Grunwalds.
Much more familiarly to me, he had sprung from two separate (and
separate remaining, though cohabiting) entities; and these even
more familiarly the archetypes of my own parents: pretty, insecure
Female, tyrannical, raging Male.

I had met Edward's mother and father the previous summer,
separately, and they existed that way, as opposing forces in his
life. In London they lived in a formal, elegantly appointed flat
near Hyde Park. His mother gave us lunch there one afternoon,
and she moved around the rooms almost as tentatively as I did.
She was a Frenchwoman, a strikingly beautiful, tall slender blonde,
speaking in heavy accent the conventional, inane diction of the
Kensington upper middle class. It always seemed a kind of camouflage (or so I recognized it), this manner and speech of her adopted
country, learned in terror and performed without much confidence
or conviction. She was equally terrorized, it seemed, by her
husband, timid, halting whenever his name came up, deeply
apologetic about herself in relation to him, particularly whenever
she had to ask her son for money because her accounts were out of
order, responding to disappointment with a gesture which expressed the perennial conflict of her existence, a simultaneous
wringing of the hands and a gay, dismissive "Oh, don't worry, it
couldn't matter less."

Simone's timidity became less strange once I met Edward's
father, or rather stood waiting to be introduced, about ten feet
from where he'd opened the door to his son and now stood shouting
in the worst language I'd heard one member of a family ever use
to another. His rage was uncontrolled, and seemingly about nothing, and not even the presence of a stranger seemed to affect it. It
had been going on like that, Edward said, once we were away from
it, for the past six months. There had been trouble at the City firm
where Roger worked, he was under stress, and recently there had
been heart problems. At the moment, and for the past year, most
of the fury had been aimed at Edward, or, as Edward put it, they

were "getting along badly." In the beginning they had had a close and affectionate relationship, if a little confusing (the doting father, the chilly husband), until a few years ago, when the course of his son's life seemed to turn away from where Roger wished it to be heading.

He was vicious about all the intellectual, poetic side of his son's makeup. He wanted Edward to succeed as a man in a man's world, which to him was the world of the City and the family firm. It was his obsession, fueled of course by his own struggles there; his son's apparent indifference to the sources from which he and his mother drew their sustenance infuriated him, smacked of ingratitude and condescension. He wasn't above calling Edward a "pansy" because he had become irredeemably intellectual. Edward fought back as best he could with the unfair ground rules (remember his heart), and they saw each other as infrequently as possible.

In the middle of October we sent our invitations for a large Halloween dinner. It was our first joint party, a kind of declaration of cohabitation. It was to be elaborate and ghoulishly camp. There would be ghostly music and ghost stories, funereal food: a side of venison to be cooked in the doll-sized Baby-Belling oven, leeks, black plum pudding, port, everything as lugubrious as we could make it, the guests of course to come in black. We decorated our basement like a Victorian funeral parlor, with crepe curtains and Dickensian wreaths, black candles and cloth, most of which was in place when the telegram came summoning Edward home. Roger had had a heart attack, had collapsed on a City street and was dead, at fifty-seven.

We didn't cancel the party. Edward sat at the head of the black table in the dim lighting, eating the awful food, being "good about it," gazing down at the forty guests in black, hearing the ghostly music and the chatter, passing the Stilton and the port, until politely he excused himself and fainted in another room.

Roger's death brought us closer. I was able to help, to listen, to let him cry, rage, get through some of the long "work" of grieving, to help him return to his friends and studies and life. It was the first time I felt that he needed me and that I was able to give him what he needed. But it also changed our lives. Because months later, when Ned and I were working toward finals, spending a lot of time at Lavender House in the frozen landscape of the Oxfordshire countryside, cooking for each other, reading, going to bed, working hard in isolation and seeing friends on weekends, settling into something calmer, solid, good, Ned heard the terms of Roger's legacy. The last gesture of this angry, disappointed man (whom, of course, Ned imagined he had killed) was to leave his only son, entirely unexpectedly, an astonishingly large fortune.

Suddenly everyone, one by one, turned twenty-one. There were parties, and parties after parties, croquet at dawn following a ball, all of us barefoot in dew-sodden grass, death-pale in long dresses and black evening clothes. There was work and exams, and after exams more parties. It was 1969, we knew now it was the sixties, and there were drugs and rock and roll, even at Oxford, mixing with the May dawn choirs at Magdalen, mixing with the seemingly picnics in punts, from which we swam, fully clothed, climbed the banks in muddied clothes, walked wet-draped into outdoor gardens of pubs to drink, and warm up, and show off. There were anarchists and hippies, Etonians in long silk scarves, a maharaja in blue satin culottes and silver buttons, there were women with month-old kohl on their eyes and whitened lips: the style of consumptive decadence which on the young and healthy looked so good. There were balls and wanderings with champagne bottles through courtyard and cloisters, stockings ripped from dancing, makeup melted and lips swollen from kissing; weeks of dawns with the music still playing and the smell of breakfasts: kedgeree, grease, eggs, bacon, tobacco, and always, always champagne. Everyone danced and drank and made love and stayed up late that May and June, and there was never enough of it. Ned and I danced, alone, waltzing on the flower-banked lawn at Lavender House to the tinny sweeps of Strauss, played on a gramophone set out on a bench; or in company, the heady, end-of-term, already nostalgic company of endless familiar faces of strangers and friends who had shared with us three years in Arcadia.

Everyone was going, leaving for the summer, to begin their lives. Ned and I were heading for New York after the summer, after a six-week trip through Europe (with my father's final grudging permission: "You are twenty-one, after all, you can do what you like").

So we went, with Wilson's fifty-pound travel allowance each, some petrol coupons and a very few addresses where we could spend the night. It was a terrible trip, sleeping upright many nights in the Spitfire, on highway lay-bys, or on rained-upon beaches and in dog-infested gardens; and it was a wonderful trip: through France and Austria, Yugoslavia, Greece, and back (starving and dirty) through Italy, France, to England. It was to be just like that for some time, Ned and I, in a little bubble car, traveling through from place to place, taking in pictures, scenery, music, restaurants, beaches and traffic jams, just him and me, twelve inches from one another in an expensive but hellishly uncomfortable vehicle, speaking in our private language, laughing in it, fighting in it, going silent, sulky, ready to kill in it, making up and going on, with all the bright world going by, just outside our window.

SEVEN

I DIDN'T KNOW what I wanted to do. I didn't know what I wanted to do with my life or whether I was going to live it with someone (usually Ned). These two questions of what you did and how many of you you were were very much connected, only I had no idea of that then. You say I should have; all decent girls in the early seventies knew these things were the same. But I wasn't taking part in history, I was my own zeit, geisted by the shark life of survival and chomping, as I say, fresh from Oxford with its cockaded hats and champagne corks, about as much a part of history as a window of chocolate squirrels (a few revelers had been made aware of the events of May when they'd strayed into Paris for ill-timed dirty weekends, that was about it), and by my ur-history with Bett and Constance, Gogi and Shrimp: the good girl and bad girl stuff; the will-come-to-no-good loners and the will-come-to-no-good players by the rules. And what were the rules? As Harriet said when she explained why the small Oxford allowance was going to come to a sudden end, "You must take your fortune from the man you're with, that is what women do."

So I was on my own, having to find my fortune by my unreliable wits, or, since I was a girl, by my looks. It was the man who found his way by his brain, thus the theory went, and the woman who found the brainy man by her face and body: Monroe and Miller were the prototype in my father's notion of things. I said I thought I'd go to New York for a while, try and use my own brain for my own fortune, leave gender, sexuality, etc., for the nonworking life. So I said, and went off to New York, and was rather surprised to find that these things were not so easily separated, in the world out there, as they ought to have been.

I had known there was a connection between jobs and sex at least since I was fifteen and asking for an after-school job assisting in a candy shop. I had watched the elderly proprietor shift from his "I doubt you'll be very useful" gaze, his suspicious and Germanic fussiness as I gift-wrapped a box of pistachios for his approval, to a kind of kindliness, at first grandfatherly but then, melting down stickily like some of his own confections, he had let his shoulders drop, given me a saliva-shiny half-smile and, shielding the unpleasant bulge in his over-ironed and likewise shiny trousers, stood next to me to "help" me wrap my package. By the time the last bright string was snipped, the kindly man had offered me not only the after-school job but, from what I could hear through all the catarrh and euphemism, a monthly income if I would stay with him in his little flat above the shop. I fled from behind the counter, knocking the gold-papered box of pistachios all over the floor, half returning to pick them up, but catching sight of his face as it resumed its scowl of displeasure and world-weariness, had fled again, to relate the incident at first in alarm and then in pretended hilarity to my worldly aunt Constance who lived two blocks away.

Thus when Peter Van Strum, after a clearly wolfish appraisal, offered me my first post-Oxford job as publicity director of his publishing business, Merlin Books in Washington Square (actually telephone sales of the backlist in a two-person office is what it turned out to be), and furthermore said that I could sleep on the studio bed in the back room until I found a place to live, I accepted on condition, as I informed him quite primly, and much to his gallant German horror, that I didn't "have to sleep with him." It was a terrible discourtesy, because Peter, as I came to know him, was indiscriminately flirtatious and far too good-hearted to take advantage of anyone.

I stayed with Merlin for six months, and then got my first "real" job, as a copy editor at Caxton's on Madison Avenue. It was an old-fashioned operation where the girls, under control of a very head-mistressy manager, were separated from the young men, not just by the interior design of the offices (we sat in hen coopage away from the real and manly affairs of the place) but by our activity, which was checking and tidying (grammatical housekeeping) the manuscripts that the young warriors had been out in the world either hunting down, if they were editors, or trading for wampum if they were reps.

It was all very ladylike and genteel. I quite like the segregation since I didn't have to deal with sex on the job, and I liked the work, not for the fastidiousness involved but because I liked sentences and grammar and all that, just as I liked crossword puzzles, and because the laborious readings through what were basically graduate school texts were a form of further education for me, which I could otherwise not afford. I read and "corrected," and therefore had really to take in, books on history, philosophy, literature. It was easy and absorbing and paid the rent. I had no ambitions to move up through the publishing ranks as an editor. I was appalled by the self-deforming behavior and appearance of New York career girls in those days, all in rip-off Chanel, overbuttoned, zipped in in bust-disguising suits, clipping around busily on little heels, bright and willing as terriers—"On-the-go, go-ahead gals," as the magazines had it. And maybe I had some leftover team loyalties to Bett in her work days when these "gals" were the enemy in the office caste system, self-congratulatingly divided from the ones who could only type or look pretty and answer the phones like Bett. I never liked them; they had all been to the right universities, were destined to marry the right men or sit at the right desks in the right firms. There'd been no struggle, no decision, they'd sold their identities to the first buyer, or so then I used to think. For myself, though I, too, had been to a "right" university, it didn't make much difference outside England, and though I was always privileged *there* because of my accent, my background, my degree, over here none of that signified. Applying for jobs, I'd always had to specify which Oxford I'd gone to. Even here, the woman in personnel had hesitated when I told her. "Not Mississippi," I said, and she nodded.

Ned, on the other hand, had been horrified by the style of New York democracy. After all, he'd been factory-raised at Eton and Oxford, won scholarships, English and history prizes since he was fourteen, got his Brilliant First last summer, and was primed, like the others in his caste, to take over the country when the moment was right. Arriving in New York in October, he'd been baffled by how little any of this counted. It was humiliating for him to be supported by me and depressing to do the only kind of work he could get: things like wrapping books in the basement of Doubleday's bookshop, getting shouted at, intimidated and, often enough, fired. Not surprisingly, he left in November, having decided to go back to England a while, and thing again.

By that time I was also writing little reviews for an art magazine. During one of my periods of nonwork, I called various magazines in whose texts I thought I was interested, and asked if they needed proofreading. At *Tempera* I was told that what they really needed were reviewers. The editor assured me that it didn't matter that I knew nothing about art, because no one else who wrote at that level did either; what was important was to be coherent. I had been doing this a few months, writing complete nonsense of the sort that can be read in any arts magazine today (the "short" reviewers are paid almost nothing and therefore tend to come from the ranks of the abusable, idealistic and unsulliedly ignorant young), when I was given my own column, a kind of roundup of interesting shows.

When Ned left we made an agreement that we would separate for six months and then see how we felt. I found I was very happy, even exhilarated, managing on my own. It wasn't a thing I automatically thought I could do. I liked my crummy studio on West Seventy-fifth Street, liked the galleries and the artists, even for a while liked my work at Caxton's and the little printed checks with the taxes removed that went into a bank and paid for what I needed. I liked waking up mostly alone, looking out of the window at the day that was entirely mine. I liked all this even more when I stopped working at Caxton's around Christmas and began to edit freelance for them. I had saved enough out of my small salary to finance myself in spartan fashion for a few months, writing my art pieces, copy-editing intermittently, eking out the time. I loved New York, walking miles in it at all hours of the day and late at night. I loved being around Bett, pretending again that we were "sisters," both living hand to mouth in a tough town. But I also felt lonely at times, and missed Ned, my Oxford friends, that life.

I wanted both here and there, and as ever had to keep moving not to feel homesick for one place or the other. I borrowed money and hocked what I could, but it was becoming clear that I'd have to have another full-time job if I wanted to stay anywhere.

And so it started again. I didn't know what I wanted. I didn't know if I wanted to live with Ned or live alone. To be or not to be two. Ned tried very hard to understand my indecisiveness. He tried very hard to understand what the exhilaration of living alone in New York had been like. But in the end, there was only one question and answer that mattered to him. "Do you love me or not?" Of course, I said. Well, then.

Actually, Ned and I did have our own third person eventually— call it, for brevity's sake, the Money. It was all right (except that it wasn't) while we were jammed up against one another going through Europe sleeping in the Spitfire. It was all right (except that it mostly wasn't) while we both were pretty poor—but then the Money appeared and made an awful lot of difference, both good and bad.

At first there was the sheer exhilaration of it. Ned bought a flat, at what seemed a modest enough price, though it was big and on two floors and backed onto a huge communal garden. We each had a separate work space, and there was one enormous room on the first floor. This one big room was to be a constant wherever we lived, and wherever I lived when I lived alone. To furnish the flat, we had some of Ned's parents' antiques from the recently sold country house, but we had to buy the rest—and suddenly buying became our occupation. After two years of living with no possessions and on little margin we were apparently free to have whatever we wanted. For a while all we did was choose and acquire: the best wool stair carpets, the most chic wallpaper, the prettiest Italian sofas and lamps, cushions and Persian carpets, decanters, corkscrews, soaps, books, mirrors and paintings. We could eat wherever we wanted and wear whatever took our fancy. When we were bored we would go shopping; it seemed full of purpose, and somehow blameless. I remember going to Barclays in Kensington and taking out the then serious sum of four hundred pounds, splitting the bills and putting the wads of twenty-pound notes in the back pockets of our jeans, getting a cab to World's End to begin our walk down the King's Road, proceeding together in and out of every shop: clothing, antique, designer furniture; using cash, checks and bank cards until there was nothing more we wanted, and we went home expended, desireless, spent. Mostly we were reasonable, we were not excessive, we thought, yet the freedom from constraint, the sensuality of days given over to spending, was excess itself.

And the flat filled up and was very beautiful; we had parties and dinners and only gradually noticed (we weren't stupid, we imagined we were being open, unsecretive, simple about it) that all this, enjoy our company and hospitality though they did, made us different, separated us, pulled us apart from our friends. Everyone was starting out; many had rich parents or private incomes, owned property and beautiful objects, but no one we knew then lived as we did. (Later, much later, many of them did, but in those days none.) And the fact that we could and did and seemed unashamed made us outcasts of a sort, islanded us and threw us more than ever upon our own companionship, enclosed us in our own cluttered, pretty world.

Ned's shame about the money was not long coming; we became uncomfortable in the beautiful flat and, once it was completely finished, edgy, constrained, confronted with ourselves and the weakness in the ties between us. The solution to all of these problems was to move, which again (and again and again) the money made possible. There was a way of having and using money that was acceptable, and we learned how to do it. We got rid of the beautiful flat and moved to run-down places that needed far more cash spending on them, but where our friends lived and likewise spent invisible cash. Within five years many of these friends had bought and sold their way up to far smarter neighborhoods and far grander houses; our mistake was to have moved faster than the others, to step out of line, to appear to be different. Calling attention to ourselves in this way, a faux pas we made in utter innocence, we committed the sin of ostentation, in England among the least forgivable.

There was not only social pressure to hide the money; there was for Ned, but reinforced by the subtle external censure, a private response. The lucre was filthy to him not only in the usual way of inherited wealth—because it violated a puritan need to earn what you have—but in this case because the message of the bequest had been mixed. After all, Roger's last words to his son had been curses, and it was hard to separate the cash from the anger. Add to that Roger's constant undermining of his son's intellectual gifts, his pressure on him to be something manly and real (like a stockbroker), and the gift, which might have financed his talents as a writer, for example, seemed unusable in endeavors which the donor loathed.

So Ned, suddenly independently wealthy, had now to go off and find manly work. Pretending that he'd never got his Brilliant First or wished to write, he went from one terrible newspaper job to another. He got himself a leather jacket, started to drink beer and listen hour after hour to the macho drivel of newshounds and photographers, to their unspeakable barroom, locker-room boasts, to their fear-sopped mockery of ideas, books, "pretensions" and everything else outside their ken. So Ned hid, along with the facts of his money, degree, knowledge of art, history, languages, his own elegance and manner, and learned how to gossip about boxing (we even went to a match to listen to the disgusting, oddly muffled sound of flesh being pulped), to tolerate talk of cunts and bimbos, wogs, yids, dagos, to write columns about old-age pensioners in collapsing housing estates and prize cabbage growers. And then, when he came home, still wearing his leather jacket and speaking the new weird language, he would sit in a dark corner of the beautiful apartment, hunched and malevolent, drinking beer and eating crisps and watching TV.

I had this problem with the Money, too, because once the fun of walking around London buying things was over, which was pretty soon, you had actually to live like that, and then by what right live like that? (I was puritanical, too.) If I lived here, was it different in kind from the way I'd lived with Ned in Oxford, simply because it was different in style and luxury? Was I suddenly now a Kept Woman? After a few months in London I got a job and could

have kept myself, but certainly never on the scale on which Ned
and I were living. I would never be able to earn enough to pay my
way with him where we were. So what was the solution? Should he
come and live with me in whatever furnished room I could afford?
Or should I just forget about it, as he said, and continue to live
with him and like it? I did the latter for a while and then, under
pressure of this inequality, as well as all the other pressures of
cohabitation, all the conflicts of two people creating their separate
identities in front of one another—of Ned figuring out manhood in
his father's terms, his terms, me figuring out womanhood in my
half-baked way (whether I'd get there faster living alone or with
Ned, whether I held to Bett's view, or Gogi's view, or Harriet's
view, or made up one all by myself)—I moved out in the first of a
series of partings and returns that was to make us, as Marianne
called it, "the longest-running show" in London, a hoary old
Mousetrap of an entertainment.

I didn't want to marry him. I thought I didn't believe in marriage
(I'd only just agreed to cook), and I certainly didn't believe in
marriage until everyone was a bit more settled. At the moment,
the only thing settled about us was our home, and that felt to both
of us too settled, a stage set of stability within which we wobbled
and careened and crashed.

I wanted to feel again the exhilaration of living alone and taking
care of myself that I had felt in New York. We agreed to a trial
separation—all our separations were "trials," unlike our returns,
which were full of commitment and final intentions despite the
increasing weight of our history. I took a place near Ned's flat, in
Powis Square, then the center of black power activism in London,
a small, tentatively gentrified hovel, but mine own. Ned lent me
some furniture and we continued to see each other intermittently.
It was all friendly and civilized.

I had a job then, and a suitor, a gallery owner I had met at a
party given by the publishing company I worked at four days a
week (the other three days I kept up with the art journalism and
the illusion of a freelance working life), and whom I found early
on, in the first throes of his ardor, ridiculous. Then, I wouldn't

sleep with him, but once Ned and I were separated he wouldn't sleep with me. His courtship was fantastical, self-parodic, as mannered as his Rupert Brooke-style looks and poses. He would say such things as "Ah"—gazing at me—"in this light I could wish I were a painter," or "Have you any idea, dear girl, what heartbreak you promise me?" and so on, all this heavy wooing of his undiminished by his clear and consistent reluctance to do anything about it once I was free to cooperate. Because of this novel divide between speech and intention, it took me the longest, unpleasantest time to understand that love was a simpleminded sport to him, involving seduction and abandonment without any intervening consummation, nor any loss of pleasure in the game through repetition. Again and again and again, so that now I really do wonder at myself, he would invite me to dinner, arrive at my flat three hours late, so that all the restaurants would be closed and all my bright looks and careful dress and makeup faded, greet me with a complex two-step of apologies and refusals to apologize, before settling down for a couple of hours of last-minute paperwork (thanking me for coffee, complaining about the desk light, waving with a regal hand), eventually sending me to bed and joining me there for a few minutes of heartfelt ruffling before sinking into his blameless rest, a rest in which I was never able to join him.

Or, after a series of broken dates, he would promise, cut off his right arm if he failed, to call for me at seven-thirty prompt with the restaurant booked or the theater tickets bought—and I would be waiting at eight, at nine, at ten, in and out of the bathroom at quarter-hour intervals to check the hair, the mascara, the expression of reproachless gaiety, while leaving the door open to hear the phone. But there would never be any phone, just a silence, a hushed house in which I performed these acrobatics of hope and distress along a wire of nerves, until even that line slackened, and I would droop, swear, resolve never again, until the doorbell rang at eleven-fifteen, when I would spin, let my heart leap and thump, receive my embrace and his declarations of mortification and crisis, wait till he made "just the quickest phone call to an Artist"—a word always capitalized for him, and capitalized upon. "Go to bed," he would say eventually, "I won't be long." And so I would—trapped in my flat, in his game, in my naïveté—take off the elaborately chosen clothes and lie under the sheets until the lord and master came to embrace me again, both of us naked now, silent, ardent, when he would suddenly sigh: "My darling girl, if you only knew what a day I've had, how tired I am," and the great, busy man would turn, and let me listen for the rest of the night to the sound of him sleeping.

Once, years later, I did demand from him some explanation, when he was an even greater, busier and yet no less flirtatious man. And he said, "Ah, how you broke my heart." "Broke your heart?" I said. "You wouldn't ever sleep with me." And he squirmed and looked askance and held his head at an angle. "Ah, can't you guess, didn't you know?" No. "It was because I never wished to sully or defile; because I always held you in such high, the highest regard."

And yet it went on—how long? long enough—while he talked of passion, even once of marriage. He would phone me at work, using his boss's voice, declare love, woo me again, flirt, break down my resistance to him: tall, fair, tormented, always suffering so for his passion, which his work, his duties, his love of his Artists prevented him from indulging.

He invited me to spend the weekend with him. The whole weekend, he promised, no catalogues, no phone calls, no work. I went, of course. How could he be hours late for dinner in his own house? The first night he showed me to a separate room. His cousin was there, he said, though he'd be gone in the morning. In the morning, they were both gone. A little note taped to the refirgerator told me where to find coffee and that he would be back from the annual village cricket match by six. At eight, accompanied by fellow players, he was back. We all went out to dinner to hear, play by play, the afternoon's adventures, and we all came home and talked more cricket until the hero, all expended, bade me sleep well and separately.

In the morning, another note on the refrigerator: another match, a promise of dinner to be made together and eaten alone. That evening I cooked the meal myself while he took his bath. I coaxed myself among the pots and pans: don't be peevish, angry, *ordinary;* wait and watch; you're younger, you don't know.

Heated by his bath, in his Errol Flynn dressing gown, he ate with me. He was infinitely grateful, ardently apologetic for my dull weekend, warmly affectionate, feeding himself with my hand in his, his eyes deep and searching, convincing me finally that we were together now, absolutely alone. After dinner he rose (he never got up, he always *rose*—tall, blond, purposeful) and went into the sitting room to put some music on. Would I be an absolute angel and bring the coffee? Ah yes, black coffee, to revive him, certainly. And fifteen minutes later, bearing the silver tray, the clean little sugar cubes embowled, the silver prongs laid out, the demitasses, the spoons and cream remembered, I entered the room and saw him on the floor, stretched out before me, silk-robe-wrapped, thick, fair hair catching the firelight, warm, contented, deep asleep. I did look to make sure his feet were covered by the leather slippers before I did it, but I did do it, set the tray down on the ottoman, waited for him to stir, waited another thirty seconds before I lifted the silver coffee pot and poured black coffee along its long fluted spout, down through the air and onto his feet. Then he rose again, very fast, checked himself lest he actually strike me, dropped his arms and, with that familiar, versatile sigh of his, said he would take me at once to catch the last train home.

Meanwhile Ned had retreated further north to Islington, where I, fresh from my own humiliations, joined him, to begin again, in humbler spirit, the familiar trek to wallpaper and carpet shops, with nothing settled between us but our separate failures in the world outside.

I loathed Islington. We weren't living in any of the grandly gloomy Georgian squares, the black, clerical-looking dwellings which had a Dickensian/Piranesian elegance, particularly in the fogs of winter, but on a street of unloved, would-be genteel suburban houses, with a kind of sour-breathed Gissing hopelessness to them and an ugly girl's big-boned, pathetic plainness. Even the street sloped hopelessly, drastically downward, toward the Caledonian Road with its self-apologetic shops which had nothing desirable to offer, barely anything edible, usable, where shoppers moved sluggishly, furtively, in and out, unwilling to linger much beyond the exchange of hypochondriacal niceties, where even the Cypriot Greek restaurant owners stared out mournfully from behind the orange rolls of slow-spinning rancid meat into the damp and yellow streets, where on Saturday nights the Guinness-dark pubs were full of black-bereted IRA supporters, and where on Sunday afternoons you would see their wives, sporting morning-after bruises under bad makeup, dragging their likewise battered kids, whining, slapped, runny-nosed, behind.

Into this setting we had come, two among many of the privileged young of the early seventies. Everywhere around us were the sounds of houses being hammered, refurbished. You'd stare into lit windows in the evenings and see, next to the shut-up, privacy-hoarding basements of the natives, the new neighbors' stripped-pine kitchens, with their bright, contemporary settings and nursery-colored crockery, their copper pots and fashionable cook-books, their ferns and miniskirted nannies, their clean and pro-gressively schooled children, their denimed husbands and wine-bearing dinner guests. I disliked the invasion by Habitat. I hated the insistent cheerfulness of it. Probably, by then, I loathed the little rustle of self-improvement that accompanied the real estate frenzy of the seventies, all the buying and selling and bettering—bettering one's standing, one's nest, getting rid of damp and listing, cracks and chips, covering everything with that relentless brightness of color and surface, that primary-painted totalitarian cheerfulness that seemed to be all that was left of the sixties, of the winds of change and the angry young men, of the desire for something new and different and egalitarian in England. Instead of the promised democracy, here was the anti-antiquarian look of the new, the mindlessly happy decor that slid in place over the unshiftable understructure of class and privilege. In Islington, so close to all the real poverty of the unemployed and their battered wives and kids, of the ritually bashed and abused immigrants, the delirious polished cotton and grinning lacquer seemed both heart-less and empty.

And inside the brightly lit kitchens I hated the dinner-party games, the competition over cooking and glassware and guests, hated the dinner-party chat, about real estate and nursery schools, or, just as bad, about politics, Labour Party strategies, as though it were some fun new board game with plastic chips and players, unreal miles away from the surrounding misery. Life in Islington seemed disconnected, dull and stifling, and, however much more politically acceptable than Kensington, no less genteel, conventional or dead.

And, of course, inside the alienation from all the nest building and Noah's-arking around us, the coupling and often enough now childbearing of our contemporaries, was my constant inability to decide on what Ned and I were up to, my wonder whether we were being swept upstream into marriage and babies without really willing it. My conflicts expressed themselves less and less in argument and more in depressions, listlessness, deadness. I used to wake up every morning in Islington and ask myself if I was going to leave or stay. To be or not to be two. Once again, among all the props of good intentions, the furnishings and improvements, inside the chalk dust of the builders, the clouds of plaster and paint fumes, was the constant question of if and when I was going. When the questioning got too insistent, or the atmosphere of doubt too unbearable for either of us, I would leave.

Why did Ned and I keep splitting up and coming back together—or, rather, since the momentum was always mine, why did I continually leave and come back? It wasn't really the circumstances, or even the Money: if I'd married him as he asked me I could have felt less "kept" (although later I did, and I didn't); nor was it my odd, erratic and undigested feminism—that was simply the way I worked it out to explain it from time to time to myself and him. It wasn't ever anything as reasonable as a reason. It was more like an illness. Whenever we were together for too long a stretch I would feel myself sicken, grow dull and listless. And then whenever I was off by myself I'd get exhilarated and recharged, but more significantly I'd feel *lifelike* again, as though I really did exist. There would be a density, a gravity to myself when by myself, which was very different from the phantom self (and not a very nice phantom at that) I became when I was too long with Ned.

Why didn't I stay apart from him? Because I loved him, because I missed him, because isolation didn't make any real sense either, and finally because I never wanted to lose him, I always wanted him there to come back to, wanted the possibility kept alive that we might one day succeed. My little forays away were really no braver than the first running steps of a baby away from its mother, the head anxiously turning back in her direction. And maybe mother/baby in this case is the right image: maybe mixed into my depressions when I stayed with Ned too long was the horror of entrapment that came right out of my long-since-fled life with Bett, and the coming and going, happiness and depression, were like being and not being with her when I was at Mirrenwood, being and not being with Hugh at Oxford. Only, bafflingly, it was when I was *with* Ned that I felt the melancholy, and when I was without him (as long as he was safely out there somewhere) that I felt complete. What I missed, mourned, when we were together too long, and what was restored to me when we were apart, was, oddly enough, a sense of myself.

So I would leave, and never stay away very long, just long enough to create for both of us the drama of parting and return, the seasickness that was for me for so long a condition of love. It had to be resolved (but that is what we always imagined we were doing—parting for good, returning for good, either/or, yes or no), one way or another, and finally, three years after we left Oxford, Ned made an ultimatum: I could marry him or get out.

I left. I found another large, light-filled room, this one in Hyde Park Square, and I promised myself that finally I would learn how to live alone.

For a while I was happy again, as exhilarated as I'd been on Seventy-fifth Street, earning my way and proud of my simple life. This time I had none of Ned's furniture. The place was bare but for a double bed and an old chipped hand-painted armoire left by the previous tenant. There was a stained carpet and no heating. I refused, beyond some painting, to better it, refurbish or gentrify. I liked it, exposed wires, cracked ceiling and all, just the way it was. I set up a desk by the big window and looked at the trees across the garden square. I was alive again; it was exciting and a little frightening and as it should be.

My work life had changed since the days of the romantic sadist. I had another four-day-a-week publishing job, editing books near Soho Square, a pleasant walk along the borders of Hyde Park and down Oxford Street. I still disliked the office politics: the systematic humiliations of the younger men by the older, the subtle abuses of secretaries and the accommodations and self-apologies of the unattractive girls. As before, looks and class came with unfair privileges, and everyone shuffled around that reality as best they could in order to keep their jobs. I wasn't the only one who suspected I'd been made an editor at twenty-four because the boss wanted to sleep with me (he was fairly direct about it, though easily dodged); it wasn't the whole story, but it certainly partly accounted for my relatively elevated status there, along with the apparent class background and good Oxford degree.

For the rest of the week I had, in theory, a book to write, and this, too, it seemed to me, had come about the old-fashioned way: unfairly. I had met my future publisher at an elegant party at the home of a friend of my father's. He was a "grand" publisher and a "grand" man and I was one of several "young things" with which the salon had been decorated. In such a milieu, affably, charmingly, expensive drink in hand, he had floated the suggestion that I should write for his firm a biography of Picasso, then still alive. This publisher's list was well-known for its picture-book nonfiction written by girls of socially prominent families, but even so, even to me, a biography of Picasso by an unpublished twenty-four-year-old was an odd notion. Yet why not write a book? I was not interested in the life and loves of Picasso, but I did suggest that I write about American artists in Paris at the same period. And so the agreement was made, and now, three days a week in Hyde Park Square, I sat reading and researching and looking out over the autumn-colored trees. How could I not be happy?

It began to seem that I was doing it for real this time, living without Ned. He was not lending me money or furniture, he was not having dinner with me at periodic intervals, he was not phoning to see how I was doing and he was not expecting me to phone. As far as he was concerned, I had turned down his entirely serious offer of marriage for the last time. It had been four and a half years since our meeting at Oxford, four years since we first lived together, three since New York, a year since we moved to Islington. There'd been enough time to figure it out.

He was gone for good. Perhaps it took me a while to understand this, that the mechanism of leaving and returning had changed once again, and that this time, though it was I who had departed, Ned had responded by leaving me, too. I began to hear about him out with other people, and though my own amorous dealings never seemed very serious to me, I suspected it might be different for him. I knew that he wanted to be married, that he was hurt by our failure, as well as infuriated by my indecisiveness. I began to imagine that in response to this hurt and fury and desire (strange as it was to me) to be "settled" in a marriage, and thereby to have the appearance at least of progress in one's life, Ned might run off and marry the wrong person, which in my egotism I imagined would be anybody who wasn't me. It was all right, I thought, for me to get my ideas straight on living alone, but his job was to hold still while I did so. Hearing that he was off and cheerful, I began to suspect I might really lose him.

And then the outside world—that fantastical place Ned wrote articles about—began to press in and diminish further my sense of the rightness of my decision to live alone. There was the miners' strike and the three-day week, there was darkness in the streets and a war-spirit mentality that was exhilarating at first, fun even, but which, as it went on, got increasingly ominous. I remember walking down Oxford Street in thick darkness that December, Oxford Street without Christmas lights, with the sound of Saturday shoppers trudging through, everything muffled, the crowds stumbling from one end of the trafficless street to the other, herded and massed like cattle coming home in the dark, and I remember the sudden terror of it: how the lit, predictable world had disappeared overnight and this thing that I was part of, the broken, hushed, jostling mass moving through the dark town like a bombed-out village populace on the move in retreat, this was reality. It was brutal and ugly and unforgiving, and it could not be survived alone.

So I saw Ned wobbling and the world wobbling and I was frightened. But it was Constance who delivered the final tap on the skull of my resolution. She had moved to London during my last year at Oxford, sick, she said, of New York, of the hardened faces, the inhuman stress, the pointless pursuits. After staying with various friends in the country, she had settled in London in a vast room overlooking the river. Here she had begun a weekly salon. Or at least tried. "They're not very bright here," she would say to me. "They don't understand it's meant to be *every* Thursday, they wait to be invited each time." She was now hard at work writing her first book, on an obscure Bedouin tribe in the Sahara.

I was going to have Christmas dinner with Constance, in order to avoid spending it at Sparrow House. I had had my annual present from the Lowells. As the years progressed I came increasingly to dread these Christmas offerings. They were worse than no present at all, being invariably part of some job lot that Harriet or Francis had come upon in the autumn and set aside for the large-scale distributions of December: faultlessly cheap, ugly, impersonal, and therefore barbed and redolent with terrible indifference. I remember a lurid plastic sponge bag, a cat-faced alarm clock, things they would never have had in the house for themselves, and one year, unforgettably, an obviously last-minute effort, a book without a jacket, some politician's memoirs, clearly already read by Francis, and not only read but, since the pages were gummed together, swollen and buckled, dropped during reading in the bath. I'd been preprogrammed for expectation at Christmas by Bett—by the high drama of last-minuteness, by her theatrical lead-ups, the continuous questioning of what did I want, the provision of which, interspersed with stated gloom over the unlikelihood of tree and presents, became what *she* most wanted, so that we both hung on the precipice of longing, waiting for rescue, which always came, eleventh-hour and with theatrical flourish, ending *her* terrible dreads of disappointment as much as mine.

But this was to be more or less a grown-up Christmas, just myself and Constance, who was in bed with flu. There was snow outside, and erratic light and heating (thanks to the miners' strike) within. Her instructions were to stay indoors; I would bring the meal, her present, and for myself, since Constance didn't drink, a bottle of wine. I was looking forward to it. We didn't get together that much in London. I came to her salons infrequently and had barely seen her since the previous winter. We had arranged to call Bett in New York, make ourselves into a little family for a while, have a nice enough time.

And we did have a nice enough time, until the subject of Ned came up, and how I was missing him, wasn't at all sure I'd done the right thing, how maybe I should have married him after all. Like too many people, Constance had been through these discussions often. She was always in favor of Ned and, despite her own preferred unwedded state, oddly unsympathetic, I thought, about the business of living alone, trying to become brave and all that. Whatever else Constance was, to me she was always heroic, not just because of the desert, but precisely because she did live alone, on her wits and with style. But now, this Christmas, fiercely, she told me it was beyond her to know what Ned saw in me, why he put up with me, what any of my friends saw in me. Maybe, she went on, Ned had finally come to his senses and realized what he'd been dealing with all these years. To this I listened humbly, backing away a little on the edge of the bed, but I did listen, amazed, and with a sense of revelation, so that all this ill will sounded like heroic truth. "Let me tell you, darling," she finally summed up, "if you don't marry Ned—although it's probably too late now—I doubt very much anyone is going to marry you. I can't imagine why he's such a fool, because he's really rather brilliant, but you're just damned lucky he is so besotted with you. You don't deserve him or anything half as good as him. If you don't grab him now, if it isn't already too late, before he really disappears, you're going to be alone for the rest of your life."

Heat in that unheated room. I sat stunned, believing she meant every word she said. I didn't think of her fever, or of the rage that can be let out from your own situation on and into someone else's, which may be felt at the time as love, as altruism, even if it doesn't sound like that to the hearer. I was horrified that she felt these things about me and horrified by the predicted life sentence, about being alone forever. I was burned and dissolved by these things and I fled, walked all the way to Hyde Park Square, miles through the snow, now sleeting in the late Christmas traffic headlights, my face streaming with ice and tears, further blurring the lights. I kept walking, keeping warm, keeping the heat of Constance's explosion, punishing, pushing, four miles to home. And it was all true. I deserved nothing and I was nothing, had nothing and never would. I would be *alone* forever.

When Ned got back from Paris I arranged to see him. Like a penitent at the monastery door I said I knew how awful I'd been, how I'd learned this now and could I have another chance.

"There's someone else," he said.

"Oh," I said. "Oh well."

"Well, what would be different this time?" he said.

"This time," I said, "we'd be married."

"You're proposing marriage now?"

"Yes," I said. "I know I have no other credibility."

"Let me think about it a few days," he said.

By New Year's Eve he said it was all right.

It was an elaborate and fractured wedding, befitting so elaborate and fractured a courtship. Bett and Hal came to stay in Islington (Hal kept saying, annoyingly but reasonably, how London looked like Brooklyn). Bett and I spent the night before in Hyde Park Square listening to Paul Simon's "Mother and Child Reunion," which would make me cry, while Hal and Ned and several others went out on the town, at least until the town closed around eleven.

We got married in the spring, at the Islington Registry, a very serious civil ceremony that was suddenly scary enough for my voice to falter when I said my lines. Ned's mother was there, my mother, my mother's boyfriend, but I did not invite Constance. Then all of us in our suits and hats went to the Ritz for champagne and pheasant. Bett looked at the "game chips" on her plate and said why'd they go to so much trouble to handmake what could be bought in a package; then Ned and I went for the night to Claridge's, had more champagne and sex in the black art deco double bath, and kippers and roses the next morning, and that night a huge party in Islington where Bett and Hal, but not Norfolk, were, and a lot of London, all catered for and dancing and carrying-on on four floors, with crashers and overnight corpses just like Oxford four years before. And then the next night the Norfolk party at the home of my father's publisher friend, Bett and Hal not there, but all Ned's family friends and relatives, and all mine, the Brit aunts and uncles, pleased, they said, that conventions had been followed, touched by that, they said, though within the decade they, too, would all come apart and divorce and do things they thought they'd never do. And more champagne and speeches, wedding cake, I in lace, long black, not white, Edwardian lace ("My dear," said Simone, "you look just like a Sargent"), and photographed thus, in black, my hand half hidden in the folds of my elaborate skirt, but clearly, and fixed for always, clenched in a fist against the day, or perhaps just the camera.

EIGHT

I WAS HAPPY reading Gertrude Stein and writing my book; happy walking through Hyde Park from my "office" to the Victoria & Albert Reading Room; happy to walk from Islington to the British Museum, putting in long days there, going out to smoke under the columns with all the other tobacco-stained and drizzled-on drudges and scribes; happy enough working by myself, out of offices with their sexual politics and class hatreds and games of humiliation. I was happy again with Ned and with the London friends I always loved. But I was still restless in London, and, when not absorbed in my work, bored with living there. Everyone's interests seemed to have shrunk since Oxford, our spheres contracted into little units of self-advancement. It was little-me-ish when elite and little-minded generally, little homes and little political skirmishes, a kind of toy town in pursuit of nothing very interesting. The more I read about Paris before the First World War or in the twenties, the more New York art magazines I read, the more I heard about what was out there beyond Islington, the more restless I got. I was also beginning to miss Bett in a new way, the more permanent London was beginning to seem.

Ned, too, seemed to be getting bored with his job, and so when, one weekend in Paris, we ran into one of the editors of a New York magazine specializing in news comment and analysis, and she told Ned there was a job possibility and would he like to try for it, he flew over immediately, and was offered, on a six-month provisional basis, an editorial position.

To both of us it seemed a windfall. For Ned it meant New York with a green card, a grown-up job involving language skills, plus big-time (not London local) news. For me it probably meant a lot more, the promised end of geo-psychic schizophrenia. I no longer had to feel pulled between London and New York, between Ned and Bett. I was going to have the two most important people in my life simultaneously in one place. *Embarras de richesse.* As Constance would have said, it was more than I deserved.

But in the meantime Ned was to be in New York on trial, while I remained in London surrounded by files and notes and finished the last chapters of my book. I was curiously content. Not only did London, and particularly London friends, seem more wonderful now that I was about to leave them, but marriage took on its happiest, easiest aspect. In my woeful state of either/or, love with solitude seemed an indefectible combination. I could idealize marriage and feel rock-safe inside it without having all the bother, distress, disillusion of living it out. I missed the physical presence of Ned, but it was not the devastation I'd known at Oxford when Hugh was gone. I truly knew Ned was there, as—except for the recent flurry of doubt which had ended in our marriage—I had always known and not always fairly counted on. Working on my book in London, not paralyzed without him, not fearing abandonment, I could have both the benefits of single, independent life and the safety and solace of being loved. It was Ned's existence in New York that set me free, despite all my previous resistance, in London.

But nothing does hold still the way you need it to. While I was at peace in London, Ned was in torment in New York, as I discovered when six weeks into the separation I flew to see him there. Life on the magazine had transformed him. He was still trembling from work when he met me at the airport, and after a perfunctory greeting he resumed the hysterics my arrival had interrupted. All the way into the city, while we bounced in the back of the cab, as the city lights and noises streamed beside us, he keened, circling and returning to the horror, the deadlines, the pressure, the word counts, the erratic directives, malevolent competition, general ill will, the fearful boss. He was not used to the boot-camp treatment, not just the systematic mangling to mysterious end of carefully rendered prose, of subtle and significant distinctions of meaning, but the constant atmosphere of guilt and fear, of error and inadequacy that corporate journalism relied on for the smooth running of business. For long and recurrent hours of that weekend visit, Ned remained in imagination still inside his office, or perhaps inside the office of his boss, humiliated, devastated, shuddering like someone sprung from a Nazi interrogation cell thrown back on the streets of Paris, still sweating and babbling from the ordeal.

I was distraught to see him so overwhelmed, and moreover to see the rock on which my transitory London happiness relied so ready to crumble. Beyond the shock to the vanity which his inability to be with me that weekend caused, there was set in place some nervousness about this plan of ours to make ends meet in New York. So convinced was Ned that he was failing at work that he convinced me of it, too, along with his sense, expressed in the absolute terror with which he regarded every aspect of this job, that the price of failure would be momentous.

But he was not failing. First his desk was moved closer to a window, then small, grudging noises of encouragement were made, and finally, at the appropriate three-month juncture, there was direct speech. Sure, they said, full of seasonal cheer, sell the house in London, bring the wife over, why not? I joined him on Christmas Eve. We had dinner at the Côte Basque and drank champagne in sleeping bags on a friend's floor. We were optimistic and cheerful and determined to succeed. My book was finished, Ned's job was on; all we had to do was find an apartment.

The money was tied up in London by one of those regulations meant to discourage tax exiles and absconders, and apart from a small rent from the Islington house we had only Ned's salary to live on. By what seemed incredibly good fortune, we were offered a special lease for a floor-through apartment in a limestone palace between Fifth and Madison near the Metropolitan Museum. It had a twenty-five-foot-square, high-ceilinged living room with parquet floors and an ornate marble fireplace, and huge ballroom mirrors on the doors; there was a kitchen and bedroom and a little terrace overlooking brownstone gardens in the rear. Because the owner of the building needed tame tenants to hold leases until he could sell off the co-ops, he offered us the place at very low rent for at least a year. And so we moved in, with no furniture but a double bed and a stereo which we bought the day we signed the lease, plus our books and clothes and a couple of rugs shipped from London. We lived in the bare, beautiful rooms as proudly as Napoleon's soldiers camping in an abandoned palace in Moscow.

There were other things about the apartment: it was thirteen blocks from where I'd lived with Bett before I went to England, where she and Hal lived now. It was around the corner from where I'd gone to school. The stationer's on the corner was where I'd bought my pencils and comics. Even the used children's clothing store of my nightmares was only two blocks away, on Madison. It seemed I'd come home, in the most elegant manner possible, but still, recognizably, home.

And then, three weeks after we moved in, signed the lease and shipped our clothes, Ned was fired. The magazine offered two weeks' salary and no explanation at all for the recent encouragement. There wasn't so much as an apology or "good luck" offered. It was as though from one day to the next Ned simply ceased to exist for them. His desk was cleared and reoccupied, like a hospital bed in a terminal ward. No one, not a boss or a colleague, said a word, except "goodbye."

After the first days of stunned fury and panic, Ned went into shock, staring morosely at the floor for hours, coming up to re-remember, try to understand what had happened. After that he began to swing between anger and depression, which got worse as the empty weeks went on. Even his skin got darker as he sat hour after hour staring at the same page of newsprint, or at his shoes, or, unsettlingly, from time to time at me, as though this were all my doing, this New York stuff, this American humiliation.

It seemed that for the first time in his life Ned had failed at something he'd set out to do, something involving his mind and labor and dedication. After so many years of school and university prizes, of seemingly duly awarded success, of gentlemanly "effortless superiority," his progress had been suddenly checked, callously, insultingly and in the face of real effort. Confronted with the characteristic brutality of American corporate behavior, it was as though his father's sneering predictions had come true: he wouldn't make it in the real world of men and money (and nothing was realer, manlier or more about money than America). Out of the shelter, this all seemed to say, Ned was hopeless.

I said what I could, tried to jostle, cheer, hold, distract him out of it. But after weeks, nothing I could offer seemed powerful enough to shake his conviction of failure, and eventually we learned simply to accommodate it. He found some freelance work, resumed a layer of good spirits, but he was fundamentally undermined. His ambivalence about his money deepened (he didn't really deserve it because he didn't earn it in the big, tough world his father admired). And just as I always suspected that I'd got my jobs and first book contract unfairly (through class and youth and looks), so he always felt it was British connections that got him the jobs that kept him going, as stringer for an English paper. Furthermore, there was now a Jack Sprat and his wife aspect to our being together in New York: me here because I was unhappy in London, him working out of London while living in New York. It wasn't just me that kept him from taking us back to England. He was stuck here, unable to face going home having failed a second time. But the division was now in place between us: my joy in homecoming, Ned's disappointment and unease; my return to America and American family, his sense of alienation, his new world of British journalists and short-term expats. I wanted to rest, let gravity fix me here; he wanted to break through American resistance to him and then get out. Though none of this was named, these were the opposing pulls with which we lived in New York.

So Ned turned, characteristically once again, to the world of men and jobs and career tribalism. Because his values weren't mine, because I wasn't suffering the way he was, I began to feel impatient. I wanted him to feel about New York the way I did. I wanted him to be like me, and I was too young to know it didn't have to be so terrible that he wasn't.

It was my limitation that what engaged him bored me, that world of journalists and "news"—gossip from the big out-there. My course was private, like my adventures. At first these were about Bett and Hal and old friends, about New York streets and goings-on, and then they began to revolve around another man. Maybe Ned's falling to pieces scared me, maybe his time of paralysis and depression felt too like Bett—set me in motion again to "save myself." Maybe his total absorption in the world of jobs and men, the way he seemed to *live* only in the part locker-room, part office atmosphere, as if everything else (private life, interior life, love life) were unimportant—maybe this basic difference in what mattered to us seemed too different. Maybe I felt abandoned by him, maybe our long history of being together and being apart made my wandering an automatic response. Maybe if I hadn't been sent to Mirrenwood when I was five, or left home when I was sixteen, maybe if my father had welcomed me, maybe if I'd stayed with Hugh, maybe if I'd been a better person, it wouldn't have happened. But I wasn't and it did.

And where was this Vronsky? Right under my feet, two floors down on the right-hand side of the building, my neighbor whom I was destined to love. I'd even carried his name in my address book for several years (he was an acquaintance of Constance's, and on her list of distinguished people I might like to meet when I went to New York the trip before last). Even the landlord had pointed out his mailbox to us. "A selling point for his damn building, I knew it," Jack said bitterly when I mentioned it.

We met decorously, accidentally, once or twice in the elevator; we introduced ourselves, met again, and then once, thus meeting, as the celebrated author looked through his letters and I through mine, he invited me up for coffee and I accepted. It was like being interviewed for a job: I was polite, witty, charming; he was polite, witty, charming, austere and unnervingly scrutinizing. He was the soul of correctness, as, a little more terrified and sixteen years younger, was I. He inquired about myself and my husband and our New York prospects. I said I had just written a book and his eyes lit briefly. When I named the subject I could feel him relaxing toward me a little further, cautioning himself not to get hopes up. I was still awfully young. And, of course, married.

We had coffee again. I brought him my book, he gave me one of his. He did not ask to meet Ned. Morning coffee became afternoon tea, became drinks, became an invitation to lunch. The intellectual premise of our exchanges submitted graciously, to the pressure of flirtation. We were playful with each other, decorously, oh so adultly courtly, bantering, courteous, the most superior playmates, pleased with ourselves in one another's eyes. It was delicious, and drawn out so it could stay that way, untinged by guilt or responsibility. So it was weeks before we even kissed, months before we went to bed. The flirtation, courtship, seduction was everything, and it was always too soon to wonder where any of it was leading.

We were both of us aware of his stature in American letters. I was deferential without being fawning (after all, he was *choosing* my company), but a certain awe and a certain respect hung like a cloud around his dark and wonderful head and clung like cologne to his clothes. My admiration for his work was genuine enough, but such admiration is a cool, abstract thing, and once I'd met the author of the esteemed prose, the works took on a weight of wisdom and beauty underived by reading alone. He gave me some (uncompromisingly) inscribed copies of his work, and in particular his latest book of essays, but I was so besotted with their author that I couldn't read any of it. The words jumped and popped around for me on the page, hold them still, concentrate though I would. I read each felicitously wrought sentence of each paragraph so many times I might have recited it by heart, but comprehend any of it I could not, as I had to confess. This conspicuous failure of mine was a disappointment to both of us, to me because I wished to please and be receptive to what was most important to him, and to him because here was a whole form of seduction closed off, a terrible waste, given the mastery of that seduction and the apparent susceptibility of the would-be object.

Nevertheless, as I say, we were both quite conscious of whom we were dealing with, and one of the characteristics of our affair was his obsession with secrecy. There wasn't the slightest gallantry in any of this; it was not my reputation he was trying to protect, but his own comfort. Whenever we went out for lunch, for example, he would lead us to the most anonymous settings, usually unfrequented coffee shops or Hungarian cafeterias, places where he was familiar enough as a customer not to be scrutinized by the managers and where the chance of anyone literary enough to know who he was coming upon him, bothering him, asking for an autograph, seeing with their very own eyes that this paragon took in food and nourishment, was remote.

Once Jack set out to charm you, there was not much you could do about it. It was not just the speed of his mind, but the playfulness, the willingness to leap, dive, flick the wrist, keep the game going. He liked talk to be like Ping-Pong, but he also liked to take the stage himself and perform. He was a brilliant mimic, and he would incorporate into his descriptions of friends, the unknown and the famous, whole chunks of reincarnation, by the subtlest shifts of body position as well as speech. What he noticed about people was unnervingly sharp, merciless, they were as though caught in the beams of a pagan god, for whom acceptance, forgiveness, was soft and unnecessary stuff. The speed and power of seeing was such that it seemed pointless trying to defend yourself against it, or to object when the play got rough. That brain was always there, on, ready to deconstruct and swallow, stomp over and cast you aside or play, dally, delight and certainly charm. All this sexual brainpower made for a kind of nerve-racking exhilaration when I was with him; it was extraordinarily exciting to please him, make him laugh or just pause and take notice in the huge sweep of his carrying-on. And it also made things scary, the speed with which his brain consumed whatever was in front of it, whether it was politics or fiction, or one's humble self got up in bows and scarves and mustering the tiny armory of one's charms.

I would sit there, nicely dressed and contained, across from him and the coffee table, holding my polite drink, and feel the wraps come undone, the room heat, spin a little as it began: Jack watching every move, me watching him watch, me beginning to risk my containment and camouflage, entering his performance, each of us performing our different selves, then retreating, noting, taking in—and all this at high speed until it became as heady and fearful and thrilling as riding a motorcycle fast at night. I had a sense of danger and of my own bravado—the "look, I'm doing it" sense— all the time. Look, I'm seducing this wonderful man, or look, I'm beginning an affair. When the touching entered in, the "accidental," and then the unguarded and truthful (all kinds of touching), the stakes upped, and the excitement.

For me he had an irresistible physical presence—tall, slender, with broad shoulders—the alertness and pent energy more predatory than athletic, and the liquid black eyes never still under thick brows. There was something wound and ready to spring about him, physically, though it was all driven by the brain, from the shoulders that bent toward you when he listened—and he always listened like someone decoding, sensing, processing vulnerability, a place to enter, overpower—to the thick tight hair that covered that cranium like excess energy. Humor could make him lean less hard at you, disarm him for a moment, but that respite of laughter was only a momentary purring, because the language itself—of humor—was really only a tribute to his own authority there, the place where he famously triumphed, won all the speed prizes, set the rules.

All this *consciousness* meant there was a lot less doing than thinking about. For me there were long runs of anticipation, of remembrance, deciphering, regurgitation. It was a smallish meal we both made a feast of, like one of those army ration biscuits meant to take you a long way in hostile circumstances. The meanest notes and phone calls had afterlives like galaxies, and each meeting, whether street-accidental or preordained, was gone over line by line, look by look, even in the moment, at least in the beginning, those hot and intense, even awful moments of simultaneity when one was simply trying to survive the emergency of actual coexistence with the beloved.

But it wasn't only the brilliance that attracted me, or the tense playfulness that let us both be self-delighted precocious children with one another, nor the ambition and achievement of his work; I was also in large part seduced by the dullest thing about him, which was how he actually lived, the monkish habits of his solitude, the grim, even depressive minimalism of his life.

I admired his fasting. I admired his stony separateness and self-sufficiency. I admired the smallness of his needs, the steadiness of his routines: his exercise weights, his evening runs, his early nights. All the symptoms of his current loneliness and depression I read as

197

choices, heroic and exemplary. I admired the way he organized his existence around the two pages a day he set himself to write, the way he kept out intruders and had an answering machine to protect him, to take his messages like a psychiatrist's in August. I admired the way he then stopped work ritually at six to ring his service, turn on his charm and attention and return his calls, then watch the evening news, eat his small supper (keeping dinners out to a maximum of twice a week) and spend the evening alone with galleys, manuscripts of friends, foreign and native.

I admired the sparseness of his living arrangements, the just so and no more of his furnishings, the blandness of what he had on his walls. I admired the just short of eccentric and therefore all the more self-effacing unimaginativeness of his wardrobe: the collegiate, always neutral shirts, tweed jackets and dark trousers, sensible footwear he wore. He looked good in good clothes, and on those few occasions we went to an elegant restaurant he would dress up in something more dashing than usual, wearing his suit and tie with a little ironic detachment as if to say, I know how to do it, you see, I simply choose not to. He wore me on such occasions with the same ironic detachment, and that made me always uncertain how much exactly he was ever engaged. I knew certainly I was anomalous in his life, amusing as long as I didn't step or make him step out of his range of comfort. "I don't live like this," he said to me once, "I don't do this," yet for a whole week when Ned was away he had abandoned his eight hours and two pages a day—for which the sick and importunate, family, friends, ex-lovers, were held at bay, and for the sake of which they held themselves at bay—in order to indulge with me in the strange thing we were doing or not doing.

And what were we doing? What was I doing, the married lady from upstairs? I was holding my breath a lot in the beginning, sitting up straight, impressing the older man with what he said he was impressed by, my "poise"—I whose heart was thumping so noisily I could barely keep account of what I was saying so "poisefully," sitting still and trying not to betray my nervousness or just run out of that vibrating room, away from the scrutiny, appetite, sleepy curiosity and sudden attention of the literary lion in front of me. And then, soon enough, all those nerves became my energy, physical, sexual. I began then to feel my own force, youth, pleasure, and I let the "posie" paralysis drop until he was no longer impressed by the calm but made wary by the wildness, the risk taking, the arriving barefoot out of the elevator to visit him, accosting him exuberantly in the street where any reader of body language could read the import of manner and dress—the more and more elaborate, "fantastical" clothing into which I changed on the chance or expectation of seeing him—as if this were all theater and rhetoric, my costume language as expressive as his was mute, and used in response to, my own version of, his language: all those coifs and curls and plumes of words and wit which he owned and used to show off, to signal to me.

Maybe I knew enough about the costs of Jack's spartan life, though it wasn't until much later that I knew it up close: the purposeful deprivation that allows you to work, the cultivation of dullness so that writing can be an escape from it, the only pleasure in an unpleasured world, really only the cessation of pain of being there, that place you have pulled down around you, made empty and ugly with loss. I certainly understood his depression and melancholy. I imagined that I hovered around the perimeters of that solitude and sadness like some ear-bitten cat, yowling and teasing from the alleys outside, a Mehitabel to his typewriter-enslaved Archie. I thought it was precisely my "recklessness" in its childish, unthreatening form that attracted him, my freedom from convention, my high spirits. And I imagined if he admired something in me other than what any number of young women might have provided, it was what I always admired in other women, some struggle to be free in the world. But it was strange, when he later wrote a version of our time together, that he ignored all that, made me into some kind of English lady/saint. It was that entirely fabricated "poise" of mine he celebrated, that and the damned English accent.

"I don't know how reckless you are," he said once. Certainly I was running risks, just by leakage, evidence in clothes and blushes. Of course, my manner changed when I was home again with Ned, though traces of escapade, the unbridled, slightly wild-eyed look of dogs and cats when they have been out all night, clung to me, along with a certain remorselessness, shamelessness, with which I imagined I was testing my rights and leash-length. And it was still all play, all games and play, except for the direction and power of it, the brutality of the infatuation, which was mutual, as I knew, and therefore too intoxicating to give up.

There was an element of St. Augustine's "Lord let me be good, but not yet" in all this. I really meant to settle down with Ned as I had vowed, but the smallness of our current life—his emotional absence from it, which left behind for us little but habit and loveless intimacy—was enough to make me feel the "not yet"—it can't be all over yet. There were these circumstances and there were the ordinary ones of any long-term relationship, the limitations and reductions of what is possible in the light of what has always been, the increasing claustrophobia of the known. Given the ghastly smallness of longtime intimacy, who hasn't longed for the crash in the china shop of the affair, the created clean uncluttered space where one may act, impersonate one's best self, do the little dance of how one might be if one were free, if life were other, if this other were one's life?

Of course, next to such monumental dignity two floors down, all Ned's rushing about, fretting, crisis of identity, seemed all the more ghastly. My comparisons between the husband and the writer were never conscious, or I might have realized how unfair they were: Ned in the process of forming himself with the help of others, next to this self-sufficient, solitary man who had done all his growing years ago. I was comparing agitation with stillness, searching with arriving. While Ned, my intellectually passionate, so profoundly intelligent and knowledgeable husband, re-donned his leather jacket and went searching for the most idiotic kind of work—"color" pieces on racing car drivers, stories of international scandal and so on—I thought yearningly of the contained, near-ascetic life going on two floors below me: the sober twilight perusals of literary journals, the rustle of foreign correspondence in a Jamesian high silence. Less absurdly imagined was the writer's self-esteem and sense of vocation to which, in my snobbery, I compared the frantic self-selling going on in my house; his self-sufficiency in contrast to all that noisy mirth-free hanging out; his worldly abdication (the money had all been made long ago, of course) in contrast to the penny-scratching going on with us. Without knowing it, I was blaming Ned for not being an artist, just when his father's jeers about his "artiness" were goading him, blaming him for a tacky ambition, for being fired, being careerless.

How much Ned knew, knowing nothing, I never saw. He knew that the celebrated author and I sometimes had lunch together, suspected I was "flattered" by it and intellectually infatuated. Perhaps he had some inkling of the romance but needed to keep it buried, needed not to have to deal with its implications just then, when everything around him was spinning. Or, perhaps, as I felt it, his heart and soul were engaged elsewhere—in that world of men and money where the real living was. I was careful with him, because that was how you were with him just then, willing to live on hold while he worked the important things out, decorously mourning the lost self-esteem, not wanting to add to it in any way, but beyond that, of course, not wanting to provoke suspicion or anger or end my idyll. I was in love with Jack, at that stage of madness even I knew enough to distrust. I was waiting for it all to calm down a little, leave the high school stage, become something if it was going to, or else disappear.

It was a short ride and it stopped fast, because under the "recklessness" I had at least a small gift for the longer view. First, the lesser consideration, but a stopping place nonetheless: the great man tired of it all, longing for his peace and routines, bored with the performing and the showing and the colors, a need for rest and the familiar governance of his world, boredom with the little bird in all her feathers and delightful youth—too much of that youth—all her freedom, her attention to him, her solitary occupation with himself. "I don't want to be the thing that you do," he once said nervously. No, we'd have to be both engaged in something else, something other than ourselves and the full-time play. I'd have to stop spinning and settle down, and then, into what? A parallel writerly dullness, miles and miles down the ladder of it all from himself? He'd end up as teacher, coach, patient father, irritated colleague. He'd end up bored, restless, confined and disengaged. I feared the disengagement, the being sent back, returned marked, not good for the long hand. I feared his boredom and the ruthlessness that came with it. He'd run through me like a brush fire, and I was too young and too unsure to get up again when he left.

And then the greater consideration: loving Ned, even in his disappearance, my faith in his return, to himself and me. I had compassion for his disintegration, though I didn't always know it. I thought I should protect him from my own wobbliness, jubilance, confusion. And I remembered Hugh and that trail of destruction— and backed off, paused with Jack, who was happy enough to pause himself, return to his habits, watch and wait.

I began to see a therapist. I was genuinely torn, I thought, between Ned and Jack, and baffled by the strength of my confusion. I was surprised that marriage hadn't settled everything for me, since for a period of at least fifteen months I hadn't woken up with the question should I go or should I stay. But the goblins were coming back, bringing new goblins like Ned's getting fired and being undone, frightened, short-tempered; like being close to Bett again, and seeng that wasn't the unalloyed filial joy I'd thought it would be. In fact, Bett and I were often fighting like old times, squabbling and exasperated as hens on a dusty road. The goblins were all my goblins and had little to do with where or whom. I thought I should figure them out.

Clarke was my first therapist. In England in those days no one had a therapist unless they were crazy. What they had to do they did with pills. My own depressions there had been susceptible to chemistry. At Northton, at Oxford studying Latin, in London, I had found antidepressants and speed good enough to carry me through my miseries. Besides, as shrinks were given to saying with irritating complacency, the thing about depression is that it eventually passes on its own. Just before I left, an American friend had told me of a miracle drug that had brought her back from the edge. It could be got from a specialist. I had been to see him, discussed Gertrude Stein's automatic writing for a while, answered his question: "After you've been depressed, are you happy?" Yes, I said, how else do you know it's passed? "All right," he'd said, and given me a prescription. "Take these to America, next time you're feeling bad try them, they might work." I had this bottle of pills with me and one day I mentioned them to my therapist.

"Lithium?" he said. "Are you serious? But you're not manic-depressive. That's a very serious drug. It has to be monitored closely with blood tests. Throw it away."

When I related the story of the pill-happy British doctor to Jack, he did not find it so amusing. There must have been some reason I'd been given the stuff; maybe I was crazy. He kept me at arm's length once I told him, and treated me on future occasions with wary politeness. A girl with a bottle of lithium (not to mention a husband) was capable of anything.

At the time I was surprised by his reaction, but then I thought maybe I'd told him about the pills as a way of getting him to back away because *I* was frightened of our getting too close. By then I knew him well enough to know how he would feel. He held himself too tightly to respond any differently.

I'd always found his caution admirable, endearing. I thought it was part of that great burden of consciousness of his; of a piece with the extremeness of his fiction and his stance in life. He knew enough and had written enough of the self-regarding niceties and restraints of the world; it was not convention that made him so fearful of emotional excess, it wasn't the *out-there* that held him back, but that self-protective center of his: the *in-there*, the woeful *I* that seemed always to be saying this isn't me, I don't do this sort of thing, I can't, I don't, I dare not. In his work he dared, and with me for a while he thought about it and imagined by the strength of that thinking he was doing it, but he restrained himself, and me, with every good reason, of course, said *we'll see*, perhaps, maybe, promising wisely, always so wisely, absolutely nothing. I loved, and in the end even relied on, this old-maidish Prufrockery of his. I had only to shake a bottle of pills at him. And really, it was *my* depths I was testing, *my* courage, not his. When I found I hadn't got the courage to run away, to leave Ned, and certainly not in such a vulnerable state, I pulled back from the situation and made Jack pull back, too.

He was utterly relieved; love was trouble, and trouble was always in his view more trouble than it was worth. He switched gears easily, we became friends, then barely acquaintances. After such a long period of meeting one another constantly by accident, at the mailbox or in the street, of seemingly brilliant materialization out of desire, we now almost never bumped into one another, just as though one of us had moved away. He withdrew himself from my life as politely and agilely as he knew how (and he had had years of practice at such affable-seeming but rock-hard withdrawal). After a while when I saw him again, he said that he was with someone else, asked about Ned and advised us to think about having children before too long. He said to stay in touch and dropped his eyes. He expressed the faintest regret in my passing, the faintest curiosity as to how it might have been otherwise, and gave a clear indication that he hoped I would not take future advantage of our after all rather brief though delightful liaison.

Some time after my affair with Jack, when Ned and I were out somewhere, a white bird flew into our apartment. We couldn't tell if it was a dove or a pigeon. I built a big cage for it from a roll of chicken wire, and it sat in the corner of our parquet-floored, mirrored, embassy-sized, otherwise pretty empty living room, talking to itself and making a mess with birdseed and droppings on the New York *Times* flooring of its cage. We took him as a sign of peace, a kind of blessing, and we named him Onan after a nice joke in Gertrude Stein, "because it spilled its seed upon the ground." But then, once it was used to living with us, we started getting Born Free notions of how we were making it weak and dependent, and when it was probably truly corrupted by domestic life we set it free. Maybe it died out there, maybe it found another benefactor. It was beautiful for a while until we started thinking about our moral responsibility, which probably killed it.

NINE

NED AND I MOVED. We went to a bigger, less elegant space, far from my childhood neighborhood, far from Bett, far from the temptations and possible confrontations of that part of town.

We settled down. Ned was working from home now, and I had a contract for a book about the work and lives of the Abstract Expressionists, depression artists and I thought of them when I was depressed myself. We would sit in matching offices, divided only by a thin wall. At the end of each morning and afternoon we would come out of our holes, meet, chat. We went to bed early. It was a version of the writer's life I'd admired with Jack—orderly, simple, industrious, not solitary of course, and not so high-minded, but Ned was no longer threatening to go back to London, because it looked like peace. As Jack knew—as everyone knew except the therapist—work solves a lot of problems, and it seemed feasible to think we were making a go of it. The dangers are past, I thought, I'm ready; but I always forgot about Bett.

Of course, Bett was "thrilled" to have me home, especially now that it looked as though we were planning to stay. Characteristically, she felt compassion for Simone, likely to be deprived of her beloved son. But Simone was a frequent visitor and a good traveler. As long as Ned seemed settled and working at something that might be heading somewhere real, she was happy enough. She made noises about our having children from time to time, but basically she accepted the situation.

She and Bett were friendly. Bett admired Simone for her elegance and style. Simone admired Bett for her uncanny youthfulness and sweet nature. Bett was always apologetic for her flat and clothes and "shabbiness" when Simone came to see her, but Simone was family now and she overcame her hesitance. Likewise, Hal and Simone got along well enough, though neither could make much of the other's accent. Simone didn't seem to think it that odd that Bett and Hal were together, or if she did she never let on. From time to time she'd wonder aloud why Bett had never married again, with those looks and so on, but she seemed prepared to overlook the impracticalities of Bett's non-French behavior. She never judged her harshly (perhaps she felt some kinship with her: age, sex, lack of education), as she did on occasion Ned and me.

Basically, the mothers thought of us as an attractive, gifted couple making forgivable mistakes on our road to inevitable success. For Bett I was the surprisingly independent inheritor of her American dream: love and marriage and financial security. Like a lot of people, she thought Ned and I were a "great couple," bound always to end up with one another. Really, she tended to see us as sort of musical comedy leads, our troubles as adorable to her as everything else about us. The dark side of the world was her private sphere; we existed in eternal sunshine. She thought so because she needed it that way.

She tried to keep her own problems away from us. When she started losing jobs that first year we were in New York, she made light of it. She and Eddy, as she called him, used to meet at the unemployment lines and go for coffee afteward, and for a while Ned's having been fired made her own misfortunes seem less terrible. If they were firing Oxford graduates, then it could happen to anybody and she needn't be so embarrassed. Then Ned got more work still, and Bett seemed unable to; the unemployment coverage came to an end; Hal, although he was meant to be driving a cab, was in and out of jobs. Things got bad. But they'd been living like that for years, hand to mouth, and however dire it seemed at any moment, history said they'd get by. Besides, now we were there, both of us making some money, and we could "lend" it to them.

I tried to tackle Bett's work problems with logic, put together a portfolio of photos of her sculpture, the heads and medallions she'd made when I was a child. I called around all the commercial sculpture places I could find, pitched her credentials and sold her over the phone. I got a long list of appointments for her to take the portfolio to, but after the first couple of interviews she lost interest. "Puppy, it's adorable of you, but I'm just no good at this stuff. I can't concentrate." It was the same thing with the nine-to-five jobs, the tempting: she couldn't concentrate. Maybe it was the ECT; she got dizzy, she was listless, depressed; she didn't know what was wrong; maybe it was "change of life."

I got her to see Clarke to talk about it. Clarke said all she really wanted to talk about was whether her daughter really loved her. "Forget about it," he said brutally. "Your mother's too old." Bett seemed to agree. She'd been to shrinks all her life, she said, they never did any good. All she needed was the doctor's signatures; the pills calmed her down. Otherwise she'd get these anxiety attacks, crying jags, "Oh, Puppy, you don't want to hear about it." She had to protect me from all that grim stuff, from herself, so that the Helen and Ned show could go on. I certainly knew what depression was; maybe Bett (and me, too) was a hereditarily hopeless case; maybe it would all get better, just pass as the shrinks always said it did. They extended the unemployment benefits; we extended the loans. Hal got some work, they got by. It was like when I was a child, only miraculously they were never evicted. Or maybe they would have been if we hadn't been there.

I think, deep down, Bett was surprised by its all being so real, by our being there, our being the age we were, our being married, being British, or at least half British, both of us. The Oxford stuff was no longer something she got to tell other mothers on the street—yes, my daughter, Oxford, England—but something she now had to live with, a toad, even, she had to swallow. It wasn't just the age differences, the differences in circumstances we had to fly over when we were together; we had to get through the strange noises I made, the strange height I had, the strange and relatively speaking good clothing I wore—clothing which I didn't get from her, or wasn't like hers. She had to get used to the fact that she hadn't been in this very direct way *responsible* for me for ten or twelve years, that I was out in that alien world, and had been all this time, without her. At first she thought it was like watching me in a school play—Helen goes to college, Helen lives in London, Helen marries Ned—but that couldn't last. It became real, and it seemed like a choice I was living out against her. Not just a one-time act of betrayal and rejection, as when I left home; those things you can forgive. Now it was actually me, part of my flesh, my otherness from her—otherness expressed in speech and appearance and dress, in realm of reference and behavior. Helen went to restaurants in London, Paris and New York, and thereby left Mommy behind. (Every time, without fail, she and I went out to lunch or dinner, always a seafood place, she would say, "I can't remember the last time I had lobster." Without fail, until eventually I'd start saying, "It was last month, with me, right here, last bloody month." And she'd stutter and stumble, "I know, I know, I mean it feels like ages.") She never, as she might have done, made fun of the accent—unless she was furious with me, when she'd spit out, "Oh, *Mummy*"; she was sort of intimidated by it, as though its strangeness made *her* the alien, the other, without rights or comforts, as though my accent put *her* in the wrong. Well, the money certainly did that. I was now on the other side—that frightening enemy side she'd been carrying out her little hit-and-run missions against for years. Now that I seemed to her to be one of them, the differences between us made her feel bad about herself, not me. Of course, *I* deserved good fortune, she always said that, it was the only credit she could take for anything, the only way she thought she could squeeze into the picture. She would say, "I'm thrilled you're a success, that you've got Ned, that you graduated from Oxford, that's what I worked for all my life; I'm the proudest mommy in the world." And I would get furious because she hadn't heard a single word I'd been saying, which was that I was *not* a fucking success, that it was often hard with Ned, that I felt as undirected and as much of a failure as she.

And now I wonder if I didn't only say those things but actually *feel* those things as a way of not leaving her behind, a way of not being cast out by her. She never gave me the right to have problems once I'd gone, had my degree, my marriage, and then, good God, my book—that was it, end of story, happy ending. She and her "messy life" as she always called it were nothing but a besmirching of that pristine surface which was her Oxford daughter, and her response was to remove herself from all the perfection, hang back, keep away, her and Hal, not to upset the precious child. And when the precious child said no, it's not so damned finished over here, she'd toss her head, laugh and kiss me.

So we fought, and at the time it felt as though I was fighting to keep her away, keep those maternal tentacles out of my reach, and that certainly was part of it—but the other part was that I fought with her in order to keep her with me, maybe even had my depressions for that reason, so that we could remain "sisters," equals, partners, even if only sparring partners. Our fights were usually the long rumbling quarreling of retired couples, with refrains and irritations, the whole point of which was sheer attrition, exhaustion of the other, but sometimes they were very bitter and we each went over the edge (but then the edge was always what we were looking for)—like the time she was going on and on about what I had or hadn't done and I said, "I'm sick of this, I never asked you to have me, you just got pregnant," as if our relationship were an inconsequential side effect of sex, and she slapped me, hard. And I think that after every one of our fights, no matter how close or far from the edge, we reestablished, in exhaustion, in despair, or in some bruised satisfaction, that we were still together—despite the accent, despite the cash, despite the lengths I seemed to have gone to get away from her, or the protective covering I needed to be with her once I was back. None of it mattered in the end. She owned me because I was her great love.

But she felt the betrayal. First I wrote my book, then Constance wrote hers, and it was as though we were doing it on purpose to make her look bad. "My whole family writes books," she'd say, forgetting Gogi and Shrimp, not to mention Hal, who still couldn't read too well. So she'd sit down again with her economics book, the big theory that was going to save the world and show them that this seemingly hopeless, living-in-the-shadows Bett was in fact all the time . . .

She sent a copy of the typescript to the White House, to NYU professors, to Galbraith. She got an embossed official reply from

209

Mr. and Mrs. Richard M. Nixon thanking her for her correspondence and good wishes and she kept it on the mantelpiece under a big formal photo portrait of me at sixteen, something she'd traded a photographer for, doing a bust of his wife in exchange, when I was about to break away to England. I looked embarrassed and bad-tempered in the picture, just as I was in real life whenever I had to look at it, enshrined and hovering over the White House card. This was not a good time to display affection for Nixon, in fact just then it was pretty unheard of. But Bett used to declare her loyalty to stunned silences at her various jobs or to friends whenever the subject came up, used to tell how she'd cried watching his departure in the helicopter, how she wrote him letters, "stood by him." I remembered how at Mirrenwood I'd be so proud of her, young and beautiful and sitting on one of the school desks chatting with the other parents about Ike. We all like Ike, he was pink and healthy and grinning, and Stevenson was always a little sinister. I remember the feeling of pride I'd had then, everyone crowding around her not just because of her beauty but because of her politics. And just as that felt warm and reassuring, this felt outrageous, this liking Nixon in 1977.

Meanwhile, something strange was also happening to Hal. He was blowing his own bubble around him, cutting himself off from everyone, using the first person singular like a battering ram. He took all the bits and pieces that Bett had first given him, added a lot of art jargon and set himself up in his own eyrie: the Artist.

He never stopped showing his slides, for one thing. It was like an identification ritual he had. Whenever he met someone for the first time he'd whip out his slides like a traveling salesman with a wallet full of the family, and with the same impulse; you may think I'm no one, he'd be saying, that I have nothing, but that's not so. You take me for a street zero but I make these tough, beautiful things, things only the magic men, the artists make. And here was what was pathetic and at the same time annoying. All that babying encouragement Bett had given him—"Honey, show Shrimp your slides"—made it impossible for anyone not to linger and effuse, as with those salesmen's family pictures. You had to say *fantastic*, or (echoing Hal) *outasight*. But then he would start to explain it to you, like a kid with a solution in long division, and you'd sit there glazing over, chirping at regular intervals. This went on for huge chunks of time, while Bett would beam and take it all in. The work really wasn't bad, it wasn't that, it was being trapped in the art lecture. There even came a point when all your "great's" and "fantastic's" began to fall on deaf ears, as Hal went on talking, because he was expecting it now and to some degree even put out that he had to explain everything to you, though it wasn't your fault you weren't an artist. Eventually you couldn't go over there, no one could, without slide shows and art lectures and Bett blissed out and catatonic. Every once in a while you'd want to shout: For Christsake, Hal, you're not fucking Michelangelo, but of course you couldn't, ever. It wasn't even enough to buy some of the work, you had to have the whole package.

So you'd sit there while Bett would feed Hal and wait on him as he talked, dusting off the slides and handing them to him, and carrying on as though it was the world's saddest story that Hal the genius should have to drive a cab. Both of them believe this now, and are incensed at the injustice. Meanwhile Ned was not writing anything serious because of his anti-artist father, though unlike Bett and Hal he had the money. The whole thing seemed likely to collapse under the weight of all that irony. Or I would, caught in the middle with guilt and defiance, and writing pretty unremuneratively myself, precisely about artists and their trials, furthering causes in art magazines, and then there's that too: you write for these people, why can't you help Hal?

The knot tightened. I was helping Bett with money I made from art writing, and I could do that because Ned was taking care of me. He could do that because his angry father died and left him a lot of money. We seemed all to be living in the house that Roger, the anti-writer father, built. But then Hal began to get pissed off with it, everyone getting to be an "artist" except him, and why didn't someone finance him? But if Bett gives Hal the money I give her and Ned gives me and Roger gave him . . . No, Hal must work, it's the manly thing to do, and soon enough, at least in his case, we are all buying into the dead father's way of thinking, begging him: For Christsake, Hal, go out and work, support Bett.

Perhaps here was where my latent hostility rose—one thing to give Bett my cash, another to fund Hal. And then Hal had his own sibling rivalry, and he always asked, Bett, how come your daughter gets not to have to go out and work?—for which there was no good answer, except I didn't have to, I got to write and live in a beautiful house. And the thing I always felt was the poor benighted Brits' problem, the class thing, here it was on American soil, here where it's always been, don't I remember? God bless the child that's got his own. But we all go on like this, more or less.

The money of Ned's made everything bad in a way, or sad, and at the same time kept the show going, the longest-running show in London, and now New York. We moved whenever life began to cramp us, whenever the marriage seemed too small, when we thought we needed more space or a different set of associations. We came to have more variables than people without money, and that kept a lot of the unchangeable problems at one (mover's) remove. We'd moved countless times in London, and already we'd moved three times in New York, always to bigger places. Even when we had separate workrooms and two floors it didn't seem big enough to house all the weather of our marriage. Now we had four floors between the two of us, two floors and a garden for living and one floor each for working in, and then later, in addition to this place, which we bought, we rented a place in the country where we could run to whenever those floors and walls closed in. We had places in London available to us, and even then, it was often the case, there didn't seem to be room to breathe. It was as though we were penned creatures or beings with very simple responses, so that whenever anxieties rose, or pressure, we would hurl ourselves at our cage doors. Of course there was always some legitimate real-world reason to move: ends of leases, tax breaks, whatever, but really it was some inner necessity that drove us, furless urban animals.

Perhaps it was a version of the constant moves of my childhood, an attempt to transform that past necessity into a virtue, a declaration of freedom. Just as I had under other circumstances with Bett, so Ned and I felt the rope of what actually was loose around us, slipped our harness again and again. If we'd known how much of a pattern this was we might have been less wasteful of time and cash and emotion, but each time we thought it was for good, that we were making a move to end all moves. Everything was always sane, logical and for keeps. Only our history said otherwise.

Thus, the brownstone. It was going to be the home-at-last home. It was so big and would take so much time to make ours, no wonder we believed in the permanence. There were four floors, solidly built by turn-of-the-century craftsmen. It wasn't grand, being at the outer edge of "safe" Manhattan, a border encampment, and inexpensive, but inside it didn't feel that way. It had stained-glass panels in the dividing doors, high ceilings, parquet, marble fireplaces, high-arched windows, stone carvings on the front of the house and a lion-headed fountain in the garden. Everything about the house spoke of feelings translated into wood and stone and meant to endure. We would live in this house and take care of it and it would take care of us; its virtue would make us virtuous and its solidity would make us solid.

We got a beautiful dog and a beautiful cat to go with the beautiful house, to keep us company until we had the children meant to please Simone and give Bett something to do. The animals were as stately and luxurious as the house, long-haired oriental creatures, self-contained and noble, Nineveh and Bertie: a blue-gray Persian cat that slept in the big bowl stolen from the Winter Palace by Ned's grandfather in the Boxer Rebellion; an orange, black-tongued chow that guarded the hallway like a Chinese dragon. We built bookshelves and hung mirrors. Everything was so elegant in the house that for a while the questions and doubts disappeared. Absolute beauty can do that.

There was another important thing about this house. It was only a block and a half from Bett and Hal, as close to coming back to live with her as possible, short of moving in. It was a declaration of my intent to *be* with her, right next door.

Now we were really neighbors, and Hal and/or Bett were over every other day while we were moving in, helping us decide on colors and placements, eating lunch with us in the garden, staying for dinner. In a way it was just what Bett and I would have wanted; there was contentment and ordinariness to it, their dropping in, our being there, to some degree sharing this with them. But there was another side to it as well. Hard to remember how much I simply willed this other part not to exist and therefore never registered, how this was simply rubbing her nose in it: the sisters and their different fortunes, the sheer horror of the unfairness of it.

It wasn't so clear. She was happy for us and happy to be with us; she felt safe sitting there on the gray sofa watching TV or putting plants in the garden with us. Besides, we were taking care of her more and more, and that's how she regarded us: half as innocent, i.e. blameless, children (not their fault she was so befuddled and unemployable, etc.), half as benefactors. You always have mixed feelings about benefactors (which is why benefactors have mixed feelings about being cast in that role, or I certainly did), and sometimes she would forget we were all this one big happy family and it would become them and us and we would be them. Oh, she hated herself for feeling such things, for feeling anything other than the familiar adoration of her precious daughter, but their situation—her not working, Hal not driving cabs or refusing to drive, wanting to paint, all that—and the inequalities must have seemed horribly unfair. Once coming back tanned from a winter holiday, we met her at the house. We all took the suitcases, and she was happy to see us but tense from her own troubles, and I won't ever forget the look she had when she saw what I'd got in London, bought in a sale and costing as much as an ordinary coat, but that was not the point, it was what it looked like: "dripping in fur," she said later. She saw the new coat I was carrying over my arm, and her face collapsed. She said with real fear and anger in her voice, "Good God, what's that?" Another spike to drive into Mommy.

During our grace period, when Ned and I were first in New York, both of us still finding our feet and Bett in jobs where her bosses still liked her, we would meet for lunch, and she would wear the rabbit coat I bought her once, which she loved (I mention this to feel better but it doesn't work) and which she still wore though the bunny was balding. It was a *grace* period, because we would both be in motion, both a little windblown, meeting for lunch. I could feel her cold cheek against mine as we greeted each other, a waft of cologne and something of that bunny fur, Mommy pink-cheeked and dark eyes shiny with cold and with the incomparable sweetness, pleasure of this, meeting her child for lunch in New York, two gals in the big city. We'd go to some Japanese or Chinese place, crowded with lunchtime business; we'd go dutch, or she would pay because she had her check, or I would pay because she hadn't. In that grace-period time we were equals, sisters, and she was working and happy and we were *in movement.* Nothing had been arranged or settled, and the endings could all have been different. But now the cycles of unemployment and depression were flattening out, getting longer, slower, slower curves, without much likelihood of rising. The skills were now skills of endurance, our places were set on the board and we were all crawling toward our final positions. Things got closer, walls and outcomes.

Bett was on pills a lot, for the anxiety, and they made her dopey. She wasn't so bright and funny so often now. She wasn't high-spirited, carefree. She didn't toss her shiny black hair on her beautiful neck, she didn't laugh with her head, she didn't move across a room like a woman of twenty. Her speech slowed, her body slowed, she slurred and stooped and slipped. Her hair became sort of lifeless, lost the shine it always had. Her skin would look tired; she would look tired. She was listless, forgetful; she was unhappy about being forgetful. Sometimes her hands would shake. She wouldn't "see" anybody; she just wanted the pills, though she never talked about it, you just knew she was on them. She would repeat herself, wander around without focus and then stay out of eyesight. And you would want to pierce through that dope, pierce through with whatever it took, words—sharp, cruel or begging— but neither the attacks nor the pleas would get through. Bett would say, "I know, baby, Mommy's just in a bad way now. Mommy just gets like this sometimes." Or "You don't understand these things. It's like a knot I get in my stomach." Or "Something bad happened to me when I was little, you can't understand, and God knows I'd never want you to. These pills take the edge off." Yeah, the edge, the shine, the light.

She would have crying fits about "nothing," about how useless she was, about how trapped she was with Hal or how trapped they both were. She didn't want to always trouble us, but Hal would tell us. "Things are getting weird again," he'd say.

We made her go with us and Hal to family therapy. They gave us a youngish doctor. He looked like the real thing, fresh from some genius degree, as dark and unstable as Montgomery Clift playing Freud, all cerebrum and sensibility as he sized us up, tried to unravel the macramé. He had a lot of figuring out to do, assessing this so-called family: Hal with his impenetrable Bronx, illiterate speech, Ned with his Eton vowels and remote manner, Bett looking wild-eyed and a little disheveled and speaking American unlike her daughter, all of us talking in different accents and dressed for different plays; Bett twenty-five years older than the rest of us, a kind of head of the family, Hal and Ned allied by their male outsiderness, their "go figure" stance vis-à-vis the troubled women, me and Bett the core knot of this knot that is like the knot in Bett's stomach, the thing Mommy just gets sometimes. Who's connected to whom? wonders the doctor, and he does his family tricks, trying to unpin or explode the family, or knock it down like a set of ninepins. For our first assignment we have to think what exactly each of us would lose if Bett got well, became happy and independent.

That was so perverse a notion it made us all laugh, though we agreed to think about it. But just that joint silent laughing at the doctor connected us a little, so that afterward in front of the clinic Hal, Ned and I stood semicircled protectively around Bett, sort of fond of one another that we were here, and almost fond of Bett that she was the cause of our being there, standing in the spring sunlight on a mild evening in April. It was as though we were all proud, as though someone had graduated or been confirmed or something, and we were all chatting on the steps full of fellow feeling after the ceremony.

We couldn't think of any benefit to any of us for Bett to stay weak and unhappy, and at the next session we all said so. Even Bett got annoyed and defended us. "I don't understand your question," she said. "They all love me; they help me; they want me to get better." The doctor shook and nodded in several directions at once, and I could feel some little hopefulness about what we were doing there leave the room. There was a young student sitting behind a smoked-glass partition recording all our movements. We couldn't see much of her, but she was writing down all the language language and body language among the group each time any of us talked. We started to become self-conscious, tried almost to mislead, as though this were all a game of them and us, them being the doctors. They were more like technicians at a recording studio. We were just the entertainment.

But we went. We went maybe just to have a shadow of that first feeling every time we got out, stood on the steps, broke up to go home. Then Bett started to be erratic about showing up, or Hal. It was as though this was too slow, as though there wasn't that much time. Or Bett would accept the gesture of our being there, that we all loved and cared about her, and push it one step further. Once, after a session, when she and I were trying to cross on a red light, I pulled her back from a car coming too fast, and she said, all flirtatious, "Why, baby, I didn't know you cared." I wanted to explode at the eye-batting vampishness of that, couldn't respond to it, couldn't say, "What do you think we've just been doing for the last hour, the last weeks?"

Perhaps we knew she was at some edge—there had to be a reason why we went twice a week, why in the end Ned gave her work helping him transcribe his taped interviews, not just so that the money wouldn't have to feel, as she always said she hated, like a handout, but so she could be with us in the house every day, half living there, sleeping over sometimes. She would work with Ned in the mornings and then wander around, sort of dazed, the rest of the time. It hurt so much to watch her disintegrate. It broke my heart to see the loveliness leaving her. It broke my heart to hear her shuffling around. Looking up at her, sometimes I would startle her, or shame her by seeing. She wanted to be with us and she wanted to be invisible.

It was hard. You wanted to save her, you wanted to return her to the air she used to breathe that made her well and beautiful. And you were furious that she was doing this, you were so angry with her. You thought she was wantonly, willfully destroying your mother, removing her, removing herself, letting her fall apart in front of your eyes. She was leaving you. You were so angry with her. She was leaving you. And all the time that anger surfaced, you exploded and exploded, and in the end you could barely even talk to her and Ned had to do it, to deal with her, like the night he took her around all the hospital emergency rooms because she said she was cracking up and had to have help. She was hysterical. And then they both came back, Ned dazed by the heartlessness of the American system, the emergency rooms, the money-first attitude toward pain; she dazed by the whiteness, the clerical pettiness, all the people waiting, sitting bunched up on laminated sofas, their eyes laminated, waiting, waiting. Clarke said, "Sometimes it's a help for people to feel the bottom; it isn't Snake Pit out there anymore, hospitals aren't the worst thing possible." But Bett came back that night in pieces, sure she didn't want to go. She said, crumpling in the doorway, her eyes swinging wildly in her head, her face contorted like a Greek mask of grief, "Don't let them send me to hell," and she meant hell, there were weird religious terms surfacing in her speech a lot these days and hell meant something real. But her face was so wildly rhetorical and she was so actressy you said, "Oh, Mommy, don't be so fucking melodramatic. You don't have to do anything you don't want to do." As if you had a clue what you were talking about.

We did the family therapy now without that much hope but we kept on going. We tried to get her to cut down the pills and she said she would. She even agreed to see a separate therapist. I think the family therapist recommended her, another student, but smart enough, because after a few sessions Bett was rather amusedly, somewhat proudly, and to me crushingly, repeating what the woman said to her. She said Hal and I were like Angel and Gogi to her, that Hal was "just like my grandmother, all kindness and love," and that "you were like my mother, cold and unloving." "Of course, baby, I said that wasn't you, only sometimes. I said I knew you loved me. She said I saw you sometimes that way, like my mother, not very loving." She would tell me this and I would explode or cry, yet there was part of me that thought it was funny that Hal would be thought of as her grandmother, like a scene from "Little Red Riding Hood." I saw Hal's long face under a white lace cap. I tried to think that her telling me I was like Gogi was just another ploy to get me to say again that I loved her, which by now should have been as obvious as anything, or else why did she always make me want to strangle her or say those things? What things? Those please-end-this-game things like when she was going on about how she wanted to kill herself, and I'd heard it every day one way or another, and said, "For Christsake, Mommy, stop threatening me with this all the time. It's just blackmail. Either do it or shut up about it." And she would look at me like I'd slapped her across the face, which was by then just a look, empty of meaning. Everything was getting emptier and emptier of meaning, like the noises about suicide. Maybe my response was an attempt to bring the language back to content, in some way, to play the film backward until image and meaning reconnected, until it became possible again for one to say, "I'm so depressed I feel like killing myself," and the other to say, "How could you say such a thing?" Bett was the little girl crying wolf, and now here the wolf is again, not Hal in Angel's lace cap but the Big Bad Wolf that really was at the door, and just about to huff and puff and blow our house down.

She came up to the country for a week, and I tried to be careful with her. We took long walks on the dirt road, with Bertie accompanying us, and sometimes Nineveh. I would be sort of in the lead, sometimes Bertie, who would cast back anxiously at me and Bett to see if we were still there. He had that worried, furrowed look chows have, and it seemed somehow touching, right, that he should trot out ahead of us and look back like that, worried, or follow behind us, keeping his pace as slow as hers. It was harder for me; I always slipped ahead, walking too fast, too firmly, trying to keep talking to her, trying to keep her going, moving along the road under the beautiful arching green, the bowers now in full leaf, sometimes dripping with rain or swaying, shsshing with a lovely noise in the soft air, going shssh, shssh and keeping us along the road, Mommy, me, Bertie the orange chow and sometimes Nineveh, looking very cross, stopping, yowling and then bouncing, trotting again because we wouldn't turn back and come home with him. Mommy talking to the animals in that sweet soft way she had—St. Francis—them understanding it, being a little worried about her, or so it seemed. All of us, trees, cat, dog, road, daughter, being gentle with her, herding her a little, keeping her going, moving, at whatever pace, while she babbled at the dog or cat like a child, a still lovely, soft, sweet, dreamy child.

Or we would walk over the hill behind the house and look at the lovely New Jersey green bursting around and beneath us and stretching county by county, the red barns dotted through the view, heightening the green, which was rich, fecund, heavy with heat already that early May, or else weeping, wet, dripping. And the lilac bushes near the house were heavy, the branches bending under the weight of all the lilac, all that perfume and deep lavender, bowing down with it, the water dripping off the black branches that were pale green underneath. Those lilac bushes were ancient, perhaps a century old, older than Shrimp, perhaps older even than Angel would have been, and every year they put forth perfumed blossoms on the black, scarred branches that glistened when it rained.

It was a rich spring. Bertie and Nineveh had taken to chasing and killing chipmunks, and there was competitive slaughter, the bodies piled by the steps of the house or hurled around the garden. Bertie was half wild in the country and would often disappear for days at a time, turning up twenty miles away, according to phone calls, but always coming home. He loved the country, and when we drove up in the open VW he would sit up in the back, chomping at the air and flies, and then, when we arrived, he would leap out and off to see the neighborhood bitches, coming back hours later, muddy, burr-covered, very pleased with himself. Alone, I would take him for long rides in the car with the top down, the Mozart pounding, him beside me in the passenger seat, sitting upright, grinning, his black tongue spraying the air in the wind we made. When Mommy came I would drive her under the trees and Bertie would lie in the back, all mannerly, paws together and deferential. He always seemed very aware, very considerate, of her.

Sometimes, when Ned was working in the barn across the road and I was in my room writing my novel (which is what the book on the Abstract Expressionists became), Bett would sit outside in the garden listening to insects and typewriters going, sitting with her book or thoughts in the sun or shade, next to Bertie and Nineveh, and keep an eye out for the local cats, who were given to sporting birds. There was a nest under the low roof of the porch, and during the time Mommy was with us it hatched. There were three or four baby birds in the nest, their parents would come and go, leaving them alone much of the time. I asked her to keep an eye on it. But she'd keep forgetting, or her mind would start drifting, or she couldn't concentrate, and whenever I glanced up I would see a cat circling the nest on the ground below. I'd come out and remind her. She would say, "Yes, yes, relax, go back to work, nothing's going to happen, I'm looking after it." And I would go back for another twenty or forty minutes and look up to see a cat circling hypnotically under the baby birds, and even Nineveh coming out of his sunshine stupor, getting vaguely interested in all that chirping. I'd come out again. Bett would look up from her book and say, "I'm here, nothing can happen." The last time, I saw the cat up the porch fence, close enough to the nest to knock it over. I ran out, shouted. Mommy said, "Oh, uh, uh, I forgot," like the dumbest kid in school, and suddenly it was more than birds, it was everything and everything that had ever been between us, and I shouted at her, "You can't look after anything, can you?" It stunned her, it cut her terribly. And it was upside down, because it was I who was helpless looking after her.

Well, of course, no, it wasn't all Peaceable Kingdom those ten days we had in the country. She slept a lot, she dreamed, she cried. She said, "Please don't leave me alone." I stayed with her. Often there would be these lovely animal silences among us all (where was Ned? always in the barn writing, always away in my memory, away in the manger), but often we would fight. We were our own weather there in that house, sun and spring, wind or storms. It rained a lot while we were there, violent heavy thunderstorms with biblical deafening crashes of thunder and hysterical lighting effects. Once when we were arguing the house was struck by lightning. It was so dramatic and so terrifying, I cowered, and Bett said, laughing, "See? You'd better be careful what you say." She thought it was very funny, but I apologized.

Sometimes she was indifferent, in another world, her own world of dreams and drugs and dreaminess. We would talk together gently when she was like this, or we'd take those walks. Sometimes she would be bitter or angry or sarcastic and we would fight, and sometimes, the scariest, saddest times, she would just sit there, shaking a little from the pills, her lovely sculptor's hands sort of abandoned in half-gesture, curving toward one another, or moving involuntarily, trembling, Bett's lovely hands held into nothingness, reaching from her plump arms, covered in the blue, cat-haired T-shirt, extending from the soft forms of her torso, into nothingness, and trembling there involuntarily, so expressively. And her eyes deep in pain under the shallowness of painkillers, and she would say, sweet and scared as a tiny little girl, "Please don't leave me alone in the house too long."

We said, "No, we'll be back soon." But once we said one hour and stayed three, and all the time I felt how she was waiting for us. I was torn, out buying her a present, something I knew she admired, a special present, but all the while knowing what it was costing her, a gift on my terms, not hers, a kind of disciplining by punishment and reward. When I came back, I gave it to her, my Mother's Day present, a hand-painted Limoges "breakfast set." She was very quiet, pleased with the gift, but the delight so muted by the terror, whatever it was (that wasn't for me to question). And I think of it, the cruelty and the desire to please and the love all contorted and coming out wrong, I think of it when I force myself to use it, when I punish myself with it these days.

She didn't want to go back to the city, but we all had to go, to pick up Simone, who was coming for a few weeks. Bett always hated the summer, as I always did when I was a child living with her: all the people with money left town and all of us with no escape had to stay. It was "hot as hell," she'd always say, and she was dreading the first blast of heat, the first exodus of all the lucky ones on Memorial Day. It was just before that holiday weekend that Simone was coming and we had to get back, to meet her at the airport, bring *her* to the country. Mommy was very quiet in the car all the way home, except for saying how much she'd loved being with us, except for her terrible gratitude.

There were people staying in our house. There was Janie, and Toni and David over from London. The house was big enough for all of us, but Ned and I were moving out for the summer to work in the country. Simone was to visit us there, where, as it happened, she had a childhood friend in a nearby village. The plan was to pick up Simone at the airport and drive her straight to dinner with some friends, then bring her to New Jersey for a few days, back to town after the weekend, where she'd see Bett and Hal, go to the theater, visit her friends, the usual things she did in New York. This picking up at the airport and bringing to dinner was all tightly scheduled. We have to go, lock up; Bett has to leave.

I'm upstairs hurrying to get dressed for the airport. All afternoon I've tidied for Simone's visit. Bett's been in the way, and now all this commotion about not being late for Simone. I can tell she feels it, that Simone is the one who counts, the good mother, the elegant, sane, cultivated one, the one who isn't a nuisance, a worry, the one who isn't falling apart and having to be looked after. Simone is the mother that everyone is looking forward to seeing, and she, Bett, is the useless, pathetic mother, around everyone's neck and ruining the lovely Helen-and-Ned picture, ruining their wonderful life when they're so lovely, even Helen, who fights and shouts but really loves her, Bett the terrible mother, now as always in everyone's way.

I'm upstairs in the bedroom. The white closet doors are standing open and I'm trying to get something on so I can hurry downstairs and leave with Ned, who's shouting from there. Bett is wandering around this room in that dopey daze of hers, her heavy, sad arms and shoulders sloping, her eyes dull, sad. Yet she's circling in some strange determined way, keeps watching me as I try to find shoes and shirt and jacket, watching me as I move around in my underwear trying to find things, weirdly, and it's getting more annoying.

"Mommy, you've got to get ready, we've got to be out of here in five minutes."

"I know, Puppy, let me look at you."

"What?"

"Let me just look at you for a moment."

"We have to go, we're going to be late for the plane."

"I know, baby, but just let me look at you."

"What is this?"

"Please."

I have to drop everything and stand there while she looks at me in this strange way, her staring at me in my bra and pants and me holding on to my anger.

"All right?" I say, furious, moving out of the pose.

"You're beautiful," she says in this spooky way that seems to have nothing to do with anything.

By now I have my clothes on and I'm heading down the stairs, but she's not moving, she hangs back on the landing. She says, "Puppy, give me a kiss."

I say, "What? We've got to go, come on, I'll kiss you downstairs."

But no, she's having this moment, this actress's moment. She says weakly, "Just one kiss."

And I am so furious I can't control it anymore, and though I am five steps down the stairs I rush back up and practically scream, *"Here's your fucking kiss."* I butt my face into hers as I kiss her, so hard it hurts us both. (It's not fair, she knows something I don't know and she doesn't stop it happening like this.) There's a look from her of utter devastation that her very own daughter . . . and then I bolt down the stairs and she comes slowly after.

That exactly was the last, the very last, conversation we ever had.

We have Simone. We take her to dinner, where everything is lovely and sweet, Ned and I enact the lovely young couple, Simone is so happy to be with us, and it's all charming, delightful, flowers and candles, laughter. But as the dinner goes on I am suddenly overwhelmed by fatigue, as though blood and light have left me. I feel drained, suddenly utterly feeble, though it is Simone who has traveled so far. And it's late when we get back to the house in New Jersey, but still not that late that it would explain it, one-thirty perhaps. Ned, Simone and I are standing in the kitchen when the phone goes, sharp and bright at that late hour.

Ned picks up the phone, holds the receiver. We look at him as his face goes, as he cries out. He wails a complaint, not at me or Simone but into the air, holding on to the receiver with one hand, pushing at his eyes with the other.

"Bett's dead," he says.

The very first, clearest sensation is of weight lifting off my head and shoulders, actual physical weight, months and months of exhaustion. A phrase comes to me, as clearly as if I'd heard it spoken: Thank God. And then immediately, the next just as real response comes to cover it: Oh God. There is an almost comical need to reach the phone that Ned holds on to, and he won't give it up, he's holding it, hugging it to himself, all the grief to himself. I see instantly how I don't exist for him at all. So much so that in order to get the phone away from him, to speak to whoever it is, I have to beg him, "It's *my* mother."

I speak to Janie, who's been trying to ring us all night, and hear how Hal called, and Shrimp went to see the body, and the police were there. It's all over and happened already. All over that afternoon, this evening, tonight. Bett's committed suicide.

Janie can't speak and I can't, I can barely breathe, there's no air in my chest, my throat. And there's Ned collapsed on a chair, beginning to sob. The minutes hold and hold, I am surrounded in unbreathable space, and stunned now by Ned's self-enclosure. Even Simone must have been, because finally she moves—she, not he—embraces me and says, as she's never said before or since, "Oh, darling."

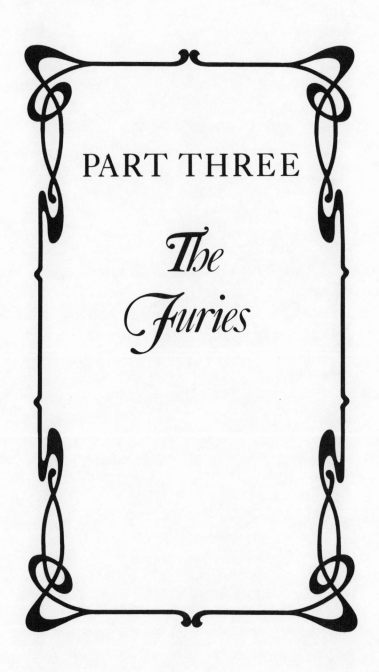

PART THREE

The Furies

TEN

A DEATH IS ANNOUNCED and nothing stops. Nothing waits. Things get hellishly, mockingly busy, as if there were fun somewhere in all of this, and you act out of numbness, panic, like treading water knowing you're going to drown but playing for time, splashing, kicking, keeping everything lifelike until the water wins and you submit, go under. Bett's dying gave us all something to do, and a kind of importance. Certainly we suddenly cherished one another, each of us guarding our own and one another's fragile significance, our tasks, our duties, our nearness to the guest of honor, dearness to the corpse. Immediately, strangely and so naturally, Hal and I and Ned became a fellowship of grief, an orphanage, a band of the chosen, Bett's only beloveds. We moved almost as one on the streets, in and out of cabs, subways, performing the death functions, taking our condolence calls, imparting the news, visiting the cremation lady, laughing together afterward at the lipstick and white powder, the clichéd embalmed look she had and brothel-keeper manner, her instant intimacy, sympathy, her gentility ("It's cleaner, dear, isn't it? Nicer . . ."), and mostly at how she wasn't anything like as real or beautiful as Bett, that corpse that conferred upon itself in dying—and by extension glorified us—something like sainthood, only not that, not martyrdom, something more ferocious, living, pagan, a godhead. She who had passed among us. And to preserve that—which we felt, which was true, which we didn't invent—Ned and Hal, brothers, were protective of me, went alone to identify the death-bloated body. "You wouldn't want to see her that way," they said. I said, "If I don't see her, will I understand that she is dead?" Because everything being so strange, nothing, not even that, was clear.

We were sort of exuberant in the heat of all this busyness we had, Hal eerily unaffected, buoyant, and me grateful that he wasn't blaming us, that he'd stopped resenting us. We were so close then, the abandoned ones, made equal in our grief and equal in responsibility, equally careful of one another. This because we'd lost her, the way you lose something you were supposed to look after. We'd all failed, and now, strangely, we were all set free. For the moment made high and set free.

I felt defiant, as though I knew what was coming, what was at stake, and what the others would think. I found the little blue address book with the names from her world, and Ned and I called them. We found a pretty church willing to hold a service for a suicide; we found a musician to play his violin into silence, a Bach partita, the most intimate, grieving sound I knew; we found a florist; we found black summer clothes. We ordered wine. Ned wrote a beautiful tribute. Simone cut sandwiches. And then I put out the photographs.

I was ashamed of losing her, ashamed of being still here without her, and so I refused to apologize. And on her behalf, too, I refused to apologize. For the suicide, the creeping away, the confession of failure, the statement that she thought she shouldn't exist. I put out all her beautiful pictures to say that we weren't ashamed, either of us. It was like when I was at school, creeping around in all those secondhand dresses, living in crummy places, how I'd always been able to feel unashamed again whenever she came to parents' day, because they'd see her, see how lovely she was, how she'd been favored. And now, doing this, it was the same, my denying she had slipped off defeated, humiliated, my insisting that not even death would change the fact, eternal, for ever and ever, every bit as eternal as this death, that she had been beloved, by those very gods that seemed so much less than loving. So I displayed her, put out the big photographs on mantelpiece and sideboard, over couches, in the hallway, everywhere the eye might look. I brought her back, filled my house with her, showed her to *them*, any of them who might be saying isn't it awful, wasn't it a waste, all of it, always. I displayed her, as a young beauty, as a still young beauty only five years back. I showed her sexy, happy. I took the largest photos I had of her and me, her gazing down into my face with so much love you could never ever think I'd hurt her, disappointed her, hastened her death. No, I made her happy, see how much she loved me, see how close we were? I had another big photo, a high glossy of Bett at some party in the early sixties with some man I'd never met, some handsomest man in the room, maybe the city, and that handsomest man in the city was sinking, falling, drowning in Bett's beautiful and smiling eyes. And that photo, too, said to all those shuffling mourners, all those funeral guests, that Bett was adored, that she was lovely and glamorous and one of the happy, and not always so sad, not always so deathly sad that she died of it. And the photo of Bett and Constance and Gogi all on the sofa at her wedding, all with those stunning legs, I put that out, too, as if to say, you see, it's a family, it has a beginning, a middle and not so finally necessarily an end, as if I were promising to keep it going, bear it forward, keep the tree of it living, as Gogi said in her letter to me, how the dying parts didn't matter as long as the tree went on. There was that, half-understood, vow and there was the other part, of me trying to slip myself into that picture, trying to catch some of that light and absolution. This is my family, too, it said to them of me, as I moved around that room in black muslin, handing out the sand-wiches, pouring the wine, keeping moving among those still islands of others, those quiet, staring clumps of mourners. This is my family, and I am not ashamed, it said. I do not feel any of the shame of this death. I am proud of my mother and (here was the empty boast) proud of myself, thus connected. *I have nothing to apologize for.*

But I was seething with apology and everyone must have known it, defiant as I was, serving drinks in this rich person's house (". . . the daughter married well and Bett with no money . . ."). I wasn't apologizing for the money or the house or my own survival, yet someone must have known something, because Gloria, Bett's long-ago best friend I hadn't seen in fifteen or twenty years (and I was so stunned to see her, so triumphant and so beautiful, like

Bett only not like Bett, alive), said, "You know I didn't come today for Bett. I came for you."

I didn't even know I needed it until I heard her words. Because with all the photos and flowers and inviting all those people (not so many really, sadly not so many at all) into this rich person's house, I was taking the lead, preempting their judgment, insisting I had nothing to be ashamed of, and she hadn't, we neither of us had, Mommy or me. I might have waited for someone to say it for me, if I hadn't been so terrified, so sure that no one would, you know, say: "It wasn't your fault."

I wonder if all that would have been better if they'd let me have her note. Not real absolution, of course, because her letter made everything all the more painful. And me all the more unforgivable to myself. But I might at least have had her tenderness, felt less outcast by her than I did those first days and days of silence. The police had removed the notes before we got there, said they were evidence needed for the criminal report (Bett being both criminal and victim). It took five days to pry even a copy from them—the cheap xeroxes on government paper. (Isn't the suicide note the property of the addressee? we asked. Not without a stamp, they said. They still have them.) At that remove I see her writing, the bold, generous, determined hand, weakening as the pills take, the arching, falling, sleepy shapes of my mother's script as she resists.

There were two notes. The one to me said:

To Helen (and Ned be with her always),
My darling, my dearest
My very dearest love in the world—
If you have felt a rage at me—it never was to me anything compared to the rage I've felt toward myself for not being able to be the mommy you were looking for. The one you once had—and still do and always will have—adoring, giving, sharing, loving and oh so proud mommy. But the desperately unwillingly hurtful person I've been instead has been so terribly—horribly far from my intent and therefore so impossible to face or admit, or have any way of sparing you from.

But the strong and loving and proud mama is always with you and always will be as you are now in my heart, loving you for everything you are—strong, beautiful, so wonderfully intelligent, elegant and capable. Gogi had the vision to see all the things you would grow to be. I had only the instincts to do anything any way I could to get the very best and love the very hardest I could, this best of all possible daughters . . .

Forgive me for what I have to do. I could be a growing burden to you and Ned. You've both done so much in spite of so little return. So little *possible* return . . .

Bett's note to me, when I finally got it, made her death clearer, made it so I couldn't think it was still part of our fight, our game, our locked horns. Not everything to do with me and her. There was self-love in this somewhere, I had only to try and find it. The Frenchman who owned the deli on her block said he'd seen her at five that afternoon (just before she took her life, according to the coroner's report), waving, smiling, stepping lively. It was late afternoon on May 31, a significant day: Memorial Day, start of the dreaded summer, Memorial for war heroes and Memorial Day for remembrance, in case anyone was ever tempted to forget—these things must have entered her choice of that day, plus Simone's being there: the "good," the surrogate mother for the soon to be motherless children, both of us, Ned and me. The end of May, month of mothers, month of Mary, month of heroes, the beginning of heat and abandonment, of the rich leaving the poor to the cities, May as in Maybe Maybe not, as in yes, finally you may, as in Mayday, the call for help and the sound of the bailout, and also, now that I think of it, as in her middle name, Maida. So two weeks after the day of her own mother's death twenty years before, Elizabeth Maida signaled Mayday, said yes I believe I may, and left for the summer, left for the duration, waving to the fat Frenchman standing in the doorway of his deli, waving, apparently happily, with a lovely smile and a strong walk, waving hello and not goodbye, and went home to write her letter and take her pills.

In the end I took her to the country for the summer, buried her there, where we'd been close and sometimes happy. I didn't think she'd want to be caught dead in a cemetery somewhere in Queens or Staten Island. Dead, I thought, she'd prefer to be caught in New Jersey. I bought her a plot in perpetuity there among the country folk, even among the Revolutionary War dead; I negotiated her into the eighteenth-century section, remembering her preference for the elegant, knowing she'd like it more than the contemporary part with its slicker, shinier, more garish stones. And *I* liked it there, all soft and weather-beaten and timeless, mossy, wistful and a little less brutal than it really was. There was a family in that part called Beauty: Constant and Eva and A. I liked her being there, so close to Constant Beauty.

The gravedigger was a nice man, young, with long blond hair and a kind of eighteenth-century manner himself, pastoral in his hippiedom and with a pretty, barefoot, blond daughter, or maybe he was out of Shakespeare, a decorative subplot in one of the late plays, the ones about lost and reunited parents and children. He helped us find a place among the ancient dead, the nation's first, on a little rise near the Beauty family. He helped us plant the peony bush above the place where the ashes were to go, below the place where the simple headstone would be, then he left me alone to put what was left of my mother in the ground.

I held the tin can in my hand for a long time before placing it in dark earth. What they give you for the ashes looks like a small labelless can of paint, enough only for touch-ups, with a wire handle that makes it swing a little when you hold it, and it swung a little over the hole the hippie dug, like some water-divining thing, some psychic's instrument for outer-body communion. It swung a little because I suddenly remembered Bett's allergy to metal, how she always had to put adhesive on the undersides of her earrings so she wouldn't get a rash. It seemed awful, suddenly, that I had her there in a tin can, for eternity, and I remembered that flash of nightmare when she had crumpled in our doorway, her face melting in terror the night of the emergency-room visits, when she pleaded with us, "Don't let them send me to hell." Well, maybe this was hell, this confining her forever in metal. And then I shook the thought and recalled that these were only ashes, were not my mother at all. And yet were, also, my mother, this appallingly little amount left, this remainderdom, remnanthood, this almost nothing that I held and which trembled in the air in a can, swinging slightly over a dark hole in the ground. It was and it wasn't Bett, and I said and did not really say goodbye.

In the city after she died it rained a lot. Outside our windows there was green from the trees behind our house, and indoors there would be a golden gray or lime-green light, a gentle mournful light of summer showers in early evening. We had cut lilacs from the country, and they drooped a little in the humidity, pale lavender inside the underwater-green-lit living room, where for weeks, until I could bear to take them down, Bett's photos were up, until they, too, lost their force, that fierceness that had protected me at the funeral. They began to wilt a little, like lilacs, to let Bett's sadness through, sad even where she was laughing. Or maybe it was my sadness that affected them, or the green light or the sweet humidity of those afternoon evenings that made, in those first weeks of grieving, the room an enchanted room, a place with its own sad music, like the funeral Bach partita, the abandoned solo violin, playing into space, making its terribly solitary imploring sounds, asserting nothing.

Those damp evenings in the first weeks after her funeral the room was still peaceful, like a small, ancient, empty church, full of Bett and my love for her. But away from this room, out on the streets, things were much harsher. I saw mothers and daughters our age, and envy would stagger me, split me apart, envy together with a savage remorse: so much love and understanding coming so late and so uselessly. And where was the person I needed to help me get through all this now? I felt the irony, but it didn't help: here was this devastating, unbearable thing and I needed my mother to make it better. I thought if she were there I could cope with this, Bett's death.

I felt searing jealousy whenever I saw them: those happy, bickering mothers and daughters in our neighborhood. I watched them waltz in and out of our stores, our coffee shops, the drugstore where Bett got her pills, where she still owed money; the bank where she had her account, where I had some savings book from

PSL. They didn't even have to be our ages, these mothers and daughters, bodies bending toward in conspiracy or away in conflict, making plans, laughing about boys, doing, as I watched and imagined them, only what Bett had longed for us to do, being so simple. Was it, had it been, too much to ask, just that, all that she wanted, to be two figures like this walking down the street side by side—not, as I usually walked with Bett, a few steps ahead, anger in my pace, impatience, she would *drag* so? "Come on, Mommy"—I had said that since I could remember, no, not at Mirrenwood, after, after I became a city child, after I learned to jump on and off buses, use my own keys, fend for myself. "Come on, Mommy." She was amused at first at my voice of exasperation, her baby, so impatient to be out on the street, out in the world, and then later the baby wouldn't slow down, and the impatience was there all the time, till the last part when we were broken, both of us, by the ending that was coming, coming, and there was nowhere for Mommy to come on to, no one to catch up with, when there was point any longer pleading, "Come on, Mommy." So I hung back, and shepherded her, the way Bertie shepherded both of us, Bertie, bounding off to show us how it could be done and then turning and dancing back to make sure we were still there and all right. My dancing backward was slower, clumsier, and by then I knew she wasn't all right.

I didn't even have to see the mothers and daughters; the streets were full of our ghosts: this block near school where Mommy crouched and spat on the corner of a Kleenex to take something out of my eye, me tearing seeing her blurred, radiant face, smelling her warm, scented skin, watching her eyes, so given to me, loving. Or here, years later, where we went for lunch once, and she so proud, introducing me to the neighborhood women, me impatient of course, where did I imagine I needed to go? Or here, this corner, where we fought, where I turned on my heel and walked off, independent, in that way that used to amuse her: my baby, and then later it became "sharper than a serpent's tooth . . ."

Oh, but it doesn't matter. What hurts and hurts and hurts and drives me off the streets is their *absence* now of her. She just isn't here any longer. *It's so hard to understand that she is gone.* That never, never, never, never, never will I see her here again, bump into her, make her laugh a the unexpected delight of our so meeting, baby and me, both of us neighbors out on the streets, doing our shopping. I'll never catch a glimpse of her slow (infuriatingly slow) saunter away from some never again so fortunate shop, her lovely head of dark hair her elegant back, and her slow, sensuous, dizzy walking, carrying something, like a lopsided carriage, looking to spill around each bend: Bett, tipping, tipsy, my delicately balanced, oh so precarious mother. So precarious she might one day disappear. And I'd never ever guessed that such a thing was possible.

I don't know where Hal was, where he went after the funeral. He was still in a sort of vacation mode about the whole thing, seemingly unaffected, anyway not shattered, numb like Ned and me, our movements and responses as slow and swollen as figures underwater. Hal wasn't staying at the apartment any longer. He gave me the keys and I went over one afternoon to pack up her things.

I was scared of what I was going to feel doing this. It wasn't just their love nest I was invading, it had also been Mommy's and mine. My legs began shaking going up the flights. It was warm, June, and the same dark cool green-marbled linoleum as had been on the steps and in the halls when we first moved there, when I was first at Wickhurst, when Mommy won Gary in a poker game, and the same oxblood-stained banisters were giving off the same smell. You could smell the cats by the second landing and the different bags of garbage that everybody parked outside their doors, brown paper bags because there weren't the black plastic ones yet, and kept waiting until they had the time or inclination to put them in the bins out on the street. So the hallways as you ascended and the warm air as it ascended would get denser and richer with the smells of old newspapers, maybe cat-peed, of kitty litter and melon rinds and coffee grounds, meat scraps and so on. It was seldom overwhelming except in high summer, but it was always pretty rich, effusive of all those private city lives. There were Ned and me living and working on four floors, and here were ten other people in a place not so very much bigger, all of them guarding their privacy, though everyone knew what everyone else had had for dinner the night before each time they came home and climbed the stairs. Our floor, the top floor, would also smell of clay a lot because Mommy kept the door open so the breeze from the little balcony could cool things off. The balcony was where she stored the beautiful oily-green clay, so dense and musty its smell could choke you even in winter if there was a fire going in the fireplace.

I was a little breathless as ever when I got to our floor. My throat was constricted and my hand was trembling as I turned the key. I felt simultaneously two things. First, that this was my real home, that I was coming home like after school, that all that England bit—Norfolk, Oxford, getting married, all that—was immaterial, like a prank I'd done and which was all over now; that I was still the New York child of Bett's coming home, going to get a soda from the fridge and do my homework. Nothing had happened—all I had to do was turn the key in the lock, push open the door and there would be Bett—"Hello, Puppy, how was school?" That was still a possibility, and everything could be all right again and not as it was going to be: a fast unstoppable fall into darkness. So, simultaneously like this, I was coming home, nothing had happened, no fighting, no leaving, no getting English, no getting married, no getting rich and therefore no getting orphaned, and then of course like the other, I was the outsider, intruder, about to open up the tomb of Tutankhamen, to break into the magic place where I'd no right to be, to disturb with my alien air the sacred, lovely site, the Bett place I'd forfeited all rights to when I left fifteen years before.

She wasn't there. The apartment was just as though she'd run off to get milk for coffee and would be back any minute. If I left the door open I'd hear her coming up, the keys jingling in her hand, her flat sandals slapping a little on the lino, her voice calling me, talking to me like she always did, as though only she and I lived there and there were no neighbors. She had no self-consciousness at all; I might have envied her that if I hadn't felt obliged to have it for both of us, would lower my voice when returning her greeting as though thereby to monitor hers, but she would just boom out or babble from wherever she was those embarrassing names for me she had, Puppy or baby or Poo: "Poo, help Mommy with her bag," or "Puppy, did Mommy lock you out?" or "Sweet Pea, why're you so dressed up in this heat?" Just like at Mirrenwood.

It was a tiny place; as soon as you opened the locks on the door you were deep inside. As soon as you stepped in one step you stood between the daybed and the broom-closet-sized kitchen. If you took two more steps you'd bump into the chair and the glass table where we ate (where they ate) dinner. I hadn't taken these steps inside for perhaps two or three months, the months that Bett was slowly caving in, crumpling, trembling, taking her pills, her eyes glazing over. I couldn't bear to see her that way, and besides she was at our house every day most of that time. So now when I looked I could see the old Bett restored, reparated, the death-reconstructed Bett. No, I couldn't see her, she wasn't here, she was gone, but everywhere in that room, grabbing me as soon as I stepped inside, were the images. At knee level when you opened the door, my mother sleeping. Fifteen years ago, before I ran away to Veronica's, I used almost to brush against her head when I got in late from some Greenwhich Village night out with Duncan, then tiptoe past her to get to my room next door, the room where later Hal made his paintings. Or when I was with Ned in the early days of our being in New York, coming in, the glass table set with four places and to the left the closet-sized kitchen, dishes in the sink and Bett turning around in there between sink and stove, cooking some "family dinner" for Hal, Ned and me, some thanksgiving or birthday when we were still all a family, when she was still Mommy, the provider, and we, at least Ned and I, were still the children, cared for by her, feted, fed. Ned, protected from home-sickness by *my* mother, who always felt for his, Hal watching TV on the other end of the bed, Bett coming out to give Ned some alcoholless concoction, some "cherry" holiday-type thing made from V8 and celery sticks or pink grapefruit and cranberries, some to him weird American thing that was all part of her charm, this lovely young, almost silly mother of his Oxford girlfriend. There were the chairs on either side of the fireplace where Hal would show Ned or me his slides, and where over the mantel was that awful, huge, bad-tempered photo of me, which Bett loved but which to me, and particularly on this day of silent entry, looked as unlovable and superior and ghastly as I felt myself to be right then. Away from it I turned my head toward the little corridor to the bathroom, the white-tiled, light-filled, quite large room where Mommy would often lie, dreaming under the soap film or bubbles or writing down her thoughts on the white semi-porous porcelain with the pencil she kept near the tub, thoughts about herself, like the ones I came upon later in her diary: "The worst thing about mental illness is that no matter how bad it gets it can never ever kill you."

In all my life, in all the twenty-seven years, this is the place I have lived the longest: three whole years between thirteen and fifteen, when I went to Veronica's. Does this fact make this place my real home? Unlike that big place where I live now with Ned, that home to end all homes, that museum and theater of the home, the site of all our aspirations for home (or all mine?). No, this is my home, every inch of it familiar to every sense and glutted with memory. Well, it's certainly small enough for me to know it intimately: only as wide as the edges of those two full-length windows in the living room and the single full-length window in my old room. Between the two windows Bett used to keep her clunky black matte wooden sculpture stand where I used to watch her making medallions or mannequin heads or bra forms, but that was earlier. Today on this June afternoon the sculpture stand is abandoned on the balcony, its clay-sticky surface gritty with city soot. Where it used to be is Bett's tiny desk with its spiral notebooks. and files of bills, where she must have sat to write her last letter, the one that begins almost with joy and gets so wobbly. I turn quickly from the desk, look at the bookshelves over the boxed-in radiator. In the other room were all my books from school and childhood, still there mixed in with Hal's art books. Here were hers, very few of them, a few Kennedy biographies, a Gayelord Hauser book, *A Gift from the Sea,* some Dylan Thomas and, of recent purchase, Nixon and economics books, but still not so very many. In the old days I used to take the hardbacks and sell them for my bus fare to PSL, but that was in that other place near the Y. Here, things were always a little more cheerful.

While I look at the books I notice the cats staring at me in that aggressive way they have; they get down from bed or table and push against my legs as if they think I'm here to feed them. It seems absurd that they are still here, sitting in that dumb, trusting, homeownership way, as though still loved and recently kissed. Maybe they were, of course, they *were* more recently kissed than me ("Here's your fucking kiss"). It's absurd, obscene, that they are still here, assuming nothing's going to interfere with the smooth running of their lives, as though she were coming back, or just absurd, obscene, that they have survived her, the way it already flashes at me as obscene that I have. It's obscene and also tender, graceful, the way she has just left everything behind, when in my rage and grief I feel like Sardanapalus, that everything, cats, books, lamps, chairs, everything should have gone, too, into the black hole we shall all be sucked into.

But they're here. I look into their bowls and see fresh crumbs of food and suppose that Hal is looking after them. I don't want to look inside the fridge. I don't want to see what she was eating, the eternal leftovers. I don't have to look, I can remember: "Honey, you ate all the cold cuts, I got them for the week" (Bett to Hal). The awfulness of this, Bett's doomed and inept attempts at managing, housekeeping. (Bett to me, a constant refrain when I was much younger, when anyone said she was extravagant: "How can you budget nothing? There's nothing to budget with.")

Nothing—I look around. She loved this apartment so much. It was always so triumphantly stylish, simple, elegant, no matter how shabby it got. I wince now thinking about her and Simone and how apologetic she used to be whenever she had Simone over for lunch, her imagining Simone was pitying her and Simone actually always quite impressed with Bett's gumption, and her youthfulness of course, and the way (though Simone wouldn't have entirely admitted this) Bett had turned her back on that pushy, demanding world of convention. But Bett hadn't exactly turned her back—had the door slammed more like.

Come on. I've got to go through her stuff and get out. I take the box I brought with me and put the little notebooks from her desk into it; I go into the bathroom and open the cabinet, put in all the eyebrow pencils, lipstick. A lot of it I throw away, but I can't bear to throw away everything. It feels so insulting to chuck anything, anything that was hers, so I take a symbolic some and tip the rest with what callousness I can find through my aching throat, tight jaw, clenched teeth, into another bag. Some of her belongings I thus disendow with her spirit, and some I take in their wholeness, though they practically burn to the touch, so much hers are they: these pathetically numerous, perfectly sharpened eyebrow pencils, each one invested with increasingly desperate value, the instruments of her agonies, her fears for her disappearing looks. Well, she disappeared before they did.

When I open her dresser drawers my knees begin to buckle. I can't do this. I have to sit down. I'm talking to myself now, coaxing myself like a pony going through mortar fire. There in these drawers I have seen/known since I was eight, that have been repainted often enough for them to stick every summer, to begin to stick now, there nesting like something a bird values and hides are the separate piles of her underwear, clean, folded, but some of them so frayed or faded or laundromat-discolored that I have to bite down hard to stop from crying. Because *I can have anything I want.* Because I would not have had to keep these, I could have gone out and bought myself—no, no, it wasn't like that exactly, it always felt to me to be Ned's money and I almost never spent it on myself. I didn't buy the luxury stuff for myself, but still, I'd never have needed to keep things until there was no life left in them. And Mommy! I remember all through my childhood how she'd throw away a cup at the first chip, any glass with a crack, anything marred. It was never worth having if it was less than perfect. I remember all this as I look at these things of hers, and the order with which they were folded. That neatness that survived the despair. There's that and there's the physical presence of hers these things convey, the immediacy and intimacy, of these things she wore so close to her skin. The bras are the worst, the bras with their ghost parts still shaping them, the ghost forms of her so dense with life, so *pressing* they can mold fabric, curve the lace, strain the stain straps, those body forms that once breathed in and out with her, held warmth, held *me*—and now are no longer, just reduced to ashes, just gone, off the face of the earth. I don't know what to do. I empty the drawer into my cardboard box and pull open another. A tired, cracked, graying plastic bag full of pill containers, probably dozens of prescriptions from the last three years. I open the bag and spill the contents out onto the dresser top. There are pills from at least twenty different doctors here. Some of the names I recognize from her bills (unpaid, once- or twice-visited shrinks). How many of these did she ever take? It's hard to say, there are so many of them, so indiscriminately, so criminally, so laxly handed out. And kept by her, saved, for what purpose? There are enough pills here to kill a family of twenty. Was she planning, then, was she hoarding? Or was she, daughter of the mad Christian Scientist, simply sampling the pharmaceuticals, waiting for the magic pill that would make it all go away? Make her go away?

I tip the contents of the other drawers into the bags for the street people. The images speed past with the fabrics and colors, T-shirts that recall conversations, unfinished dresses she was making, whole bags of colored threads for her sewing machine, old patterns, pins still in them, old skirts, and jeans that recall her beautiful body to me and make me crumble like a lover over the remains of some dead beauty. I find the Dior nightgown I gave her the previous Christmas, and for a second there is something like reprieve. It is still in perfect condition—saved as a rare luxury among all this worn and dead clothing? Or refused, the inadequate gesture of the unloving child? Am I hurt that it is unworn? Or merely relieved that it is there, proof of some kind that I was capable of kindness? For this last reason, I think, but maybe for all these reasons, I put it in the box to take with me; likewise the Limoges cup and saucer and plate I gave her only a couple of weeks ago. Everything here has contradictory pulls for me, my chest is really hurting now and it's still hard to breathe. I'm putting things into my box, some things into the garbage, some things into a pile on the bed for some later visit. I don't know what I'm doing anymore, my head it swimming, black shapes like bird wings strike across my eyes. There won't be any later visit. I'll never come here again. I'm looking my last, I know that. I see the rabbit coat I bought her, now five years old and ripped, and again I feel simultaneously relieved that it exists and reproached by the state it's in.

I am dizzy now, in front of the closet shelves with their stacks of photos, those photo books of her work I made for her and she never used, those designs of hers for topless sandals and cubist dresses, all those inventions and escape plans going back to the early fifties, all ways of breaking out, escaping this, all cracked now, yellowing, grease-stained or dusty, but all *kept,* hung on to, through evictions, through thick or thin as though there were something in them still, some hope still, some key if only she could find it. Or maybe by now they were just souvenirs of a time when things *were* hopeful. I don't know anymore. I put them in the box. I take a pair of my mother's high-heeled shoes, with the shape of her toes and the grime of the soles still imprinted, place them too in the box. I look at the pair of rubber boots she has worn all rainy spring. I bend down and touch the black masking tape over the place where the boots have split, appalled how they have been repaired, these cheap rubber boots mended with such dire hopelessness, to keep out the wet, keep out the cold. I can't take any more of this, I pull my hand from the boots, close the closet door, leave the piles on the bed in some order for Hal, take my bags and box and go. I think if anyone sees me on the stairs I will cringe like the criminal I feel. My nose is running and my eyes. I really can't breathe now. At the bottom of the stairs I wipe my face on the Dior nightgown, breathe slowly like they teach you in yoga, take the remnants of my mother home.

That night, when Ned is out at some meeting, I lie in bed alone, wearing the Dior nightgown and feeling her presence in the room, right by the bed. It is loving, consoling, but it has extremity to it. It isn't remote or detached or comforting in that way, like a mother touching her child with an outstretched, distracted hand. It's as passionate as I am. There is sobbing and apology. She is *so sorry*, she had no choice. And I am *so sorry*. I feel the pain in my chest where the tears are coming from, breaking through my throat and spilling quietly, regularly, down either side of my face into the pillow. Every time I breathe I feel this extra weight in my chest. It feels like her to me, lying with me, feeling what I'm feeling, as though we were one. Sometimes even when I am not crying but only lying there I feel this pain and weight and presence and then the pain disappears and I know I am no longer without her.

I get up. I am not crying now. I am kind of exalted. I go to the bathroom and I take her box with me. I put it on the sink counter and stand in front of the mirror, touching her things. I put on her earrings with the Band-Aid tape against the metal. I pick up her eyebrow pencils and then I use one on my brows. I put her Blue Grass cologne behind my ears. I put on some thin chain necklace that Hal gave her—no, that was the locket, I left that there, the gold chain was something she bought herself. When I put these things of hers on, they disappear as things, they become magic only, conduits, ways of connecting. I try to put on her high heels but my heels stick out like the ugly stepsister in Cinderella and I'm afraid I'll hurt the shoes. I touch the bra but I don't put it on because I'd feel like a pervert. I put on her blue T-shirt with cat hairs still on it and the little rips in the seam and some dribble stain, probably also from a cat, the last thing my mother got to mother. I'm standing there with one of her shoes half on and her blue T-shirt over her nightgown and her earrings and necklace and perfume and makeup on, pressing myself into whatever is left of her, trying to take her heat and smell and body shapes into me, like some cannibal, like some early Christian getting the Eucharist all wrong, like some drag queen, like some old tart, now with her lipstick on my mouth and my eyes streaming her makeup, like that, hobbling up and down on the one high heel across the room, like that I go back to bed, collapse on the sheets, taking my mother or all that is left of her into bed with me.

Ned and I left the city, went back to the country, and she stayed with us there. She was both inside me and around me in all the green and heat of the countryside. Inside that green I was like someone incandescent; something in me was spinning, throbbing, *dense*, pumping out so much love and grief, but love more than anything else, so painful that my chest hurt constantly and my throat ached. I felt everything buzzing then, pulsing, croaking, swaying, as though my terrible love and grief set the whole countryside into heat and noise and light, and that the light and heat and noise wound and wrapped around me, kept me sealed to itself, protected, apart from everyone else, and then set me down at different times during the day, set me down gently into ordinary life.

But I had only to begin to feel Bett or think of her and the whirlwind would start, very quietly, and build and build, and soon I'd be rapt and away, high and flying and in my strange pain, a kind of natural, universal pain, like childbirth, as though I were part of the earth and the wind and the light, and all their pain of being, all their heaving and sparking and making light and heat and air, were mine—I was creating the day out of my pain for Bett, converting my body into an instrument of mourning and affinity with everything around me, and the animals felt it, the trees felt it, that we were all one, Bett's spirit, too, which was with me, cradled me, held me like that for weeks: in light, in love and pain, and off the ground.

I was never so connected to the country as in those first weeks after Bett died. I felt nature pushing in, impinging everywhere, the heat and humidity that came in at every opening, the spiders living in the bathtub, anchoring their webs to the ends of the toothbrushes, strands wrapping over the bristles, reclaiming you in the night, reclaiming you the way she reclaimed you every night in your sleep. Or the moths weaving cocoons in the bathroom window frames, the windows open enough to all the tiny living, killing, dying, reproducing creatures of nature. There was some wholeness then to inner and outer, no boundaries, some message and force pushing in from outside, demanding oneness. And time, too, pushed against boundaries, so that when those cobwebs and moth corpses made powdery white dust along the white gloss window-sills, I would be again at Mirrenwood, with its ancient, repainted white windowsills, the insects on it dead or giving birth and us little girls dressing in our white underwear behind the dotted Swiss bathroom curtains, brilliant in the morning sun. And here in this farmhouse now everything pressed in, white summer morning light and green of vines and branches, the odor and heat, of green expiring, exhaling humidity, and the heat of mourning, the dampness, numbness, the irresistible yielding to it, inside and outside becoming one in grief, from early morning until night, those hot humid nights when sweating and crying and the dampness outside all was one thing. At night the daytime green became a darkness, lit by fireflies, drawn by all that moisture in the meadows beyond our window, or by the large pond where the frogs croaked to one another in huge, nearly obscene noises, loud, upheaving, sexual noises, choral, crowded, a kind of mockery, grotesque accompaniment to the nighttime tears.

Sometimes Ned and I made love, our bodies slipping against one another like stones underwater, sweating and pumping like the hot world outside. Only inside ourselves we were broken, trying to find balance, to connect through the sensations of our skin, knowing ourselves lost inside the drowning grief and the thumping engine-hearted nature, hot, heavy, green, brutal, all around us.

The pain wasn't only about Bett, it was us, too, the heartbreaking, blind way we groped, our faces swollen from crying or heat or lovemaking, but swollen as a battered face is swollen. We were numb, too, as battered people are, and it hurt and dismayed and maybe even embarrassed us a little that we could only fumble sexually toward one another, like hobbling ogres across a deserted landscape, like Goya monsters, in all this dark green grieving. We were our last hope of relief from pain, and we turned toward one another almost callously, as though sex were the organism's response to the absolute sterility of death. But death was more fecund than we, and there was no love in the lovemaking, no comfort, no compassion. I tried not to remember how we were when Ned's father had died, how different we had been then, and how being in love had seen us through that devastation. It wasn't just an absence on Ned's part, it was his exhaustion, the sense of separateness I'd first seen the night we heard of Bett's death. He just wasn't with me, any more than I, wrapped in grief, was with him. We denied it, made allowances for our stunned state, but it had an ominous quality to it, as though there were a second loss coming, clearly, overwhelmingly. I would have turned to Ned if I'd been able, but all his embraces pushed me further and further inside myself, while what was simply there around me—the heavy air, the breeding frogs, mice, moles, raccoons, spiders, gnats, the black snakes that died under cars on the black tar road, the dogs and cats, the lilac bushes and overhanging trees, the noises of the countryside and then the memories there, the places I'd been with Bett, all those benign messages for forbearance I heard in the outer world, all the bright fireflies and phosphoric marsh plants, all those stars and sweeps of cloudy gauze in the sky, all the moonlight and engining, pumping, screeching in that countryside at night—all this seemed more embracing, more loving, more motherly, fatherly, more like an intimate, a lover, than did Ned.

I could have drowned in that wet green grieving summer, if it had held still for me, kept its arms wide. Instead it seemed to shift gradually, and then, more wildly, turn its face to spit me out. Things began to happen, time returned, and emergency. No longer did things feel safe. There were freak accidents and freak storms. Ned, gesturing to a friend in the living room in the country, snagged his finger on an old fishhook attached to a rod hung on the wall and had to be driven to the hospital to have twenty stitches. There were flash floods and sudden biblical lightning storms just as in the days when Bett was with us here, the end of May. The huge ancient barn where Ned worked was struck, and burned to the ground one night only hours after he'd left it. In the meadow where the barn sits, where the rain pelts down, a crowd like a lynch mob gathers to watch the firemen and the flames that blow wildly under a torrential sky. In the city, someone breaks into the house, takes nothing, but leaves the living-room window open and a kitchen carving knife on the bench in the hall. And in California my aunt Veronica, now seventy-five, bored and depressed by growing old, follows Bett's lead and commits suicide.

I am falling deeper and deeper into the green hole, the mourning sickness, the green sickness, spinning and nausea. I am hanging on through words, writing again, picking up the old narrative of my novel, but changing it for my purposes, writing about a well-heeled mother trying to convince her broken daughter that she cannot just stop, but must go on. I am switching the roles and speaking to Bett, but I am talking to myself, too, reanimating my dead mother so that she can be with me again, in whatever disguise, so I can hear some maternal voice saying all will be well.

That summer Ned's financial adviser came to stay with us a few days. We had been living stretched since the spring before, by the house, by Bett, and always Gordon had come up with schemes to cover expenses. We depended on Gordon and his inventive juggling. He was so upright, so reliable, we always felt safe, lucky to have him, lucky to be able, thanks to him, to think about other things. But this visit he was not so sweatless, but strangely disheveled, a little wild-eyed. He said he wasn't sleeping well, doing all these deals, the client list growing, the constant traveling. But that didn't quite explain his new state. When he left we found an empty bottle of scotch in his room, a thriller and a single sock. In our new helplessness we could only register these things; we weren't capable of caution.

Gordon came to see us again when the summer was over, when we were back in the house on Ninety-fifth Street. He sat in the kitchen with us and put his head on his arms. He said there would be no more money because the capital was gone. Just gone. He'd taken the power of attorney Ned had signed for him when we left New York and removed the cash, doling from the top to keep us quiet all summer. He'd had every intention of repaying, only things hadn't gone that way. He looked dismantled, damp and puffy. He began to cry. He said he would pay back every cent, we had to give him time. He was sorrier and more ashamed than he could say. As a gesture of good faith he wrote us a check for five hundred dollars. Then he left, saying he would be in touch at the end of the week.

We heard nothing from Gordon for a fortnight. Then Ned went out to his home in the Bronx to find him. He found the wife and kids, but not Gordon. Ned conferred with lawyers, with other outraged clients, did what he could to trace Gordon, but Gordon was gone, and so was the Money.

Ned was so ashamed he could not tell anyone. Everything seemed lost now, not just the money but the dead father's trust. Ned didn't look after what his father left him, any more than I could look after what my father left me. Only Bett had nothing to do with my father, as my father had nothing to do with me. No, Ned lost his money and I lost Bett, and for the moment all we could do was rent out the house on Ninety-fifth Street, live somewhere on the slender margin between cost and income, and try to figure everything out.

Somewhere Ned is furious with me. *My* mother's death and *his* punishment. They're all angry with me, it feels. Or maybe, in my terrible guilt, which is now the way my grief expresses itself, I see their anger everywhere.

My father: the day after Bett's death Ned had called him in Norfolk. He never said, "Let me speak to Helen," he never called back later, he never wrote a letter. Within the week I had tender notes from everyone in Norfolk but him. The silence seemed a stunning indifference.

At Christmas we exchanged our greetings, I received another plastic sponge bag, and a card from Harriet signed by him also. We rented out our house, and Ned disappeared to London. I went to stay in a friend's loft while they were out of town for the holidays.

It was a strange place, a large white loft at the back of a building. There were no windows, only trompe-l'oeil shutters, painted eternally shut. There was no way to know if it was day or night, or that it was winter. What I knew vaguely was that it was Christmas. I knew that Bett was dead and how she had died; that part of that was my fault absolutely and I would never be able to repair it. The running battle, the long argument was over, and she would always have the last word, there was nothing I could ever say to her again that she would ever hear; everything that was going to happen between us had already happened and would be fixed forever somewhere in a big white room where there was neither day nor night—a room like the big white room of my Mirrenwood nightmares, where I'd pulled down the shades to blot out the light. I had blotted out the light and now I had to run and run around a rubber track inside a big white room away from the thing like an ambulance, like a garbage truck, the mechanical-jawed creature that was chasing me down, run as I can, scream as I can, try to wake.

That is where, that first Christmas, alone in a borrowed, sealed-off loft, suddenly a thousand times alone and cut off from everything, I understood in a different way how Bett and I were sisters, and that her fate was going to be, had to be, mine. It was there, lying awake at 5 A.M., or noon, or six or ten in the evening, in artificial light, that I began actually, literally, to hear the razor blades in the bathroom cabinet beckoning, crooning like sirens. And I would go and just stare at them and try to figure out how they were making the sound.

Ned returned for the New Year, and we were alone again with each other. We were fighting all the time, as worn as bad tires, thin-skinned, likely to puncture, explode, send the vehicle into a ditch at the slightest roughness of surface. There was no belief to sustain us. Too many bad things had happened. There had not been enough respite to digest it all; Bett, Veronica, the loss of money, and now, it seemed, of each other. It was nothing to say that we were touchy; there was electricity coming off us day and night, both of us.

I like to hear him doing things, typing his new articles, talking in the phone, calling to Bertie. I like him at that distance, feeling he's safe, content for the moment, absorbed inside his life. When he's with me, when he comes upstairs to say or bring something, there's an exhaustion to him, a weariness that I feel responsible for and helpless about. Often I want him to tell me that this hell will pass, that things will be all right again, that things will be all right between us. But really I want him to say those things. I don't dare, don't feel I have the right to ask.

Often enough we are still tender with each other, at least for moments at a time. I always think he's a nice man, a nice man in over his head and getting scared, a kind man reduced to unkindness. He thinks his life is broken, that it is all leaving him, his gifts, intelligence, the cash and privileges, all his universe of knowledge and art and order. It is a lot to have gone awry, to have smashed up on the shoals of the new world, to have lost to an unworkable love that has become an unworkable marriage.

To himself, he was wrecked, a weeping, ruined man with no prospects. That was one version of it for him. The other was that we were simply taking a break in the country. Things could be worse, we would say from time to time. We both have our health, we can sell the house eventually, when the real estate slump is over, and now, look, we are free, free to do what we've had too much choice previously to do, just get on with here and now. And maybe this will all be some circuitous route to happiness. We'd say these things and kiss and feel better, and then some wave of all that had happened would strike and we'd be off, fearful, defending, shouting, fuming or disappearing, too afraid to speak, too afraid of our thoughts even to be in the same room, but now, unlike any time before, with no place, no extra real estate, no cooling-out or temporary shelter to run off to. Like most people in the world, we were suddenly, and unfamiliarly, stuck with things as they were.

When we couldn't talk to one another any longer without anger, we would talk to the animals. Ned would address the dog or cat and thereby let me know that he was all right, that his feelings were still intact. We could speak affectionately to these creatures because they seemed to us innocent in ways we no longer seemed to ourselves. For long stretches we would simply, wordlessly, cohabit and let other noises be our form of communication. So Ned would rattle dishes or run water in a certain way to let me know that he was all right, that the heaviest griefs had lifted slightly, enough to let him get on with whatever simple tasks there were before him. When there was a lot of slamming of doors or knocking things over, I would know enough to stay away and say nothing. I was not sturdy enough to take on the weight of his unhappiness, and I was learning to keep my own devastation to myself. We did keep ourselves away from each other, often enough it seemed simply as a ploy to avoid murder, but it was unfamiliarly, brutally lonely. It was as though we had, with Bett's death, forfeited any right to human comfort, our own included, as though at best we could address the animals as innocent bystanders to our crime.

[. . .]

I did go, eventually I did. I went because there was no other way to do it. I went pretending and even half thinking I wasn't really leaving, just off on a business trip—to see the English publisher who had accepted my novel. On the train to London I wept, through the countryside, through northern Italy into southern and then northern France, wept and even bled all over my *wagon-lit* sheets as though there'd been a miscarriage, as though there really was a corpse. I felt myself surrounded by shapes of every fear I have ever imagined, some triggered by memory, others pure dread: abandonment, extinction. But at the end of it, at the edge of the fear—the fear that was and was not, thanks to the strength of defenses: denial, numbness, depression, so that it is little like the approaching English sky, dense, dark blue, gray, white, then dark again—was a piece of something shiny, a little excitement, a tiny, flapping, tinselly seduction of "freedom," whatever that might mean, out there, whenever I might be granted the strength to use it.

ELEVEN

IN LONDON I CONCENTRATE on disguise, on appearance; I see friends one by one and am careful not to unravel so much I will never be whole again. There is much danger in compassionate company. If you let go, if you lean, if you take comfort, life the other side of your own shut door will be unbearable. You may not even make it to the underground.

I need outside corroboration. I need women to have lunch and tea with, women who appraise my clothes and appearance and say I seem fine. Here particularly, where people don't risk so much, move so much, "chop and change," my chaos looks like courage, and I am applauded like some half-serious entertainment. From safe within their lovely homes, they see me wandering my own heath, and it all comes across as on the edge, romantic. Men are warier, or wiser, and appraise me only as prey or outsider. As the latter I constitute some threat. Women should behave thus and so, and thus and so I am good only for adventure. (You could not settle with her; she is not the settling kind.) If Edward cannot domesticate his wife, then far be it from any of these to take over. It is, to some extent, perceived as Edward's failure that I am left flying around London like loose shrapnel, like a loose marble in a tin box; good for dinner chat (but don't get her started on anything because the bubby, frothy surface—well, even they can see the dark waters below that will put out the flames of seduction), and good of course for sex, but not really for any bond further—she's a little punchy from her recent past (something about a suicide, wasn't it?) and this separation seems messy. Not to mention the foreign connections. Where does she live anyway, New York? She seems right but is not right, not quite right, not quite one of us, though of course all the more interesting, for some things, for that.

And what I feel is: this is good for tonight. Tomorrow I can make it to that drinks party on the strength of this. And then there is a dinner after the drinks party, so I needn't wander sad and a little tipsy home alone, but will be anchored, safe at some cloth-covered table eating off matching china, dressed in pleasant clothes, chatting through the time: okay therefore for the next thirty-six hours, then I can call this or that one for lunch on Saturday, dinner with so-and-so and that leaves only Sunday, perhaps something will turn up. Better not go away for the whole weekend again, the sadness tends to hit even then when surrounded by the sheltered others, when faced with children and mealtimes and landscape. Whether I want these things or not I want the things these things seem to provide: peace, or at least absence of pain. But I am not good over the long haul, over an entire weekend I'm liable to lose my momentum, break down, cease to be charming or amusing (as is the unspoken contract for weekend guests) and hit the pain, become the problem, use up their sympathy along with their food and drink, and go home unbuffered by any illusion that things are getting better.

So I'm talking all day long and drinking and dining at the homes of friends or giving in my basement home little dinners, as though Ned were just temporarily away. I don't *know* yet how to switch from being Mrs. to my former self or my real self, whatever that may be. I am further from that self than I ever was before. Certainly in my "real" incarnation I would never give these point-less dinners—that's the English costume party which one must attend in the proper costume, whether guest or host. There is no correct garb for the single wife, the not quite divorced, not quite abandoned, female. There isn't yet either the dignity of being single, if there *is* any dignity to it, and in any case being single here is for women "like one" considered only a temporary state. It's absurd to imagine I won't be married again, within the year, they say, so there are counselings, sympathies, confidences about their own affairs and introductions. Here is love and kindness, but no image of a way to be that I can yet recognize. Instead, I am leaner, better dressed (for power games, for seductions, for dinner parties), than ever I was as a "married lady." My clothes and makeup are a form of weaponry only; hostilities are on. The world is once again red in tooth and claw, and there will be survival only of the fittest. I wear a disguise, of sturdiness and sexiness and carefree charm, but inside I feel wounded. I want warmth and reassurance, but not scrutiny.

With men it seems you have to trade sex for company. I don't know that this is what's happening. I think these are "interesting" evenings, "dates" even, in my mother's parlance. But I am not good at casual sex, I don't like it. It's like behaving well at dinner parties and weekends in the country, a form of good manners. But the old me is still there, and this sexual willingness is only part curiosity (as to what is out there after all these years, as to whether one is desirable and by whom—all that suddenly-single syndrome, famous in scandal and song); the other part is victim behavior: my horizontality because I have been run over, a form of helplessness that may even be seductive in itself. No, I say to an old married friend, you must be crazy. But I'm the one who's crazy and I am persuaded. I sense the expression of the friendship transformed in his touch: the friendship comforts as the fucking horrifies. "This isn't really happening," he reassures me, excited by my lame protests, "it's just a dream."

It's all just a dream. I "know" people for years, or at least I believe I know them, until suddenly I am with them naked, and there's a whole other dimension to acquaintance. There's a bond made from such secrecy, a strange truth gets spoken and the language shifts. Lies and politeness disappear and you are left with your naked friend and your naked expressions (after years of properly dressed and addressed expressions) of affection. You have entered the criminal classes, where there is of course a code of decency and so on, but still you are in an underworld after years of "straight" behavior. It is strange how many other criminals are out there, parading their propriety in the daytime, moving around with a different kind of freedom and access at night. You are now an insider here, which only goes to show what an outsider in the other world you've become.

I dream about Ned, as I am to dream about him for years and years to come. In these dreams he is always angry and I am always sad. The rage I receive as a form of Bett's rage, and my sadness is appropriate to these double losses. Sometimes these dreams fix me for hours afterward and I am shaken and possessed all day. Then, I was in it every moment, frightened for him as for myself, frightened of his madness in both senses of the word, and of how far it could lead. Sometimes I thought it was lucky there was so much earth and sea between us. When, infrequently, we spoke, we were painfully careful not to touch real feeling. We spoke of our joint property, the house on Ninety-fifth Street, our joint friendships, our financial arrangements, and, a little sarcastically, our best wishes for our health and recovery.

It seems so unnatural to be alone, that's the irony of it. It seems shameful and bizarre only five years after marrying, when marrying had seemed the bizarre thing, and possibly the more shameful. And look, now I am alone in a big white space with a novel about to come out. Look, I am a single writer, and still young—as young as Gogi was when she divorced, young enough to start again. But I can't start, I am stalled, in pain, and howling for my mother like at Mirrenwood, as abandoned, as aware of the big black car disappearing through the trees now as then, as unsteady on my legs now as then; and then Ned has gone off, too, and though I can feel the relief of that (the same horrifying "thank God"), I also feel the love and loss. I am so accustomed to our intimacy, to the constant conversation of bodies and heads. I am so used to my existence in relation to his. I am still an object in a sentence governed by a man. First it was a woman, then it was a man, and now they're both gone. And here's the irony, because here is where I always wanted to be. Ever since I first admired women, it was for that ability to do it singly, cut a swath, create their *own* breeze when they passed. Constance, Gogi (despite Bill I always thought of Gogi as single), they were able not just to survive alone, or hobble sweetly like Bett, but to triumph, to have love and lovers and still the self. Perhaps I should have admired women for staying married or keeping marriages going, but it always seemed too easy to me, and me too with Ned, too easy to have any merit. And that's a joke, too, because easy is one thing it never was.

[. . .]

It has worked, this perverse thing I've done, or worked enough. It's such a gift to feel so numb, because I haven't any mourning left in me—only the resolution to work, to "go on" with my life. For all this purity I need a new place to write, to finish my new novel, about "gaiety" and ruthlessness. I find a mews studio with skylights where I can go to work. I go out with a handsome film star, someone recently voted "the nation's heartthrob." He's acting and I'm acting and it's all glamorous and flattering and more mimicking of fun through movement. I have energy for all of it now, for writing in the daytime and dressing up and laughing at night. I'm not a crushed soul, I think, I've saved my own life. The near-miss of the thing is exhilarating.

I finish my novel while the snow falls on the skylights. I am working day and night now in artificial light, the daylight blocked by snowfall. I am in my own darkness, pushing like a mole, harder and harder and as though something is hurrying me on. Never have I worked so fast. Something is chasing me. I feel it at my back and in the dark weight of snow overhead, and I'm so busy staying ahead and away from it I haven't time to be curious what it is.

When my book is finished I give it to my agent and go out to dinner with the heartthrob. I think it is safe now to unspin, untauten. We go to a Greek restaurant two blocks from my new place. We talk about my novel, his film, and the wine's going down and the conversation's livening up, while all around us from the street are strange sounds like bombs going off which might, we think, be the IRA. Afterward we walk home along the two blocks that curve toward my house. We're swaying with them, both of us, serpentine. We drank more than we thought in those short, sparky two hours, and as I get closer to where I live I see around a bend the street full of fire engines and firemen and I can smell the burning. Maybe it *was* a bomb, I think, but I don't see any ambulances and it's sort of all over. As I get nearer the place where the firemen are it looks more and more like having something to do with me, like being right next to my house, my side of the street. And then it seems to be right next to the big house that is in front of my studio, but that's still standing, and I keep walking like a tipsy woman, which I am, until I finally see that it *is* my house. We walk through the gate, both silent now, on the path toward the studio, still not quite getting it because there isn't a house there at all, just a smoldering, smashed shell of walls under piles of skylight glass (the cracking explosions we had heard), and in among the heaps of glass are blackened legs and backs of furniture, charred remains of books and papers, shoes, clothing. Dazed as I am, I shake off the heartthrob's restraining arm and walk through this uneven ground of stinking, wet, black shapes, say hello to the firemen, and under the rooflessness, inside the ruined walls, try to get past them, thinking, I'll deal with all this tomorrow, still heading for the bedroom, which doesn't exist anymore either, but just directing myself toward the sleep I'll need to face this new weird thing when I can. And maybe the firemen think I'm shocked or fatally dumb; they lead me to the kitchen of the big front house, sit me down in a chair and bring the CID man to ask me questions.

"What enemies did you have?" he asks. "Who knew your movements? What was being written on the typewriter we found on the top of the pyre?" Then the constable comes over to voice his suspicions about the owner of the big house in whose kitchen we sit. "He was here all the time and says he didn't hear the fire. They heard the fire ten houses down, but not him." Still, this is not the clincher, which is: "The bloke's over thirty and still living with his mum." Afterward the heartthrob takes me home. We drink an awful lot of brandy, and sometime around 4 A.M. fall asleep.

I went back in the morning, dressed in all the clothes I now had, what I'd been wearing last night. It still smelled of fire, burnt plastic and firemen's foam, and everything looked worse in daylight. There was nothing left of the snow-covered roof but twisted lead and piles of blackened, greasy glass. Standing inside the walls, now mostly down to the foundations, you could see what had happened last night in the space of two hours. The CID people came by and said they had found petrol and the door lock still locked. They figured whoever had done this had watched me leave, then entered through the only window there was. They'd taken all my clothes from the closet, all my books from the shelves, and piled these under the round table where I'd been writing my book. Then they'd poured petrol over the typewriter and table, the bed and the sofa, and set them alight. All the furniture that had been there was just springs and burned limbs. Under the remains of the worktable were remnants of clothing, a bit of smoked red silk, dead, curled shoes, fragments of manuscript pages, a blackened diary and charred passport, fire-eaten luggage and, on top of this pyre, my typewriter in expressionist contortion, its metal arm curved and twisted like something out of *Richard III*.

It hit me then. Everything was gone. All my clothes were gone. All my dresses, skirts, shoes, coats, underwear. All my books, notebooks, papers, phone book, were gone. Everything in the bathroom was gone. I would have to buy a toothbrush and a change of underwear just to get through the day. Then I would have to figure how to telephone whomever I was meant to be seeing that week. I was supposed to go to Paris in ten days' time. I'd have to telephone friends in Paris. I didn't have a passport, their phone numbers or my diary. I was probably meant to be seeing someone for lunch today and dinner tonight and I couldn't remember who. To call the people in Paris I had to call people we knew in New York. To call New York, I'd have to call people in London; I had to call people in London to call people in Norfolk. I had to sit down, borrow a pen and a piece of paper and write down all the numbers I had in my head and then try to reconstruct a larger circle and a larger. I had to try to remember where I was going this week and tell those people, first finding the number, first remembering the name. I had to stop being dazed because my memory was all that I had. I had to get cash from somewhere to buy a change of clothes, to continue into tomorrow. At some point I had to register all this, remember and adjust to the loss of everything.

And then it also came to me. There'd been no way out of this skylit studio, only one window and one door, and if I'd been asleep when whoever it was came through the window, I'd never have got to the door. Then I would have been gone, too, part of this charred stinking mess. I sat down on the remains of something, getting grease and charcoal on my only clothing, and thought about this. I looked again at the way the arsonist had piled everything under the table and the typewriter, as though the novel were the cause of the anger. He'd gone through my clothes, shelves, bedclothes, and purposely made a pyre under the place where I was writing. The novel had escaped but everything else had been set on fire. Who could have been so angry?

The police decided the man in the big house had hated the owners of the little house because they were millionaires and had parked their fancy car and flashed their champagne once too often. Class, of course, explaining everything in England, that and the fact of him still living with his mother. (Well, both of us were still living with our mothers.) Then they said maybe this was the "Queensway arsonist," seven local deaths in the past year and a half. They never figured it out. I figured it out, not consciously but in every other way.

The day I went through Bett's things after her death, the things survived and she was gone. Here it's the reverse, but like that day it's the clothes that hit hardest, the burnt scraps of silk, the scorched camisoles and melted bracelets. I pick out a rhinestone earring and two eaten-through nightgowns from the ashes. I must save some of this. The burning of my clothes, particularly these pretty clothes, "going-out" clothes, "intimate" clothes, is almost the worst, partly because my work in some form did escape. But these have been torched as though fate did not want me to be pretty, social, sexual, as though above all this were the outrage, my recent erotic self, when it was Bett who was the beauty, and by childhood compact I the vacant-faced worshipping companion. This is the lesson I take. As in Greek myth I'd transgressed where there was only one goddess. Men were hers, and if she couldn't have them any longer, then neither could I. This place, the studio where I imagined I could work hard, be safe and independent, go out with my film star, all this was an affront. All the moving out and starting over and daring to be okay, all the end of mourning, was an affront. In my grief and guilt and current devastation I turned Bett's love into this message of anger. Even under the love of her suicide letter, I now read only the wild, destructive anger that should have flashed out freely but had turned against its owner. The bolt that should never have been bent toward herself had now flown straight and down, and burned everything with it.

Some suggest I should try to see the arson as a kind of gift, a cutting of traces, an unburdening, a new start. But I've had enough new starts and I don't react in this fine spirit. Perversely, I try to play the footage backward, to restore. I borrow from the heartthrob, from my publisher, and I seek out the shops where I bought clothes months and months before, hopelessly trying to find identical things, as though I imagine by this means the destruction can be undone. But it's too late, everywhere, everything's moved on and I can't keep it all still, let alone retrace my steps, replace what's gone.

Even when my novel, spared the flames, is bought and the English edition of my first novel is about to come out, I feel dazed, preoccupied. There is a party for the book, and everyone I know and like and some I don't come to it. It should have been fun, but I couldn't reach it. I hadn't got myself out of the ashes yet and I didn't understand the well-wishes. I felt I was impersonating someone else in my new clothes and apparent success. I walked in and out of the rooms among all the literati, smiling at the photographer but feeling peculiarly numb, and fraudulent. I felt this was all about and for somebody else.

The book was praised by the reviewers. That was good because it meant I could go on writing. It was bad because I didn't feel I deserved it. It was just arbitrary fortune. I was beginning to feel that only terrible things were real, and that anything good that happened didn't count at all, skimmed off the top of my head and flew back to wherever it came from without landing at all.

The outside life continued, though I really only hobbled through it, with the heartthrob until the press got hold of that and it had to end, and then with a playboy of a sort, whose previous girlfriend looked down in larger-than-life photography over the bed. None of this was me.

All through that spring and summer I struggled with the unease of being in one place and feeling I was being dragged somewhere else. Part of me wanted terribly to stay. When the divorce came through there would be a little money. I could put a down payment on a flat and get a mortgage. I could write my books and go to my parties and be with my friends. I began to look for a place to live, another home, a real home that I could own and live in. I found the perfect flat and at the same time the perfect car, just like the one I'd had in New Jersey and driven around in with Bertie and Mozart before the suicide. Then I realized I couldn't really afford the perfect flat, though it had a certain look of where Ned and I had lived in New York, a redemptive little aura of a prettier past. It was a hard, long decision not to take it, and when it was sold a couple of weeks later the person that bought it turned out to be Ned. Just (painful) coincidence. Only there were no more coincidences. Envy, mixed with anger, was what Bett had felt about Ned and me, and everything Bett had felt was what I was being led now, step by step, to feel.

A friend said maybe I should go and talk to Bett, "have it out." She gave me the name of a famous psychic, and I went along to an ordinary, genteel, terraced house in Chelsea, where a small, pert woman with a businesslike manner invited me into a room of flowered wallpaper and little chintz-covered chairs.

I sat across from her and she closed her eyes. Of course I've said nothing to her, and I am only thirty; there's no reason to assume anyone in particular is dead. Her eyes open and shut like a doll's. She stares past my head and begins to speak; her voice is clipped, matter-of-fact. "You're an actress, aren't you?" I am relieved, she knows nothing. "No," I say, "I am a writer." "But you're a very good actress," she insists. I wait. She says she has summoned "my dead" to where we are and she begins to name them. "Two grandfathers," she says, "one short, one tall; two grandmothers, one who loves you very much. She is looking directly at you right now. There is a child, about seven years old, that never came into the world." Relief again, this is wrong, but then I think I remember a pregnancy scare (or failure) around this time. She names a woman who might be Veronica. I begin to think I have so many dead she can't go wrong. She is quiet for a while and then she says, "Your mother is here." The hair on the back of my head begins to prickle. I am waiting. The part that is still resisting wonders how could she take such risks, and then, how can she possibly know? "Your mother is trying to talk to you." I swallow hard. Perhaps she senses a change in my breathing, my attention. I am hanging tightly to my doubts because I really don't want to cry. "Your mother says"—all this in the same flat, wire reader's voice—"she's so sorry for what she had to do. She had no choice. She is very sorry to have hurt you. She says she is free now. She says she can move, she is happy. She is able to be herself now. She just couldn't be the person she wanted to be before." Phrases of Bett's last letter come home, her way of speaking arrives in this stranger's British voice. The woman still has her eyes closed. My tears are coming now, but I am silent. I don't want to believe this is happening. What can I do with it if I do? "Your mother says again how sorry she is for all the pain she's given. She says you must try to get rid of the anger." Anger? I have no anger, I think, just these tears. "She says you must forgive her." Forgive her, it is she who must forgive me. The tears come and come and I listen. On and on she goes, never hitting a false note, while I sit crying quietly. Then she says, "Your mother says you must go to the dentist and the gynecologist." And on this practical note, my mother disappears.

The psychic opens her eyes and looks at me. Then she closes her eyes again. "You know," she says, "it's extremely unusual, but all these dead people have their backs to you, except one, a tall, older woman." Gogi, I say to myself. "She is the only one looking straight at you." The psychic opens and closes here eyes again, waits. "She says, 'You don't know which way to go, do you?' Does that mean something?" I say I don't know. She opens her eyes again. She looks totally drained, exhausted. I am beyond questioning any of this now. I am simply sitting on the floral chintz, crying.

"Go home now," she says, "go home and sleep. When you wake up you will feel at peace. You will have a great sense of peace."

She hands me a Kleenex. I hand her the money. On my way down the stairs I meet her next client, a fidgety, carrot-haired man, who seems to think he's in a brothel. Outside the light is dazzling, disorienting. I go home. I lie down. I do not sleep. I do not feel peace.

I felt a little jangled, jumpy. I had dinner with friends, didn't talk about what had happened or think about it much. I got to bed late and I woke late, tired. I thought about the previous day but I wasn't preoccupied with it, it came and went among errands, phone calls, the ordinary things of the day. Around five I felt very drowsy and I lay down to take a nap. I must have slept the psychic's sleep, because when I woke I felt not just peaceful but something far stronger. I felt my mother in the room, unmistakably. I could smell Blue Grass and I felt overwhelming love, no fear at all, but a great happiness that she was with me. My body began to tingle strangely. There was a peculiar warmth on my legs and in my throat. I began to breathe rapidly, ecstatically. I knew that what was happening was real and that it was she with me. I felt intense joy and the strange heat for perhaps thirty minutes. Then I began to look for her, really try to see her. I looked at the evening light on the bedroom curtains, at the ceiling, the mirror, knowing she was right there and expecting momentarily to see her. I got up, feeling pressure in my solar plexus, almost painful, and my throat. I was not sad but ecstatic, transported, still looking for her. I went and got a photo of her that I'd brought with me from New York, one taken outside our building on Ninety-fourth Street about ten years earlier. She was wearing her young clothes and looked no more than thirty and she was smiling in the photo, her slightly sad, beautiful smile. Her face in the photo was perhaps half an inch high, but as I looked at it, it began to get larger. It also became a kind of holograph and I could actually see her face moving, her mouth forming the smile and her eyes alive, still slightly sad but smiling. I was beginning to cry and my tears were making the photo jump so I could no longer see her expression. When I wiped my tears I saw her face moving again, speaking something to me, something very happy, very loving. Then in the photo she began laughing, a very tender, delighted laugh. I was holding the photo about eight inches from my face and my mother was moving inside it, speaking, laughing. It didn't feel as though the photo had come to life but as though the photo were only the first second of a little silent movie, that we had gone way beyond the photo into the movie, that the movie was being made then and right there in that London room. Her body did not move, just her face and head. The part of me that wouldn't believe any of this was long gone. I was simply looking with my heart beating in my chest and throat, and I felt great, great joy.

And then it stopped, stopped long before I wanted it to, before I stopped crying. It all stopped by itself and started to fade, and she faded, grew still, until everything was still, the Blue Grass was gone and the motion in the photo. The photo became just a photo again, a piece of glossy paper.

That night I had to go to a fancy dinner party. I was still stunned, and very high, and when I met a handsome writer there I felt he was a gift from my mother. He took me home and talked to me all night in the garden of his London house. We stayed up until dawn and we liked each other very much. I really believed Bett had something to do with this. I was believing all sorts of things by now, like that suddenly I was under her divine protection.

We were lying in the long grass in his garden one night, early on, when I was still imagining that this easy ending was going to happen. I really was beginning to see myself together with him in the cozy setting—the book-lined study, the view of the river—somewhat prematurely, as it happened, because as we were lying there under the stars, kissing and on the verge of going upstairs, he began to confess. Not the worst, but not the best social disease. I should know, the choice was mine. And so eager was I to be saved that I did think about it, the heroic act, binding yourself to a lover through disease, sexual demarcation. Yes, I did actually think about it. And then I thought, maybe I had enough problems and I didn't need more help in my own undoing. I let the "perfect man" go by. Doing so, I realized maybe he wasn't one of Bett's conciliatory gifts, the farewell gesture after our reconciliation. I thought instead he might be one of her little jokes.

I guessed from this I wasn't supposed to glide back into London. I guessed I was supposed to finish up the business in New York. And at the end of the summer, the beginning of autumn, right on Persephone Mean Time, New York is where I went.

TWELVE

SO I WENT BACK to New York. Left the dinner parties and the literary events and the wild spinning, left the pavements that seemed more and more to slant upward under my feet, the skies that bore down, left the place where gravity and logic had gone haywire, where I had gone haywire, left the glitter and the terror and went to the eye of the storm to try to understand what was happening and how I could turn it around.

A week before I went I called the storage company where everything I'd left behind me in New York had been held: furniture, books, clothes, a lifetime's worth of accumulation, everything that was left of where and what I was, everything that hadn't been burned in London. They were barely apologetic, the storage people, just embarrassed, defensive, fearful of a lawsuit; they'd been meaning to write. After Ned took away his furniture and paintings, shipped all that to London, sometime thereafter, they didn't know quite when, sometime in the past few months it seemed there'd been a theft in the warehouse. They were very sorry about it, and they were still trying to trace the crates, but the part of the warehouse where my things had been had been emptied.

Well, whom do you keep telling of such things? It's not dinner-party conversation after a while, it's just terrifying, shaming. You think there has to be a reason why all this is happening, on both sides of the Atlantic, a reason you're not making up. You don't believe in coincidence very long, you start to believe in conspiracy, only not of this earth. You believe it, and very fast you accept, because there's no argument with ghosts, and because secretly you believe you deserve all this and more. You don't complain, and you barely tell anyone. You've stopped grieving and objecting long ago. It's the disgrace and inevitability of the misfortune that you feel.

In New York I began to look for an apartment to sublet for six months. I intended to go back to London after that, after whatever was going to happen happened, when my second novel was scheduled to come out. I had nothing in storage anywhere except the car I thought I'd use the following summer in London, keep there or take back with me here or maybe sell it. I'd already paid the garage owner three months in advance for storage and I wanted to let him know my plans. I wrote and then I tried to phone him. He didn't exist anymore, and the place where a dozen cars had been kept was now empty. I called the London police. They took down the particulars and told me the man was a famous thief. Was I insured? Not yet. And this was all getting funnier by the minute. Do you give up? Give in? Can't you guess? Go on, have a guess. They advised me to get a private detective to work on the case. But I didn't bother, the case was pretty well wrapped. And now here I was looking for Moriarty on home ground.

I asked the rental agents to show me places downtown, in neighborhoods I'd never lived in, which had no Bett, no Ned associations, where I thought, even yet, that I'd make another new start. They showed me lots of lofts, full of light and skyline, but I didn't want any of them. The one I thought I liked had almost no light. It was a long, dark tunnel with a double bed and a writing table, with two chipped canisters that had once contained laughing gas, with a library full of books on meditation, prayer, on death and dying cheerfully. It had been the last home of a famous filmmaker who'd been filmed there as he struggled with cancer. I found out all this after I took the loft, but my first feeling about this dark place was of its homeyness, its rightness. I thought it was a good and peaceful place. I thought it was beautiful. The absence of light somehow didn't matter to me, it gave it privacy. I didn't recognize it as a burrow and a place for penance. I just thought all the blackness was downtown and hip, and that in this dark, silent place I'd be able to write.

I couldn't write. This had never happened to me before and it seemed like yet another thing I suddenly couldn't count on. I had nothing to say, or I had too much and couldn't make anything of it. I sat in the dark loft at a table in the middle of the room, switched on the lamp and sat, waiting for words. I sat like a rabbit in that room waiting to unfreeze. This lasted five days. On the sixth, a Sunday, I decided I needed a drink, and since I couldn't buy alcohol I went into a bar alone. I'd never done this, but I was terrified by the prospect of my own unaided night thoughts and oblivion seemed urgent. I had no intention of sitting drinking in the bar; it was for later I needed the anesthetic, for solitude, for sleep. I sat at the bar across the street, dealt with the stares and ordered two double cognacs. Two? Yes, two, I said. I tipped them one after the other into my mouth, got off my stool, paid, walked back to the loft trying not to choke, and spat the brandies into a glass so I could drink them and my own spit at my leisure and be escorted into my dreams.

[. . .]

Memories of Bett poured and burned through me. They surrounded and entered me, and I had no sense of my separateness from them. Not even a historical sense of separateness about the time when she was alive or the different countries we had lived in: our discrete dancing ten years ago; Bett flying between despair and mania and I "safe" in London blackening my lashes for dates or looking at stair carpets, bopping around my "adorable problems" like one of the Bobbsey twins. "Puppy write to Mommy, Mommy's blue" may have been all the indication I'd had of her monstrous misery. Did I feel excused from blame for that? I didn't let myself off so easily. It was only worse that her despair had been so long-lived, so familiar to her, hoary and unshiftably heavy overhead. I tried now to unload some of it onto myself, a kind of late gesture, but heartfelt. And of course there was more to it than that. It was also a way I had of being with her again, by living with that living death of hers. These horrifically vivid memories, this secret underpinning of my uncannily youthful, childlike mother, became my way back to her, the beginning of my shuffling, ash-eating, prodigal return. I took on her despair as a sign of kinship much as earlier I had taken on my father's height and accent. I was Bett's sister/daughter again, dark, depressed, and eventually suicidal.

I should emphasize that in the hellish months that followed I was not simply unwinding (unraveling) from all the recent upheavals. This was something new, this bonding with Bett, catching up with Mommy. There were to be no more clean new starts, but only backward motion, toward the dead mother (earth in my mouth and under my nails), back to the real equality, that immortal sisterhood of ours.

I was unable to go on inventing my own life anymore. Being back "home" where all the English manners, the restaurant and bed behavior, the contests of chat and style, simply disappeared into the general pot of indifference, this sudden simplifying was made easy. I shed the trappings of my own life and took on hers, both in penance and in love. Her poverty began to obsess me, and I didn't simply mimic it but took it on to the point of real and eroding panic about money. Like Bett, I could neither work nor concentrate. I watched my money thin until homelessness became another fear. I added to my miseries her terrible sense of isolation, her hopelessness about herself and her prospects. Occasionally I would shake out of this state, dress up again, spend some money, get a haircut, have a few evenings with friends. But the effects of these excursions into normalcy never lasted because my heart wasn't in them, and whatever I wore felt like a costume for a costume party, something you'd put away in the back of the closet until next year. I couldn't, as they say, keep up appearances. Instead what slipped in and stayed with me were those last days of Bett's when she was getting heavier, when the makeup didn't adhere and the shine was gone. I felt my way into that and got heavier, blearier, too, doom-laden. The London shine was long gone and I knew it; I took on shame with the sadness and refused to see old friends when they came through, concocted insulting excuses. It was as if the London self was dead and all I had to show them was this creature from the crypt. And when I did see them, as sometimes I did, dismay became the content of our evenings, laced with forgiveness and a lot of worry, and the pain of my solo homecoming would redouble in self-reproach and self-contempt, just like Mommy.

Of course, my own dismantling, disintegration, registered with me fully and wounded me further. I felt all the sliding steps of my destruction, and yet I could not halt it, or even argue with it. At best I could camouflage it for a night or two and then scuttle back to the site of all my despair, to the drink and self-loathing and the terrible sense that there was no way out or through or back, because we were sisters, because we shared everything, and Bett was dead.

It got so I didn't want anyone to see me, not just the English friends, or the former Ned-and-Helen New York friends, but anyone I knew. I began to leave the house only when it was dark, to hug the sides of the buildings when I walked through my neighborhood. (That neighborhood! With its reeking fast-food shops and dead-faced City Hall workers, the crowds that filled the streets on workdays and then completely vanished at five forty-five and every weekend.) I'd slip through those streets on speedy errands, on snatch-and-grab missions, bolt back to my tunnel and the borrowed furniture. There money panic forced me to try to work, but I couldn't do it. I had no belief to sustain me. And the more I couldn't work and the more the person I had been disappeared from the mirrors day by day, the more I slipped level by level closer to the ultimate horizontal.

I felt simultaneously too visible and unrecognizable. When I was a child Bett could disappear into her dark face, as though the life and light had been turned off. When that happened she aged suddenly and hugely, her jaw went slack and her sockets hollow. Sometimes it was frightening, as she must have known, because on those depressive days she wouldn't even go out, lest she be seen in this "true" monster guise. And that was how I felt now, too, lightless, heavy, with my own mark of Cain, a face like a Sicilian village in mourning, and I couldn't fix it, couldn't mascara or blush or lipstick my features into life, and so could only hide and slope and fear recognition like some swamp crawler of a child's nightmare, some hunchback or troll that had swallowed the girl/person I'd been.

Autumn through spring I led this anti-life. For nine months, long enough to give birth to a new, terrible self, I dug myself deeper and deeper into the pit I'd fashioned, trying and failing to work, trying to combat consciousness, trying and failing to stop a relentless descent. In May, as the anniversary of Bett's death approached, I fell new levels downward and for the first time began to feel real fear about where I was heading. I sought help from a psychiatrist, whose offices were far uptown, but in my current state the long subway rides would depress me more than staying at home. On the trains I would see my own hopelessness everywhere, and over the edges of it, menace and lunacy. On the streets around the stations I began to sense that the mad ones, the bag ladies and muttering drunks, recognized me, looked at me in a special way, wise to where I'd be ending up. Sometimes I'd hear in their speech splinters of my own past, voices of teachers, of my mother's friends, and once, most bizarrely, out of some anoraked ruin sloping against a supermarket wall, I heard the accent of my former British lover, the perfect fruity enunciations of Peter O'Toole, whose voice I now noticed his had always resembled. On these excursions to and from the shrink, it was as though all the elements of my life had been spun around and were washing up in haphazard spittle, haphazardly aimed, or as if some large, whole glass had been shattered and the shards were everywhere, still reflecting light, still able to draw blood.

To this psychiatrist when I went, twice a week, I would tell stories, narratives of childhood and adolescence, as remote from me as TV dramas. There were beginnings, middles and ends, familiar villains and heroes, but nothing that registered with me as organically mine. In my new deadness, my new identification with Bett, my sense of connection to my past (as to any sane present) was as severed as if an operation had been performed. The best I could manage was to hobble like an amputee, occasionally feeling the ache of phantom limbs.

I saw this shrink and told my stories, rode the hot, terrible trains, avoided the increasingly intimate lunatic eyes all summer, from May until August, making sure in daughterly penance that I got the full hellish effects of that particularly hot and airless New York summer. The excursions through the city to talk about an unfelt past or an unshifting present seemed finally hopeless to me and I said I thought I would "terminate" the "therapy." "I don't think you should leave," said my therapist, in what struck me even then as an act of blackmail. "I think if you do, you will commit suicide."

Such was the help. I had described the contours of my trap to her and she had added the proportions and lock of the lid. She had not cut out eyeholes in the cardboard, she had not demonstrated that I could simply stand up and climb out, she had entered the box with me and let me know that her fears of its impregnability were even stronger than mine.

I decided to leave the city, a sidestep maneuver, at least away from the crowded misery and reflecting eyes. I was sure I had to refashion my life out of material other than self, the skins of former selves that jammed my closet, the account of former selves that brought my therapist to her pronouncement of doom. I sublet my tunnel and answered an ad for a post-Labor Day rental on Cape Cod, where I'd never been but which sounded like one of those good, clean, godly places where the wind would clear the demons. The photos of the house confirmed this to me. It was a clean, spare no-place of light and bare walls, glass and pale wood looking out on sea and sky. The summer merrymakers would be gone and I could be solitary with salt air and windblown sand, perhaps find my own zero point and from there begin to rise, to work, to come back to the human race.

Perhaps the emptiness of Cape Cod matched my own or perhaps we were like bodies of water finding a common level and I could stop drowning and begin to float. In the beginning I was always afraid, buzzed by constant anxiety brought on by the "nothing-ness," the undefendedness of myself in it, the absence of noise and clutter that left room enough for anything to happen. When the menace lifted, I began to feel a neutrality in the emptiness and then later something more soothing in the light and silence, a sympathetic, sort of institutionally encouraging aspect. I began to have thoughts that were not all jagged pieces of panic, and slowly I began to feel "safe" enough to think them. After nearly two years of hit-and-miss and abandoned pages ever since I left London to "face" the Furies, that curiously conceived task that was now so vague and certainly still neither finished nor started, I was beginning to work again, at least for a few hours at a time.

I was always frightened at night, which fell solidly, earlier each evening, reducing the universe to what was lamplit around me. Alone in that curtainless glass-sided house, I'd be spooked by my own reflection, all that stood between me and the black, curving sea, between me and the long dirt road up which any traveler on a mission of murder might stray. At night I lost my invisibility in that house, both to myself and to others, certainly lost my sense of connection with a universe, which seemed to embrace or at least accommodate me during the day, but which dropped me back in a terror-filled box at night.

I was on the edge of the world, and on those black autumn nights I could see it, round and twinkling at its Provincetown point. That curve sheltered me, barely inside my own edge, especially at night when thoughts not of murderers nor of ghosts but of my own disintegration kept my heart beating noisily in my ears. Reflected in every glass wall, my wild and gloomy face set above the horizon, interrupted by birds and ships, I was yet terrorized by my own absence. In the darkness I seemed to cave in upon myself. And it was always clearest at night that I would have to put myself back together here and soon or else forever fly around, a collection of shards and splinters. Many times I could bear very little of such clarity and at six or seven in the evening, after hours of exhausting alertness, of struggle with night fears, I would get into bed and watch sitcoms until boredom (or drink) brought on early sleep and maximized the amount of daytime I would have for tomorrow . . .

What was I so terrified by? Whatever it was, it came howling in at four o'clock with the screaming winds off the water. At 4 P.M. that late October and all of November, when the view of the sea and sky disappeared with heart-lurching suddenness and my cage contracted to its evening size, every foot of which could be measured by a creaking floorboard, in they would come, promptly, like guests for tea, the demons, my shapeless (because I dared not scrutinize them) dreads. But if I didn't look them in the eye, I overheard them well enough, and what they seemed to speak of were terrible things to come. Dread of the future was the content of the messages from the banshee winds and the chatter inside my head, and not even the TV laugh tracks could altogether drown it out.

But then day would come again, and the glorious view of clouds and sea and sunlight—with gulls gliding inches from my window as slowly as Christmas angels on wire—would be returned to me and I to it, and I would think all the night fears had been worth this morning restitution.

I worked, I read, I took long walks along the edge of the sweetly curving bay; I watched light on foliage until there was no foliage left, and then I watched light on rocks and sand. I drove round and round the dune roads at Race Point, racing myself in a kind of dolphin's splashing solitary ecstasy with life. I was lonely often, but at least, until nightfall, not mad. It was the Persephone business all over again, on a daily basis, descent into darkness and deliverance into light.

Sometimes my nighttime dreads accompanied me even in sunlight. I used to enjoy watching the socializing of gulls, those crowded end-of-day gatherings when the wet sands below my window would be tracked by hundreds of three-pronged feet and the pecking and shrieking, strutting and cold-shouldering, would go on with all the busy propriety of a big-city cocktail party. But the birds that were comical in groups became ominous when sighted singly. One morning there appeared on a post near the deck of the house an enormous sea eagle, black, evil-eyed and cruelly beaked, who remained, apparently uninjured and therefore seemingly with some private purpose, for three days, and whom I passed, watching him watching me, at close and cautious range whenever I left the house. It was after he disappeared that I saw one morning alone on the sands below me two large ravens, "twa corbies," as I remembered from the Middle English poem, the harbingers of death. Not long after that I began to play a game with myself, a game out of nowhere, that a white bird was a good omen, a black bird bad. It was a cheerful enough game to play by the seaside, where gulls far outnumber crows even in autumn, but soon the black birds began to obsess me. The game shifted, too, and soon it was "white bird means you'll survive, black bird you'll die." A white bird could cancel out a black bird, but if you asked the question seriously and then looked at the sky, the answer would be the answer and you'd be stuck with it. I didn't know where the terms of this game were coming from (survive what? die from what?) but they got stronger the longer I stayed. Once, driving too fast, with a truck overtaking a car in the oncoming lane, I heard posed near my head, in a distinct and entirely serious voice, the question "Do you want to die fast or slow?" "Slow," I said aloud, and passed the truck unscathed.

That autumn, from Halloween through hunting season, death thoughts were with me constantly in strangely primitive, childish form, and yet I was not aware of feelings of doom most of the time, but of healing. I'd accepted the solitude and the conditions of what I felt were my recovery. I'd stopped drinking and smoking, didn't eat meat or sugar or caffeine, so that even the symptoms of what I'd thought were a grumbling appendix had disappeared. I slept well, if at oddly early hours, walked a great deal, worked. I went through the nights with less and less terror and through the days with increasing pleasure.

In December I sent out Christmas cards to all the people I hadn't seen in England and Europe and New York. My months of solitary confinement had made my friends vivid to me again and I suddenly missed them terribly. It was an unusually emotional and broadcast greeting I sent out that year and I was surprised at my own intensity. There was some valedictory quality to the gesture, as much as an attempt to take back what had been relinquished in my strange battle with myself. I felt such love, writing to the people I loved, sitting there, in that familiar silence, thick emptiness, high above the pinkening, blueing, twinkling cove, that I myself wondered at where I thought I had disappeared to, and where I thought I was heading. I was saying hello with such passion, I might have been saying goodbye.

In the third week of December I sent half a novel to my publisher, closed up the house and set off for New York. Some crisis was over, I thought; I could return, play again, be among others. I was as eager as a recovered child to get back to it, back where "everyone" is, where the game's still going on. I thought something had happened in this seaside retreat and that the sentence had been lifted, the insanity fled. I thought there was nothing now to stand between me and ordinary happiness but the recent return of that grumbling appendix, dismissed by the local doctor as stress, but now on the long drive home taking the form of violent cramps. But even these didn't really interfere with my optimism as I left the winds and birds of Truro and headed, one hand on my kicked-in stomach, one hand on the wheel, toward the siren lights of New York.

PART FOUR

Alone

THIRTEEN

DECEMBER 21.

She felt my stomach. She said, "What's this?"

"What?"

"This hard thing. Could you be pregnant?"

"No." I was still smiling.

She looked at her watch. "I want you to go for a sonogram now. It could be nothing, a looped bowel, anything. I want you to bring the sonogram back here before four o'clock so I can see it. It's got to be then because I've got a plane this evening and I have to be out of here by four-thirty. Okay?"

"Where are you going?" still chatty.

"The Virgin Islands."

"How lovely."

"Yes." I guess she looked at me oddly. It was hard to tell because I didn't know her. She was one of the young doctors at the center, and upmarket place where some architecture firm had highlighted all the pillars and Romanesque barreled ceiling, where all the tots wore black designer jumpsuits and played with the Swedish wooden toys the center provided. I'd been there once before for a tetanus shot and the pediatrician, the only staff member on duty that day, gave me a lollipop afterward. If there was something bad going on with me, this would be the last place to make me feel it.

The nice lady at the sonogram office apologized for the coldness of the cream, asked if the thing they push around on you hurt me at all. I thought it was all courtesy. I was courteous and cheerful back. It wasn't until she said goodbye and "Good luck to you" that I began to be apprehensive.

Then I left the office and tried, on a sleeting Friday before the long Christmas weekend, and at twenty to four, to get a cab. I had my sonograms under my arm and they were getting wet. Cabs speeded by and sent slush and mud on all of us at the street corners. I hailed everything on- and off-duty, and then in panic chased an off-duty driver down, showed him the big, now-soggy manila envelope with the radiologist's address on the top left corner. "See, *radiology*, see this." I shoved the corner of the envelope at him so he could read. "I've got to get to a doctor ten blocks away." He started to roll up the window. I was shouting and the sleet was making it look like I was crying, too. "I may have cancer," I shouted at him, and the window went all the way up and he drove off. I got another cab, without going through all this, fifteen minutes later. And it was there, in the back seat skidding along toward the doctor, that I realized what indeed I might have. And it was then, for the first time, I felt that thing that was to become absolutely familiar to me ever since, just a little baby form of it, fear of hearing the words, not fear of having the illness, fear of the sentence (in both senses), not the execution.

I went into the empty waiting room. Her door was open and she was waiting for me. I took in everything in my beginning fear, I watched her, I wondered how she'd phrase the terrible, TV-drama words. I might have been auditioning her for a play, so observant, so detached from my own part in this, did I become.

I thought it was *interesting* (where was I?—still in the cab or somewhere, not quite caught up with what was happening) that she used the most hackneyed phrase, really said it. It was like watching a movie now, a very, very odd sensation of not really being in the movie, about an attractive long-blond-haired doctor with a nice practice trying not to be late for her flight to the Virgin Islands, who has nevertheless a truly unpleasant, truly unfestive duty, and she must, because she is a serious doctor, perform it. She said, "I don't know how to tell you this." And it was true, she didn't, or rather I didn't know how to hear it. She said, "I've spoken with the radiologists. You've got a large tumor on your left ovary."

After the speed of the cabs and the sleet, the panic to get back here in time, it was suddenly terribly slow, the time it took to hear things. Fast in a sense, but very slow, because I could watch the words come one by one out of her mouth. I could see the effort she made behind them and then would stop making when a whole, glib phrase would glide out. There were holes in the time we sat there, wide holes in which she could fall and I could fall, down to a ground where the words connected to implications. Slow, slow time for speech to cease to be speech and become fact.

And I was so slow to catch on.

"I've made an appointment for you tomorrow morning with a specialist. He treated my sister-in-law for the same thing. Look," she said, going from fact to florid (the same bad scriptwriter), "you're about to begin a journey through hell. All we can hope is that it isn't a long one. And it may not be. You don't have to die from this."

And still, dragging behind, I said, "You mean I can't die from it, is that what you're saying?"

"No," she said, and here she actually laughed, "you certainly can. Yes, indeed. But you don't *have* to. My sister-in-law was treated and she's fine now."

I didn't ask about treatment. The doctor would tell me all that tomorrow. And besides, she was upset by all this. I wasn't even a patient of hers and I was putting her through this, and then there was that flight she had to get.

"I don't want you to be alone tonight," she said. "Will you be with someone?"

I said I would. She said again she didn't know what to say, but she had to leave. She said she was very sorry, and I said it was all right and not to worry, and have a good Christmas.

The whole thing seemed fantastic to me. You could just cut along the dotted edge between three and four-thirty and none of this would have happened. Ovarian cancer, she said. I'd never heard of it. I didn't know if it was really bad or just pretty bad. I didn't know if I could just get on with things, all those people I was going see, Christmas, all that, sort of put this on hold somewhere, think about it, deal with it later. It was odd, like a funny thing that happens on the way to somewhere, a story, a thing to tell. But not yet then a thing to live. Even the damn pains that had brought me to the doctor had gone. And now this. I couldn't make anything of it. Yes, it was bad, that was for sure. Yes, it would sink down, sink in, but all that was slow, and by musing at it, at the out-of-left-field suddenness of it, I was sort of keeping it at bay.

I had a date with Shrimp that evening, and because my tunnel was still sublet I was going to stay in her apartment for the week she'd be away. I went to the place I'd stayed the previous night after my drive from Cape Cod and took a bath, changed, got her Christmas present and went over. I knew I couldn't mention any of this to her, because she'd be terribly upset. She, too, was going off somewhere and it wasn't the sort of information that would make for rest and relaxation. She was over eighty years old, and even if she was my nearest family, I couldn't tell her.

She asked how the doctor was and I said all okay. We had dinner. It went on like that, and all the time everything that had happened was welling up inside me. And I thought: Oh yes, this is exactly how it's going to be. You cannot reach out. People will be frightened. This is something you have to go through entirely alone.

The next morning in the waiting room of the specialist there were a group of us, and except for one middle-aged couple sitting grimly by themselves, stiff with worry, an oddly high-spirited social atmosphere. People stood up and walked around, flipping through magazines and talking to one another, excited more than frightened by the recent and absurd news in their lives. It was a Saturday morning, and perhaps everyone's appointment had been scheduled at the last moment, an emergency crowd, not yet settled into leaden acceptance. A large, pretty blonde in a silk dress, like a hostess at a garden party, confided cheerfully, amazed at her situation. "I'm in the fourth stage of it," she said, in the tone of what do you think of that? "I haven't got a hope in hell. I don't even know what I'm doing here. I should be on an island somewhere, or on a trip around the world." The whole thing was unbelievable to her, and perhaps to us, looking at her, plump and creamy-skinned, polished, coiffed and radiant, while in the corridors, on trolleys and in the rooms we had all glimpsed on our way up to this doctor's office, there had been the recognizably ill, the frighteningly color-bled dying.

They were cheery in the examination room, too, both the doctor and his nurses. I was in this strange good mood myself, as though it were my job to make everyone feel better. I was Pollyanna, irrepressibly looking on the bright side. "At least I'll lose some weight." "You certainly will," said the nurse. "I get to keep the tits, don't I?" "Sure you do." I was told about surgery and chemotherapy and it all sounded like a course of beauty treatments and everyone was quite jolly about it. And yet I had seen what I had seen on my way up to the doctor's rooms and I knew I didn't want to be in a cancer hospital. It was a place that would take you out of your garden-party clothes, hide your lipstick and turn you into gray, rumpled bedding. Once they had you, they took your colors away, put you in a world like early TV, black-and-white, reduced, fuzzy imagery on a tiny screen. I didn't know what all the merriment was about in that office; it felt like a trick, even my part in it, like Pleasure Island in Pinocchio before everyone grows ears and gets shipped off for the slaughter.

I visited other specialists attached to other hospitals. One doctor couldn't stop joking, said the surgery was no big deal and rapidly changed the subject to talk about his sailing. But later he told the friend who referred me she had to get me into surgery immediately, it was all very serious. After more of this, I chose a doctor, highly recommended, gruffer in manner but straightforward. Yet even his offices were sunk in whimsicality, with embroidered upbeat slogans on the walls and dozens of teddy bears crammed on tables and along the floorboards, teddy bears in all colors and sizes with hand-sewn costumes and funny props. There was a large moving-image screen of lakes and forests and waterfalls in the waiting room, and in the bathroom, set on top of the bathtub and running the length of the room, a huge Christmas display, winter wonderland with elves and reindeer, with Christmas lights blinking on and off in every color.

It seemed to be party time at all the doctors' offices. There were jokes and slapstick everywhere, and all in the effort to make up for what was actually at stake. It was perverse and it was scary.

And during all this, Christmas was going on, with dressing up and bringing presents, drinking and brave faces and laughter. There was dancing on Christmas Eve and a lot of picture taking, to record, I suspected, a last Christmas, a last time we were all together, a last time I, at whom the camera was pointed too often, would be dancing at all. Though my friends were buoyant with me, they were also horrified. Later I would feel bad to be the one introducing this premature and ugly reality into their living rooms and phone conversations; but just then, and particularly after the solitude of the last year, I was gratified, delighted by the love and attention. For a while I was as indulged as a child, and I was like a child with it, a happy, spoiled, suddenly precious (because I might any minute disappear), blessed child at the center of everything. They were all miserable about it and they all surrounded me with cheer. It was like we were all going to do this thing together, that they didn't want to leave me alone with it, but would come as far along the road of it as they could, until the point where I'd have to go on without them. Nothing about this cancer was the least as anyone might have predicted it, nothing leading up and nothing during, nothing at all after that first, strangely formulaic phrasing of the blond doctor. But this friendship, unstinting, immediate and unconditional, was the most surprising thing of all.

I had an overwhelming need to speak to Ned. Despite the divorce, the acrimony, the three years of hostile silence between us, he was still, and especially now, the person I felt closest to, knew the best, who knew me the best, still the person I loved the most. The illness and its implications brought me quickly to a place where feelings were so clear and strong they could be heard over the chatter of regular life with its procrastinations, clutter and denial. I needed to tell this terrible thing to Ned, needed his outrage on my behalf. But the years and trivia that had been swept away were only my years and trivia, while his, of course, remained intact. His first response was not horror but a weariness, a request for me not to bring this up now. He really didn't want to deal with any of these things but of course he couldn't help it. He told me later how he was drawn into it, by terrible dreams, by people at cocktail parties in London offering him consolation, as though we were really still together.

But we weren't together because he was in the death-free zone, where there was all the time in the world, nothing but pink, hazy future, and you could simply cast off the past. Until Bett's death, I'd been there myself, I knew very well what a pleasant place it was.

This new place I was in was quite different. There was high emotion and fear and a lot of drudgery: the sudden world of doctors and waiting rooms, insurance forms and constant appointments, of boredom muffling terror. It was a world full of portents, too, secret codes and deciphering, where you read professional faces for "true" information, learned doctors' euphemisms and what their sudden silences could mean. All words were scanned for some double entendre, some secret message from out there. Taxis passed many street signs and you read them, sometimes with irony, sometimes not: Passenger Terminal, No Exit, No Through Road, Road Narrows, Dead End, Complete Stop Ahead. The bird business had calmed down, mostly because you were in New York, where there were only pigeons, speckled, piebald, dirty, neither black nor white, ambiguous as the present prognosis.

A friend offered me a room in her house for the week before surgery was to take place. My loft was still sublet. Another friend had offered to have me after the operation, until I was walking and could find somewhere else to stay. About this irregular housing, I remember well the heavy irony of one of the specialists I'd consulted. "Oh, very clever of you," he said. "I didn't plan on this situation," I told him. "Look," he said, another one with fundamentalist vocabulary, "you're going to have to walk over hot coals to survive this. So you'd better find somewhere to live and get organized."

Surgery was on January 3. There was a last party on New Year's Eve, a last hit of fun and glamour, makeup and fancy dress, before hospital time and hot coals. I'd been out every night in a high, slightly crazed mood and this was the last fling. It was some LA producer's party with a lot of show-biz types. I remember watching the faces light up and then dim all night in sequential greeting, watching actors and agents "working the room," watching everyone mime a good time, surrounded by the props of a good time, the expensive food and champagne and party favors, how I felt cheated, tricked, because this party had somehow failed to be good enough, a wonderful last party that could send me buoyant into where I was going. I was angry at those people for faking everything, for having a fake good time, when life was so precarious, when there were so few chances. Leaving with my friends, I actually began to cry slightly, like a child who had been promised something, because this last party that was meant to be good had been bad, and it all mattered terribly much and there might never be a New Year's party again.

I had never been in a hospital in my life, never had my tonsils out or visited a sick friend. The day before surgery I went to get things I thought I would need. I bought books and classical tapes for the Walkman (Verdi's *Requiem* with the face of a crucified Jesus on the cover was one memorable choice), as though this were a long train trip on which I might be bored. And I was obsessed for some reason with buying lipstick, though I almost never wore it. I tried on colors at the Bergdorf counter as though lipstick had some magic power to keep death away, as though you could be too glamorous for bad news.

So I wore my lipstick the evening before surgery as my friends sat in the patients' waiting room with me. We drank and we smoked and we were all in the same hung-over spirits. And then we separated. And as we separated you could see in their faces the same acting fatigue as I'd seen on the faces of the guests at the New Year's party. They were exhausted, they needed to go home, but they had waited until the very last moment so it would seem less that they were leaving than that they were being sent away under protest.

And so I was suddenly alone, putting on a green hospital gown, answering questionnaires, shuffling off to EKG and X ray, having loathsome enemas and being shaved, smelling those hospital smells and seeing hospital sights, and yet still somehow cheerful enough because we still didn't know how bad it would be, because it was all new, and therefore, at some level at least, all sort of interesting.

FOURTEEN

I WAKE AT SOME POINT the following day and see a circumference of friends' faces bending and peering anxiously at me, as distorted as by a convex mirror. I recognize the image from movies and I remember being at some level amused by the recognition. But the distortion isn't just drugs, it's alarm on these dear faces, private knowledge. These kindly faces welcoming your consciousness also disinvite it. There is a kind of hush in the room which does not bode well. I am swaddled in bandages, and I feel soft and wounded, filleted, oozing. I fall in and out of consciousness and people change their places on the chairs around my bed. Doctors say a few things to me, but I am more aware of some kind of avoidance, of averted eyes, hasty retreats.

I was too drugged to be in pain that first day, but not too drugged to understand what had happened, that it was worse than they'd expected, both ovaries, appendix, some bit with a funny name, the whole reproductive system out, five-hour operation, dire prognosis. Somehow I took all that in without horror.

But it's the pain you wake to now, not so much the news, the pain from the clamps and the cut. You're wrapped in swaddling and there's a big wound under that, and something aches and then screams. You sort of scream, too, dully, and go under, come up again not to pain but to understanding. It's worse than they expected. Yeah, it's worse, but you're alive, wrapped in blood and gauze and alive. And for some reason this makes you happy. In and out you go from there to not there, and every time you return you're grateful, sometimes ecstatic, like the worst, like the nightmare, is over.

I remember still this strange joy just being there, alive, more or
less conscious, whatever the treatment, whatever the prognosis.
Those doctors were far more depressed than I was. I had my
friends, cheerful now because I was. I had more flowers in my
room than they knew what to do with, banks of them, messages
from friends in New York and London. I had constant visitors and
phone calls all day. I even had flowers and calls from the heartthrob,
in town then and proposing to visit me, with a tube hanging from
my nose and urine trickling into a bottle: no, thanks, later, thanks,
though the nurses would have been thrilled. People I hadn't seen
in months, sometimes years, came to visit, I was a draw, my fifteen
seconds of celebrity of a kind I didn't want. I felt helpless, and the
more they got excited by my news, the worse the sentence seemed
to be: not much time left, have you heard? There was kindness
and there was morbid sensation and I knew which was which.
People sat at my bedside being philosophical. "Why me?" you
must be asking yourself. But I wasn't, I was asking myself something else, something along the lines of why aren't I hysterical,
why am I taking it so well? Maybe I didn't believe it still, flowers
and gossip notwithstanding. Why was I so damn cheerful when the
doctors couldn't even manage a civil phrase, all their pre-op jokes
spent, all their merriment long gone? And where did I get that
piece of saintliness that day I consoled the family of a girl who
shared my room, down in the operating theater to remove what
seemed the biggest tumor in the world, when she'd arrived screaming in pain and looking like she'd swallowed a basketball? The
mother and two sisters waiting for her to be brought up, nice black
ladies holding hands, sort of moaning. "Look," I said, though no
one asked me, "what's the worst thing that could possibly happen?" They didn't want to say. "The absolute worst?" I asked. I
answered for them. "That she dies, right?" They began moaning
again. "But you know, don't you," I said, "you know in your
hearts, don't you, that no one really dies, ever, because their spirit
lives always. Death isn't important," I said, and they nodded at
me. "She'll never die, she'll always be with you." They came over
to my bed and took my hand and thanked me and we waited
together. Where did I get such things? I said it with absolute

conviction, maybe I'd seen God when I was under the knife, but I knew it was true, even if I died it didn't matter *really* because something would continue, like Gogi, like Bett, through love, through the people you've loved. And I was so sure of this thing that it set me free—or almost free, because when their daughter/sister came back and the doctor told her the tumor she had was benign, I felt joy for her and her family, but also, I must confess, a heavy pang of envy.

Was this all shock, denial? Was it some kind of stupidity on my part? I just wasn't devastated the way I should have been. I was in pain, I was angry at nurses and doctors and I was fearful of the unknown, but I was also mysteriously high on something and in a state that in retrospect, because it lasted beyond the first week, beyond the first months, through the whole damn business, I can only call and recall with infinite gratitude, a state of grace. I remember, too, thinking, again and again, through those terrible and yet not so terrible months, that horrendous as this was, it was still better than where I'd been, that dark, terrible depression of the last two years.

Some days I just couldn't cope and I would stay in bed all day, watching television or reading or sleeping. I slept a lot because the drugs knocked me out, and I had deep and heavy dreams. Sometimes I'd dream I was ten and Bett was with me and we were happy, or that I was with Ned in the earlier days and we were happy. Sometimes I dreamed sad, sad dreams that they were both gone and there was nothing I could do ever to have them back again. Then I'd wake up dazed and heartbroken and yet happy to have been so close to them again as they essentially were, as I essentially was, with no lines broken between us and everything natural and loving.

Sometimes waking I'd forget where I was and have to remember, and that was always the hardest, that reindoctrination of being here, now, with this thing, alone and going to die, with this cancer thing like a huge ugly raven's suit I'd have to harness myself into, a carcass of huge black bird wings into which I'd strap my arms and torso, a heavy ugly costume I'd carry through the day, that weighed me down and made me clumsy and, except in dreams, never forgetful. I maneuvered in it as best I could, kept my spirits up as best I could, but it wasn't like when I was free, it wasn't like when I was loved and loving of Bett or Ned or any of those people I saw in my dreams and got to be with for a while.

How I would cheer myself up. I learned to give myself the most distance I could from this thing they all said was going to happen to me. I'd say, "It isn't today you have to die," and therefore I could take that day for myself. Or, "It isn't today you have to do chemotherapy," and I could have that day, and forget for some of the time the huge raven wings to which I was harnessed all the same.

Sometimes I was afraid because I did not know how to die. It was the same kind of fear you have before an important exam. I didn't know how to do it, how to disintegrate, give up pieces of myself one by one. I didn't understand what would be asked of me, the expertise, as though dying were something I'd not only participate in but orchestrate. Dying didn't seem a transitive business to me, but something I had a limited amount of time to learn about. I don't mean dying gracefully or with dignity, I just mean going, going that wasn't sleeping. They said I was going to die and they indicated it was going to be soon and I just wasn't ready, I was unlearned, untutored. How give up strength, will, surrender body functions piece by piece? I was afraid I was going to blow it, this dying. It wasn't like childbirth; there were no classes for it.

I was aware of this dying business always. It wasn't as though I was insisting *not me*, only *not yet*. There were things once this dying became my future I couldn't do, like sit still through movies and plays. I couldn't deal, but literally, with "last acts." I couldn't go to restaurants and take the chair that faced into the wall, I'd have to be able to see out, otherwise the coffin aspects would unnerve me. It was all right with elevators, but places that looked onto walls unnerved me. And yet I don't think I ever "thought" I was going to die. I "knew about" it, had heard it said by experts, but it didn't ever become a part of me. I never made a will, I never wrote farewell letters. I never "put my affairs in order." But I did once or twice think of my life and what I'd managed to achieve. It was pretty little on the obit scale of things—three books which might get mentioned in some small press somewhere when I went, but not the real stuff. I didn't think of "achievement" as any form of journey from childhood to here, not the spiritual journey; I thought in terms of the people that I'd loved and who had loved me: that was what my life had been about, absolutely: Bett, Gogi, Shrimp, Veronica, Hugh, Edward, Jack, my closest friends, lovers. What made me saddest about dying was that I'd never get to meet and love or be loved by anyone else again. That was what "all over" meant. Not the books unwritten or the places not seen, but the people I was never going to love. I'd wasted a lot, and I had certain regrets. I'd been dealt a good hand and I'd thrown too many good cards away. But I'd loved a lot and I'd been loved, and in the end, which this seemed to be, that was all that mattered.

Coda: Out of "hell," "safe." A year after my last chemotherapy I am visiting my mother's grave in the company of my first lover in two years. I talk to Bett, while he waits in the car, and tell her it is over. I say this gently. I say I have survived. I say we are on separate sides of the grave now. I say goodbye. As I get into the borrowed car to drive down the mountain to the place we are staying (an hour away) it begins slowly to rain, then storm, a tremendous biblical storm, thunder, lightening, total darkness in the afternoon. It is almost ridiculous except that it becomes increasingly terrifying as cars drive at fifteen miles an hour in sheet rain. The full headlights of an enormous truck then flash behind me. With almost no visibility, he is driving fast, bearing down on me downhill, horn honking. There is nowhere on those turning country hills to pull over. I speed up, every corner looks like the last. I drive, he pursues mile after mile. At last I find a verge to pull onto. I drive out of his lights and let the juggernaut go past.

ABOUT THE AUTHOR

JANET HOBHOUSE wrote four novels and two works of nonfiction, including *Everybody Who Was Anybody: A Biography of Gertrude Stein*. She was a contributing editor of *ARTnews* and *Vogue* and was a fellow of the New York Institute for the Humanities. Ms. Hobhouse died in 1991.